INTRODUCTION

TO THE

GREGORIAN MELODIES

A HANDBOOK OF PLAINSONG

Da Capo Press Music Reprint Series

INTRODUCTION

TO THE

GREGORIAN MELODIES

A HANDBOOK OF PLAINSONG

BY

PETER WAGNER

SECOND EDITION, COMPLETELY REVISED, AND ENLARGED

PART I

Origin and development of the forms of the Liturgical
Chant up to the end of the Middle Ages.

TRANSLATED BY
AGNES ORME AND E.G.P. WYATT

New Introduction by
Richard Crocker

Da Capo Press • New York • 1986

Library of Congress Cataloging-in-Publication Data

Wagner, Peter, 1865-1931.
  Introduction to the Gregorian melodies.

  (Music reprint series)
  Reprint. Originally published: London: Plainsong & Mediaeval Music Society, 1901.
  Includes index.
    1. Chants (Plain, Gregorian, etc.)—History and criticism. I. Crocker, Richard L. II. Title.
III. Title: Origin and development of the forms of the liturgical chant up to the end of the
Middle Ages.
ML3082.W1313 1986   783.5   85-17520
ISBN 0-306-76284-6

This Da Capo Press reprint edition of *Introduction to the Gregorian Melodies* is an unabridged
republication of the edition published in London in 1901, here supplemented with a new
introduction by Richard Crocker.

Published by Da Capo Press, Inc.
A Subsidiary of Plenum Publishing Corporation
233 Spring Street, New York, N.Y. 10013

INTRODUCTION
to the
DA CAPO EDITION

The name of Peter Wagner is as closely linked to the restoration of Gregorian chant around 1900 as is that of the Benedictines of Solesmes — although the work of Solesmes is much better known. Also better known is the antagonism between Wagner in Switzerland and the Benedictines in France, even though they all engaged in a common cause — the restoration of the chant to the state of beauty and respect that they, at least, believed was due. This seems to us to be a broad issue and one largely resolved, at least in principle. Around 1900, however, the issue took very specific form, involving very specific arguments and protagonists. It is to these that Wagner alludes in the first paragraph of his Preface to the Second Edition: "If in the decades of the previous century it might seem as if learned investigations into Gregorian Music were for ever condemned to remain unfruitful in practical results, such apprehensions will no longer be entertained after the events of the last few months." (The Preface is dated October 1901.) A fascinating account of these events, from the point of view of the Benedictines of Solesmes, was published by Dom Pierre Combe (*Etudes grégoriennes* VII, 1967).

Various scholarly researches on the chant were proceeding apace in the last decades of the nineteenth century. The immediate issue concerned the practical application of this research, and specifically the endorsement by the Pope and the Sacred Congregation of Rites of particular chant books. The publisher Pustet of Ratisbon (Germany) held a virtual monopoly on publication of the chant books officially recognized by the Vatican, and these books contained the Medicean version of the chant that had resulted from the sixteenth-century reforms. One hard-fought issue was whether or not these versions had been supervised by Palestrina — for if they had been, then their authority was enhanced by Palestrina's great prestige in Catholic music of the nineteenth century. A case was made in the 1890s that Palestrina had not actually endorsed the Medicean versions. But the fate of the Gregorian researches hung on the question of whether Pustet's privilege would be renewed, thereby perpetuating the Medicean versions (which were increasingly recognized as far from the tradition preserved in the earliest chant manuscripts). Intensive efforts were made by the Benedictines and their supporters, as well as other scholars and Catholic officials, to prevent this from happening; and all these parties had great cause for rejoicing when, on 17 May 1901, Pope Leo XIII signed an open letter to Dom Delatte, Abbot of

Solesmes, acknowledging the importance of the research for the future practice of the Church, and encouraging any who wished to pursue chant research *solerter et libere* ("skillfully and freely"). The Solesmes Benedictines took this as support for their cause; but the terms of the letter were broad, as shown by the fact that under them Wagner applied for and received papal blessing on his Gregorian Academy, which then opened in November 1901-a month after Wagner had hailed the papal action in the Preface to his Second Edition.

The scholars were agreed, then (and had convinced the Vatican) that the official chant of the Church should be restored according to the evidence of the earliest manuscripts, rather than according to later expedient revisions-or still worse, in some simplified form in accordance with modern ideas of practical church music. But the melodies (even when restored according to manuscript evidence) were still difficult for modern singers to understand and perform. In addition to restoring the Gregorian melodies, the Benedictine scholars of Solesmes-Dom Mocquereau in particular-were in these same years working out a theory of rhythm, and system of notation and performance, which produced attractive and persuasive results. The Benedictines sought official endorsement of this system along with their versions of the melodies. But since Dom Mocquereau's theories lacked firm documentary and historical support, they were resisted by other scholars, especially Wagner, who seems to have been in part responsible for their exclusion from the new Vatican edition of the *Graduale* issued in 1908 under Pope Pius V. Wagner did not believe that exact rhythmic versions of the chant could be made yet-certainly not in the manner of Dom Mocquereau; Wagner had his own ideas about how the problem of rhythm could be approached but unfortunately these, too, were not founded on sufficiently good documentary evidence.

In these turbulent events of the years just before and after 1900, when Wagner was writing and revising his *Introduction to the Gregorian Melodies*, we can observe his remarkable combination of complete dedication to scholarly method with passionate devotion to the chant as sacred music of the highest order. Writing as a practicing Catholic, Wagner seems to have admired Gregorian chant as the music most appropriate to the Liturgy. This love of the chant comes through on every page, and-after the great difficulties we all experience with documentary and historical materials-continues to be an inspiration. It is in terms of this love that we can best understand Wagner's bitter aspersions cast from time to time on the "harmonists," the musicians who developed medieval polyphony. In terms of our present understanding of medieval polyphony, aided by a half-century of knowledge of the sources and of increasingly good performances, we may now find Wagner's judgment unreasonable; but I must admit that after spending much time with chant, the thought sometimes comes that music is primarily melody, and everything after monophony was a departure. More important, and more abiding, is Wagner's emphasis on the liturgical function of chant. He stressed, on one hand, that the chant was the best musical complement of the liturgy, and on the other hand that the chant must be understood in terms of, and with the help of, liturgical knowledge. This emphasis has guided research on medieval music ever since—and not just in chant but also, and especially, in the study of polyphony. Furthermore, the idea that some kinds of music can and should be understood in terms of an extra-musical function (such as liturgy) was a fresh idea in 1900, after a century of intense development of a German symphonic style that claimed music to be the self-sufficient expression of the highest truth. Nowadays, however, extra-musical functions are a commonplace in music and scholarship about it.

In his Preface, Wagner hoped his book would encourage the extension of knowledge about chant, and that it has certainly done. One result, of course, is that some of his own ideas have been superseded. He believed firmly in the idea that Gregory the Great (died 604) was a central figure in the formation of the repertory of chant that bears his name. Wagner was also ready to argue at any moment for the close connection of Gregorian chant with the chant of the synagogue, which he took to be its immediate origin. We are now more keenly aware of the distance—in time if not in other aspects—that separates Gregorian chant from the synagogue; and we are more ready to entertain the idea that the Gregorian repertory as we know it from manuscript sources of the ninth and tenth centuries may have assumed that form only in the seventh or eighth centuries, some time after Gregory. But these are historical interpretations that—in the absence of any firm data for those centuries—vary from one scholarly generation to the next. Wagner formulated the crucial proposition of the argument, in Chapter XI (p. 177): ". . . if we may assume that the Gregorian chant was not substantially altered before the ninth century, the time of our oldest noted MSS," and this assumption remains central in the debates ever since. Contemporary discussions of "oral tradition" in chant revolve around the question of what kind of change, and how much, took place in the seventh, eighth, and ninth centuries; modern opinions vary between "some change" and "much change," where Wagner assumed "no change." But since direct evidence is lacking, the disagreement remains one of opinion and assumption. And if Wagner on one hand stipulated the use of musical notation in the period 600-800 (which we no longer believe), on the other he acknowledged that memorization and "oral tradition" played an important role throughout much of the Middle Ages.

While various other of Wagner's interpretations (including those on tropes and sequences) have been superseded, his work, including Volume II on paleography and Volume III on the melodies, remains the most comprehensive, systematic survey of Gregorian chant. In Willi Apel's standard work *Gregorian Chant* (1958), he paid homage to Wagner's work; and Apel's reads in many respects like a commentary of Wagner's, carefully exploring and assessing musical details that arise out of Wagner's treatment. Most of the extensive research on the chant since World War II has taken the form of articles or monographs on specific subjects; or else of basic scholarly tools, such as the inventories published by Dom René-Jean Hesbert—(*Antiphonale missarum sextuplex*, 1935, and *Corpus antiphonalium officii*, 1963-79)—works in which Wagner would have greatly rejoiced.

One of the most prominent features of Wagner's work is his drive to make sense out of the recalcitrant data of historical documents—particularly recalcitrant in the case of the history of chant. He moves forcefully from the data to a clear, consistent, and credible interpretation, asserting how Gregorian chant must have been based on the Book of Psalms, how it must have included, from its beginnings, both solo (responsorial) and choral (antiphonal) styles, how the repertory must have been fixed in the time of Gregory the Great, how the features of the classical repertory came about as the best expression of the liturgy. Perhaps we now disagree with some, or all, of these assertions; in any case, we are more likely nowadays to say "could have been" instead of "must have been." But while applying corrective caution, we need to be reminded by Wagner of the importance of making *some* kind of sense out of the data, representing as it does a once-living practice of singing.

Page after page of Wagner's work is illuminated by his knowledge of the chant manuscript sources. In his time there were few bibliographic tools for surveying manuscript sources, and new ones were still being discovered and analyzed. His knowledge of sources was unmatched then, has not often been surpassed since, and is still impressive in our own day, when the data of musical sources has gained ever increasing importance. And his comprehensive sense of the meaning of data can still instruct us in principle as well as in practice: in pursuing a current line of research we still check back in Wagner to make sure we have covered the topic.

RICHARD L. CROCKER
Berkeley, California
January 1985

INTRODUCTION

TO THE

GREGORIAN MELODIES

A HANDBOOK OF PLAINSONG

BY

Prof. PETER WAGNER, Ph.D.

SECOND EDITION, COMPLETELY REVISED AND ENLARGED

PART I

Origin and development of the forms of the Liturgical
Chant up to the end of the Middle Ages.

TRANSLATED BY

AGNES ORME and E. G. P. WYATT

LONDON: Printed for The Plainsong & Mediæval
Music Society, 44 Russell Square, W. C.

PREFACE TO THE SECOND EDITION

Since the first edition of this book appeared circumstances have considerably altered. If in the last decades of the previous century it might seem as if learned investigations into Gregorian Music were for ever condemned to remain unfruitful in practical results, such apprehensions will no longer be entertained after the events of the last few months. Science and art alike owe lasting thanks to our present renowned Ruler, the Pope; by a providential decision he has so utilized the results of learned investigations and the skill of practised exponents of Church music as to make a true reform of the liturgical chant possible.

We stand at the opening of a new era in regard to liturgical and ecclesiastical music. The head of the Church has given it clear direction and aim. It is to be hoped that many workers will now devote their powers to the service of the Gregorian restoration, and not least, that the enthusiasm of the movement may encourage the scientific study of the liturgical chant; for the field is immense, and the workers are still few. May the second edition of this book have the result of extending in ever-widening circles a knowledge of the magnificent history of the liturgical music, and of its worth and beauty.

I have endeavoured to remove the defects of the first edition, of which I myself am most conscious, and to perfect the book as far as possible. Numerous journeys have enabled me to make use of manuscript collections, especially those of the National Library at Paris: in other cases permission was willingly granted me to examine manuscripts at home. The result is, as will be seen, an entirely new book. Not only has the material grown so much that a division has become necessary, but the treatment also has become much more detailed; so that the whole work has now become a *Summa Gregoriana* in a small compass. The aspect of the book being thus entirely altered, I long hesitated whether I should not change its title. Finally, however, I decided to retain the former title in order to show the connection with the first edition, particularly as the general arrangement of the material remains the same.

The present First Part deals with external history and liturgy, and lays the foundation; as compared with the first edition, besides being in more direct relation to the sources and being able therefore better to represent the development that has gone on, it also brings out more forcibly the importance of the liturgical side. It was the works of Cardinal Tommasi, which, though still valuable, have remained almost unknown to the historians of music, that showed me the road along which every historian of liturgical music must go. I hope in this way that, by using all that is best in ancient and modern research, I have described the history of development of an important section of the Liturgy in such a manner that the description corresponds with the actual course of the history. The careful reader will himself find out how much fresh matter has come to light. But the book itself must demonstrate the absolute necessity of always keeping in sight the development of the Liturgy in dealing with the history of the matter in hand. If any one attempts to proceed in a different fashion, he must inevitably fall at every turn into capricious and prejudiced ways. Recent literature can produce instructive examples to prove this to be so. It will be to his own injury if the historian of music refuses the valuable help which the historian of the Liturgy is able to give; and I venture to assert that many difficult and disputed problems of plainsong history will finally be solved by the latter and not by the former.

In this way this First Part has reached a form which it is hoped will prove useful to those who, without being professed students, wish to acquaint themselves with the history of the Liturgy.

The Second Part of the book will be quite new; it will have as its subject the manuscripts of the liturgical music, their contents, and the study of Gregorian forms. As in the present Part, there will be included much that is new from sources which have not been used hitherto. The reader will thus be put in a position to examine the manuscripts of the liturgical music for himself. Much that is said in the First Part will then be elucidated and completed : I allude especially to the information which the melodies themselves give concerning their history, as contrasted with their external history which is more especially contained in the First Part. The Third Part, which will be devoted to the Gregorian theory, will considerably improve and amplify the corresponding section of the first edition.

Freiburg in Switzerland, October 1901.

P. WAGNER, PH. D.

Professor at the University
and Director of the Gregorian Academy.

TRANSLATORS' PREFACE

The translators desire to express their deep obligations to the Reverend W. H. Frere and the Reverend G. H. Palmer for the trouble they have taken in revising the translation and reading the proofs.

CONTENTS

INTRODUCTION

The expressions 'Gregorian Melodies,' 'Gregorian Chant,' denote the universal liturgical Chant of the Latin Church as, starting from the practice of the first Christian centuries, it was ordered and fixed under Pope Gregory I. (†604), spread from thence to all churches of the Roman Liturgy, and was used everywhere until recent times.[1]

In the proper sense, the term 'Gregorian' should belong only to those melodies which come from Gregory's own hand or from the Roman *Schola Cantorum* founded by him. But it was right that this his honourable title should be extended to the later medieval melodies, which were composed in consequence of the establishment of new feasts or for similar reasons, and were included with the older ones, because they more or less preserved their essential characteristics.

In recent times many books of liturgical chant have been altered, not only in secondary matters, but also in the most essential particulars, and the contents of these books cannot be called Gregorian. For these alterations continually reveal that the intimate connexion of the Gregorian forms with the Liturgy has been misunderstood, and that contemporary part-music and the theory that underlies it have triumphed over those characteristics of the Gregorian Chant which are bound up with the artistic views of earlier times, and especially over the rights which belong to melody which is intended for unison singing. Thus the gulf which divides the modern form of the melody from the Gregorian is certainly much greater than is usually supposed.

The most important formal principle on which the Gregorian Chant is constructed is the contrast (which governs the whole medieval liturgy) between solo and chorus music, with the consequences resulting from it, or, in other words, between responsorial and antiphonal music.

---

1 The designation 'Gregorian Chant' *(Carmen Gregorianum)* is found already in a bull of Leo IV. (847—855). The activity of Gregory I. in Church music is testified to by the Venerable Bede : of which more in Chapter XI.

The rubrics of the Missal and Breviary, which embody the tradition of more than 1500 years, still prescribe solos for certain parts of the Service, and chorus for other parts; but since the 17th century almost all the music books, ignoring this fundamental distinction, have so curtailed the solo melodies that only chorus melodies remain; moreover, since then, the liturgical Cantors (who from early Christian times have always been practised singers,) have come to execute constantly the melodies which were intended to be sung by a choir. [1]   It is precisely its power to correspond with the changing demands of the Liturgy, and to interpret all its different moods, which forms the chief title to fame of the Gregorian Chant. [2]   There are other equally important alterations in the modern editions, which have to do with the modes, the rhythm and the words; for these are now treated not according to the rules of the unison music, but according to those of the part-music of the later Middle Ages. [3]   Finally, the musicians of the 17th century had lost all knowledge of the laws of Gregorian composition; they often laid hands on the liturgical chant from motives which were by no means praise-worthy, not to speak of their method of work, which at every turn left behind it traces of arbitrariness and want of principle, and destroyed the beauty and symmetry of the original.   Consequently the facts of liturgical and musical history alike make it impossible to call the chant of the modern books 'Gregorian,' in

---

1 See what has happened in the later choral books in the case of the solo chants of the Mass,—the Gradual and Alleluia.   No distinction is made between them and the Choir chants,—the Introit, Communion &c.

2 None of the later developments of Church Music has succeeded in corresponding so closely with the Liturgy.   This in itself should suffice to make the Gregorian Chant appear to us Catholics to be worthy of special honour, even though our musical apprehension, through being bound up with modern music, has some difficulty in becoming familiar with it in one respect or another.   But this difficulty (as I can prove from many years' intercourse with singers of the most different types) is not nearly so great as is usually supposed, and is more than counterbalanced by various advantages.   There is no better school of Church music than the performance of the Gregorian Chant; if only it keeps well away from that caricature of the proper pronunciation of the Latin, with its angular roughness and ugliness, which is unhappily so wide spread, and undeniably indeed is almost necessitated by our modern editions of plainsong.   There is no better method of bringing the singer to understand the admirable masterpieces of the Catholic Liturgy than liturgical and musical explanations given from time to time in practising Gregorian music.

3 It must not of course be thought that there is no other difference to be found between unison and part-music besides that which is implied by those designations.   The principle

so far as they have (as is unfortunately the case) 'reformed' what was characteristic of the medieval form of the liturgical chant.

In the Gregorian music two equally important forces meet,—the liturgical—for it has grown out of the Liturgy, and, with it, attained strength and greatness; and the musical—since it shapes itself on the principle of unisonous melody. These do not hinder one another, but enter into a harmonious league together. Thus the Gregorian Chant is the musical art-product of the Church.

The German name for this music, 'Choral,' comes from *chorus*, the Latin term for the body of singers whose duty it was to beautify the liturgical service. This term was then transferred to the space where they took up their position, which was in front of the Altar. In Monasteries, Cathedral and Collegiate Churches the liturgical singers still have their place *in choro*. So it was natural to call the music, which in old times was without exception Gregorian, 'Choral' music. But the German name 'Choral' has always had a more general sense; for example, the Protestants have claimed it for their German hymns. It is therefore best to add to the name 'Choral' the designation 'Gregorian' for the medieval Catholic Melodies.

The Latin terms are: *Cantus Gregorianus, Cantus choralis*, and *Cantus planus*; the last refers to its ancient mode of execution, since the difference in duration of the single notes was not so great as was the case in Figured music; it flowed more equally and evenly. [1] The French likewise say 'Mélodies Grégoriennes' or 'Plain Chant,' the English 'Plainsong.' The Italians have formed yet another name, 'Canto fermo,' from the Latin *Cantus firmus*, which in part-music means the melody adopted as the basis of the whole composition, which is usually taken from Gregorian music.

In the Middle Ages, especially before the invention of part-music, roughly speaking before the 12th century, only general designations were in use, such as *Musica, Cantilena, Cantus*, with or without an adjective such as *ecclesiasticus*. A distinguishing name was not found to be necessary for the liturgical chant, until there was beside it another kind of music,

---

of unison involves a number of important consequences in the case of unisonous melody, while a melody which is intended to form part with others in an artistic whole, demands on that account an entirely different method of treatment.

[1] An author of the 13th century, Elias Salomon, gives the following *Regula infallibilis* with respect to this: 'Omnis cantus planus in aliqua parte sui *nullam festinationem in uno loco patitur plus quam in alio*, quam est de natura sui; ideo dicitur cantus planus, quia omnino planissime appetit cantari' (Gerbert, *Scriptores*, III, 21).

the *musica mensurata*. As a matter of fact it is from this period, the 12th—13th century, that the phrase *Cantus planus* comes.

The purpose of this book is to be an introduction to the scientific understanding of this music. It aims at expounding the glorious creations of the medieval masters of singing, which are interesting in more than one respect, by describing their origin and their growth, their artistic peculiarities and their liturgical value. After what has been said, no further justification is needed for not extending the scope of the following exposition far beyond the Middle Ages. But the early printed books of the end of the 15th and of the 16th century must be taken into consideration, since they still contain the Gregorian Chant.

Further, the plan of the exposition cannot be doubtful. The Gregorian Chant belongs to two branches of scientific study, the history of the Liturgy, and that of Music : therein lies its peculiarity and thereby is fixed the method which we must follow. Speaking generally, we may say that the method adopted hitherto, of treating the Gregorian Chant historically, has been one-sided, because it has confined itself almost exclusively to a statement of musical history, instead of taking into consideration at the same time the accompanying liturgical conditions. In a word, the history of the origin of the music must be placed in the framework of the development of the Liturgy, the Mass as well as the Divine Office; for these are the two branches of her worship for which the Church has especially supplied the music. It will often be found that this method of treatment proves of great advantage in gaining a knowledge of the subject, and easily solves a number of problems which, from the point of view of musical history, are beset with great difficulties.

Thus the first task which this INTRODUCTION TO THE GREGORIAN MELODIES has to take in hand is to show the history of the origin of the different Gregorian forms in conjunction with the liturgical factors which accompany them or evoke them. This forms the contents of the First Part, which concludes with the origin of the latest forms of liturgical chant, viz. the Sequences and Tropes, and the Offices in poetical form.

CHAPTER I

PSALMS AND PSALMODY IN THE FIRST CHRISTIAN CENTURIES [1]

The oldest part of the Church's music is Psalmody: it is as it were a bequest left by the Jewish Church, before its fall as a political and religious power, to the rising Christian Church. Our Lord Himself had taken part in the liturgical practices of the Jews, and even at the Last Supper recited psalms with His disciples. In various places the Apostle S. Paul exhorts the faithful to offer to the Lord 'psalms and hymns and spiritual songs.' [2] In a similar manner the heathen who entered the Church became familiar with the Psalter, so that in time the knowledge of it spread wherever Christian communities arose. It formed the treasury from which everyone drew, whether in private or public devotion; and thus the Psalter acquired an importance in the Christian Church, which far surpassed that which it had possessed in the Jewish.

---

1 The earliest written liturgical melodies that we have are of the 9th century; the writings of the older Christian authors however are rich in valuable notices of the liturgical chant of their time. Most of these are collected in the work *De Cantu et Musica Sacra* (S. Blasien 1774. vol. 2) of the Benedictine Abbot, Martin Gerbert, of S. Blasien in the Black Forest. His treatment of them is not now in accordance with modern requirements, but the work is still valuable as a collection of materials. Further, the sources of the history of the liturgy are also of importance to us, as the development of the liturgical chant was throughout dependent on the development of the liturgy. Among modern works I have made use of the histories of the Breviary by Bäumer and Batiffol (both 1895), and Pleithner (1887), the various writings of Probst on the history of the liturgy, and especially the liturgical works of Cardinal Tommasi, as they were prefixed, for example, to each volume of the Maurist edition of the Works of Gregory the Great (*ed.* Gallicciolli. vol. 9—12. Venice 1772—4), from which I shall always quote in future.

2 Eph. v, 18; Col. iij, 16; 1 Cor. xiv, 26; also S. James v, 13. The Pauline expressions *Psalmi, Hymni* and *Cantica spiritualia* are synonymous; in yet later times psalms are called *Hymni* or *Cantica.* Chevalier, *Bibliothèque Lit.* I, 23.

On the same level with the psalms are placed the other lyrical portions of Holy Scripture, particularly those which are called to-day the Canticles of the Old and New Testaments. Among them are veritable pearls of religious lyrical poetry. Those of the Old Testament were already in high esteem among the Jews, and the gospel-canticles are mentioned by Christian authors. [1]

Psalter and canticles thus became the foundation of liturgical prayer and chant. They have kept this place of importance ever since. The most ancient book of liturgical chant which has come down to us, the *Codex Alexandrinus* in the British Museum, which belongs to the 5th century and was intended for the precentor, contains besides the psalter the following 13 canticles: 1 The song of Moses after the passage through the Red Sea, *Cantemus Domino, gloriose enim* (Exod. xv), 2 The song of Moses before his death, *Audite caeli quae loquor* (Deut. xxxii), 3 The prayer of Hannah, the mother of Samuel, *Exultavit cor meum* (1 Kings ij), 4 The song of Habakkuk, *Domine audivi auditum* (Hab. iij), 5 The song of Isaiah, *Confitebor tibi Domine* (Isai. xxvj), 6 The prayer of Jonah, *Clamavi de tribulatione* (Jon. ij, 2), 7 The song of the Three Children in the fiery furnace, *Benedictus es Domine* (Dan. iij, 52 vulg.), 8 The song of Azariah, *Benedictus es* (Dan. iij, 26 vulg.), 9 The song of Hezekiah, *Ego dixi, in dimidio* (Isai. xxxviij), 10 The Prayer of Manasses in the Apocrypha, *Domine omnipotens*, 11 The *Magnificat*, 12 The song of Zachariah, *Benedictus Dominus*, 13 The song of Simeon, *Nunc dimittis*. [2] If we open a liturgical music-book to-day and consider the text of the chants, we see similarly that even in the parts of the liturgy which appeal most nearly to the personal devotion of the individual, *i. e.* in the chants, the Book of books presents the unchangeable standard, which makes any deviation into subjectivity impossible. The offering which the liturgical singer made to God the Father in the name of the Church in the first centuries, inspires his heart even now: one century has passed on to the other the songs inspired by the Holy Ghost, and to the end of time they will form the strong stem round which all Church singing centres, and from which it draws strong and healthy nourishment.

---

1 In the *Ecclesiastical History* of Eusebius (v. 32) an old author is mentioned (who wrote against the heresy of Artemon) as evidence for the antiquity of the belief in the deity of Christ, &c; 'Psalms and songs of the brethren, compiled from the earliest days by the faithful, which extol Christ the Word of God, and ascribe the Godhead to Him.'

2 Beside these there is also mention of the morning hymn *Gloria in excelsis*, of which later. On the canticles *cf.* Bäumer, *Breviergeschichte*, 126, and see a list of the

Have these texts from the earliest day been sung, or were they only recited ? At the religious exercises in which for a long period they joined with the Jews in the synagogues, the Christians without doubt joined in the psalmody which was customary and in use there. But it is not agreed whether or not there was singing in the assemblies in which they celebrated the Eucharistic sacrifice. Amalarius, [1] the liturgist of the 9th century, takes the negative view: 'Without Singers and Readers and the ceremonial of to-day, the blessing of the bishop or priest sufficed to bless the Bread and Wine, with which the people were refreshed to the salvation of their souls, as it was in the first ages, in the Apostles' time.' It is no doubt true that at that time, when the Christians formed a community persecuted by the State, there was good reason for keeping the religious assemblies simple and inconspicuous.

However, this did not always remain the case : as soon as circumstances allowed, the musical art was admitted into the sanctuary. *The Century which created the great basilicas also inaugurated an artistic development of the liturgical Chant.* The liberation of the Church under Constantine (Edict of Milan, 313) made it possible for the arts to be brought into the service of Christianity. The liturgical forms quickly developed, and an artistic psalmody spread over the world. Eusebius († 340), who was a witness of the budding life of the Church, says [2] that 'the command to sing psalms in the name of the Lord was obeyed by everyone in every place : for the command to sing psalms is in force in all Churches which exist among the nations, not only for the Greeks but also for the Barbarians;' and further, [3] 'throughout the whole world, in towns and villages and in the fields also, in short, in the whole Church, the people of Christ, who are gathered from all nations, sing to the one God, whom the prophets foretold, hymns and psalms with a loud voice, so that the voice of the psalm-singers is heard by those standing outside.' In the letter of S. Basil to the Neocæsaræans we learn also [4] that psalmody was held as much in esteem by the Lybians and the Thebans, in Palestine, Arabia, Phoenicia and Syria, as by those dwelling on the Euphrates; and Pope Leo I. speaks of 'Davidical psalms which are sung in the whole Church with all piety.' [5]

In psalm singing all the people took part, as the statements of Christian authors show beyond all doubt. It was particularly at the vigils that

---

canticles in use at Constantinople, Milan, and in Gaul, in *Revue Bénédictine* 1897, 389.

1 Amalarius, *De Off.* III. 1. (*Patr. Lat.* cv, 1101).   2 *Ad psalm.* 65. (*Patr. Gr.* xxiij, 647).   3 *Ibid.* 658.   4 *Ep.* 207, 3. (*Patr. Gr.* xxxij, 763).   5 Gerbert, *De cantu,* I. 65.

the general psalmody was used; there it was an effective means of keeping
alive attention and devotion. The Church historian Sozomen [1] relates
how S. Athanasius succeeded in escaping while all were singing in the
church, and the pursuers considered it unlucky to lay hands on him under
such circumstances. Further, women and maidens were not forbidden
to take part in the psalmody. S. Ambrose remarks with regard to the
command of the Apostle that women should be silent in the congregation
of the faithful, [2] 'but they also do well to sing their psalm: it is sweet for
every age and suitable for either sex . . . and it is a great bond of unity
when all the people raise their voices in one chorus.' Another time [3] he
compares the church to the sea, as the chant of men, women and children
resounds in it with loud reverberations, at the responsorial singing of the
psalms. With like enthusiasm Gregory Nazianzen and John Chrysostom [4]
speak of the general psalm-singing of the whole community without
distinction of age or sex, and the Fourth Council of Nicaea allows the
laity to take part in the Church chant. [5] Where this practice did not exist,
zealous pastors urged its introduction, as for instance Caesarius of Arles. [6]
Venantius Fortunatus praises the activity of S. Germanus of Paris, who
let clergy, people, and even the children, join together in the psalms.
(*Clerus plebs psallit et infans*[7]). Others on the contrary interpreted the
words of the Apostle more strictly, and extended them to the chant in
church: thus the *Didascalia 318 patrum* (*c.* 375) expressly forbade women
to take part in psalmody. [8] Some forbade women to sing loudly enough
for their voices to be heard, *e.g.* Cyril of Jerusalem. The Catechist
Isidore of Pelusium (5th century) thought that women should only be
allowed to sing in church on the ground that their inclination to gossip
might otherwise lead them to talk during the service: but that as this did
not suffice to keep them from offending, it should be forbidden them.
The Council of Auxerre later in the same century altogether forbade
chanting in Church by women and maidens. [9]

---

1 *Lib.* iij, *cap.* 6. (*Patr. Gr.* lxvij, 1047).   2 *In Ps.* 1. (*Patr. Lat.* xiv, 968).
3 *Hexaem.* iij, 5. *Patr. Lat.* xiv, 178.

4 In his *Exposition of Psalm* 140 (*Patr. Gr.* lv, 425) he informs us that this psalm
was known to nearly every one by heart, and was sung daily in the evening assembly.
5 Gerbert, I. 39.

6 His biographer Cyprian says: 'Adiecit etiam atque compulit, ut *laicorum populari-
tas* psalmos et hymnos oraret, altaque et modulata voce, instar clericorum, alii Graece, alii
Latine, prosas antiphonasque cantarent.'   (*Patr. Lat.* lxvij, 1008.)

7 Venantius Fortunatus, *Poema in laud. cler. Paris.* (*Patr. Lat.* lxxxviij, 104).

8 Batiffol, *Hist. du Brév.* p. 6. note.   9 In 578; Gerbert, *De cantu,* I. 40.

From the pre-eminent position of the psalms in prayer and chant, it is easily understood that it soon became a custom to learn them by heart. The Fathers addressed exhortations to monks and clergy to do this, and also to youths and maidens who wished to dedicate themselves to the service of God. Pachomius, who wrote the first monastic Rule, bound his monks to learn the psalter. [1] According to Epiphanius, the monks of the East spent their time in chanting psalms, frequent prayer, and the recitation of the Holy Scriptures, all of which they said by heart; [2] and Jerome gives the monk Rusticus the advice: 'Never let the book disappear from thy hand or thy sight; thou must learn the psalms word for word by heart.' [3] For the nunneries we have evidence of this practice in the *Vita Euphrasiæ*, who upon her request for admission into the Convent received the answer that she must learn the psalter if she wished to stay. [4] Jerome gives the women of the convent of S. Paula at Jerusalem great praise for keeping strictly to the fulfilment of this obligation: 'No sister may remain, if she does not know the psalms.' [5] Even little girls were bound to it, as is shewn by Jerome's advice to the Roman matron Laeta with respect to her daughter. [6] The second council of Nicaea was only laying down an indispensable requirement when it made the bishop's consecration conditional on his knowledge of the psalter, [7] for the Archbishop Gennadius of Constantinople even refused ordination to the priesthood on these grounds. [8] Gregory the Great also denied a priest consecration as a bishop for this reason. [9]

There was scarcely any usual practice of the Christian faith, in which the psalter did not occupy a position of honour; especially this was so with the night-and day-hours, which were dedicated to common prayer and chant. We know from Cassian [10] that many Eastern monks used to sing each night 20 or 30 psalms or more. Even in funeral rites psalmody was in use. For this there comes from the East the witness of S. Chrysostom, who explains [11] 'If the faithful are keeping vigil in the church, David is first, middle and last. If at dawn any one wishes to sing hymns, David is first, middle and last. At funeral processions and burials, David is first,

---

1 *Patr. Gr.* xl, 949. Pleithner. *Ælt. Breviergesch.* 142.   2 *Patr. Gr.* xlij, 829.

3 *Patr. Lat.* xxij, 1078.   4 Bolland. 13 *March.* (*tom.* II, 267).

5 *Epist.* 108 *ad Eustoch.* (*Patr. Lat.* xxij, 896.)

6 *Ep.* 107 *ad Laetam, (ibid.* 871.)   7 Gerbert I. 166.

8 Nicephorus. Call. *Hist. Eccl.* xv, 23 (Gerbert *l. c.*), (*Patr. Gr.* cxlvii, 68)

9 *Ep.* 48. (*Patr. Lat.* lxxvij, 778.)

10 Cassian, *De Coen. Inst.* II, 2. (*Patr. Lat.* xlix, 77.)

11 *Homil.* 6. *de poenit.* Gerbert I. 64.

middle and last.   In the holy monasteries, among the ranks of the heavenly warriors, David is first, middle and last.   In the convents of virgins, who are imitators of Mary, David is first, middle and last.'   A beautiful passage in his exposition of the Epistle to the Hebrews (*Hom.* 10) refers to funeral rites only : 'Consider the psalmody that thou usest at that time (of the burial): *Turn again then unto thy rest, O my soul, for the Lord hath rewarded thee;* and again, *I will fear no evil, for Thou art with me;* and again, *For thou hast been my defence and refuge in the day of my trouble.* Consider what these psalms mean.   If thou truly believest what thou sayest, then it is unnecessary to mourn and weep.'   The Apostolic Constitutions prescribe for funeral rites the use of psalms 12, 114, 115, etc., which are still in use on such occasions.   From the West we have the account of the burial of S. Cyprian, and a great amount of testimony from the catacombs. [1]   The use of the psalms at household prayer in the Latin Church is attested by Tertullian, who exhorts Christian married people to emulate one another in psalm-singing. [2]   It was customary to sing psalms in the same manner before and after meals, and before going to sleep, as for example Clement of Alexandria tells us. [3]

On the other hand, as far as the *Mass* is concerned, the readings from Holy Scripture and the Prayer of the Celebrant took up a great deal of space, and there was not much scope left for the singing.   During the communion of the faithful, however, psalm 33 was sung, on account of the words *Gustate et videte, quoniam suavis est Dominus* (v. 9) ; and Tertullian mentions the psalmody between the lessons and the sermon [4] (the *gradual* of to-day); but all other chants at mass are of later date.

The prominent use of the psalms [5] is to be explained not only by Jewish tradition, which in many respects was a model for the Christians, but also by their contents.   Special attention has rightly been called to the fact that there is actually no religious mood, which has not found its poetic and devout expression in a psalm.   This observation is ancient;

---

1 Pleithner *l. c.* 73, draws attention to the peculiar fact that Justin Martyr quotes only very inexactly the words of the other books of the Old Testament (probably only from memory), but the psalms almost always exactly word for word; in fact he quotes whole psalms quite accurately.   Pleithner rightly explains this phenomenon by the daily use of the psalms in devotions.

2 *Ad uxor.* ij 8. *(Patr. Lat.* i, 1304.*)*   3 *Stromata* 7. Gerbert, *De Cantu* I. 141.

4 Probst, *Liturgie der ersten Jahrh.* Tübingen. 1870, p. 363.

5 S. Chrysostom tries to explain why the psalms are not only recited but sung : 'When God saw that many men were lazy, and gave themselves only with difficulty to spiritual reading, He wished to make it easy for them, and added the melody to the

Athanasius [1] has already summarized it in the following words: 'The words of this book (the psalter) include the whole life of man, all conditions of the mind and movements of thought . . . If thou art in need of repentance or confession, if sorrow or temptation befall thee; if anyone has endured persecution or has escaped by hiding; if anyone is sad or troubled, or if good fortune has returned to him; if the enemy is conquered, and he wishes to offer to the Lord praise, thanks and glory—for all this he can choose material enough from the psalms, and offer to God what they contain as his own work.' Ambrose [2] calls the Psalm 'the blessing of the people, the glory of God, the praise of the people, the applause of all, the language of the assembly, the voice of the Church, the sweet sounding confession of the faith, the devotion full of authority, the joy of freedom, the cry of rapture, the echo of bliss.'

Abuses might occur from the participation of all the people in the psalmody: the chant might easily degenerate into a shout and into mechanical singing. Against this the Fathers always insist that psalmody must be sung not only with the mouth, but also with the heart, according to the direction of the Apostle. [3] But a man's deeds should also agree with what he sings, as it says in the book of Wisdom: 'Praise is not seemly in the mouth of a sinner.' Origen enjoins, [4] 'He alone is worthy to sing psalms to the Lord, who does not utter the coarse sounds of sin, whose tongue does not blaspheme, and whose spirit is disinclined to luxury.' Similar utterances are found in Eusebius, Ambrose and Chrysostom. [5] Very beautifully are these thoughts expressed in the formula used at the blessing of the liturgical singers: [6] '*Vide ut quod ore cantas, corde credas, et quod corde credis, operibus comprobes.*'

Prophet's words, that all being rejoiced by the charm of the music, should sing hymns to Him with gladness.' *In Ps.* 41. 1. (*Patr. Gr.* lv, 156.)

1 *Ep. ad Marcellinum.* (*Patr. Gr.* xxvij, 42.) Indeed the whole letter deals with this theme in greater detail.   2 Preface to his *Commentary on the Psalms,* (*Patr. Lat.* xiv. 24): '*Psalmus enim benedictio populi est, Dei laus, plebis laudatio, plausus omnium, sermo universorum, vox ecclesiae, auctoritatis plena devotio, libertatis laetitia, clamor iocunditatis, laetitiae resultatio.*' The Manichaeans rejected the Old Testament and with it the psalter and psalmody, on which account S. Augustine especially blames them. *Confess.* ix, 4. (*Patr. Lat.* xxxij, 766).

3 '*I will sing with the spirit, and I will sing with the understanding also.*' 1 Cor. xiv. 15.   4 *Hom.* 6 *in Judic.* (*Patr. Gr.* xij, 977.)

5 S. Augustine says very beautifully in his exposition of Psalm 32 : '*Cantate vocibus, cantate cordibus, cantate oribus, cantate moribus.*' *Patr. Lat.* xxxvj, 277. There are other utterances of this kind in Gerbert, *De Cantu.* I. 236 foll.

6 The decree of the 4th council of Carthage, *cf.* Gerbert I. 239.

For the development of the liturgical chant, as for Western music in general, it was important that instruments should from the beginning be excluded from the liturgical assemblies of the Christians. The noisy, luxurious character which belonged to their use at heathen theatres and banquets accorded ill with the seriousness and modesty of the Christians, who shunned everything connected with sensual pleasures. 'We want,' says Clement of Alexandria, [1] 'only one instrument, the peace-bringing Word alone . . . not therefore the old psaltery, trumpet, drum, and flute, which are dear to those who are training themselves for war.' Eusebius [2] says also, 'We sing God's praise with living psaltery, inspired cithara and spiritual songs. For more pleasant and dear to God than any instrument is the harmony of the whole Christian people, when in all the churches of Christ we sing psalms and hymns with harmonious minds and well tuned hearts.' Eusebius says this in opposition to the custom of the Jews, who had formerly allotted a prominent place in psalm-singing to instruments; and he then continues : 'These are the psalmody and the spiritual songs, which are customary with us, in accordance with the direction of the Apostle. Our cithara is the whole body, by whose movement and action the soul sings a fitting hymn to God, and our ten-stringed psaltery is the veneration of the Holy Ghost by the five senses of the body and the five virtues of the spirit.' Chrysostom uses a like figure, in a passage in which he compares with splendid effect the effects of spiritual and of profane music : [3] 'Here no cithara is needed, nor tightened strings, neither the *plectrum*, nor any instrument at all; but if thou willest, thou canst make thyself into an instrument, if thou mortifiest the flesh, and strivest with the body after beautiful harmony.' An author of the 4th or 5th century says explicitly, [4] 'In the churches the use of instruments in singing is excluded, and only the simple chant allowed.' [5]

---

1 *Paedag.* ij, 4. (*Patr. Gr.* viij. 443.)

2 *In Psalm* 91. (*Patr. Gr.* xxiij, 1171 foll.)

3 Psalm xli, 2. (*Patr. Gr.* lv, 158.) In his exposition of Psalm 150 (*Patr. Gr.* lv. 497) Chrysostom says, 'Now those instruments were then tolerated because of their weakness, and because they stirred them up to love and harmony, and incited their mind to carry out with joy what was profitable : and because by such inducements they were led to a high pitch of zeal.'

4 Pseudo-Justin *Resp. ad orthod. quaest.* 107. Gerbert I, 212.

5 As regards such utterances of Christian authors, it should be noted that Christians were long compelled by external circumstances to adopt a hostile attitude towards instruments, as everything depended on their not lifting for their enemies the veil of secrecy which hid their meetings. If Christianity had come into the world without the thousand difficulties which actually beset it ; if instead of gradually conquering them it

No objection was made to the use of dignified instruments in private devotion, as the further observations of the Alexandrian catechist make clear : [1] 'If thou canst sing or chant psalms to a lyre or cithara, thou wilt incur no blame, for thou dost imitate the Jewish King.' [2]

The teachers of the Church endeavoured to exclude from the music everything of a noisy or sensual character. In particular they were opposed to chromatic music, which must have been used then in profane music, though long before Christ the enharmonic and chromatic had lost their prominent position, and made way for the diatonic. In regard to this the monition of Clement of Alexandria is classic : [3] 'Only modest and discreet harmonies are to be admitted, while on the other hand weak and enervating ones are to be avoided. For with their impure and artificial intervals they lead men on to an over-refined and effeminate course of life; on the other hand, sober modulations tending to self-restraint do not encourage intoxication and dissoluteness. Chromatic and frivolous scales, such as are the fashion in immodest drinking-bouts where people deck themselves with wreaths, and the music of the wantons, must always be avoided.' In spite of this, here and there in oriental congregations there must sometimes have been a great deal of noise at divine worship; at any rate at Miletus in the time of Athanasius the hymns were accompanied by clapping of hands and

---

could have taken possession at once, church music would certainly have had an entirely different development, and, in particular, Christians would have made use of the whole apparatus of the instrumental music of their age, and would have purified it from the stains which defiled it, just as they did not reject on principle other intellectual acquisitions which antiquity had made. It is no mere chance that, as soon as external circumstances allowed, instrumental music was actually brought into church, and it is very remarkable that even the organ, composed of flutes, was admitted. It was popular especially in ancient times at secular concerts, and was introduced into the church by the Byzantine Rulers, who endeavoured to adorn divine worship with all possible magnificence; thence it spread into the whole Christian Church. It immediately attained the rank of a liturgical instrument, and it has, not merely in modern times but ever since then, exerted a remarkable influence on the development of Church music. It is known that in the middle ages other instruments also were turned to liturgical use in the chief strongholds of Church music, (e. g. in England and at S. Gall.) It would be a task well worth undertaking to investigate from original authorities the use made of instruments in medieval services.

1 Clemens Alex. *Pedag. l. c.* The lyre and cithara were in the time of the Emperors what the lute was during the Italian Renaissance, and what the pianoforte is to-day,— the best instrument for social purposes in every way; while the flute, the liturgical instrument of the heathen feasts, was held in abhorrence by the Christians.

2 Probst *l. c.* 262 : 'The prevailing tone of the Agapes and feasts was found to be reconcileable with singing and instrumental music.' 3 Clemens Alex. *Pedag. l. c.*

dance-movements, a custom against which the saint constantly fought. [1]

The execution of the psalmody in the earliest times of Christianity was almost exclusively entrusted to a single person. This oldest form of Christian psalmody, the *psalmodic solo*, is a copy of the practice of the synagogues; and the precentor in the Christian communities is the successor of the Jewish precentor in the Temple and the Synagogue. The method in which psalmody was performed by the Jews can be seen to-day, for instance, in the 135th Psalm, every verse of which ends with the words 'for His mercy endureth for ever.' These formed the refrain sung by the people to the first part of the psalm-verse performed by the soloist. The psalmodic solo with interpolated phrases for the people (or exclamations, as in Psalms 32 and 88) is thus an old tradition of the Jews. Its adoption into the Christian service is easily understood, as at first the Christians continued to take part in the liturgical exercises of the Jews, and many a cantor who performed his office in the Synagogue may later have placed his skill at the service of the Christian Church. A positive witness to this is given moreover by the Jew Philo, and the Christian historian Eusebius. According to the former, the psalmody of the Jewish sect of the *Therapeutae*, which he describes, was of great importance : since their liturgical customs were built upon a Jewish foundation, we must accept the fact that the solo psalmody came down from the Synagogue. The same kind of psalm-singing was almost exclusively in use in the Christian services of the first centuries, and Eusebius says expressly that the description of Philo coincided exactly with the Christian practice of his day. [2]

The Precentor in the Christian liturgical assemblies began by giving out the title of the psalm which he was to render. It was so in the Greek as well as the Latin Church. S. Ambrose often explains the title of the psalms on which he is preaching, and which he had before caused to be sung by the soloist, as in the case of psalms 54, 65, 88, and 92. [3] For the

---

1 Theodoret, *Haeret. fab.* 4,7. (*Patr. Gr.* lxxxiij. 426). It was the general custom in the East to accompany religious chanting in this manner and with instruments. The old Jewish temple-chant was no exception to this.

2 The part referring to the psalmody of the *Therapeutae* in the Ecclesiastical History of Eusebius ii, 17, was compiled from Philo, *De vita contemplativa.*

3 A reminiscence of this is preserved in the present forms of the Liturgy, as *Incipit lamentatio Jeremiae prophetae, Lectio Epistolae b. Pauli Apostoli ad Romanos, Sequentia ·S. Evangelii secundum Joannem.* The S. Gall MS. 381 gives (p. 98) among the *Versus ad repetendum* to the Introit *Jubilate (Dom. ii post albas)* the second time, the ℣. *Canticum psalmi resurrectionis,* the title of Psalm 65. With this compare what Cassiodorus remarks in the second chapter of the Introduction to his *Exposition of the*

answers of the people to the part of the precentor, the Greek authors have the designations ὑποψάλλειν, ὑπηχεῖν, ὑπακούειν, the Latins *succinere* and *respondere*; and this kind of psalm-singing is called by the latter *Cantus Responsorius.* As regards the Church of Jerusalem, this psalmody is mentioned in the second half of the 4th century in the journal of the pilgrim Silvia (or Etheria) (*c.* 380); [1] and the Apostolic Constitutions(*c.* 400) say expressly, that the people are to chant the Psalms after the *acrostichia.* [2] This responsorial chant might take various shapes. If the people responded to the precentor verse for verse, a form arose which is similar to the present mode of saying the Litany of the Saints; it offered no difficulties and was already known to the Jews. [3] However the *cantus responsorius* was more frequently practised in the form in which the congregation always answered with the same refrain. [4] This might be taken from the psalm, or contain a sentence from elsewhere. In choosing them, according to the witness of S. Chrysostom, [5] preference was given to those texts in which a sublime dogmatic thought found expression. Thus the cry *Amen*, received from the Jews, [6] the *Alleluya* added to certain psalms, and the short doxology *Gloria Patri et Filio*, were each of them at first a *versus responsorialis.* The church historians [7] agree in mentioning an example of such responsorial chant on the occasion of the persecution of Athanasius

---

Psalms : 'Usus ecclesiae catholicae Spiritus Sancti inspiratione generaliter et immobiliter tenet, ut quicunque eorum (i. e. of the psalms) cantandus fuerit qui diverso nomine praenotantur, lector aliud praedicare non audeat, nisi psalmos David. Quodsi essent proprii, id est aut Idithun aut Filiorum Core aut Asaph aut Moysi, eorum nomina utique praedicarentur, sicut in Evangelio fit, quando aut Marci aut Matthaei aut Johannis vocabula pronuntiantur.' (*Patr. Lat.* lxx. 14).

1 'Psalmi resp0nduntur', she says in her description of the Night Office (*cf.* the extract in Duchesne, *Christian Worship*, p. 492); she mentions the *psalmus responsorius* in the same connexion (p. 501 etc). On these terms of Silvia *cf.* Dom Cabrol, *Etude sur la Peregrinatio Silviae*, Paris 1895, pp. 59 foll.

2 ii, 57. Καὶ ὁ λαὸς τὰ ἀκροστίχια ὑποψαλλέτω, 'And let the people sing the acrostics.' Sozomen calls the short responses of the people *akroteleutia.* Probst, *Lehre und Gebet in den ersten Jahrhunderten*, p. 262, explains : '*Acrostic* signifies usually the beginning of a line of writing, but sometimes also the end of it.'

3 Pleithner, *Ælt. Geschichte des Breviers*, 65.

4 Psalm 94, *Venite exultemus Domino* is thus sung to-day at Mattins.

5 Chrysostom on Ps. 117. (*Patr. Gr.* lv, 328.)

6 Already in the time of the Apostle Paul, strangers and those unversed in prayer responded *Amen* to him who led the singing or praying, to show their association with him. 1 Cor. xiv. 16.

7 Socrates, Sozomen, and Theodoret, as well as S. Athanasius himself. Gerbert I. 47.

and his Christians in Alexandria : the saint gave the order that the deacon should precent a psalm and the people answer after each verse *quoniam in æternum misericordia eius*, 'For His mercy endureth for ever.' In Antioch also this practice was known. When in the Emperor Julian's time the relics of Bishop Babylas were being conveyed thither, the people responded to the precentor with the verse, *Confounded are all they that worship carved images and that delight in vain gods.*

In the Latin Church the *cantus responsorius*, the psalmodic solo with intercalated verses sung by the people, was in use from the beginning. It may have been the first preachers of the Gospel in the West who introduced the psalm-chant there, as far as it was suitable for providing the assemblies of the Christians with chanting. Already Tertullian, who may be regarded as the witness for the Latin practice,[1] mentions the *cantus responsorius.* Augustine testifies in several passages to its use in the Milanese Church : expressions such as *voces psalmi quas audivimus* (executed by the precentor) *et ex parte cantavimus*[2] (referring to the interpolated verse of the people), or *Psalmo quem cantatum audivimus, cui cantando respondimus,*[3] are not uncommon in his writings. Isidore also, the great representative of the Spanish Church, informs us of the great antiquity of this use, and certainly describes the responsorial psalmody exactly in its original form.[4]

The *cantus responsorius* was employed by special preference annexed to a lesson; uplifted by the words of the Holy Scriptures, the people had an opportunity of offering to the Lord in melody their exalted feelings and pious resolutions; further, the chant brought variety, and prevented fatigue and flagging of attention. The precept of the Apostolic Constitutions may be understood in this sense, that 'After every two lessons someone (other than the reader) shall always sing the hymns of David, and the people shall join in at the last words of the verse.'

The psalm-singer, *psaltes, psalmista* or *cantor, praecentor, pronuntiator*

---

1 Thus Bäumer, *Breviergesch.* 41. Tertullian, *De orat.* 27. (*Patr. Lat.* i. 1301.)

2 *In Psalm.* 26. 2. (*Patr. Lat.* xxxvi. 199,) *cf.* Tommasi in *Op. Greg. M.* vol. xi *praef.* xxxvij.

3 *In Psalm* 46. 1. (*Ib.* 525.) Further examples from the writings of Ambrose and Augustine in Tommasi, *praef.* xxxviij foll.

4 *De offic.* i. 8. 'Responsoria ab Italis longo ante tempore sunt reperta (i. e. the responsorial chant has not been brought from the East to Italy like the antiphonal chant, but has always been in use there) et vocata hoc nomine, quod uno canente, chorus consonando respondeat., *Patr. Lat.* lxxxiij. 744.

psalmi, psalmorum modulator et phonascus, as he is called, [1] enjoyed liturgical privileges in the East and in the West. The *Therapeutae* chose for this office only men who had the recommendation, not merely of artistic ability, but also of a worthy manner of life. [2] Similarly in the Christian Church an order of church singers developed. They were at first certainly not identical with the *lectors* who had to read the lessons from the Holy Scriptures. In a letter, ascribed to S. Ignatius, [3] to the inhabitants of Antioch, the *cantors* are enumerated with the *lectors* among the minor orders : it says, 'I greet the subdeacons, *lectors*, *cantors*, doorkeepers and exorcists.' Here *lectors* and *cantors* are different personages. In the Apostolic Constitutions [4] also they are always kept separate. It seems that some wished to show their skill in leading the singing, who had not been called to it : for this reason the council of Laodicea (*c.* 350) exhorts that, except the canonical singers, who mounted the platform and sang from the parchment, no one should sing alone in church (*Can.* 15). According to this the precentor had his own raised place, so that all could see and hear him. Already this had been the case in the Synagogue, [5] and so it continued in the middle ages. In another passage (*Can.* 23) the same council defines the work of the *lectors* as 'reading'; that of the *cantors* as 'singing.'

The contrast between lectors and cantors, which stood out clearly at first, disappeared later, and the result was that one man was *lector* and *cantor* at once : [6] according to Zonaras the lectors of his time occupied themselves more with chanting than with reading. [7] In Alexandria the office of *lector* and *cantor* might be given to Catechumens even, but elsewhere only to those who were baptised. [8] With the Latin Fathers the use of the designation *lector* for the Soloist was quite usual.

---

1 Pleithner, *Ælt. Gesch. d. Breviergeb.* p. 62.

2 Eusebius, *l. c. Cf.* also Gerbert, *De Cantu* I. 20.

3 *Patr. Gr.* v, 908.

4 *Ap. Const.* viij, 28. Chap. 47 urges them to avoid gambling and intemperance. In the Liturgies of Mark and James also, the 'psalmists' are reckoned among the Church orders.

5 Amalarius, *De off.* iij, 17. (*Patr. Lat.* cv, 1123).

6 Sozomen, iv, 3. reports this of a Martyr, Martianus. (*Patr. Gr.* lxvij, 116).

7 Gerbert, *De Cantu* I. 33.

8 This shows that the *cantor* was not employed during the Mass proper. In the Gregorian Roman Liturgy also, the *cantus responsorius* appears only in that part of the Mass which precedes the Offertory. (On the transformation of the *Antiphona ad Offerendum* into a *Cantus responsorius*, see below).

In the Roman inscriptions of the second half of the 4th century the cantor is often commemorated with words of praise. '*Psallere et in populis volui modulante profeta*' is on the gravestone of one Leo, who in later life became a Bishop; on that of a deacon, Redemptus, is

'Dulcia nectareo promebat mella canore,
Profetam celebrans placido modulamine senem.'

From the beginning of the 5th century there comes an epitaph on an Archdeacon Sabinus, 'Who chanted psalms in artistic style and sang the holy words to manifold tunes.' Of another it simply says 'He was singer of the songs of David.' [1]

A complete innovation in Church music was made by the *choral psalmody*, which came into prominent use about the middle of the 4th century. It consisted in the alternation of two choirs in the execution of the psalm verse, each in turn taking up a melody which was the same for each choir and for all the psalm verses. This also was inherited from the Jews. David in his time had ordered the separation of the temple-singers into choirs, who evidently sang the psalms in chorus, and responded to one another (I Chron. vj. 31. foll.); and psalmody by alternating choirs was well known to the *Therapeutae*. [2]

We possess two traditions as to its adoption in the Christian services. According to Socrates [3] it is said to have been S. Ignatius who introduced into the Church the custom of executing hymns in alternate chorus. It was shown him in a vision that the angels sang to the Holy Trinity in alternate chorus; and he introduced this method of singing into his church, from whence it passed to all other churches. Theodóret [4] on the contrary ascribes its introduction to Flavian and Diodorus, two monks of Antioch at the time of the semi-Arian Bishop Leontius (344—357). Both accounts agree in saying that the new mode of singing spread from Antioch, and that is doubtless correct. The tradition of Socrates has found little credit; [5] and as regards that of Theodoret it is supplemented [6] by a statement of a contemporary of Flavian and Diodorus, Theodore of Mopsuesta, that the two monks brought over the new mode of chanting from the Syrian to the Antiochene Church.

In the first half of the 4th century there existed in the great churches of the East, Alexandria, Jerusalem, Antioch and Edessa, communities of

---

1 Duchesne, *Christian Worship*, pp. 169,170.   2 Eusebius, Philo *l. c.*

3 *Hist. Eccl.* vj, 8. (*Patr. Gr.* lxvij, 692).

4 *Hist. Eccl.* ij, 19. (or 24) (*Patr. Gr.* lxxxij, 1060).

5 Gerbert, *De Cantu* I. 41.   6 In Nicetas, *Thes. orth. fid.* v, 30. Gerbert *l. c.*

pious men and women, who united in a common life in order to serve God with greater fervour in seclusion from the world. In Syria they were named *Monazontes* or *Parthenae*, and it is well known that the beginnings of the monastic orders lay in such associations as these. Their influence was very great in the formation of liturgical customs : amongst other things, as we shall presently see, the introduction of daily vigils is traced back to them; hence also arose the need of combined psalmody in the form of alternate chanting. Thus it was from Syrian monasteries that choral psalmody was transferred by Flavian and Diodorus into the Church of Antioch.

Choral psalmody in the form of alternate chanting has from the first borne the name of '*antiphonal* chant.' The word 'antiphon' used to be translated simply by 'alternate chanting.' But that cannot be its original meaning. Antiphon is an expression that comes from Greek music-theory, and to 'sing in antiphons' was equivalent to 'sing in octaves.' [1] In the first centuries after Christ, Greek music was world-wide music, just as Greek was the world-wide language, and it prevailed in Greece and Rome, Asia Minor and Africa; so musicians in Syria certainly knew what 'antiphon' meant. One must therefore suppose that the original form of the Christian Antiphonal was chanting in octaves. Support is given to this view by the fact that alternate chanting combined with chanting in octaves may be proved to have existed in the early centuries, and even earlier among the *Therapeutae*. In the description of their vigils, Philo-Eusebius [2] remarks as follows : 'All at once on both sides rise up . . . and form two choirs, the one of men, the other of women. Each choir chooses as its leader and cantor one who is distinguished as well by the dignity of his person as by his skill in music. Then they sing hymns to God, composed in different metres and melodies, sometimes all together, sometimes answering one another in a skilful manner. Next . . . they form the two choirs into a single one . . . as did the Jews when they went through the Red Sea. One is reminded of this company by the choir of pious men and women, as throughout the singing and the alternation of the melodies the deeper sound of the men's voices and the higher sound of the women's voices singing together compose a sweet and true musical symphony.' Now seeing that Eusebius not only accepts the utterances of Philo on the

---

1 Pseudo-aristot, *Problem.* 19. 39. in Jahn. *Mus. Script.* (Leipzig 1895). p. 100 : The consonance of the octave is antiphonal, and antiphony arises when men and children sing together, whose voices are distant from one another, as, for example, the *Nete* e from the *Hypate* E.   2 *l.c.*

chanting of the *Therapeutae*, but represents the practice of his time as agreeing with the description of Philo, without doubt in the first half of the 4th century there was octave-singing in the Christian Church, and that not only in the responses of the *psalmus responsorius* made by all the people; it is still more certain that boys were very early brought up to psalm-singing. After the liberation of the Church under Constantine it is especially found that in churches, both of the East and West, boys with their fresh and penetrating voices were employed for reading the lessons and singing the chants. They were trained for this task in special schools, where they lived together under the supervision of the clergy. Most of the Church dignitaries passed through these *lector*-schools; in fact clerical education began with them. Felix of Nola, Eusebius of Vercelli, Popes Liberius and Siricius, and many other holy men were *lectors* in their boyhood. For these customs in the East we have the testimony of the pilgrim Silvia, who calls the boys *pisinni*, [1] and in the Apostolic Constitutions (viij. 4) boys are ordered to sing the *Kyrie eleison* in the presence of the rest. Somewhat later, in the time of S. Augustine, the responsorial psalmody after the lesson in the Mass was entrusted to them. [2] An African inscription of the beginning of the 6th century mentions a *lector* of 5 years old. [3] A decree of the Second Council of Vaison (529) deals with the singing boys, [4] at which it was decided, under the presidency of S. Caesarius, that priests who had charge of a parish should, as was customary in Italy, take *juniores lectores* and instruct them in psalmody, reading etc. A Lyons inscription as early as the year 552 speaks of a *Primicerius scholae lectorum* : [5] the like were to be found at Reims and other churches. The historian of the Vandal persecution tells of 12 singing-boys from Carthage, who on account of their faith, through the treachery of their teacher Teucharius, had to endure much hardship [6] (about 480). Gregory of Tours praises the pains taken by the Bishop of Lyons, Nicetius, to enable boys to take part in the chants of the psalms and the antiphons. [7] The Rule of S. Benedict contains particular directions with regard to them. [8] Consequently there can be no doubt that at least from the 4th century onwards, singing by boys was usual throughout the whole Church. But if

---

1 Duchesne, *Christian Worship*, p. 493.

2 *Sermo* 352. (*Patr. Lat.* xxxix, 1550. *cf.* also xxxiv, 1049).

3 De Rossi, *Bulletin* 1880. p. 20, 21.

4 Labbe, *Concil.* iv, 1743.   5 Duchesne, *l. c.* p. 348.

6 Victor of Utica, *De persec. Vand.* v, 10. (*Patr. Lat.* lviij, 248).

7 Gregory of Tours, *De vitis patr.* 8. (*Patr. Lat.* lxxj, 1040).

8 According to Chap. 45 the boys who sing wrong are to be beaten.

the boys sang together with men there was naturally a chant in octaves. *Antiphon therefore must be understood to mean a chant in which two choirs of different voices relieved one another in turn and afterwards sang together, thus entailing a singing in octaves.* Later the alternating of the chant was more esteemed than the real feature that was characteristic of this antiphony; and thus this is the meaning which thenceforth remained bound up with the expression. [1]

From Antioch psalmody in alternating chorus spread over the whole Christian world, both in the Greek and the Latin Churches. Already by 375 it was known throughout the whole East, as may be seen in the above-mentioned letter of Basil to the inhabitants of Neocesarea. Basil had introduced among them the chanting by a double-choir; and when they reproached him for this innovation, he reminded them that the psalms were then everywhere so sung. His description gives a clear picture of both kinds of psalmody: [2] 'But as for your reproach respecting the psalmody, I can reply to that, that it is arranged in harmony and agreement with all the Churches of God. At night the people rise and go to the House of Prayer, and, when they have prayed, they turn to psalmody. And sometimes they sing psalms, divided into two sections alternating with each other, and sometimes they leave it to a single person to sing solo, while all respond. And when they have thus spent the night in different kinds of psalmody, they all intone the Psalm of penitence as from one mouth and one heart . . . moreover if this is the reason why you separate yourselves from me, then must you likewise separate yourselves from the Egyptians, Libyans, Thebans, and the inhabitants of Palestine, Arabia, Phoenicia and Syria, and from those who dwell on the Euphrates, in a word, from all those by whom the vigil services and the common psalmody are held in honour.' Here attention is called to the fact that the common psalmody was especially in the nightly vigils. Antiphonal and responsorial psalmody are mentioned together in the contemporary *Didascalia 318 patrum*, [3] where, in accordance with the prevailing custom in the East, women are forbidden συμψάλλειν and συνυπακούειν, to join in singing and in the responsorial refrains. Theodoret mentions a peculiar form of antiphonal chanting where in a monastery consisting both of Greeks

---

1 But Bryennios the Byzantine Theorist of the 14th century, still calls tones which stand in the relation 2 : 1 by the name 'antiphon.' *cf.* Reimann. *Vierteljahrsschrift für Musikwissenschaft.* (Leipzig. 1889). p. 380.

2 *Epist.* 209. 3. (*Patr. Gr.* xxxij, 763).

3 Batiffol, *Hist. du Brév.*, 6.

and Syrians, they each sang the psalms in their own language, repeating it verse by verse antiphonally. [1]

At Constantinople *S. Chrysostom* introduced antiphonal chanting towards the end of the 4th century. Before his call to Constantinople he had the opportunity of making himself familiar with it at the place where it could best be heard, namely at Antioch. In his new sphere of work he was able to make new psalmody all the more useful because the Arians had made a great success of their antiphonal songs. As leader of the psalmodic choir-music he appointed the music-master at the Court. [3]

The merit of making the West acquainted with the antiphonal chant belongs to S. Ambrose of Milan, who at the time of his persecution by the Empress Justina (386) instructed those who were faithful to him, and who had shut themselves up with their pastor in his church, in the singing of antiphons and hymns. [4] From Milan the new practice spread quickly into the other regions of the Latin Church, thanks to the favourable position of the city geographically and to the authority of its bishop. Its use in almost all the Churches of the West is shewn by the witness of a contemporary of Ambrose, his secretary and biographer Paulinus. [5] Rome would not separate herself from the general movement : the night office was in early times celebrated there publicly, and certainly chanted in alternate chorus, as everywhere else. [6] Perhaps the council which took place in 382 in Rome, and at which there were present Greek and Syrian Bishops to whom antiphonal chanting was familiar, gave the impulse in introducing it into the Roman Liturgy. A generation later, under Pope Celestine I (422-432), it found admission into the Roman mass. [7] But here it was only an addition and intended to make the service more artistic; and its use in this way presupposes its use in the Divine office, and particularly in the Vigil, for which it was created, and with which it spread. The numerous monasteries which speedily covered the countries of the Latin

---

1 Theodoret, *Hist. Relig.* 5. Gerbert, *De Cantu* I. 179.

2 Sozomen, *Hist. Eccl.* viij, 8. (*Patr. Gr.* lxvij, 1536). 3 *Ibid.* (1538).

4 Augustine, *Confess.* 97 (*Patr. Lat.* xxxij, 770).

5 Paulinus, *Vita. Amb.* 13. (*Patr. Lat.* xiv, 31).

6 The Vigils are mentioned as early as the *Canons of Hippolitus* which according to Batiffol go back to the end of the 2nd century (*History of the Brev.* 42,), according to Bäumer (*Breviersgesch.* 32) to the beginning of the 3rd century. Further, Jerome, the liturgical adviser of Damasus, had learnt the Eastern practices in Bethlehem : *tota Ecclesia nocturnis vigiliis Christum Dominum personabat* he says in his letter to the Deacon Sabinianus (*Patr. Lat.* xxij, 1195).

7 *Lib. Pontif. ed.* Duchesne, i, 230.

Church then disseminated antiphonal chanting everywhere, even among the secular churches. [1]

Just as the psalmodic solo was connected with the chorus-refrain, so in like manner the *cantus antiphonus* was made more interesting and richer. The custom of singing a short solo-melody before the psalm, which enabled the singers to grasp more easily the psalm-melody, and was then further repeated after each of the verses performed by the alternate chorus, formed most probably part and parcel of the choir-psalmody from the beginning. This is confirmed by the fact that psalms and antiphons are spoken of as different things, as early as the 4th century. [2] Here the refrain which interrupts the alternating chant of the psalm is called antiphon, according to the use which has prevailed ever since. Accordingly the rule of S. Benedict (529 or 530) speaks much of *antiphonam imponere*. Thus it says in the 47th chapter: 'The psalms or antiphons are to be started *(imponat)* by each one in turn after the Abbot'. With this new meaning agrees the strange etymology given by an anonymous writer of the 6th century [3], who identifies the word absolutely with *anteponere*—'to prefix', or 'make to precede', because the antiphon precedes the psalm ; so does the form which is used in the oldest MSS of the Rule of S. Benedict, viz. *antefona.* [4] Together with the original sense of the word the remembrance of its origin has also disappeared.

From the expressions quoted it is not clear, whether the antiphon was repeated after all the verses of the psalm, or only after some of them. The former is certainly the original use. [5]

Of less importance was a third kind of psalmody, the *Cantus in directum*, or, *directaneus*, which consisted in the psalm being performed from beginning to end without responsorial or antiphonal additions. It

---

1 To quote an example : When S. Agricola, Abbot of Lerins, became Bishop of Avignon (about 660), he took care that in the Church of Avignon, for the canonical hours and other liturgical occasions, psalmody in alternate chorus should be introduced, as was customary in monasteries and 'had been admitted into the Roman Church by Damasus.' Mabillon, *Acta SS. Ord. Bened. Saec.* iv, *praef.* no. 210.

2 This is so in the description of the Liturgy of Jerusalem by the pilgrim Silvia (*c.* 385) *cf.* Cabrol. *l.c.*

3 Gerbert, I. 46.   4 *Cf.* the edition of Wölfflin (Leipzig, Teubner, 1895).

5 As is well known, the canticle *Nunc Dimittis* is now sung with the antiphon *Lumen ad revelationem* at the procession at the feast of Candlemas in the same manner ; the *invitatorium* also is a reminiscence of it. As we shall presently see, the old theory implied the repetition of the antiphon in the psalmody after each verse. This is indicated also by the Greek name for antiphon, τροπάριον (from τρέπειν, 'turn').

also appears to be of later origin, for it is first mentioned in the Rule of S. Benedict. This prescribes, in the 12th chapter, that at Sunday mattins Psalm 66 shall be sung *in directum* without antiphons; in like manner are Terce, Sext and None to be sung in the smaller monasteries. (Chap. 17). Clearly the founder of the order wished to prevent the brothers from becoming fatigued by the repetition of the antiphon after each verse of the psalm, which moreover would have taken up a disproportionate amount of time. We meet again with the *psalmus directaneus* in the rules of S. Caesarius and of S. Aurelian. [1] It is prescribed also in the Ambrosian Breviary and was sung, as a rubric directs, by both choirs together and not alternately. [2] Many liturgists have pronounced as their opinion that the psalmody *in directum* was an ordinary recitation without any melodic embellishment. [3]

The monasteries were the headquarters of psalmody; it was in them that the liturgical forms were fixed, in the West as in the East. Here the requisites for beautiful chant were earlier available, and also the regulation of this part of the worship of God was here more necessary than among the Christians living in the world. The first church song-schools arose in the eastern monasteries, and others after their pattern followed in the West. The education of the brethren in the chant was the duty of the cantors. The impetus which church music received after the middle of the 4th century is to be traced finally to the activity of the Syrian and Egyptian monasteries. Antioch and Alexandria were the centres of the movement; they represent for the Churches of the East what in the 7th and 8th centuries the Gregorian song-school became for the West. It was from Antioch that antiphony had set out on its victorious career in the whole Church; and in Alexandria the art of chanting so flourished that strict ascetics prophesied the decline of religious life. Thus Pambo, abbot of the Egyptian monastery of Nitria in the 4th century, bitterly reproached one of his monks, who while selling in Alexandria the products of his monastery, had listened to the magnificence of the chant in the monastery of S. Mark, because he then wished to introduce into his own monastery the chant of the *Canons* and *Troparia* which he had heard there; and Pambo thought it a great crime for a monk to be occupied with such things. [4]

---

1 *Patr. Lat.* lxvij. 1102, and lxviij, 395.

2 Beroldus, *Ordo Mediol. Ecclesiae* in Muratori *Antiq.* iv, 886. [or *ed.* Magistretti, 44.] The Ambrosian antiphoner published in *Paléographie musicale* vol. v, of the 12th century, also prescribes the *psalmus directaneus* frequently.   3 *e. g.* Tommasi, vol. xj of the *Op. Greg. M.* praef. xxxiv.   4 Gerbert, *Scriptores* I. 2.

The Monks on Sinai also kept aloof from antiphonal chant, strictly refusing everything that went beyond the simplest performance of the psalms. [1] Fortunately for liturgical music, such views were not held generally; on the contrary, in other monasteries of the East and West great stress was laid on a·beautiful and correct execution of the psalmody. S. Benedict, with rare penetration, understood how to bring the beauty and sublimity of the liturgical functions into harmony with severe monastic observance; thus he created a rule which was in accordance with the spirit of the times and remained full of vigour, while those of his predecessors gradually disappeared; and in chapters 7—19 of this rule he occupied himself very fully with the arrangement of the liturgical psalmody.

The secular churches were not behind the monasteries in zeal for dignified and beautiful church-music. In particular, it was usual to educate boys in the performance of these duties : their singing gave especial brilliancy to the liturgical assemblies. In Carthage, about 484, there were among the numerous clergy many *lectores infantuli*, who rendered good service in the psalmody. An inscription at Lyons of 552 has already been cited which mentions a *primicerius* of the *schola lectorum*, and one in Spain speaks of a *princeps cantorum*. [2] As to the state of things in Rome, it is certain that there were liturgical singers there at a very early date. Even if the foundation of a song-school by Pope Silvester (314—336), as Panvinius and others relate, cannot be historically proved, yet its existence in the 2nd half of the 4th century is very probable. [3] The introduction by Pope Celestine I of antiphonal chanting for the Introit of the Mass presupposes a choir of instructed singers. Pope Xystus (432—440) established *ad catacumbas* a monastic community, with the intention that it should make regular use of the day and night psalmody. [4] In close proximity to the basilica of S. Peter there arose under Leo the Great (440—461), the successor of Xystus, a monastery, dedicated to S. John and S. Paul, the members of which had the charge of the liturgical prayers and chants in the Pope's church. [5] Such were the beginnings from which the Roman

---

1 Bäumer, *Breviergeschichte*, 127.   2 Duchesne, *Christian Worship*, 348.

3 Gerbert, *De Cantu* I. 36. 'Although at the time of Pope Silvester and later there were several large basilicas in Rome, yet they did not each have their own clergy or monks to perform divine worship . . . Further, the daily psalmody was not yet at this time customary in all monasteries, for till then the single basilicas did not possess the income necessary to support colleges for singers. So a *schola cantorum* was founded, which was common to the whole city ; and if a station, procession or feast was celebrated in a basilica, all the singers went there and performed the office and the mass.'

4 Duchesne, *Lib. Pontif.* I. 236.   5 Duchesne, *ibid.* 238.

song-school descended, which later became so flourishing and influential.

More detailed statements on the musical form of this psalmody are unfortunately not forthcoming in the writings of the ancient Christian authors. We understand their silence: they were not musicians by profession, and had more important things to do than to report on something which everyone had the opportunity of hearing daily in church. Consequently, until far on into the middle ages the liturgical chant had a hidden existence; while outside in the world profane music enjoyed universal attention, the liturgical chants were bequeathed from *cantor* to *cantor*, from monastery to monastery. Peaceful and unmoved by the sound of secular music, they were handed down from generation to generation. Professional musicians knew only profane music, while the liturgical music was in other hands, viz. those of liturgical personages, and seldom stepped outside the doors of the House of God. Thus it came about that musical composers did not trouble themselves about the liturgical chant until the time of the Carolingians, because they had nothing to do with it, and did not know it from personal experience.

In the early days, no doubt, one must assume customs analogous to the Jewish use. It would naturally happen, and be in conformity with Jewish tradition, that the part of the soloist took a richer musical form, and assisted the development of virtuoso technique. Similarly it is to be supposed that the psalmody in which the whole community took part bore a more simple character. Elaborate melodies would here have proved to be only hindrances.

The view that church music until far on in the Middle Ages knew only the forms of simple recitation, such as developed naturally out of the pronunciation aloud of the liturgical text, is tenable only so far as the first centuries are concerned, and in the case of some ultra-conservative monasteries of a later date. But it cannot be maintained for most monastic communities and for the secular churches subsequently to the middle of the 4th century. Apart from anything else, it would have been very strange if the Church, after her liberation and while enjoying the protection of the secular power, had not outgrown the simpler forms of chant, which had only been a necessity as long as she was obliged to be content with a hidden existence. Church music could not stop at this point, when all other arts prepared to offer the best that they had to the God of the Christians. In the basilicas of the 4th century, into which were collected all the glory and magnificence which man could give, the old, almost melancholy, melody no longer was found in place. We have followed the course of antiphonal chanting in its triumphal march through the whole Church; but the striving after richer and more beautiful forms and ways of expression was not confined to this branch alone.

A passage in the 'Confessions of S. Augustine' is often brought forward to confirm the view that before the 4th century richer melodic forms were unknown to church music. And yet it says just the opposite. The great bishop mentions a tradition, according to which S. Athanasius made the *lector* sing the psalms with such moderate inflexion of the voice, that the psalmody was like speaking rather than singing. [1] Isidore of Seville copies the passage and puts as a correction 'the primitive church' instead of 'Athanasius.' [2] But what does the passage prove? Hardly that at the time of Athanasius psalmody was still bare of more developed melodic forms. If the Saint thought it necessary to give special instructions to the precentor about his psalmody, we must conclude that otherwise, without special directions, he was not accustomed to sing the psalms so simply. Thus the observation of Augustine directly presupposes a melodic way of performing the psalms in the Church of Alexandria. What Athanasius wanted was an innovation, or a return to primitive practice, anyhow something which at the time of Augustine was regarded as strange and unusual, as we learn from taking the whole context together. Accordingly Augustine is witness to the fact that about the year 400 the liturgical singers performed in other styles than the mere simple forms of recitation, which restricted their skill and ability to a minimum.

There are not wanting positive witnesses among Christian authors who describe the melodic development of church music in a manner not reconcileable with the idea that it was restricted in its method of performance to a mere recitation. Eusebius calls psalmody μελῳζεῖσθαι, [3] an expression which implies more than mere recitation. In another passage he says: 'We sing the psalms in melodious tones' (ὁμόφωνον μέλος ἐν ταῖς ψαλμολογίαις ἀναπέμπομεν. [4]) Chrysostom calls the Psalms 'prophetic songs which are sung with much harmony of the voice and in suitably composed melodies.' [5] In the Latin Church Augustine even knows of different kinds of reading. He occasionally uses the expression *solemniter legere*; thus he mentions that on Good Friday the Passion was

---

1 *Confess.* x, 33. 'Tam modico flexu vocis faciebat sonare lectorem psalmi ut pronuntianti vicinior esset quam canenti.' (*Patr. Lat.* xxxij, 800).

2 *Patr. Lat.* lxxxiij. 762. 'Primitiva ecclesia ita psallebat, ut modico flexu vocis faceret psallentem resonare, ita ut' etc.

3 *In Psalm.* 65. (*Patr. Gr.* xxiij, 647). *cf.* above p. 14.

4 *In Psalm.* 91. (*Patr. Gr.* xxxiij, 1174).

5 *Homil. ad Antioch.* 59. Gerbert, *De Cantu* I. 31.

solemnly read. [1]   This can only mean such a performance as is nearer to singing than to ordinary reading.   This being so, the methods of performance which are not comprised under the term *lectio*, and psalmody in particular, could claim a still more melodious character.   This is also shown by the context in which he brings out the simplicity of the Alexandrian chant under Athanasius.

That the saint was very susceptible to musical effect is shown by the oft-quoted passage of his 'Confessions' [2] where he describes the lasting impression made on him by the antiphons and hymns which had been introduced into the Milanese Church by Ambrose : 'How I have wept at the hymns and songs (*cantica*), deeply moved by the voices of your sweet-sounding church music !   Those voices forced an entrance into my ear, and with them the truth into my heart.   They awakened emotions of warm devotion and tears which benefited me.'   And yet again the saint had scruples on account of the deep emotion and tears, which he declares to be the effect of the sensual impression made by the chant, and 'While I seek to protect myself from this deceptive impression, I err again through too great severity, and to such an extent that I desire to banish from my ears and from the Church all the sweet melodies to which the psalms of David are sung with us *(melos cantilenarum suavium, quibus Davidicum psalterium frequentatur);* and it seems safer to do as I have often been told Athanasius, bishop of Alexandria, did; for he made the singer of the psalms chant with such moderate inflexion of the voice, that his performance was like speaking rather than singing.   On the other hand, when I remember the tears which I shed at the songs of the Church in the first days of the recovery of my belief, and when I am moved not so much by the chant as by what is chanted—then I again perceive the great use of this arrangement.' [3]   Thus the saint found himself temporarily hesitating whether to consider the art of chanting allowable or not.   At any rate the Milanese chant which he was considering was far advanced beyond the simplicity which he ascribes to the chants of Athanasius.

According to Cassian, who gives a fairly full description of the liturgical uses of the monasteries of the East, and is also a competent witness for the end of the 4th century, the archaic kind of psalmody was still undoubtedly held in honour in the Egyptian monasteries.   He adds

---

1 *Sermo* 218, i. (*Patr. Lat.* xxxviij, 1084). To-day the performance of the Passion and the Lamentations of Jeremiah in Holy Week is still a *lectio solemnis*.

2 *Confess.* ix, 6, 7. (*Patr. Lat.* xxxij, 769. foll.).

3 *Confess.* ix, 33. (*Patr. Lat.* xxxij, 800).

however that in other monasteries certain psalms were lengthened by antiphons and the addition of special 'modulations.' [1] The last expression has a special importance for us : it can only mean the singing of an elaborate musical phrase; and thus this remark of Cassian *is the most ancient witness to the existence of melismatic chant in the liturgy of the office.* It deserves to be noticed that Cassian is speaking of the Vigil, the predecessor of Mattins, which throughout the middle ages and up to the present time has been the chief home of melismatic chant in the Divine Office. Solo-psalmody at the vigil is not once referred to : the context, as well as the association of it with the antiphonal chant, shows undoubtedly that Cassian had the choral psalmody in his mind. But if already in the 4th century the tendency to a melismatic form of melody existed in this branch, then we are almost compelled to assume that the same was the case with regard to the solo-singer.

Cassian does not stand alone in his statement. The Rule of S. Benedict contains similar definitions, the tenor of which on careful consideration cannot be doubted. It must not be forgotten here that the great founder of the order was much attached to the practice of the monasteries of the East; and so the information to be found here is evidence also for the 5th century. Again it is the Vigil that is in question. With regard to it the Saint directs (Chap. 10) that in summer in the time from Easter till the beginning of November only one lesson (instead of three) is to be read, and that from the Old Testament; and a *brevis responsorius* (*psalmus*) is to follow it. The respond attached to the lessons in the nocturn must thus have been in other cases a longer one and it was only the need of a shorter *officium nocturnum* for the week days in summer that caused him here to prescribe a shorter respond. His direction is only to be understood by taking the short respond to be (as it has been ever since) melodically simple, in contrast to that which was customary on other occasions, and which must have been richer. If the melody of the usual responds were then only syllabic, the saving of time thereby obtained would have been infinitesimal, even if the text were shorter; but such a

---

[1] 'Quidam enim vicenos seu tricenos psalmos, et hos ipsos antiphonarum protelatos melodiis et adjunctione quarundam modulationum debere singulis noctibus censuerunt.' *Inst.* ij. 2. (*Patr. Lat.* xlix, 78). This passage moreover can be cited as proof that the antiphons were at first repeated after each verse of the psalm ; there is no lengthening of the office to speak of when they are only sung before and after the whole psalm. The special addition of melismatic passages (tropes) to a verse is still preserved : thus the versicle after the hymn in certain parts of the office, for example at Evensong, is recited indeed on one note, but on the last syllable a neum is added.

saving was certainly effected, when the responds were elsewhere retained in their richness, but here were only to be sung in a simple (or nearly syllabic) form.

Not much later than the rule of S. Benedict is that of Paul and Stephen, of the 6th century. We gather from it a valuable note which is the complement of the former one, and also proves what a delicate sense there was of the requirements of the different parts of the liturgy. It says : 'What is to be sung is not to be exchanged for any sort of prose or any thing like a lesson; and what is prescribed for use after the manner of lessons is not by our own presumption to be turned into tropes or singing.' [1] Two ways of performing liturgical texts are here named, both of which found place in the service; it was considered necessary to give direction where each was to be used. The more simple is called *lectio*, the richer is chanting proper, in which the art of the developed melody is to be used. *Tropus* is the name for melismatic embellishments of the kind that Cassian describes.

Again, attention must here be drawn to the different parts played by the solo and the choral chant in the *ensemble* of the Liturgy, as they developed apace from the 4th century onwards. The cantors certainly made use of the opportunity given them by the free public exercise of Christian worship, to set forth their skill in a conspicuous light. For the choral psalmody simple melodies still remained a necessity, as in this case regard had to be paid to singers who were not especially gifted or educated musically. But for the solo-singers a melody which only moved along syllabically could not permanently be sufficient. It would have been out of keeping with the splendour which was now being introduced into the services. The texts of the solo-chants, the psalms, belonged almost exclusively to the species of prose, or at least at that time they were conceived as such. But while a metrical text (as the ancient Greek music testifies) tends to bind down the melody to the requirements of the prosody of the verses, prose on the contrary is favourable to a prolongation of the text by enrichment of the melody. [2]

---

1 *Patr. Lat.* lxvj, 954. 'Non omnino oportet ut quae cantanda sunt in modum prosae et quasi lectionem mutemus, aut quae ita scripta sunt, ut in ordine lectionum utamur, in tropis et cantilenae arte nostra praesumptione vertamus.'

2 The melismatic form of melody was already known to the ancient Greeks, and indeed its use coincides with the dissolution into prose of the ordered language of poetry. It is well known how Aristophanes makes merry over the *melismata* of Euripides (*Frogs.* 1309 foll., εἰειειειειειλίσσετε). The Egyptians, as early as the 3rd century before Christ, were acquainted with melismatic passages on the vowels, and moreover in their liturgical

It is possible to go even further, and put the question whether, since the solo-chant was used in the Church three centuries earlier than the choral chant, the artistic and more or less developed chant in the Church is not more ancient than the simple. A ground of support for this opinion might be seen in the fact that those very chants which the history of the liturgy shows to be the oldest, the Gradual-responsories of the Mass and the responsories of the Office, belong to quite the richest pieces which the Middle Ages have handed down. [1]

The chief point at which the melismatic chant is used is the Alleluia. The singing of the Alleluia descends from the liturgy of the Synagogue, [2] where it was connected with a number of psalms. These alleluiatic psalms [3] have still in the present edition of the Bible the superscription 'Alleluia.' At the adoption of this custom in the Christian Church no one ventured to translate the Hebrew word into Greek or Latin. The Jewish Christians may have brought many Alleluia melodies with them from the Synagogue into the Christian Church, and many Alleluia *jubili* of our choral manuscripts may contain a Jewish kernel. It has already

---

chants in honour of the gods. Demetrius Phalereus (†282), §71. *cf.* Gevaert, *Mélopée.* p. xxviij.

1 There is clearly no need to claim for the 4th and 5th centuries the richness of the Gregorian solo-chants, which are unmistakeably the work of accomplished singers such as the Roman Song-school possessed. But we may at once dispose of the objection that chants of this kind were first introduced by these schools. If this were the case, it would be hard to understand why, for example, the antiphonal chants of the Mass, such as the Introit and Communion, are melodically simpler, although they were executed by the singers of the *Schola Cantorum*, and were fixed by them. The difference in style is the result of the strong contrast between solo and choral music, which governed the liturgy long before the time of the *schola*. The still simpler construction of the music of the *Gloria, Creed* etc. may be similarly explained. They were sung, as the *Ordines Romani* testify, not by the *schola*, but by all the clergy assisting at the Altar. Moreover not the slightest evidence has yet been brought to show that the liturgical chants of the manuscripts were first composed under Gregory I. His work, as will be shown at the proper time, has quite a different character: it is composed of several *strata* of different dates; the gradual-responsories belong to its oldest portions, as is shown by their text. It may further be remarked that under the Emperor Justinian the choir of the Cathedral Church of Byzantium was composed of 111 *lectors* and 25 *cantors* (Gerbert, *De Cantu* I. 33). It was thus more numerous than the Roman *Schola Cantorum*. At any rate the 25 *cantors* were all solo-singers; the 111 *lectors* had the care of the choral psalmody.

2 Isidore (*De Off.* i, 13). says: 'Laudes, hoc est alleluia, canere, canticum est Hebraeorum.' (*Patr. Lat.* lxxxiij, 750).

3 Basil mentions, in his Epistle to Marcellinus, Pss. 104—106, 110—115, 118—134, 146—150. Gerbert I. 57.

been mentioned that the Alleluia was readily used as the response of the assembly to the psalm-verse of the soloist. In conformity with this the Egyptian Monks responded the Alleluia only at the alleluiatic psalms. [1] The Alleluia was indeed frequently used as an exclamation of Christian joy—pious parents taught their children to sing the Alleluia in their earliest youth; [2] the sailors shouted it from afar on the sea; [3] and Christian armies went to battle crying it aloud; [4]—but its chief place was in the Liturgy. But in contrast with the East, where in the middle ages it was still sung daily even on Good Friday and at burials, [5] its use in the Latin Church was restricted. It was sung everywhere at Eastertide, and is still lavishly employed at that season in the liturgy. For the other seasons of the year there were different customs. According to the testimony of S. Isidore it was sung daily in Spain, except on fast days and in Lent; in Africa only on Sundays, except at Eastertide; and in the Rule of S. Benedict it is forbidden only in Lent. In his writings S. Augustine very often speaks of the singing of Alleluia at Eastertide: in one of these he calls the festal chant of Alleluia an ancient custom of the Church. [6]

From the very first the Alleluia chant has been melismatic. The contrary supposition is opposed to all that has been handed down to us as to the pecularity, effect and importance of the Alleluia-singing. The singing in *melismata* was called *jubilare*, and the melismatic melody *jubilus*, and various mystic explanations were given of the use of these terms. Augustine says in his exposition of the 99th Psalm: 'He who sings a *jubilus*, speaks no words, but it is a song of joy without words; it is the voice of a heart dissolved in joy, which tries as far as possible to express the feeling, even if it does not understand the meaning. When a man rejoices in his jubilation, he passes from some sounds which do not belong to speech and have no particular meaning, to exulting without words; so that it seems that he rejoices indeed, but that his joy is too great to put into words.' [7] This passage demonstrates the general human need of the

---

1 Cassian, *Inst.* ij, 11. (*Patr. Lat.* xlix, 101).

2 Jerome, *Ep. ad Laetam.* (*Patr. Lat.* xxij, 871).　　　　3 Gerbert, *l.c.*

4 Thus S. Germanus inspired the Britons to battle with the Anglo-Saxons and Scots. Bede, *Hist. Eccl.* I, 20. (*Patr. Lat.* xcv, 49).　　　5 *Patr. Lat.* lxxviij, 468.

6 'Quod nobis cantare certo tempore solemniter moris est secundum ecclesiae antiquam traditionem.' *In Ps.* 106, 1. (*Patr. Lat.* xxxvij, 1419).

7 *Patr. Lat.* xxxvij, 1272. 'Qui jubilat non verba dicit, sed sonus quidam est laetitiae sine verbis: vox est enim animi diffusi laetitia, quantum potest experimentis affectum non sensum comprehendentis. Gaudens homo in exultatione sua ex verbis quibusdam, quae non possunt dici et intelligi, erumpit in vocem quandam exultationis

jubilatio. Other passages of the same author concern its use in the service of God. In his exposition of Psalm 32 he exclaims : 'And for whom is this *jubilatio* more fitting than for the ineffable God ? He is ineffable, for speech is too poor for Him; and if speech cannot help thee there and thou darest not be silent, what remains but to exult so that thy heart may rejoice without singing words, and the immeasurable breadth of joy may not experience the restriction of syllables ?' [1] Jerome expresses himself in the same manner : 'By the term *jubilus* we understand that which neither in words nor syllables nor letters nor speech is it possible to express or comprehend how much man ought to praise God.' [2] A very clear and important passage on the *jubilus*, of pre-Gregorian date, is to be found in Cassiodorus in his exposition of Psalm 104. He is thinking there of the long drawn *Alleluia-jubili*, and exclaims : 'This (the Alleluia) is peculiar to the churches of God, and specially suitable for the holy feasts. The tongue of the singer rejoices in it; joyfully the community repeat it; and, like something good of which one can never have enough, it is renewed in ever-varying *melismata.*' [3] There was thus in the middle of the 6th century a kind of Alleluia in which the liturgical singers could display their skill, and which knew manifold varying modulations. Far from being a recent importation it had already become the subject of some regulations. One can understand that on specially joyful feasts a more extensive use was made of the *jubilus* than at the others.

These passages of Augustine and Cassiodorus imply that the Alleluia is an independent and extremely richly-developed chant, which is not accompanied by a text: the contrast between it and the word is expressly prominent. This is also brought home to us by the designation 'Alleluiatic song,'

---

sine verbis; ita ut appareat, eum ipsa voce gaudere quidem, sed quasi repletum nimio gaudio, non posse verbis explicare quod gaudet.'

1 Augustine, *In Ps.* 32 : 'Et quem decet ista jubilatio, nisi ineffabilem Deum ? Ineffabilis enim est, quem fari non potes : et si eum fari non potes et tacere non debes, quid restat, nisi ut jubiles, ut gaudeat cor sine verbis et immensa latitudo gaudiorum metas non habeat syllabarum ?' (*Patr. Lat.* xxxvj, 283).

2 Jerome, *In Ps.* 32 : '*Jubilus* dicitur, quod nec verbis, nec syllabis, nec litteris, nec voce potest erumpere aut comprehendere quantum homo Deum debeat laudare.' (*Patr. Lat.* xxvj, 970).

3 Cassiodorus, *In Ps.* 104 ; 'Hoc ecclesiis Dei votivum, hoc sanctis festivitatibus decenter accommodatum. Hinc ornatur lingua cantorum; istud aula domini laeta respondet et tanquam insatiabile bonum, tropis semper variantibus innovatur.' (*Patr. Lat.* lxx, 742.) Cassiodorus confirms the connexion of the Alleluia with the *Jubilatio* in another passage : 'Ecce iterum alleluiatica nobis gaudia redierunt; ecce brevi praecipitur, ut Domino totius psalmi jubilatione cantetur.' (*Patr. Lat.* lxx, 735).

which the historian of the African persecution of the Christians hands down.[1]

From the words quoted from the Rule of S. Paul and S. Stephen we see that the singers had *written directions* to show in each case whether the *lectio* or the complete melodic execution was to be employed. There is no need to take these to be a specific musical notation ; general directions would have sufficed. [2] Since the number of the liturgical melodies, as well for the Office as for the Mass, would have been only a small one— even in the medieval MSS. we find the same melody set to the most different texts—the tradition by word of mouth might do instead of a written one. Only later, when the chants became regulated, did it become necessary to have them written down. Hence the order quoted from the Council of Laodicea, according to which only the liturgical singer *who performed from the parchment* should sing during the service, is not to be understood to imply that they were in possession of written melodies. They had the text on a leaf before them ; they themselvès added the melody to it.

There is no trace of a musical notation in the most ancient liturgical piece of writing which has come down to us. This is preserved on a papyrus of the Archduke Rainer of the beginning of the 4th century, and gives us an insight into the responsorial psalmody as it was performed in the East about 300 ; the leaf contains on one side the *acrostichia* to the festival psalms of Epiphany, on the other side that for the feast of S. John the Baptist, which in the Egyptian Church was celebrated the day before the Epiphany. On the *recto* stands the following text.

ὁ γεννηθεὶς ἐν Βηθλεὲμ καὶ ἀνατραφεὶς ἐν Ναζαρὲτ, κατοικήσας ἐν Γαλιλαίᾳ, εἴδομεν σημεῖον ἐξ οὐρανοῦ. (τῷ) ἀστέρος φανέντος, ποιμένες ἀγραυλοῦντες ἐθαύμασαν. (οὐ) γονυπεσόντες ἔλεγον. δόξα τῷ Πατρὶ, ἀλληλούϊα, δόξα τῷ Υἱῷ καὶ τῷ ἁγίῳ Πνεύματι, ἀλληλούϊα, ἀλληλούϊα, ἀλληλούϊα. [3] On the other side of the leaf : Τυβὶ ε : Ἐκλεκτὸς ὁ ἅγιος Ἰωάννης ὁ Βαπτιστής, ὁ

---

1 Victor Uticensis, *De Persecut. Vandal.* relates of a cantor singing the Alleluia : 'Quodam tempore paschalis solemnitas agebatur, et dum in quodam loco qui regia vocitatur, ob diei Paschalis honorem nostram sibimet clausam Ecclesiam reserarent, comperiunt Ariani . . . et tunc forte audiente et canente populo Dei, lector unus pulpito sistens Alleluiaticum melos canebat; quo tempore sagitta in gutture jaculatus, cadente de manu codice, mortuus post cecidit ipse.' (*Patr. Lat.* lviij, 197).

2 In spite of this it is worth notice that, according to Victor of Utica, the singer of the Alleluia holds a *codex* in his hand. See the foregoing note.

3 'Thou who wast born in Bethlehem, brought up in Nazareth, and who hast dwelt in Galilee, we saw thy sign in the heavens; when the star appeared, the shepherds keeping watch by night marvelled; falling on their knees they said : "Glory be to the Father, alleluia, glory be to the Son, and to the holy Ghost, alleluia, alleluia, alleluia."'

κηρύξας μετάνοιαν ἐν ὅλῳ τῷ κόσμῳ εἰς ἄφεσιν τῶν ἁμαρτιῶν ἡμῶν. [1]

It was thus customary to write antiphonal melodies on single leaves for certain feasts; in our case, only the *acrostichia* are given, the psalm itself would have been familiar to those present. Bickell [2] supposes that the festival psalm was sung at the beginning of the Liturgy between the Old and New Testament lessons, so that we have here the most ancient form of the gradual responsory of the Mass. The *acrostichion* for the feast of S. John is not long, and was repeated after each psalm-verse; that for the Epiphany is divided into three parts, which are used as responsories one after another for so many parts of the festival psalm. This, according to Bickell, was Ps. 32, as responsories. According to Bickell's ingenious conjecture, the enigmatical words (in parentheses above) τῷ and οὐ contain a reference to the psalm-verses at which the ensuing part of the *acrostichion* is to be used. After the first 5 verses the choir repeated each time the first of the three portions, from ὁ γεννηθεὶς to ἀστέρος; and from the sixth which begins with τῷ, the second portion was responded as far as γονυπεσόντες; the third portion finally was the responsory for the last part of the psalm which (v. 16) begins with οὐ. It is further worth notice that the doxology forms the conclusion of the *acrostichion*, because later it was always connected with the psalm.

---

1 On January 5th. 'Chosen is S. John Baptist, who preached repentance in all the world for the forgiveness of our sins.'

2 Bickell, *Mitteilungen aus der Sammlung der Pap. Rainer.* 1887. vols. II & III.

CHAPTER II

THE HYMNS

Besides the Psalter and the other lyrical portions of Holy Scripture, there are yet other songs mentioned in the past Christian centuries. It cannot be ascertained what kind of hymn it was that our Lord sang with His Apostles on the day before His Passion. [1] The Apostle Paul speaks of a *charisma* of psalm-singing, [2] by which he means new songs which were the product of the solemn devotional mood. Tertullian relates that at the *Agape*, 'after the lighting of the candles and the washing of hands,' each might come forward and praise God from the Holy Scriptures, or following his own inspiration. [3] Origen testifies that 'the Greeks in Greek, and the Romans in Latin, and each nation in its own language prayed to God and sang hymns to Him with all their might.' [4] Such improvised songs have been rightly seen in many parts of the New Testament, [5] as for instance in the 4th and 5th chapters of the Apocalypse etc. [6] The world of

---

[1] S. Matt. xxvj. 30. S. Mark xiv, 26. The Priscillianists professed to possess it, but S. Augustine declared it to be apocryphal (*Patr. Lat.* xxxiij, 1034 foll.). When Charlemagne wished to know where this hymn was preserved, his liturgical adviser Alcuin told him in answer that it was contained in the prayer (S. John xvij.) which our Lord addressed to his Father for his disciples (*Patr. Lat.* c, 428. foll.). Perhaps the hymn was that prescribed in the Jewish liturgy for the Passover (*Ps.* 112—117, conclusion of the Hallel).

[2] 1 Cor. xij, at the end.   [3] *Apology* 39. (*Patr. Lat.* i, 540).

[4] *Contra Celsum* viij, 37. (*Patr. Gr.* xj, 1574).

[5] See Bäumer in the *Kirchenlexicon* of Wetzer and Welter, (2nd ed. VI. 521); his article 'Hymnus' should be referred to for the whole of this Chapter. Probst also gives a detailed account of such songs, *Lehre und Gebet in den 3 ersten Christl. Jahrh.* (Tübingen, 1871.) 256 foll.

[6] According to Eusebius (*Hist. Eccl.* ii. 17.) the *Therapeutae* also had this kind of 'new psalms;' and he adds that not only did they understand the older hymns admirably, but also composed new ones 'in manifold metres and very fitting melodies.'

thought introduced by Christianity offered thousandfold inducements to creations of this kind, and has never ceased to inspire gifted and pious Christians to magnificent poetical productions. All the later songs which are not taken from Holy Scripture, such as the hymns, sequences, the Ecclesiastical folk-songs etc., are closely connected with these creations of primitive Christianity.

Poems of this kind were frequently called psalms, as the expressions 'psalms' and 'hymns' were for a long time often used in the general sense of 'spiritual songs.' It was only gradually that the word Hymn acquired the meaning of metrical poetry intended to be sung in praise of Christian truths or events. Originally the conception of a hymn was a wider one. [1] Thus the two songs mentioned in the Apostolic Constitutions (vij, 47) were called hymns, i. e. those which were sung at the liturgical morning and evening prayer, and which are the originals of our *Gloria in excelsis* (of the Mass) and of the *Te decet laus* (conclusion of the Sunday Mattins in the Benedictine Breviary). A very old evening hymn is the *Lumen hilare* (Φῶς ἱλαρὸν ἁγίας ὁόξης). Clement of Alexandria is celebrated as the composer of two hymns to the Redeemer and the Instructor, [2] the former of which is a particularly admirable example of the most ancient hymnody. The martyr Athenogenes composed a poem in honour of the Holy Trinity. [3] About the year 200 lived the Egyptian bishop, Nepos, whose hymns and psalms were still beloved in the time of Eusebius. [4] Later than this is Methodius (†311), of whom a poem on Christ and the Blessed Virgin is extant.

As early as the third century non-biblical poetry of this kind had taken root, and enjoyed such popularity that the Council of Antioch (269) found fault with Paul of Samosata, the Bishop of that town, for having abolished it in his Church 'on the ground that these psalms were not taken from the Davidic psalter, but were of later origin.' [5] On the other hand this popularity soon gave the heretics the opportunity of pressing their doctrines upon the people by means of hymns. In the 2nd half of the

---

1 S. Ambrose defines the hymn thus : 'Cantus cum laude Dei. Si laudes Deum, et non cantas, non dicis hymnum. Si cantes, et non laudes Deum, non dicis hymnum. Si laudes aliquid quod non pertinet ad laudem Dei, etsi cantando laudes, non dicis hymnum. Hymnus ergo tria ista habet, et canticum et laudem et Dei.' Gerbert, *De Cantu* I. 74.

2 *Patr. Gr.* viij, 681. foll.

3 *Ibid.* xxxij. 205.

4 Eusebius, *Hist. Eccl.* vij, 24. (*Patr. Gr.* xx, 693).

5 Eusebius, vij, 30. (*Patr. Gr.* xx, 709 foll).

the 2nd century, Marcion and the gnostic Valentine, who came to Rome about 153, spread heretical psalms, of which Tertullian speaks. [1] A complete gnostic psalter of 150 psalms originated from Bardesanes (†223) and his son Harmonius. [2] The apocryphal acts of the Apostles (c. 200) contain many gnostic psalms. S. Epiphanius knew of similar works of Hierax. [3] Songs of this kind wrought much mischief, as the false teachers understood how to give them an attractive musical form. It was Arius in particular who thus made so many followers, and with regard to whom S. Ephraem said that the false teachers had veiled the plague of destruction in the garment of musical beauty. S. Athanasius also complains of his exquisite songs. [4]

In order to destroy the disorder from the roots, the Council of Laodicea (between 361 and 381) forbade, in its 59th Canon, anything to be sung in the liturgy which was not contained in Holy Scripture. [5] The result of this decision was that most of the compositions of this sort, and those of catholic origin among them, were lost. The name given them by the Council is *Psalmi idiotici*. But other pastors did not fail to appreciate the good which was attainable in this way, and strove to cut off the excrescences and to retain what was essential, to clothe orthodox doctrine where possible in still more beautiful forms, and have it sung to yet more beautiful melodies. This procedure thereupon became the victorious one, and this is the standpoint which the Church has adopted all through the middle ages and down to the present time. Not only has she received into the inner circle of liturgy songs and hymns which do not come out of Holy Scripture, but she has permitted the faithful to render to God laud and praise, repentance and penitence, thanks and prayer, in the vulgar tongue; though there have been times when there was a wish to restrict the people's singing in the Church to a minimum, or even to banish it altogether.

The most prominent hymn-writer of the East is S. Ephraem Syrus (306—373). Not only did the Syrian hymnody reach its zenith in him,

---

1 *Liber de carne Christi*, 17 and 20. (*Patr. Lat.* ij, 781 and 786).

2 Sozomen, *Hist. Eccl.* iij, 16. (*Patr. Gr.* lxvij, 1090).

3 *Heresies*, lxvij, 3. (*Patr. Gr.* xlij, 175).

4 *De decretis Nicaeni synodi*, 16. (*Patr. Gr.* xxv, 451). It has already been mentioned above, that in Miletus hymns were accompanied with clapping of hands and dance movements. *Cf.* p. 13.

5 A Spanish provincial council in the 7th century took the same standpoint, and in the 9th century the opponent of Amalarius, (Agobard of Lyons,) of whom more will be said in this connexion.

but his poems became of great importance for the development of the new form in the Greek and Latin Churches. Already in his lifetime they became naturalized in the Syrian liturgy; in the later collections they occupy the first place. As most of the works of the older Eastern hymn-poets (like those of Bardesanes and Harmonius) came to an end with the gnostics and other heretics, so Ephraem's hymns belong to the oldest which are still in liturgical use. He found successors in his own Church : pre-eminent among them were Cyrillonas (2nd half of the 4th century,) Balæus, Rabulas and Isaac the Great (1st half of the 5th century) and James of Sarug (521).

The important effect which the Syrian hymn-poetry had on that of later date is in the rhythmical structure of the poetry, which was entirely dominant in Ephraem's hymns. [1] The line is not founded on the ancient law of quantity, which combined long and short syllables with one another and formed them into various feet, but on the principle of accent and enumeration of syllables. The alternation of accented and unaccented syllables, of *arsis* and *thesis*, is its formal element of construction; while further, there is an equal number of syllables, or at least of accented ones, in the verses which correspond with one another. This new poetical form of rhythmical poetry, which is claimed by a prominent investigator to be of semitic origin, [2] was to be a pioneer for future times. The style of language which underlies it has a specially musical character, and thus shewed itself extremely fruitful in giving musical form to the liturgical chant throughout the middle ages.

Ephraem's contemporary, Gregory Nazianzen, transmitted it to the ecclesiastical poetry of the Greeks without quite giving up the old classical form of poetry. [3] His successors, the Byzantine poets of later times, went further in the same direction. It was S. Hilary of Poitiers (†367) who made the Latin Church acquainted with the hymnody which had spread from Syria all over the Greek Church. Banished by Constantine to the East, this indefatigable opponent of Arianism had the opportunity of acquainting himself with the Syrian and Greek hymns, and of noticing the happy influence which they had on the people. On his return home

---

1 See Hubert Grimme, *Der Strophenbau in den Gedichten Ephräms des Syrers* (*Collectanea Friburgensia* II, Freiburg, Switzerland. 1893), where the different poetical forms of Ephraem are analyzed.

2 W. Meyer, *Anfang und Ursprung der Lat. und Griech. rythmischen Dichtung*, (*Abhandlungen der Bayr. Akademie der Wissenschaften, Munich.* 1885.) p. 270—450.

3 Grimme, *l. c.* 77. foll.

he translated some of these into Latin and added some new ones. The Spanish liturgist, Isidore of Seville, calls him explicitly the first Latin hymn-writer [1], and S. Jerome was acquainted with a book of hymns by him. [2] They are almost all lost, except a few which were discovered in 1884 by Gammurini in a MS. at Arezzo (which also contains the *Peregrinatio Sylviae*). Hilary found no right understanding of his compositions among his own people; [3] and so it was not he but S. Ambrose who determined the brilliant development which the new form was to take in the West. In the days of necessity and fervent prayer, when he had shut himself up with his faithful flock in his basilica to save it from being taken possession of by the Arians, and made them acquainted with antiphonal psalmody, he also taught them to sing some hymns composed by himself. [4] He was able by these to inspirit the people so much that the Arians accused him of having bewitched them. [5]

The contrast is great between the hymns of Ambrose and those of Hilary. Those of the former are complete and perfect works of art in their contents and form. The characteristic of these hymns is that they are Christian thoughts clothed in glorious language, which is at the same time simple and popular, and composed in classically antique form. They all consist of 8 stanzas, of 4 lines each; all the lines are written in Iambic dimeters. As the hymns of Ambrose found many imitators, the name 'Ambrosian' became an appellation of hymns composed in the style of S. Ambrose's poetry. [6] Opinions are still divided on the point as to which of these

---

1 *De offic*, i, 6 : 'Hilarius, Gallus episcopus Pictavensis, eloquentia conspicuus hymnorum carmine floruit primus.' (*Patr. Lat.* lxxxiij, 743).

2 *De viris illustribus*, (*Patr. Lat.* xxiij, 699).

3 According to a statement of S. Jerome (*Patr. Lat.* xxvj, 355). Hilary spoke of the Gauls as 'in hymnorum carmine indociles.'

4 Augustine, *Confess.* ix, 7. (*Patr. Lat.* xxxij, 770.) Paulinus, *Vita Ambrosii*, 13. (*Patr. Lat.* xiv, 31).

5 Ambrosius contra Auxentium, (*Patr. Lat.* xvj, 1017). 'Hymnorum meorum carminibus populum deceptum volunt. Plane nec hoc abnuo. Grande carmen istud est, et quo nihil potentius, quam confessio Trinitatis, quae quotidie totius populi ore celebratur.'

6 This designation is met with as early as the Rule of S. Benedict, and Walafrid Strabo (*De Reb. Eccl.* in *Patr. Lat.* cxiv, 954) says in regard to it : 'In officiis quoque, quae b. Benedictus abbas ordinavit, hymni dicuntur per horas canonicas, quos Ambrosianos ipse nominans, vel illos vult intelligi, quos confecit Ambrosius, vel alios ad imitationem Ambrosianorum compositos. Sciendum tamen multos putari ab Ambrosio factos, qui nequaquam ab illo sunt editi.' The term 'Ambrosiani' always means only the hymns, never the other chants of the Milanese-Ambrosian Liturgy. Later writers have not heeded this, and because some medieval authors ascribe to

'Ambrosian' hymns have had the Saint himself for their author. [1] It is certain that the four hymns

Aeterne rerum conditor
Deus creator omnium
Jam surgit hora tertia
Veni redemptor gentium

are due to Ambrose, as they are attested by Augustine. [2] Biraghi, [3] a Milanese savant, has, on account of the agreement of the oldest Milanese liturgical books, adjudged 14 more to Ambrose, besides the four above-mentioned hymns; these are given below, in order to make clear the present condition of the question. [4]

Splendor paternæ gloriæ	*Hic est dies verus Dei*
Nunc sanĉe nobis spiritus	*Viĉor, Nabor, Felix, pii*
Reĉor potens, verax deus	*Grates tibi, Jesu, novas*
Rerum deus tenax vigor	*Apostolorum passio*
Amore Christi nobilis	*Apostolorum supparem*
Illuminans altissimus	*Aeterna Christi munera*
Agnes beatæ virginis	*Jesu corona virginum.*

In the footsteps of Ambrose trod *S. Augustine* (†430), who composed a song against the Donatists (about 393) which he calls a psalm, but which may also be regarded as a hymn: '*Omnes qui gaudetis pace, modo verum judicate.* [5] His contemporary, *Paulinus* Bishop of Nola (†431), was the author of a book of hymns, [6] which has not come down to us. Outside the circle inspired by Ambrose stands his elder contemporary *Marius Viĉorinus Afer* (†370), among whose works are to be found three hymns to the Holy Trinity, [7] without metrical or rhythmical construĉion, which

---

'Ambrosiani' a measured (in modern phraseology 'bar'—) form, have expressed incorreĉly the view that the chants of the Ambrosian Liturgy were sung in modern bars.

1 *Cf.* Ulysse Chevalier, (*Poesie liturgique du moyen age, Rhythme et Histoire.* 1892), wh ɔ gives complete information on the disputed point. p. 69. foll.

2 Augustine, *Retraĉ.* i, 21, (*Patr. Lat.* xxxij, 618). *Confess.* xi, 12, (*Patr. Lat.* xxxij, 777). *De natura et gratia*, 63, (*Patr. Lat.* xliv, 284). *Sermo*, 372 (*Patr. Lat.* xxxix, 1663).

3 Biraghi, *Inni sinceri et carmi di S. Ambrogio*, Milan. 1862.

4 Biraghi's conclusions have been simply taken for granted by Dreves (*Aurelius Ambrosius*, Freiburg 1893). The remaining musical part of the book is unsatisfaĉory both in its form and in its contents.

5 *Retraĉ.* i, 20 (*Patr. Lat.* xxxij, 617).

6 Gennadius (5th century) *De viris illustribus*, 48, ascribes to him a *hymnarium* (*Patr. Lat.* lviij, 1083). This Paulinus is not to be confounded with the biographer of S. Ambrose of the same name. .   7 *Patr. Lat.* viij, 1139. foll.

perhaps approach nearer to Hilary's type. From them portions are taken to form the *Officium de Trinitate*. Hymns are also ascribed to Pope Damasus († 386) ; [1] some of them penetrated to the medieval Liturgy, such as *Martyris ecce dies* for S. Agatha, *Decus sacrati nominis* for S. Andrew, and *Jam dudum Saulus* for the Conversion of S. Paul.

The most prominent hymn-writer of the time immediately following Ambrose is the Spaniard *Prudentius* († after 405), who still dealt solely with the forms of the classical poetry of the ancients, and occupies a more independent position than Ambrose. He is the author of two collections of hymns, the *Cathemerinon* (hymns for each day) and *Peristephanon* (hymns in honour of the Martyrs). Some of his hymns penetrated to the Spanish, and later also to the Roman Church, which uses the following hymns of his :—

> *Ales diei nuntius* (Sunday Lauds)
> *Audit tyrannus anxius* ⎫ Holy Innocents
> *Salvete flores martyrum* ⎭
> *Nox et tenebrae et nubila* (Wednesday Lauds)
> *Lux ecce surgit aurea* (Thursday Lauds)
> *O˙ sola magnarum urbium* (Epiphany)
> *Quicumque Christum quaeritis* (Transfiguration).

Most of these hymns are made up of single strophes of longer poems. The Latin hymnody of the first centuries may be said to end with Prudentius. Its further history will be dealt with in the 10th chapter.

How were the old hymns *sung?* In Syria and Greece the hymn-music must have approached closely to the Folksong of those countries. At any rate, as later ages have held, melodies which were in use among the people were turned to this use, in order to make the hymns themselves popular. We know nothing further in regard to their music, but the poetical forms, which were often complicated, appear to have introduced a great variety of melodies.

In the Latin Church the hymns have from the first had a more distinctly popular form. The division of the poem into lines of equal construction, of the stanzas into an equal number of equally constructed lines,—such a formation is in a high degree popular. It demands a melody which can be repeated for all the stanzas, and which reflects the single lines in their extent and structure. Generally each syllable of the text receives one note only : that is the norm for the Folksong of all times, and for melodies which are sung by large multitudes such a formation is in

---

1 Chevalier, *l.c.* 67.

some sort a necessity. Whether Ambrose and his successors also composed the melodies for their hymns, or whether they resorted to popular melodies, it is certain that their melodies were simple in form. The melodies of the hymns in the Ambrosian Breviary are of a like simple structure, and many of them may go back to the 4th or 5th century, especially those which can be proved to have been sung to texts written by Ambrose.

CHAPTER III

A GENERAL SURVEY OF THE DEVELOPMENT OF THE LITURGY AND OF THE LITURGICAL CHANT IN THE MIDDLE AGES. [1]

The development of Ecclesiastical Chant from the beginnings which have been so far described was completed in the Greek and Latin Churches in different ways. Yet until the Great Schism (about 1050) there were influences on the Latin Liturgy from the Greek, *i. e.* the Byzantine, which were not without musical results. The question how much the Latin Liturgies in their oldest forms are on the whole indebted to the Greek has not yet received comparative investigation.

There are two facts to be especially borne in mind with respect to this : first, until the end of the 3rd century the liturgical language in Rome was Greek, and Latin was only secondarily thus used. S. Paul wrote his Epistle to the Romans in Greek, not in Latin, and all the religious documents preserved to us from early Christian Rome are written in the Greek language. Accordingly at first the Liturgy at Rome was performed in Greek, and thus they sang in Greek.

Secondly, the first and most complete development of the liturgical chant took place, as we know, in the countries of the East; it was from thence that the alternate chant of the psalms and the antiphons penetrated to the West, into Italy, Gaul and Spain; and the hymns also. . Many roots therefore of the liturgical chant of the West extend to the East, to Jerusalem, Antioch, Alexandria and Constantinople.

---

1 The sources for the material which occupies the following chapter on the history of the Liturgy in the Middle Ages are the following : the *Ordines Romani*, the old Roman books of ceremonial (printed in *Patr. Lat.* vol. lxxviij), the Gregorian mass book, the *Liber Sacramentorum S. Gregorii Magni (ibid.)*; the writings of the medieval liturgists, Amalarius (*Patr.Lat.*vol. cv.) etc. Of connected compilations I again mention the valuable works of Cardinal Tommasi; the *Origines du Culte Chrétien (Christian Worship)* by Duchesne; the Histories of the Breviary by Bäumer and Batiffol; Gerbert *De Cantu* vol. i. also contains much material.

Under these circumstances it would be surprising if the chant of the
Latin Church at first had been of an opposite nature to that of the Greek
Church. On the contrary, everything points to a near relationship between
them. Even after the introduction of antiphonal psalmody and hymnody,
the chant of the Latin Church did not remain absolutely unaffected by
the Byzantine; and it is easy to define the different stages of the
development.

On investigating the texts especially of the Roman Mass, the fact
emerges that they are with few exceptions drawn from Holy Scripture,
especially from the Psalter. [1] But whence come the others? There is
good reason for saying that most of them are translations of a Greek
original; especially the circumstance that the Masses to which they belong
may be proved either to be derived from the East or to be in many ways
composed of Greek elements. Their melodies may be divided into two
classes: those which follow the musical laws of the remaining chants which
have their texts drawn from the Bible, and those which have melodic
peculiarities of their own, especially modal ones. Without doubt the
chants of the first class were already known in Rome; when the Mass-
music was set in order, and the arranging of the liturgical chant, the fixing
and correcting of the melodies extended to them. They have been
welded into an organic unity with the other parts of the book of the Mass-
music, and are not musically distinguishable from them. To this class
belong the Introits *Ecce advenit* of Epiphany, *In excelso throno* of the
following Sunday, and probably also the Christmas Alleluia ℣. *Dies
sanctificatus etc.* [2]

Entirely different circumstances attended the second class of Mass-
chants, which can be proved to have been first taken into the Latin liturgy
under the Greek Popes of the 7th and 8th centuries, after the settlement
of the Roman Ecclesiastical chant. According to the *Liber Pontificalis* [3]
Sergius I (687—701) introduced a procession before the Mass on the four
feasts of the Blessed Virgin, the Annunciation, Assumption *(Dormitio)*,
Nativity and Purification. At the procession of the Purification our most
ancient manuscripts [4] still contain antiphons which are very instructive as
to the point in question. One of them runs Χαῖρε κεχαριτωμένη, *Ave gratia
plena*, θεοτόκα παρθένε, *Dei genitrix virgo*, ἐκ σοῦ γὰρ ἀνέτειλεν, *ex te enim
ortus est*, ὁ ἥλιος τῆς δικαιοσύνης, *sol iustitiae, etc.* As verse to it is sung

1 More of which later. 2 On the Greek origin of the corresponding feasts
cf. Duchesne, *Christian Worship*, 257.
3 *Liber Pontif. ed.* Duchesne, i, 371. foll. 4 *Patr. Lat.* lxxviij, 653.

Κατακόσμησον τὸν θάλαμόν σου, Σιῶν, *Adorna thalamum tuum, Sion,* καὶ ὑπόδεξαι τὸν βασιλέα Χριστόν, *et suscipe regem Christum,* etc. The Latin verse is still prescribed for the forementioned procession. Most of the chants of the feasts of the Elevation of the Cross imported by the above mentioned popes, and many chants of the Palm-Sunday Procession, the antiphon *Crucem tuam,* and the Good Friday *Improperia* in which the choir still answers the complaint of the Saviour to His thankless people with the exclamation *Agios o Theos, Sanctus Deus* etc., came under the same category. The melodies of these chants, as handed down in the Medieval MSS. entirely betray their Greek character, and shew that they were later additions to the Latin Mass. They follow modal laws which are throughout different to those which govern the other Latin chants.

In addition, we meet in the oldest documents of the Latin chant numerous Greek elements. The most ancient ceremonial book of Roman origin, the first *Ordo Romanus,* prescribes for Easter Even the performance of the lessons and chants in Latin and Greek;[1] for the Easter Vespers the Alleluia verse Ὁ κύριος ἐβασίλευσεν *(Dominus regnavit.* Ps. 92*)* with the ℣. Καὶ γὰρ ἐστερέωσε *(Etenim firmavit);* for the vespers of Monday in Easter week the Alleluya verse Ὁ ποιμαίνων τὸν Ἰσραήλ (Ps. 79 vv. 1, 2, 9 & 10) and the same for Tuesday, Friday and Saturday of the same week. [2] Manuscripts of non-Roman origin but of the Roman Liturgy confirm the use of Greek chant in the Latin Church. Not infrequently we find the Greek *Gloria* and *Credo* (usually written in Latin character); I refer to *Cod. S. Gall.* 381, 382; the MS. 9449 of the National Library at Paris etc. Also at S. Blasien in the Black Forest the *Gloria* was sung both in Latin and Greek. [3] A troper of Montauriol even has the Greek *Sanctus* and *Agnus Dei* provided with neums. [4] The above mentioned Paris MS. (it belongs to the 11th century) has a number of chants in the Greek language [5] for the Mass of Pentecost, in addition to which

---

1 *Patr. Lat.* lxxviij, 955.

2 *Ibid,* 965. Likewise in the *Liber responsalis Gregorii M. (Patr. Lat.* lxxviij, 772). In the first half of the 12th century it was still the custom in Rome at the assembly following the Easter Vespers, in which the Pope entertained the company present, to sing a Greek sequence, Πάσχα ἱερὸν ἡμῖν σήμερον. *Ibid.* 1045.

3 Gerbert, *De Cantu* I. 382. As to the celebrated Greek Mass which was celebrated until the 18th century in the Abbey of S. Denis at Paris (*cf.* Fleischer, *Neumenstudien,* ii. 54.) the connexion of the psalm-verse with its melody at the Introit undoubtedly points to a redaction which cannot be earlier than the 16th century; it is probably a question of translation from the Latin. 4 *Cf.* Daux, *Deux livres choraux monas- tiques des* 10me *et* 11me *siècles.* (Paris, Picard, 1899). *pl.* ii.

5 The scribes seldom knew Greek, and so these renderings of Greek texts in Latin

the *Codex* 1235 *nouv. acquis.* of the same Library, of the 12th century, indicates for the Circumcision the Alleluia verse *Dies sanctificatus* in Greek.[1]

The Greek rites have exerted a yet more lasting influence on other Latin liturgies. Hitherto but few detailed investigations have been made about it. The results of enquiry up till now give good grounds for supposing that further interesting and important discoveries are to be made in this way as to the history of Church music as well as to the Latin liturgies.[2]

The invasion of the Latin Church by Byzantine music which had the most important consequences took place in the time of the Carolingians : from the 8th century onward in Gaul and Germany we meet with Byzantine music and theory at every turn. As we shall presently see, even the sequences and tropes may perhaps be founded on the Byzantine music.

After the Greek Church had thus from the first given manifold support to the Latin chant and assisted in developing it, the sub-division of the two Churches followed, which led to their final separation. Since the Greek schism the liturgical relations of both churches have ceased, and in Church music they have each gone their own way, the Greek to experience the very deplorable influence of Turkish music, the Latin, while resting on the foundation of the Gregorian Chant, to bring the resources of the musical art to a wonderful development.

In the Latin Church there early grew up four forms of the Liturgy : the *Roman,* the *Milanese* or *Ambrosian,* the *Gallican,* and the *Spanish,* later

---

characters teem with mistakes of every kind. In the Paris MS. 9449 the Introit *Spiritus Domini,* which is provided with rich tropes, is followed by the subjoined text (fol. 49) : 'Natis thos o theos ke dios corpis this tesan ey extri autu kepye thosan oy me sontes autu a proposo tu autu. Gratias agamus alme Trinitatis semper. Pneupma tu kyrriu. Doxa patri ke yo ke ayo pneumati. Ke nim Kea im ke ystus oeo nathon oeo non amen. Pneuma tu kyrriu eplyros empti oygumenu alleluja. Keu thu tho tho sincraton panta tin nosin akyiphonis alleluia, alleluia, alleluia.' Then come other tropes to the same Introit, the Kyrie *Cunctipotens genitor Deus,* and the one of which the tropes begin with *Theoricam practicamque vitam,* also the Greek *Gloria in excelsis (Doxa in ipsistis theo kepi gis eudokia,)* the Alleluia Verse *Emitte Spiritum* and its Greek translation, another Alleluia Verse 'Agalliaste tho theon thon boyton ymon, halalizate tho theos Jacob, labethe psalmon termon metha cithara.' The other chants too of the same Mass have a text partly in Greek, partly in Latin.

1 *Fol.* 123 : 'Ymera agios menin epiphanem ymon de utheenni kepros kenim ysatheton kyrrion othissi methos katelthinphos megalim epi thin gi.'

2 A beginning has been made by Dom Cagin in the *Paléographie musicale* vol. v. The most interesting example of such a borrowing from the Greek Church is offered by the *Sub tuum praesidium confugimus,* which Cagin gives in the form of the Greek original and in the Latin of the 10th, 12th and 14th centuries.

called *Mozarabic.* Each of these liturgies, following the primitive Christian practice, made prominent use of music. Thus in the Middle Ages there was a Roman, an Ambrosian, a Gallican and a Mozarabic chant. The question of their origin leads back to the question of the origin of the four liturgies. For a long time it has been acknowledged that the traditions of many Gallican and other churches, tracing their existence back directly to the Apostles and their immediate successors, are to be banished to the sphere of legends. As to details there is no agreement at present among liturgists. This can be easily understood, for it is only recently that interest of investigators has been directed to the history of the Liturgy and rites.

There is no doubt that the Latin Church was founded from Rome. We have a witness to this in a very old document, a letter of Pope Innocent I. to Decentius (416), in which he says : 'It is clear that in all Italy, Gaul, Spain, Africa, Sicily, and in the islands which lie between these, Churches were established by those alone whom the venerated Apostle Peter and his successors had made priests.' [1] With this agrees the result of the comparative study of the most important formularies of prayer of the Mass, of the oldest constituent parts of the Canon : they betray a common origin. But does this common characteristic concern only their forms of prayer, or is it wider-reaching ? Here investigators disagree. According to one view the different Latin liturgies had a broader common basis in the first place, a Latin primitive liturgy, whose chief peculiarities are preserved especially outside Rome in the so-called particular liturgies, while in Rome itself were adopted new rites, deviating much from the primitive Latin one. This view is put forward by G. Morin, [2] and particularly by P. Cagin, [3] who confirms it with a great display of liturgical knowledge. Less different from it than appears on the surface is the view of Duchesne, [4] who accepts two liturgical centres in the Latin Church, Rome and Milan, as the Gallican and Mozarabic liturgies were largely tributary to the Milanese. For us the difference is not of great importance. It is an unmistakable fact that the kinds of chant are very similar to each

---

1 Given in Ceriani's *Notitia liturgiae Ambrosianae,* p. 77. foll.

2 Morin, *Les véritables origines du chant Grégorien.*   3 *Paléographie musicale,* vol. v.

4 See Duchesne, *Christian Worship,* and an article in opposition to the *Paléographie musicale* in the *Revue d'Historie et de litterature religieuses,* Paris. April, 1900, p. 31. Duchesne especially combats the idea that Rome has changed in liturgical matters while other Christians have kept more faithfully to the customs received by them from Rome. But the history of liturgical chant affords convincing proof of this.   One need only think of Amalarius and the surprise caused him by his study of the Antiphoners of Corbie and Metz (more of which later).   On the whole, no Church has been so fruitful in

other; they are like children of one father, and the expression 'dialects' applied to the different liturgical chants is a happy one. As far as we are acquainted with them—of the Mozarabic and the Gallican chant we do not know much,—the Ambrosian and Roman-Gregorian have been fully preserved for us—they agree essentially in the treatment of the words of the text, the modes, the rhythm, etc.

Yet it is not improbable that the liturgy which was in use in Milan in the Middle Ages varied but little from the ancient Roman liturgy which originally spread all over Italy. As far as the music goes, the result would be that the Roman and Ambrosian chant were at first more or less identical. This supposition is supported by the fact that in the MSS. of the Roman liturgy Milanese and Roman elements have grown so closely together that it would be difficult to cut out the parts belonging to the Ambrosian without destroying the whole Roman collection. Pre-Gregorian and medieval Milanese resembled one another so closely that the remains of the pre-Gregorian chant, which till the 11th and 12th centuries were to be found at different places in the Italian Peninsula, were looked upon as regular Ambrosian pieces. [1] But while the Milanese chant came down almost unaltered far into the Middle Ages, the Roman further developed into the form in which the medieval MSS. present it, and which, as we shall see, is the work of the Roman *Schola Cantorum*.

The kinship of the forms of the chant of the four Latin liturgies is particularly striking, inasmuch as the root-forms of the liturgical chant prevail alike in all liturgies. All have *solo* and *chorus*-chant, and agree in giving to them the names of *Responsorial* and *Antiphonal* chant; in all, the responsorial chant is *richly developed melodically*, as is suitable for a soloist, while the antiphonal is simpler, more or less syllabic, as befits chants which are to be practicable for those who are not skilled singers. This contrast was so real in the Middle Ages that wherever in the MSS. an A (antiphon) is found marked at the beginning of a chant, a more simple melody may be looked for; but a rich one on the contrary wherever there stands an R (respond). [2]

---

liturgical innovation as the Roman. So there is often a contrast between primitive-Roman, *i.e.* the Roman use as it existed in Churches outside Rome, and the new-Roman, *i.e.* Roman rites as they appeared in Rome itself as the result of changes in the original use.

1 Morin *l. c.* p. 13.

2 It is necessary to keep quite distinct the performance, also by a soloist, of liturgical pieces such as the Versicles, and the Lamentations of Jeremiah, which belong

How can this remarkable fact be explained ? The single possibility which can be seriously considered lies in the hypothesis that *both kinds of melody belong to the ancient constitution of the Latin liturgy. There must have been richer melodies for solo, and simpler ones for chorus, before the liturgy began to develope in different directions in different localities.* The common liturgical ground occupied by both forms of melody will not allow of any other explanation. But here we fall back to a very remote date, no later than the 5th century. As has been pointed out already, the beginnings of this movement go back to the 4th century, and as regards the responsorial chant they reach back to Apostolic times. [1]

The principal forms of the common worship of God are the Mass and the Office, the service of the Altar and the devotions for the Hours. Connected together at first, as a Vigil and with an Eucharistic celebration following, they were soon separated, and developed outwardly in a different manner. Their original connexion is however still apparent in the present form of the Mass, for the actual celebration of the Sacrifice is preceded by a section consisting of readings from Scripture, psalmody, and prayer, the same elements which originally composed the Vigil, and to-day still compose the Office. In the case of the music especially, the Mass and the Office have arrived at different results. The examination of these will make clear the destiny of the liturgical chant in the Middle Ages.

---

neither to the antiphonal nor to the responsorial chant, but to the class of the 'lesson' and are essentially different from the pieces of chant. The Lamentations stand in the Office of Holy Week in the place where in other cases a lesson is always to be found, and, like the lessons, are always followed by Responds; this is the best proof that they are not to be placed in the same class with the chant of the Office or of the Mass. On the *Responsoriolum* see later.

1 In order not to be misunderstood I again emphasize the fact (*cf.* above, p. 31, note 1) that I do not wish to refer back to the 4th century that degree of melismatic music with which the solo chants of the Middle Ages are enveloped. Without doubt here also a development from simpler beginnings took place, the traces of which we can still follow. But it is only by ignoring the most certain facts of liturgical history, that the melismatic formation of melody can be made out (as has constantly been the case of late) to be the product of the 8th or 9th century. The question as to how the melismatic chant was dealt with in the Middle Ages will be treated of in the second part of the 'INTRODUCTION': it will suffice to remark here that the addition of *melismata* on the last words of the texts of the liturgical chant (*cf.* p. 34), which is mentioned as early as by Cassian, has throughout remained the most important form of the melismatic technique of the whole Middle Ages; and that a highly developed musical interpolation of this kind may quite well go back to the practices of the Jewish precentors.

CHAPTER IV

LITURGICAL DEVELOPMENT OF THE CHANTS OF THE MASS IN THE MIDDLE AGES.

THE INTRODUCTORY CHANTS OF THE MASS

The oldest writer on music who speaks of the liturgical chant of his time, Aurelian of Reomé, of the 9th century, puts together in the last (20th) chapter of his *Musica disciplina* [1] the different forms of the Mass music, and discusses them in the order in which they come in the Mass. His statement is as follows : 'The Office of the Mass consists in the first place of the *Antiphons* which are called *Introit.* They received the name from being sung at the entrance of the people into the basilica, and they last until the pontiff and the other ecclesiastical dignitaries in their rank have entered the church in regulated order, and have occupied the places belonging to them. Then the *Litany* is sung, in which God and Christ are entreated *to have mercy upon the people,* upon which the priest, in imitation of the angel who announced *Glory to God in the highest, and on earth peace towards men,* begins this very song with voice setting forth Salvation. Next is chanted the *Responsory* which is called *Gradual* after the steps *(gradus)* from which it is sung : because among the ancients the singers, like the speakers, used to take their place on such raised steps. Thus it is said of Ezra that he placed himself on the wooden steps, which he had made, in order to speak from. Hence we speak also of the *Gradual Psalms,* which, according to the literal interpretation, are so called because they were sung from the steps. The *Alleluia* we received from the Jews, to whose language the word belongs. It means

---

1 Printed in the *Scriptores* of Gerbert i, 59. It is clear that Aurelian in the above-mentioned statement is following a Roman source ; and this may be gathered in particular from the relation in which he places the Introit to the Procession, which is an ancient Roman arrangement.

'Praise God,' and out of reverence it was not translated into any other language; it is very fittingly sung before the Gospel, that the minds of the faithful may be prepared by this song for the reception of the words of Salvation. The chants which the Church sings to the Lord over the oblations offered are called *Offertoria*. This custom is an imitation of the ancient Fathers to whom was given the direction—'When a feast and festal day is celebrated, then ye shall sound trumpets over your sacrifices, and your memorial shall be before the Lord.' At the administration of Communion, the *Agnus Dei qui tollis peccata mundi, miserere nobis* is first sung, that the faithful, who partake of the Body and Blood of the Lord, may with the uplifting of their voice praise That which they receive in their mouth, and in order that they may honour Him Who is turned into bodily food for them to taste, and Who, as the Church teaches, came down to be crucified, to die, and to be buried. At its conclusion yet another chant is sung, which is called the *Communio*, so that, while the people are receiving the heavenly blessing, their souls may be exalted and uplifted by sweet chanting to sublime contemplation.'

These are the chants of the Mass in the 9th century in Gaul and in Rome, for in the time of Aurelian the Liturgy prevailing in Gaul was the Roman. He does not mention the *Tractus*, because it was an alternative to the *Alleluia*; but it already existed in the 9th century. In the same way the *Sanctus* is passed over, probably because it belongs originally to the Preface with which it is immediately connected, as may still be recognized in the case of its oldest melody. The *Credo* on the other hand was not yet included in the Liturgy of Rome in the 9th century as a mass-chant, and it is on the whole the latest chant of the Mass. However, its musical arrangement, as Aurelian depicts it, is older than the 9th century; it rests upon the liturgical measures taken by Gregory the Great (†604),and is inseparably bound up with his settlement of the Liturgy of the Mass.

If we glance at the chants individually, they are seen to fall into two well-defined groups. The oldest go back to the *psalmody* and were originally whole psalms [1]; they differ from one another only in their musical execution. In one case they were performed by a soloist to whom the choir responded with a refrain—we recognize here the *Cantus Responsorius:* in the other the choir was divided into two parts, which relieved one another in turn in performing the psalms—this is the *Cantus Antiphonus*. To the responsorial Mass-chants belong the Gradual-responsory and the Alleluia; to the Antiphonal, the Introit, Offertory and Communion. The Tract

---

1 The *Alleluia* alone may perhaps form an exception.

forms an exception, as it was sung later by the singer, without repetitions by the choir, straight through from beginning to end. These three forms have to this day never disguised the fact that they owe their origin to the psalms: their texts are still taken with few exceptions from the Psalter or the canticles. The other groups of Mass-chants are more like Hymns, and some of them are actually called hymns,—as for example *Hymnus Angelicus (Gloria in excelsis)* etc. The psalmodic parts of the Mass music have varying texts: as a rule each Mass has its own text for the Introit, Gradual, Alleluia (or Tract), Offertory and Communion. They are therefore called the *Proprium* and are now divided into the *Temporale*, *i.e. Proprium de Tempore* (Feasts of our Lord), and *Sanctorale, i.e. Proprium de Sanctis* (Feasts of Saints). The other group never changes its texts: for this reason it was placed in contrast to the *Proprium* as *Ordinarium Missae*; it includes the *Kyrie, Gloria, Credo, Sanctus* and *Agnus Dei.*

The contrast in character between the *Proprium* and the *Ordinarium Missae* is shown in their liturgical position, as well as in the manner of their execution. The chants of the *Proprium* are early enough to form part of the arrangement of the Mass made by Gregory the Great; they form an essential constituent part of the Mass, so that there is no such thing as a Mass without Introit, without Gradual, without Alleluia (or Tract) etc., disregarding the last days of Holy Week, which liturgically stand on a peculiar footing. The liturgical importance of the pieces of the *Ordinarium Missae* is less: it was built up only gradually, and, from the Gregorian Sacramentary on to the Mass book of the Council of Trent, there are many masses found in which no directions are given to sing the *Gloria* or the *Credo.* The significance of any particular feast is much more clearly shewn in the varying elements which compose the *Proprium;* for example, it is often the case that the Introit at once leads the way, with a dramatic vividness, into the realm of thought belonging to the feast. Further, the pieces of the *Ordinarium* were of less value from the musical point of view. The *Proprium* alone is contained in the oldest liturgical books of chant; it has formed the iron frame-work of the Mass music from Gregory's time to the present day. The *Ordinarium*, on the contrary, has a very changeful history to record. In Rome at first, as will be shown later in detail, it was sung not by the *Schola* but by the ministers assisting at the altar, or else by all the people, as was the favourite custom in Gaul. As the household of the Greek Popes of the 7th and 8th centuries contained also Greek clergy, this explains the fact, already mentioned, that these chants of the Ordinary were in many places also sung in Greek. The

Roman origin of this custom is expressly shewn by an ancient anonymous writer of Tours. [1] On the other hand the performance of these chants by the clergy and people had a reflex effect on their melodic form : this was at first quite simple and syllabic, and demanded no particular skill.[2] From the moment when the choir of singers supplanted the clergy and people in their share of the chants of the Mass, and took over the execution of all liturgical chants, that is from the 11th—12th centuries, there began to appear in the Chant-books some melodies for the *Kyrie, Gloria* etc; but they were set as a rule quite at the end, as evidence of their late adoption. These were rich and beautiful; accordingly the older and simpler ones were degraded to ordinary days and to Masses for the Dead.

An alteration, of much importance both liturgically and musically, was made when the papal singers at Avignon went to Rome with Gregory XI. in 1377, and took with them the new art of harmonized chant which was flourishing in France; from that time it gradually became the custom to sing the chants of the Ordinary in harmony. Strangely enough, the *Ordinarium* thus composed in harmony was called simply 'Missa' : this reveals the fact that the Ordinary had become the principal part of the Mass from the musical point of view. This development did not bring with it any particular gain, for it is a merely unnatural circumstance that since then the chief emphasis artistically has rested on the chants of the Mass which do not necessarily belong to it and are to some extent liturgically superfluous. What a far more grateful field would have been offered to composers in the variable texts of the Mass ? Though it is true, they would have been able to perform their works only once or twice during the year. [3]

We must now deal with the historical development of the chants of the *Proprium* as well as of the *Ordinarium*. In so doing it is advisable, in order to bring out their connexion with the Liturgy, to take them in the order in which they follow one another in the Mass, and not to discuss the two groups separately.

INTROIT

THE ANTIPHON

'First comes the *Antiphona ad introitum*, as is appointed for various

---

1 In Martene, *De ant. eccles. ritibus* I. 102, referring to Christmas. 'In missis cantatur *Gloria in excelsis* . . . . nos canimus illud graece *juxta morem antiquum Romanae ecclesiae.*'

'2 The 2nd part of the 'INTRODUCTION' will show this from an Italian MS.

3 This is only one of numberless injuries that were inflicted on the Liturgy by singers who were accepted only on the ground of their musical skill.

seasons, for festivals, and for ordinary days.'[1]   Thus begins the Gregorian Mass-book, the *Liber Sacramentorum*. [2]   In like manner the introductory Mass-chant in the *Ordines Romani* and in the medieval liturgists is called *Antiphona ad introitum*, Antiphon at the entrance—*i. e.* of the celebrant to the altar. 'It has received its name from the approach of the priest to the altar', says the author of the *Micrologus de ecclesiasticis observationibus*. [3] Later the chant itself is called *Introitus;* to-day the expression is no longer used of the priest going to the Altar, but simply of the opening chant of the Mass.   In the Middle Ages it had yet another meaning : it often served as the name of the whole part of the Mass which precedes the *Oratio*, and the reading of the Holy Scriptures. [4]   It is not difficult to say how this meaning arose : the Mass began originally not with a chant but with reading, and the whole section which was prefixed later is the Introduction (*i. e. Introit*) to the Mass.

As regards non-Roman liturgies, with the Greeks of the Middle Ages the Mass opened with the chants of the *Monogenes*.   The Ambrosian rite has a formula which is only in part similar to the Roman Introit, the *Ingressa*.   It consists merely of a melody without a psalm or psalm-verse, from which it follows that it is of later origin ; for antiphons without psalms or psalm-verses were not customary till later.   In Spain, in many parts of Gaul, and in England the Introit was called *Officium*. [5]   The old Gallican liturgy as handed down to us by S. Germanus of Paris (†576) opens the Mass with an *Antiphona ad praelegendum*. [6]   Sometimes instead of *Introitus* the name *Invitatorium* [7] is used, which formerly belonged only to the opening chant of the Choir Office, but which also corresponds well with the function of the first chant of the Mass.

---

1 'Inprimis ad introitum antiphona, qualis fuerit statutis temporibus, sive festis diebus, sive quotidianis.'

2 *Patr. Lat.* lxxviij, 25.   According to Probst, *Die ältesten Römischen Sacramentarien und Ordines*, (Münster 1892, p. 386.) the first *Ordo Romanus*, as it appears to-day, was a working up in the 8th century of the ceremonial appointed by Gregory the Great himself. Duchesne, *Christian Worship* 146, similarly regards different pieces as additions of the 8th and 9th centuries.

3 *Micrologus*, 1, (*Patr. Lat.* clj, 979).

4 Thus Amalarius : 'Officium, quod vocatur *introitus*, habet initium a prima antiphona, quae dicitur *introitus*, et finitur in oratione, quae dicitur a sacerdote ante lectionem.' *De off. eccles. iii*, 5. (*Patr. Lat.* cv, 1108).

5 *Cf.* the English MS. Graduals, *e.g.* the *Graduale Sarisburiense* of the Plainsong and Medieval Music Society, (London), Aurelian, cited above, p. 51, and the author of the *Musica Oddonis* (Gerbert, *Scriptores* I).   6 Duchesne, *Christian Worship*. 190.

7 In the 5th *Ordo Romanus*, (*Patr. Lat.* lxxviij, 986).

As we have noticed, the Mass began in the Greek, as well as in the Latin Church, with readings out of Holy Scripture in imitation of the Jewish liturgy. To this, testimony is borne by Justin Martyr, according to whom 'On Sunday all came together from the town and from the country, and the writings of the Apostles and the Prophets are read, as long as the time allows,'[1] and by the Apostolic Constitutions (II, 57). But Basil remarks that the reading was preceded by something of great importance for the Holy Mysteries.[2] This may have been psalm-chanting. In fact, in the liturgy named after him, the Mass is introduced with chanting by the Cantors.

In the Latin Church the Holy Sacrifice began with readings in the time of S. Ambrose and S. Augustine. The former relates in a letter:[3] 'On the following day, it was a Sunday, after the readings and sermon I dismissed the catechumens,' etc. Here the Milanese Church knows no chant before the reading. Augustine gives a similar but much clearer description:[4] 'Easter-day arrived, and in the morning when the people were assembled in numbers in the church . . . I went there. The church was full, and resounded with the joyful voices of all, who (on account of a sudden miracle) on all sides gave thanks to God. *I greeted the crowd*, and when all had become quiet *there was solemn reading from the Holy Scriptures*; when the time came for *my sermon*, I said only a little,' etc. According to Tommasi these words relate to an occurrence in the year 425. For a long time after the settling of the introit in the Roman Mass the old practice was still kept up in the Gallican Church. Thus in the Church of Trier in the time of Bishop Nicetius, at the beginning of the 6th century, the introit was not yet known: the *Vita* ascribed to Gregory of Tours[5] relates of Nicetius: 'Sunday came, and behold, the King (Theodobert) stepped into the church with those who had been bidden by the priest to keep away from Communion; the readings which the old Canon had appointed were read, and the gifts were offered at the altar of God,' etc. Nothing is here said of a chant before the readings. The oldest Ambrosian *Ordinarium Missae*[6], after the *Gloria* and the threefold *Kyrie* which follows it in the Milanese Mass, before the *Dominus vobiscum* and the *Oratio super*

---

1 *Second Apol.* at the end.

2 *Patr. Lat.* lxxviij, 266.

3 *Epist. 2. Class.*, 20. (*Patr. Lat.* xvj, 1037).

4 Tommasi, *l. c.* xij, *praef.* 3.

5 *Patr. Lat.* lxxj, 1080.

6 See Ceriani, *Notitia Liturgiae Ambrosianae,* (Milan, 1895.) p. 3.

populum, still has the rubric : *Incipit Missa canonica*, which shows that what precedes is a later addition.

The oldest trace of the existence of the Introit in the Roman Liturgy is a passage in the *Liber Pontificalis*, according to which Pope Celestine I. (†432) ordered that the 150 Davidical Psalms should be sung before the oblation antiphonally by all, which till then had not been done, as only the Epistle of Paul was read out, and the Holy Gospel.'[1] Here the introduction of a psalm at the beginning of Mass is spoken of. Perhaps a division of the Psalter among the respective Sundays and holy days was connected with it. At any rate it is always a whole psalm that is in question, not merely a couple of verses.

The way in which this psalm was originally performed may be seen from the designation 'antiphonal,' which is first found in the later MSS. of the *Liber Pontificalis;* but the uniform witness of the Middle Ages testifies to the performance of the Introit by two choirs, alternating with one another in the execution of the Verses. As in the 5th century the melody, which introduced the psalm, and was specifically called Antiphon, certainly belonged to antiphonal psalmody, this must be taken to have been the oldest form of the Introit.

According to the liturgical writings of the Middle Ages, the Introit was performed in Rome, from the time of Gregory the Great onward, as follows : when all the preparations for Mass were finished and the candles were lit, the *Schola Cantorum*, the *Paraphonistae* and the boys placed themselves in two rows before the Altar, according to their rank, and the chief of the singers, the *Prior Scholae*, intoned the antiphon to the Introit. At this moment the Pontiff, with his retinue, proceeded from the Sacristy

---

1 *Liber Pontificalis, ed.* Duchesne, i, 230. It is not possible, with Gevaert, (*Origines du Chant liturgique*, 14), to refer this to the original introduction of antiphonal Chant into Rome, as it is explicitly concerned with the Mass only. Antiphonal chanting was everywhere first introduced for vigils : there is its home and its original place ; there it was a sort of necessity. Its addition to the Mass presupposes its use in the Office. The explanation of the passage given by Morin (*Véritables origines du Chant grégorien*, p. 46) is also not satisfactory. According to him, the introductory chant of the Mass in Rome was older, and Celestine only added a psalm to it : at first it had a form like the Milanese *Ingressa*, which up to the present possesses no psalm or psalm-verse. Against this view must be set not only the fact already noted, that the *Ingressa* is unknown to Ambrose, but also the fact that in that case the existence is assumed in the first half of the 5th century of a form of chant which is unconnected with a psalm. Now, except the hymns, there was no such thing at that time. It accords much better with the description given in the documents of that time, if we see in the *Ingressa* the result of a later arrangement.

into the church. On arriving at the Altar, and after adoring the Holy Host, he gave a sign to the *Prior Scholae* that he was to start the *Gloria* (at the end of the psalm). Bowing to the Pontiff he obeyed his command. At the *Sicut erat* the Pontiff went from the Altar to his seat, and the whole concluded with the antiphon. This description in the *Ordo Romanus I.* [1] is clear, but may be supplemented by notes in the remaining *Ordines* and other sources.

The antiphon was sung in its entirety before the psalm : the custom of only intoning it before, and never singing the whole until after the psalm, is of later date, and belongs only to the Office and not to the Mass. [2] Whether the whole psalm was sung, or only a few verses, and in that case how much, depended on the Pontiff, who gave the singers a sign to break off and sing the *Gloria*. The antiphon was repeated after each verse. An old description of the Mass from the Monastery of Corbie, [3] which refers, it is true, only to the Bishop's Mass, remarks at the Introit : 'At a sign from the Bishop the psalm is begun by the precentor, and the Introit which alternates with it'. It does not follow for certain from this, that it was thus performed in Rome also, but it would agree very well with what we learn of the antiphonal chant in general. [4] At the doxology, which on feast days was divided by the repetition of the Introit before *Sicut erat*, [5] one or several verses were added, the so-called *versus ad respondendum* or *repetendum*, [6] also called *versus prophetales*, [7] until a deacon gave the sign

---

1 *Patr. Lat.* lxxviij, 941.

2 Tommasi (*l. c.* xij, *praef.* 6) is inclined to suppose a repetition of the antiphon before the psalm, so that each of the two choirs of singers performed it once ; else it would not have been an antiphonal chant. The repetition by the chorus of the beginning part, sung by the soloist, may be proved in the case of the responsory. According to Rhabanus Maurus (*De Instit. Cler.* I. 33), antiphon and responsory were only to be distinguished from one another by the fact that at the latter the verse was sung by the cantor, and at the former by a part of the choir ; therefore Tommasi concludes that in the antiphonal chant, that is to say at the Introit, the antiphon must have been repeated before the psalm, or possibly, he thinks, it was divided into two parts which were assigned to the two choirs. However, this opinion seems hazardous, as neither the *Ordines Romani* nor the liturgists say anything which can be held to support it.

3 *Patr. Lat.* lxxviij, 242.

4 This will be treated of in the 9th chapter.

5 I. *Ordo Rom.* (*Patr. Lat.* lxxviij, 950).

6 So they are called in the oldest books of Mass-Chant, *e.g.* in Tommasi, vol. xij. *Cod. S. Gall.* 380 and 381, *Cod. Einsiedl.* 121, *Cod. Paris. Bibl. Nat.* 9448 etc.

7 *E.g.* the 2nd *Ordo. Rom.* (*Patr. Lat.* lxxviij, 970) and Amalarius, *Eclogae de Officio Missae* (*Patr. Lat.* cv, 1318).

for the *Kyrie*.[1]   A last repetition of the antiphon ended this elaborate chant.

The treatment of the Introit-antiphon with psalm, as the *Ordines Romani* show it, like the existence of the chant itself, is based on the circumstances existing at Rome. It was considered fitting to fill up the time, till the beginning of the Mass proper, with chanting, [2] which might be longer or shorter, as was needed. But when the Roman liturgy of the Mass, and the chant belonging to it, spread outside Rome, there arose the need of shortening the chant, because the ceremonies no longer lasted so long. [3] This is not the only abbreviation instituted in the 8th and 9th centuries in France, in order to fit the rites of the Pope's Mass to the simple needs of other churches. As regards the Introit, it is these circumstances which account for the fact that in the bulk of the MSS. of the chant of the Mass which are preserved to us, after the antiphon, only a single verse is set down besides the *Gloria :* this is the custom which of course exists at the present time. To-day the antiphon is only sung *before* the verse and *after* the doxology which is attached to it.

Traces of the Introit in its original and more extended form were however still preserved in the Middle Ages. The *Consuetudines antiquae Cluniacensium* contain the direction to repeat the Introit at the principal Mass of Sunday, half after the verse and the whole after the *Gloria*; and according to Durandus [4] it was sung three times in some churches,— before the verse, then after it, but only in an incomplete form, and again after the *Gloria* in the complete form. In the English churches up to the 16th century it was repeated entire after the verse and after the *Sicut erat* at all Masses, with the exception of ferial days and the Passion Season. [5] A custom of this kind, which recalls the original Roman

---

1 2nd *Ordo. Rom. (ibid)*.

2 In an old exposition of the Mass, the purpose and task of the Introit is thus stated : 'Quoniam animus ad multa divisus, tumultibus curarum saecularium perturbatur, et non statim, ut ecclesiam ingredimur, omnium huius sollicitudinum possumus oblivisci ; quo purius et attentius puriorem atque attentiorem orationem ad Dominum fundere videamur : quod Antiphona ad Introitum decantatur et suavi modulatione interposita.. praeparatio est et exercitatio animorum : ut animus populi a mundanis cogitationibus, his omnibus paulatim avulsus, ad coelestia cogitanda ac desideranda trahatus. (In Tommasi, *l. c.* xij, *praef.* 4).

3 It was only partially possible to preserve the various ceremonies of the beginning of the Pope's Mass in France, for example in places where the stations were copied, as was done in some cathedrals, Mainz, Trier etc. *cf.* Bäumer, *Breviergesch.* 316.

4 Tommasi, *l. c.* xij, *praef.* 6.

5 An English MS. of the 14th century (*Cod. Brit. Mus.* 17001, cited in the P & M.M.S. edition of the *Graduale Sarisburiense*, plate A) adds to the Introit *Ad te levavi* after the

practice, existed all through the Middle Ages in the Church of **Lyons**, and among the Premonstratensians and Carmelites;[1] in this the distinction was usually made that, on the chief great feasts only, the Introit was sung in its entirety three times over, before and after the Doxology; otherwise only half was sung after the verse, as Durandus says.

A trace of the original Introit survives in the custom of putting in Missals and Graduals, not the symbol $\bar{V}$. (*versus*) before the verse of the Introit (as at the Gradual responsories), but ps. (*psalmus*), although for a long time nowhere had more than a single verse been sung. This is already found in one of the oldest books which has come down to us, the Gradual of Rheinau, of the eighth century.[2]

It will be interesting to subject the text of the Introit antiphons to a closer examination. For this purpose we will take a manuscript which is accessible to everyone, the S. Gall *Codex* 339, of the 10th century, which is published in the *Paléographie musicale*, vol. i. As will be seen from the tables at the end of this book, this book contains pieces of chant for 201 days of the Church's year, and, since Thursday and Saturday after Pentecost have two Masses each, for 203 Masses. But the number of Introits is only 149, as many are sung in more than one Mass : 54 or 56 Masses have no Introits of their own. Of these 15 (or 13) come from the *Temporale* and 39 from the *Sanctorale*. The repetition of one chant in several Masses may be explained by the fact, that new formularies were no longer considered necessary for newly introduced feasts : already existing texts, with their melodies, were just taken over for them. This method was systematically followed from the 12th century onward, and from it arose the *Commune Sanctorum,*which from this time took its place in the chant-books of the Mass, along with the *Temporale* and *Sanctorale*, as an independent constituent part. As the arrangement of *Codex* 339 shows, the *Temporale* and *Sanctorale* are not yet kept separate, feasts of our Lord and feasts of the Saints are not yet divided into two groups, as was the custom later, but are joined together just as they follow one another

---

verse *Vias tuas*, this rubric : 'Repetatur officium, et postea dicatur *Gloria Patri* et *Sicut erat* : tertio dicatur officium. Et hoc per totum annum observetur, tam in dominicis quam in festis sanctorum, et in octavis et infra, quum chorus regitur, et in omnibus missis de S. Maria per totum annum, nisi a dominica passionis domini ad missam de tempore paschali.'

1 Tommasi, *l. c.* xij, *praef.* 7.

2 *Cod. Rhenaug.* xxx of the Cantonal Library of Zürich, printed by Gerbert in *Monumenta vet. liturg. Alem.* i, 362 foll.

in the Church's year. The number of Masses of the *Sanctorale* which possess no Introits of their own is almost three times as great as that of the corresponding Masses of the *Temporale*. From this we may conclude that, at the time when the new Masses were arranged, more new feasts of Saints were added than feasts of our Lord.

Of the 149 different Introit texts of *Cod.* 339 of S. Gall, by far the greater number are taken from holy Scripture; at least 143 are so,—102 of them from the Psalter, and 41 from other books of Holy Scripture, or perhaps even 45, counting allusions as well as citations. [1] The rule that the texts were taken from the psalms or from other parts of the Bible cannot be laid down as universally true. Only this much is undoubted, that the Introits of the oldest feasts of our Lord have their texts taken by preference from the historical and other books; the later Masses as well as most of those of the *Sanctorale* have texts from the psalms. When texts were to be found in the Bible, containing a direct reference to the feast to be celebrated, it was natural to choose them : see the Introits for Christmas, Easter, Ascension-Day, and Whit-Sunday. But for the feasts of the Saints recourse was had to the psalms, because in them might be found a glorification of every sort of Christian virtue. Thus psalm 44 praises the nobility of virgins, and the oldest feast of the B. V. Mary, which was celebrated on the octave of Christmas, takes from it the texts of all its variable Mass-chants. Such characteristics of particular psalms were carefully noted in the arrangement of the texts for the liturgical

---

1 The Introit *Ecce advenit* is a translation from the Greek (*cf. Lib. Pontif.* i, 289); the Introit *In excelso* is the same, or else an allusion to Isaiah vi, 1. The Introit *Gaudeamus*, which has a parallel in the Introit *Laetemur omnes* which later MSS. have for the Conversion of S. Paul (*e. g. Graduale Sarisburiense*, 177) and which is also a Milanese Ingressa (*Paléographie musicale* v, 16), may also be a translation from the Greek office; for S. Agatha is a Sicilian Saint, and in Sicily there existed many Greek rites in the Middle Ages; to these may be added the Introit *Benedicta sit* (de SS. Trinitate), from Tobit. xij, 6, and the Introit *Dicit dominus, sermones* (de S. Clemente) which is inspired by Isaiah lix, 21. The Introit *Salus populi* must also be of Greek origin (*Dom.* xix. *p. Pent. & fer.* v. *p. Dom.* iij. *Quadr.*). The Introit *Salve sancta parens* which appears in the MSS. from the 12th century onwards, comes from the *Carmen paschale* of Sedulius (Book II, *v.* 63 in *Patr. Lat.* xix, 599), and is the only example of an Introit in metrical form. It consists of two hexameters, but in the second verse the conclusion *tenet per saecula cuius* is changed to *regit per saecula saeculorum*. The word *regit* substituted for *tenet* comes from the explanation of Sedulius' poem by Remi of Auxerre, (*cf. Revue d'historie et de littérat. relig.* IV, 1899, I, 95); the rest had to be changed for the sake of the conclusion. For other uses of parts of the *Carmen paschale* in the liturgy, see later.

chants. [1] Moreover the Psalter was, from the beginning, the chant-book of the Church, so that it was always drawn upon for Masses of no especial significance.

The Psalter has been especially employed for the Introits of Lent and of the Sundays after Pentecost. As to the latter, it is striking to observe that the order of the Sundays corresponds with the order of the Psalms. This order is followed up to the 17th Sunday after Pentecost, and after that time abandoned. Thus the Sundays after Pentecost are divided into two groups, from Sundays 1 to 17, and from Wednesday in the following Ember week to Sunday 24. We shall meet with similar arrangements of the psalms in other Mass texts also.

The relation of the Introit-verse to the Introit itself is as follows: when the Antiphon is the beginning of a psalm, the succeeding verses of the psalm were used as Introit-verses. But if on the other hand the text of the Introit is taken from the middle of the psalm, the first and the following verses of the psalm form the Introit-verses. This observation is already made in an old manuscript of the Vatican;[2] it may be seen from this that in the later Middle Ages the knowledge of the formal principles of the construction of the Introit had not yet disappeared. The study of the *Versus ad repetendum* is, in this regard, of special interest. For example, the Introit of the First Sunday in Advent *Ad te levavi* is taken from psalm 24, vv. 1—3. The Introit-verse *Vias tuas Domine* follows at once in the same psalm as v. 4, and in like manner the ℣. *ad repetendum, Dirige me* which is v. 5 of the psalm: on the other hand the Introit *Sicut oculi servorum* comes from ps. 122, vv. 2 and 3, the Introit-verse *Ad te levavi* forms the first verse of ps. 122, and the ℣. *ad repetendum,*

---

1 They were always given particular titles according to their contents and their liturgical use. Thus Alcuin, the liturgical adviser of Charles the Great, in his order of the Psalms for weekdays (*Patr. Lat.* clj, 563 foll.) calls

Ps. 2 *Quare fremuerunt gentes* the Psalm 'de Incarnatione.'

  34 *Judica domine nocentes* the Psalm 'de Passione.'

   3 *Domine quid multiplicati* and ⎱

  29 *Exaltabo te Deus* the Psalms 'de Resurrectione.'⎰

   8 *Domine Dominus noster* the Psalm 'de Ascensione.'

  44 *Eructavit cor meum* the Psalm 'de S. Maria.'

  18 *Coeli enarrant* the Psalm 'de Apostolis.'

  32 *Exultate iusti* and ⎱

  78 *Deus venerunt gentes* the Psalms 'de Martyribus.'⎰

 123 *Nisi quia Dominus* the Psalm 'de Confessoribus.'

2 Tommasi, *l. c.* xij, *praef.* 7.

Quia multum repleta est is v. 4. The Introit texts which are not taken from the Psalter are in most cases joined to verses of a psalm which was already taken up for the Gradual, Offertory, or Communion of the same Mass.

According to the directions now in force, the Introit is first begun when the Priest reaches the Altar and begins the first devotions. In the Middle Ages it was sung while the Celebrant with his retinue proceeded from the Sacristy to the Altar. In a certain sense the older custom is still carried on in the Masses of Easter Even and the Vigil of Pentecost, which have no Introit, because on these days the Priest goes to the Altar during the singing of the Litany; hence no further chant is necessary for the 'Entrance,' and accordingly in the Rheinau Gradual there stands here the rubric *Ad Introitum Litania.* [1] In some Gallican churches it was even customary to sing the Introit while the celebrant was putting on his vestments in the Sacristy, and only when the choir had reached the *Gloria Patri* did he proceed to the Altar with his assistants. [2]

The musical composition of the Introit was settled by the manner of its performance. It is a chorus-chant executed by the *Schola* : and accordingly it is observable that the Introit melody of the MSS. is more than mere recitation, and clothes the words of the text with a melody suitable to them. It is never as rich as the solo-melody of the Responsory or Alleluia : nor as simple as the oldest *Kyrie, Sanctus* and *Agnus* melodies, which were sung by all present at the Altar, and by the people also, and were therefore syllabic recitative; it is on the contrary a true choir-melody, intended for all the singers of the *Schola*. The psalmody following the antiphon falls into the same category: it quite conforms to the character of choir-psalmody, but it is somewhat richer than that of the Office, for in that case forms were necessary which were within the reach of everyone, even of those who were not very skilful in singing.

The Kyrie Eleison

Immediately upon the Introit there follows the *Kyrie eleison*. 'Inprimis dicitur *Introitus* . . . deinde *Kyrie eleison*,' says the Gregorian Mass-book. [3] It comes from the Greek Church, where it was sung very frequently, and not in the Mass alone. In the liturgies of Mark, James, &c., [4] it was a cry of all the people. As it is common to all the Latin liturgies, it is justifiable

---

1 Gerbert, *Monum. vet. lit. Alem.* i, 383.

2 *Patr. Lat.* lxxviij, 251. *Ritus antiq. Missae celebr.* of the 11th century.

3 *Cf.* above p. 54.   4 Menard in his Commentary on the Gregorian Sacramentary. (*Patr. Lat.* lxxviij, 267).

to conclude that it belonged to the oldest Latin rites, and, as it is composed of Greek words, it may have been already extant in Rome when Greek was still the liturgical language there.

In the Gallican Mass the chant of the Kyrie was inserted between two other chants, the Thrice-holy, *Trisagion*, and the Canticle *Benedictus Dominus Deus Israel*. [1] The *Trisagion* was precented by the Bishop, and sung first in Greek and then in Latin; as it is to be found in this place in no other liturgy, it may here be ascribed to Greek influences. The Canticle *Benedictus*, which during Lent was replaced by the *Sanctus Deus angelorum*, at least in Paris, has survived in the Mozarabic liturgy on the Sunday of S. John Baptist in Advent; the Ambrosian has no longer any trace of it.

The *Kyrie* was in general use in Gaul from the time of the Council of Vaison (529), which prescribed it for all Masses, as well as for Mattins and Vespers. [2] The order concerning it proves its use in all the Churches of the East and Italy. Among the latter is the Milanese, for in the books of that rite the *Kyrie eleison* occurs after the *Gloria in excelsis*, after the Gospel, and at the end of Mass. In this the Ambrosian rite resembles the Greek, in which likewise it was often sung in the Mass, after the Gloria, after the Gospel, and before the conclusion of the Mass, after the Communion. [3] It must have existed in the Mozarabic Mass, as we may conclude from the intimate liturgical relations of Gaul and Spain; it has maintained its position now only in the Mozarabic Vespers.

The primitive Latin and old Roman use of singing the *Kyrie eleison* outside the Mass, still exists in the present Benedictine Office in the Vespers for Easter-day, for which it is prescribed as early as the 1st *Ordo Romanus*; [4] it was still sung, in more recent times, instead of the *Deus in adjutorium meum intende*, wherever the last traces of the Medieval Frankish-Roman liturgy has survived, *e. g.* in Besançon, Chalons-sur-Marne, Cambrai, also among the Premonstratensians and Carmelites. [5] It was finally

---

1 Duchesne, *Christian Worship*, 192.

2 Can. 3. 'Et quia tam in sede apostolica quam etiam per totas Orientales atque Italiae provincias dulcis et nimium salutaris consuetudo est intromissa, ut *Kyrie eleison* frequentius cum grandi affectu et compunctione dicatur : placuit etiam nobis ut in omnibus ecclesiis nostris ista tam sancta consuetudo, et ad matutinum et ad missas et ad vesperam, deo propicio, intromittatur.' The same Council prescribed the *Trisagion* for all masses, not only for the public ones, to which up to this time it had alone belonged.

3 Ceriani, *Notitia liturg. Ambros.* 3 & foll.   4 *Patr. Lat.* lxxviij, 965.

5 Ortigue. *Dictionnaire du Plain-chant.* 736.   Compare also the essay of Pidoux in the *Tribune de St. Gervais.* (Paris. 1900.) p. 294.   The ninefold *Kyrie* at the beginning

abolished in Trier, through the adoption of the present Roman Breviary (1888).

The introduction of the *Christe eleison* goes back to the organizer of the Roman Liturgy, Gregory I. There were some who reproached him for needlessly imitating the Greeks in his reforms; but he justified himself to them in a letter [1] in which he pointed out that there was a difference between his practice and that of the Greeks: they sang only *Kyrie eleison*, not *Christe eleison*; also they sang the *Kyrie* altogether, while he had it sung by two clergy and responded to by the people. With this agrees the statement of the first *Ordo Romanus*, [2] according to which the chorus of singers chant the *Kyrie*, not, as at the Introit, the *Prior Scholae*. At the Introit the singers continue to chant; at the *Kyrie* an indication is given that, while the whole *Schola* intoned, those who continued the singing were others than the singers themselves, *i. e.* the people. It was not till later that the choir of singers appropriated the chant of the *Kyrie* altogether to themselves, and the participation of the people ceased.

In the oldest *Ordines Romani* nothing is said of a threefold *Kyrie* and *Christe* as prescribed to-day. Both were sung as time demanded, a larger or smaller number of times, and then the celebrant gave the sign to break off, or to sing the *Christe*. This custom was retained in the Pope's Mass, the rite which is described by *Ordo I.*, and in the Bishop's Mass. [3] The fixing of the number of the invocations at three apiece is contemporary with the introduction of the repetition of the *Kyrie* after the *Christe*. In the 9th century the present use was already known in Gaul, for Amalarius mentions the final *Kyrie eleison*, and explains the disposition of the invocations by a reference to the Holy Trinity: 'therefore the singers say *Kyrie eleison*, 'Lord, Father have mercy upon us, '*Christe eleison*, 'have mercy, Thou Who hast redeemed us with Thy Blood,' and again, *Kyrie eleison*, 'Lord, Holy Ghost have mercy.' [4] As Amalarius had gained his knowledge of the Roman rite on the spot, and had even received instruction from Archdeacon Theodore who was always present

---

of the Easter Vespers was abolished by the Franciscans in the 13th century; and as their breviary gradually obtained supremacy, the old use disappeared from the Roman Liturgy. Bäumer, *Breviersgesch.* 323. The Manuscripts (and the Breviary of Trier till 1888) have for the Lauds of the 3 last days of Holy Week a touching chant set to the *Kyrie eleison.*

1 *Epist.* ix, 12. (*Patr. Lat.* lxxvij, 956).
2 *Ibid.* lxxviij, 942.
3 *Ordo Rom. I.* (*Patr. Lat.* lxxviij, 942) and *Ordo V.* 6. (*ibid.* 987).
4 Amalarius, *De eccles. officiis*, iij, 6. (*Patr. Lat.* cv, 1113).

at the Masses of the Pope, [1] we can easily conclude that he had in his mind the Roman use of his time in his symbolic explanation of the disposition of the *Kyrie*-chant ; and that accordingly, about the year 830, the invocations of the *Kyrie* in Rome were already ordered in the manner which has obtained ever since. The direction given in the *Ordo* published by Duchesne, [2] which is somewhat older than Amalarius, leads to the same conclusion : it expressly mentions that the *Kyrie*, the *Christe*, and again the *Kyrie* are always to be sung three times, once by the *Schola* and the other two times by the *Regionarii*. According to this, the limitation of the *Kyrie*, *Christe*, and *Kyrie* to three repetitions was effected in Rome about the year 800 at the latest.

In the liturgical documents of the Middle Ages the *Kyrie* was also called *Litania*. In the Greek Church it is the answer of the people to the petitions of the Officiant. Moreover in the Latin liturgies its repetition has a resemblance to the Litany, and indeed in Rome they come into organic connexion with one another in the Stations. It was the custom there that the Pope should pontificate not only in his own, but in other churches. In this case the people assembled in a church named by him beforehand, and, after the *Oratio ad Collectam* [3] had been said over them, they went in a long procession to the church in which the Pope meant to celebrate Mass,—the Station-church. During this, psalms were sung, and other chants, among them the Litany of the Saints. [4] We are still reminded of the ancient use by the titles of Masses ; for example, of the last three days of Holy Week in the Missal, *Statio ad S. Joannem in Laterano*, etc. The connexion of the *Kyrie eleison* with the Litany may be clearly seen on Easter Even; this *Kyrie* is nothing else but the conclusion of the processional litany. After the *Agnus Dei qui tollis* and the *Christe audi nos*, the rubric follows in the Missal: 'Hic cantores solemniter incipiunt *Kyrie eleison*.' The same is the case on the Eve of Pentecost. The melody of the Easter *Kyrie*, as the MSS. give it, still has echoes of the Litany of the

---

1 In 831 or 832 Amalarius was sent by the Emperor Louis to Rome on a liturgical mission. The details are to be found in the prologue to his *Liber de ordine Antiphonarii* (*Patr. Lat.* cv, 1243. foll.).

2 Duchesne, *Christian Worship*. 458. foll. According to Duchesne, this goes back to about 800 or even earlier.

3 This is the origin of the prayer now called *Collecta*, after the greeting *Dominus vobiscum*.

4 On the Stations *cf.* Probst, *Die ältesten Röm. Sacramentarien.* Münster. 1892. p. 324 foll., or Mönchemeier, *Amalar von Metz* (Münster. 1893. p. 126).

Saints.   On the Station-days [1] the *Kyrie* needed not to be sung by itself, as it was contained in the Litany.   In the other churches the connexion of the *Kyrie* with the Litany was not so prominent, and in time was forgotten, as the Stations were a specifically Roman institution.

The melodic character of the *Kyrie* is due to its having been appointed to be sung by all present.   It was at first a simple recitative chant.   When later the *Schola cantorum* executed the *Kyrie* alone, the singers were naturally no longer contented with the simple syllabic melody, but created richer ones, such as are contained in the oldest existing manuscripts.   Further they took care always to use a more or less festal melody, according to the character of the day.   This development arose especially from the fact that the Roman singers sang on the last syllable of the word *Kyrie* a *melisma*, suited to an expression of entreaty.   The Ambrosians however continued to sing the *Kyrie* as well as the *Gloria*, *Credo*, and *Sanctus* in a syllabic fashion only, that is, in its oldest and simplest form. [2]

GLORIA IN EXCELSIS DEO

The angelic hymn was sung in the Greek liturgy in the morning office, and its use goes back to the first centuries, as it is mentioned as early as the Apostolic Constitutions (VII. 47).   It was also used at solemn and private thanksgivings in the East as well as in the West. [3] It was only later that the singing of the *Te Deum* took this place.

Its introduction into the Roman Mass, according to a note of the *Liber Pontificalis* unworthy of much credit, was due to Pope Telesphorus (†154); and it certainly was sung at first only in the early Mass of Christmas Day, [4] no doubt in memory of the song of the angels in the fields at Bethlehem at the birth of our Lord.   Its use was extended by Pope Symmachus (498—514) to Sundays and the feasts of the Martyrs.

---

1 'Quando litania agitur, nec *Gloria in excelsis Deo* nec *Kyrie eleison* post Introitum, nec *Alleluia* cantatur, excepta litania maiore.' *Ordo Rom. I.* 25.(*Patr. Lat.* lxxviij, 950).

2 'Unicam servant notam' says Radulphus Tungrensis, *De Canon.observ. Propos.* 23. Durandus of Mende (*Ration.* v. 233) indicates that neums of this kind (so he names the *melismata*), sound best on the vowels *a* and *e*, and recall the *Alleluia* and *Kyrie*.

3 Chrysostom, Hom. 3. on the 18th chapter of the Epistle to the Colossians. Gregory of Tours, *De Gloria Confessorum* i, 63.(*Patr. Lat.* lxxj,762), says that priest and people, at the discovery of the body of the martyr Mallosus, sang the *Gloria* with joyful hearts.   When Charles the Great visited Pope Leo III in 800, the Pope, after their mutual greeting, began to sing the *Gloria*. See Anastasius Bibliothecarius, *De Leone III.* (*cf. Patr. Lat.* lxxviij, 570).

4 Duchesne, *Lib. Pont.* i, 129.   *Cf.* also 130 note 3.

This also rests on the authority of the *Liber Pontificalis*. [1] But this permission concerned bishops only; priests might sing it only on Easter Day, when they represented the Pope, and on the day of their installation in priestly functions. [2] On the days on which Mass was preceded by the Stational procession, the *Gloria* dropped out, even in the case of the Pope's Mass, as may be seen from a rubric of the Gregorian Sacramentary. On the other hand the Papal Mass has the *Gloria* again on the Sundays in Advent; at any rate this was certainly the case in the first half of the 12th century. [3]

In the first half of the 11th century a movement sprang up in France with the object of obtaining leave for priests to sing the *Gloria* as often as the bishops. Berno of Reichenau (†1048) supported it energetically, and declared that it was a strange thing to allow priests to sing the *Gloria* on Easter Day, and not on Christmas Day, when it was sung for the first time by the angels upon earth: it was nowhere forbidden to priests by Holy Scripture or by the Popes; and if it was forbidden only because it was not customary in Rome, the Creed also should not be permitted, for that also did not then form part of the Roman Mass. [4] This movement was successful: at the end of the same century the *Micrologus de ecclesiasticis observationibus* [5] makes no longer any difference between bishops and priests. It prescribes the *Gloria* for bishops and priests, for all feast days with complete office, otherwise than in Advent, the season of Septuagesima (*i.e.* the time from Septuagesima to Easter), and on the festival of the Holy Innocents (which was looked upon as a festival of mourning in the Middle Ages). As the author of the *Micrologus* everywhere makes the Roman use prominent and follows it, we can scarcely go wrong in supposing that in his time the *Gloria* was sung in Rome as often by priests as by bishops. The reason why the *Gloria* was not sung in Advent while the *Alleluia* was—as is known to have been the custom from this time onward—is mystically expounded by ritualists. The non-use of the *Gloria* sets forth the sadness of the Patriarchs who awaited the Incarnation of the Saviour, while the *Alleluia* contains the hope of

---

1 *Ibid.* i, 263.   2 *Patr. Lat.* lxxviij, 949, and Duchesne, *Christian Worship.* 166.

3 See the *Ordo* of Benedict the Roman Canon and Cantor, of the first half of the 12th century (*Patr. Lat.* lxxviij, 1027).   4 '*De quibusdam rebus ad Missae officium pertinentibus.*' *Cap.* 2. (*Patr. Lat.* cxlij, 156. foll.).

5 *Cap.* 2. (*Patr. Lat.* clj, 978 foll.). As to the author, who was for a long time considered to be Ivo of Chartres, *cf.* Morin in the *Revue Bénédictine* of 1891. 385. foll., who thinks it was Bernold of Constance.

deliverance ; so says an exposition of the Mass. [1] The real reason is that the *Alleluia* is an older and generally adopted constituent part of the Mass, while the *Gloria* is always considered only a secondary mass-chant. At the present time this character of the *Gloria* is shown by there being many Masses in which it is wanting. It is only sung on days of special joy [2] ; while it is missing in Lent, Advent, and elsewhere on ordinary days.

According to *Ordo Romanus I.*, the Pope precented the *Gloria* while turning to the people, [3] as at the *Dominus vobiscum.* At the *Gloria* this custom has disappeared, but it has been retained at the salutation of the faithful. According to the second *Ordo*, the choir continued *Et in terra pax hominibus.* [4] It is remarkable that the celebrant should himself start the *Gloria* : at the *Kyrie*, as we have seen, he signed to the singers when they were to intone it. The choir which takes up the singing after the intonation of the celebrant cannot be the choir of singers, for the 2nd *Ordo* always calls this the *schola*, while here it speaks of the 'whole choir.' By the latter must rather be meant all the clergy assisting at the Altar, to whose share the other chants of the Ordinary fell. Accordingly the oldest *Gloria*-melodies had the character of syllabic recitation : it was a recitation performed with raised voice rather than a chant. The richer melodies are of later date, and show at the first glance that they were meant to be performed by the choir of singers. Moreover Ralph of Tongres (2nd half of the 14th century) says that the *Gloria* (and *Sanctus*) in the gradual of Gregory the Great had only a few notes ; the richer melodies he considers to be the work of secular singers and without authority; he praises the Carthusians who rejected the new melodies of this character. [5]

From the Roman Mass the *Gloria* spread to the Mozarabic and Milanese. In the latter it was called *Laus Angelorum* [6] and was performed by the *Magister Scholarum* quite alone, according to the *Ordo* of Beroldus (12th century) : it was thus a kind of reading. Only on the chief festivals did the *lectors* sing the second part, from *Suscipe deprecationem nostram*

---

1 Hugo Cardinalis, *Explic. Missae.* 6. *Cf.* Gerbert, *De Cantu* I. 360.

2 When in 1198, the Monastery of S. Blaise in the Black Forest wished to introduce the *Gloria* for the Feasts of the Annunciation, Purification and of S. Blaise, as they fell *infra Septuagesimam*, they had to ask for the special permission of Pope Celestine III. See Gerbert, *ibid.*

3 *Ordo Rom. I.* 9. (*Patr. Lat.* lxxviij, 942).

4 *Ordo Rom. II.* 6. *ibid.* 970.

5 *De Canon. observ. Prop.* 23. Gerbert. *l.c.* 383.

6 In the oldest Milanese *Ordo. Cf.* Ceriani. *l.c.* 3.

onwards. [1]   The Gallican liturgy replaced the *Gloria* by the *Trisagion*. [2]
In the Church of Bethlehem the *Gloria* belonged to the daily Masses,
and even to those in memory of the dead. [3]

It has been already mentioned that in many churches of the West
the *Gloria* was sung in the Greek language; and also that this observance
probably goes back to the Greek clergy who ministered in Rome in the
7th and 8th centuries. [4]

---

1 *Ordo* of Beroldus. *ed.* Magistretti. p. 49.

2 Duchesne, *Christian Worship.* 192.

3 Gerbert, *De Cantu.* I. 381.

4 *Cf.* above, p. 63. This use may be proved for all countries of the Gregorian
liturgy. For England the Winchester Troper (Henry Bradshaw Society, p.60) is a proof,
and according to Gardthausen, *Griech. Paléographie.* p. 422, the Greek *Gloria* was sung
in the Monastery of S. Martial at Limoges in the 10th century.

CHAPTER V

The Chants between the Lessons

Between the lessons from Holy Scripture which follow the *Oratio* of the Celebrant, there are inserted two chants, which were performed by the soloists with repetitions, like a refrain sung by the choir of singers. They thus belong to the class of the *Cantus responsorius*. The first is called *Responsorium Graduale*; the second is the *Alleluia*, which in times of penitence and in Lent is replaced by the *Tractus*. There are always *two* chants. This is striking, and the reason of it is that in earlier times more than two lessons were read. First came a prophetic lesson ; after it a chant was prescribed ; the *Epistle* followed, after which another solo was performed, and then the *Gospel*. Thus the three lessons were separated by two chants. Later the first, the prophetic lesson, disappeared, probably in the 5th century, in the Roman liturgy as in the Byzantine, [1] but not without leaving traces behind. Until the 12th century some MSS. preserved three for certain feasts : for example, at the Masses of Christmas, of S. John Evangelist, of S. Silvester, and of the Epiphany ; this survival moreover is attested also by the medieval ritualists. [2] On certain days in Lent and in the four Ember-week masses they are retained up to this day. Now it is very significant that both chants have been preserved, although the real reason for them no longer exists. The regulator of the Roman liturgy sanctioned the twofold chant, and the Church has not abolished it to this day, as a proof of the regard which she bears towards the chant.

All three lessons are to be found in the Mozarabic liturgy : the chant between the two first, the *Lectio Prophetica* and the *Apostolus*, is called the *Psallenda*. In the Milanese liturgy there were usually two lessons before the Gospel, and between them was sung the *Psalmellus* or *Psalmellus cum versu*. In Africa it was usually called *Psalmus*. All these names

---

[1] Duchesne, *Christian Worship*. 168, 195.　　　[2] Gerbert, *De Cantu* I. 387.

indicate the contents of the chant, which was a psalm, while the Roman name *Responsorium* points to the method of performing it.

THE GRADUAL RESPONSORY

The *Responsorial Solo* in the Mass is of apostolic origin, the most ancient of all the chants of the Mass. We know how, in imitation of the Jewish liturgy, a solo from the psalmist was inserted between the readings from Holy Scripture in the Christian assemblies, to which the celebrant and those present listened in silence. [1] The chant of the *Responsorium* of the Mass is, from the first, present on its own account, in contrast to the Introit, Offertory and Communion, which were introduced later, with the object of filling up the time taken up by the ceremonies. [2]

That the *Responsorium* of the Mass at first comprised a whole psalm, is shown beyond doubt by several statements, particularly some of S. Augustine. The *precentor* sang in turn the verses of the psalm for the day, and the congregation answered each verse with the refrain. In his sermon 176, S. Augustine explains : [3] 'We have heard the first lesson . . . then we sang the psalm in which we mutually incited one another by singing with one voice and one heart, *O come let us worship.*' The last words formed the refrain sung by the congregation to the part of the soloist. He is still more explicit at the beginning of his exposition of ps. 119 : [4] 'It is a short psalm which we have just heard sung and to which we have responded.' Longer psalms were also sung in their entirety, as may be concluded from his exposition of ps. 138, which he begins thus : [5] 'I had arranged that a shorter psalm should be sung by the *lector*; but he, as it appears, in a moment of perplexity performed another, and I preferred to follow the will of God shewn in the error of the *lector* rather than my own. Accordingly, if I have detained you somewhat by the length of the psalm (ps. 138 has 24 verses), you must not blame me for it, but perceive that God does not put a strain upon us without benefit.'

From this and other passages it seems to follow that the refrain of the congregation always comprised a whole verse. In his exposition of psalm 42, [6] Augustine mentions as the refrain *Inimici mei dixerunt mala mihi,*

---

1 *Ap. Constitut.* II. 57.

2 Duchesne, *Christian Worship.* 169.

3 *Patr. Lat.* xxxvij, 950. A passage in sermon 176 mentions the same thing : 'audivimus *Apostolicam lectionem,* audi *psalmum*...audistis *Evangelium*' (*ibid.* 927).

4 *Patr. Lat.* xxxvij, 1596.

5 *Ibid.* xxxvij, 1784.

6 *Ibid.* xxxvj, 444.

'*quando morietur et peribit nomen ejus* (v. 6): in the *Enarratio* 2 *of* ps. 29: *Exaltabo te Domine quoniam suscepisti me, nec iucundasti inimicos meos super me*[1] (the opening verse); in the exposition of psalm 25: *Ne perdas cum impiis animam, et cum viris sanguinum vitam meam.*[2] This refrain is taken from the last part of the psalm (v. 9), and confirms the above statement that the psalm was sung in its entirety.

The evidence also shews that in the Roman Mass, before its regulation by Gregory the Great, the soloist performed a whole psalm. In the 3rd sermon on the anniversary of his accession, Leo the Great (440-461) says: 'We have sung the Davidical psalm (the 109th), not for our own exaltation but to the glory of Christ the Lord.'[3]

As we have seen, the number of the Introit-verses, until long after the Mass-reform of Gregory, depended upon the time taken up by the accompanying ceremonies and the prayers of the Pontiff; the shortening of the psalm did not come in until the simplification of the rites, adapted in the first instance for the Papal Mass, was an established fact. But in the case of the Responsory of the Mass, as far as we can trace back the Gregorian Mass, we find it in its present form, i. e. as *an introductory chant with a single verse*. The Gregorian Sacramentary[4] prescribes simply the *Grad(u)ale*, and all the known MSS. without exception, beginning with books of Rheinau and Monza in the 8th century,[5] indicate in the chant which is marked ℞. only one verse, and that is marked ℣; they never, as at the Introit, indicate a psalm (Ps.). The ℞. *Ecce quam bonum* is the only one which has two verses.

The question has not yet been solved, at what date the abbreviation of the Mass-responsory took place, and yet it is one of the most important in the history of Plainsong. I do not either pretend to be able to give a definite answer, but an attempt to solve it cannot be avoided here. On considering the rich melodic garment which clothes the Gradual-responsory in all MSS., the conclusion suggests itself that the abbreviation and the highly melismatic form are closely connected,—that the shortening took place at the time when the melismatic style came in for this Chant, and in order to avoid extending it to an excessive length. A psalm performed in this way would probably have made this part of the Mass immoderately long. If this supposition be correct, it is only necessary

---

1 *Ibid.* xxxvj, 216.　　2 *Ibid.* xxxvj, 191.

3 *Patr. Lat.* lxxviij, 25.

4 *Patr. Lat.* lxxviij, 25.

5 Gerbert, *Monum. vet. lit. Alem.* i, 362, and Tommasi, *l.c.* xij, 214. foll.

to determine the date of the abbreviation in order to be able to put a date to the *introduction of this rich melismatic style into the responsorial Mass-chant.* As the Graduals of Monza and Rheinau, containing the texts of the chants, equally with the later noted MSS., only know of the one Gradual-verse, the alteration of style cannot have taken place after 700.

But there is more to be said as to the abbreviation of the responsorial chant. The fact that in all MSS., without exception, only one verse is marked, forces one to conclude that the melodic extension of the Mass-responsory belongs to the medieval Roman Order of the Mass from the beginning; later alterations of this Order may always be recognized by deviations and variations in the MSS. As it is certain that the founder of the before-mentioned Order was Gregory I., the abbreviation of the Mass-responsory from a psalm to one verse of a psalm, cannot have been carried out later than 604, the year of Gregory's death. The study of the texts of the Gradual offers support to this conclusion. It would agree well with the character of Gregory's reform, if he himself had given the impetus to the abbreviation.

But one must go back still further. The documents of the non-Roman Latin liturgies know only the shortened form. The old Order of the Mass of S. Germanus of Paris (†576) mentions the responsory as being performed by boys [1], but not as a psalm; so that—granting the connexion of the richer form of melody with the abbreviation—the richer solos must be claimed as existing in the Gallican Church by the middle of the 6th century. Now since Pope Leo the Great is shown to have been accustomed to the whole psalm, we must place the abbreviation of the text and the introduction of the full melismatic style in the Mass-responsory *between 450 and 550.* It is quite unnecessary to look to Graeco-Byzantine influences for the explanation of the event: the *Alleluia* had already for a long time represented the rich melismatic chant in the Mass, and it was natural similarly to elaborate the other solo-chant. Moreover the Gradual-psalm was far advanced beyond a form of simple recitation and was tending towards a richer style of composition by 400, as Augustine teaches us (*cf.* p. 28). And in this connexion the very important fact must not be left out of sight that in the Latin liturgy the melismatic style and the solo-chant always appear together, just as the antiphonal psalmody always wears a simple form of melodic dress.

Another possibility is that the abbreviation of the psalm and the rich elaboration of at least the first part which precedes the verse, and is at

---

1 Duchesne, *Christian Worship,* 194.

the same time the refrain, arose out of the appropriation by the choir of the response of the congregation. The history of the *Ordinarium Missae* proves that, from the moment when the people, or the priests assisting at the altar, resigned their singing functions to the choir, the liturgical text exchanged its syllabic dress for a richer one. Thus it would not be inconceivable that, when the congregation left off singing the refrain to the responsorial psalm, the *Schola* made it more ornate. In this case it is possible that the solo part had already a richly developed melismatic form, and that the abbreviation of the psalm was caused by the elaboration of the refrain melody alone. But as there had been a choir of singers in Rome, at least ever since Celestine I, the appropriation by them of the refrain, and therefore the transformation of the responsorial style, must again be placed in the second half of the 5th century.

The shortened chant is no longer called *Psalmus responsorius*, but simply *Responsum*, *Responsorium*, or *Responsorius* (*sc. cantus* or *versus*). Besides these, there are the names *Gradualis* (*sc. cantus* or *versus*), or *Graduale* (*sc. responsorium*[1]), which refer to the place from which the soloist performed his office. This was called the *Ambo* (ἀμβώ, from ἀναβαίνειν to mount), or *suggestus*, or *pulpitus*, and was reached by steps (*gradus*[2]). The *reader* of the Gospel placed himself on the topmost step, the *singer* of the Gradual on one of the lower ones; also the *lector* whose duty it was to perform the other lessons.

The original custom, allotting the performance of the Gradual to a single singer, was soon given up. Isidore of Seville[3] as early as the 7th

---

1 The *Gradual* has nothing to do with the Gradual psalms. (Ps. 119—133).

2 Such *Ambones* are still preserved in the Churches of S. Maria in Cosmedin and others; in S. Clemente in Rome, the *Ambo* has two desks, one turned to the west towards the Altar, presumably for reading the Epistle, and the other standing lower and turned to the east, probably for singing the Gradual and Alleluia; for Durandus (4. 20. 8) says the Alleluia is to be sung towards the east (Tommasi, *praef.* p. 15, in vol. xij of the *Op. S. Greg.*). Where there was no *Ambo*, the Gradual was sung at the steps of the Choir, as at Reims (Tommasi, *ibid.*). Walafrid Strabo thus explains the word : 'Ambo ab ambiendo dicitur, quia intrantem ambit et cingit,' an explanation which clearly owes its origin only to his ignorance of Greek. In Gerbert (*De Cantu* ij, p. 534, *Tab.* iv.) an *Ambo* is figured. The *Ambo* of the basilica built by Constantine on the Vatican in honour of S. Peter, bore the inscription : 'Scandite cantantes Domino, Dominumque legentes; Ex alto populis verba superna sonent.' (de Rossi, *Inscript. Christ. Urb. Rom.* vol. ij).

3 Isidore, *De Off. Eccl.* i, 9 : 'Responsoria hoc vocata nomine, quod uno canendo chorus consonando respondeat : antea autem id solus quisque agebat, nunc interdum unus, interdum *duo vel tres* communiter canunt, choro in plurimis respondente.' (*Patr. Lat.* lxxxiij, 744).

century teaches us that in his time it was sometimes sung by two or three singers. But in Rome the old custom lasted on for a long time. According to *Ordo Rom. I.*, before Mass, announcement is made to the Pontiff while still in the sacristy, which singer will execute the solo;[1] and in like manner it says later : 'The *Cantor* ascends the *Ambo* with the *Cantatorium* (the book with the chants of the Mass), and sings the *Responsorium;* if he can perform it by heart, he need not take the *Cantatorium* with him.'[2] Amalarius, who is a witness for the use of Rome in the 9th century, knows only a single singer of the Gradual.[3] We first meet with two Gradual singers in Rome in the 12th century, as prescribed in the eleventh *Ordo Romanus* for the Masses of Maundy Thursday and of Easter Day.[4]

In Rome, according to the passages quoted from the *Ordines Romani*, the senior members of the *Schola* always officiated as singers of the Gradual; in other places simply the *psalmists*, or in the Church of S. Germanus at Paris, boys, or in other Gallican Churches, deacons.[5] In North Italy also it was a favourite custom to train boys for the work; in Milan it was also sung by subdeacons, deacons and archdeacons, and on Easter Even by the Archbishop himself, as is shown in the *Ordo* of Beroldus of the 12th century.[6] Gregory the Great considered it an abuse that the office of singer should be executed by deacons : they ought to concern themselves more with preaching and the distribution of alms. By a decree of 595 he ordained that in future only subdeacons, and when they were not to be had, members of the minor orders, should officiate as *Cantors.*[7] But this regulation did not long remain in force, for in many liturgical books of later date we see not only *clerici minores* and subdeacons, but also

---

1 *Patr. Lat.* lxxviij, 940.

2 So I understand the expression 'sine aliqua necessitate' of the *Ordo Rom. II.* 7. Amalarius, *De Eccl. Off.* iij, 16. (*Patr. Lat.* cv, 1123) speaks of *Tabulae* which the singer held in his hand : by this must be meant the cover of the binding of the *Cantatorium* ; and in fact e.g. the S. Gall *Cantatorium, Cod.* 359, has a valuable binding of ivory tablets. *Cf.* note 6.

3 Amalarius, *ibid.* cv, 1117.   4 *Patr. Lat.* lxxviij, 1040 & 1044.

5 Duchesne, *Christian Worship*, 196.

6 Beroldus : 'Finita lectione puer magistri scholarum acceptis tabulis eburneis de altari vel ambone positis per clavicularium hebdomadarium, vestitus camisiolo ascendit pulpitum, ut canat psallendam. Et hoc semper, excepto in Quinquagesima et in dominicis diebus Quadragesimae, in quibus lectores canunt, et in Annuntiatione S. Mariae, quando duo subdiaconi et totidem notarii cantant, si archiepiscopus adfuerit. Si vero defuerit, duo notarii et duo lectores cantant.' *Ordo* of Beroldus, *ed.* Magistretti, *p.* 49. foll.

7 *Patr. Lat.* lxxvij, 1335.

deacons and even priests invested with the office of *Cantor*. In the nunneries of France the Gradual was not infrequently sung by the nuns, a practice combated by Pope Zacharius in a letter to the Major-domo Pippin. [1]

According to the liturgical documents of the earlier Middle Ages the execution of the Gradual was as follows : the *Cantor* sang it from the beginning as far as the verse; the First *Ordo Romanus* contains the rubric 'The Gradual-responsory is sung to the end by him who begins it.' [2] The choir repeated the part of the *Cantor*. After this came the verse, performed by the *Cantor*, after which the responsory was repeated. For a long time the repetition of the beginning part was observed wherever the Roman rite was used, as may be seen from Amalarius: [3] 'After the verse is ended, the *Succentors* (the singers who responded to the *Precentor*, the first singer) repeat the *responsorium* for the second time from the beginning and sing it to the end.' The *Consuetudines* of the Cluniac Order gave the same directions; also Bishop Sicardus of Cremona (†1274). [4] In England the repetition of the first part of the Gradual by the choir before and after the verse was still customary at the same period, as the rubrics of the chant-books there show. [5]

But before the 13th century the custom had already begun of leaving out the repetition after the verse if another chant followed, such as the Alleluia or Tract; it was only when this did not happen that the old use was retained. The *Rituale* of the Canons of S. Peter's, Benedict (*Ordo Rom. XI.*),[6] a valuable witness to the Roman use in the first half of the 12th century, directs the repetition in Lent, but only for week-days if no Tract follows. On other days accordingly it was omitted. The Premonstratensians and Carmelites followed this use down till recent times. [7] Elsewhere however, the repetition was soon universally abandoned ; and the Missal of the Council of Trent sanctioned the performance of the Gradual-responsory [8] which was general in the later Middle Ages, *i. e.*

---

1 Tommasi, *l.c.* xi, *praef.* 11.

2 *Ordo Rom.* i. 26. (*Patr. Lat.* lxxviij, 950).

3 Amalarius, *l. c.* iij, 11. (*Patr. Lat.* cv, 1118).

4 Tommasi, *l. c.* xij, *praef* 13.

5 *Cod. Brit. Mus. Addit.* 17001. *Cf.* above, p. 59, note 5.

6 *Patr. Lat.* lxxviij, 1039. This *Ordo* is addressed to Cardinal Guido de Castello, who ascended the Papal throne in 1143 as Pope Celestine II.

7 Tommasi, *l.c.*

8 As a result of this, there was a verbal *non sequitur* in the Gradual and Missal. The Gradual-responsory of the Mass of S. John Baptist runs : 'Priusquam te formarem in

without any repetition. This circumstance has conduced most of all to the suppression of the old name, and to the bringing in of the appellation 'Gradual,' which gives no indication in regard to the musical form of the piece. To-day the Gradual is started by one or two singers, after which the choir takes it up. As a conclusion by the soloist alone sounds unsatisfying, it is always the custom for the choir to join in with the soloist again at the end of the verse. This practice dates from the later Middle Ages : it is already mentioned in the above-named English MS., which adds that after the intonation of the precentor the choir begins again from the beginning, thus repeating the intonation.

If the Gradual had, as an exception, more than one verse, it was repeated after each verse. To this category there belong, besides the ℞. *Ecce quam bonum*, some chants which early acquired the name of Tract, although the witness of ritualists leaves no doubt that, properly speaking, they are Gradual-responsories; for they clearly prescribe the repetitions which are charactistic of responsories, and which the Tract has never had. But as the chants in question all fall in Lent, the use of the name Tract is easily intelligible. Among them is to be reckoned the *Domine exaudi orationem* of Wednesday in Holy Week, which is called *Gradale*, in the oldest MSS., *e. g.* those of Rheinau and Monza, [1] or else *Responsorium*, as in Amalarius, who in his exposition of the ceremonies of that day expressly mentions the *Responsorium*, and ascribes five verses to it. [2] After each verse, the first part was either partly or entirely repeated, as befits a *Responsorium*. This is proved by the *Consuetudines* of the Monastery of Corbie, [3] which call the chant *Tractus*. The same

---

utero, novi te : et antequam exires de ventre, sanctificavi te. ℣. Misit dominus manum suam et tetigit os meum, et dixit mihi.' It is thus logically incomplete. Originally the first part was repeated after the verse, and completed the sense. A Leipsic MS. Gradual (in the Library of S. Thomas' Church) expressly prescribes the repetition after the verse for this Gradual.

1 Gerbert, *Monum. vel. lit. Alem.* i, 381, and Tommasi, *l. c.* xij, 219.

2 Amalarius, *De Eccl. Off.* i, 11 (*Patr. Lat.* cv, 1009) : 'quarta feria post Palmas, quae habet varietatem et adjectionem unius lectionis et *unius responsorii cum quinque versibus*,' and towards the end of the chapter : 'Responsorius secundus quinque versus habet.'

3 *Consuet. Corbeiens. Mon.* (See Martene, 3. xij, 32) : 'Feria iv sequenti cantabunt duo monachi *Tractum* ad magnam missam *Domine exaudi;* mox ut cantaverint primum versum, conventus repetat eundem versum et cantabunt; et post praedicti duo monachi alium ℣. et conventus repetet tractum in medio, sc. *Et clamor meus*, et sic usque in finem praedictus tractus cantabitur. Et post praedicti duo monachi iterum incipient principium primi versus de dicto tractu et conventus cantabit eundem versum.'

holds good of the chant *Domine audivi auditum* of Good Friday, which has also been called *Tractus* since the 10th century. Before that, it was called *Responsorium* or *Graduale, e. g.* in the Gelasian Sacramentary, in the Antiphoners of Rheinau and Monza, and in Amalarius. The *Rituale Corbeiense* directs as to this, that after each verse the whole of the first part shall be repeated, or the second half of it. Both chants were later called *Tractus*, only because by that time the proper Gradual had lost all but one of its verses, and these, being longer, seemed to bear a likeness to the Tract. The Antiphoner of Monza also calls the responsory *Beata gens* a Tract.

If now these Tracts are properly responsories, then all those also which use the same melody or its *motif* in the MSS. (and printed books) are only in an improper sense called Tracts,—that is all the Tracts of the 2nd Mode. In their structure and true manner of performance they are Gradual-responds; and in them there is preserved a valuable relic of the early medieval method of singing; for here, as in general, Lent proves to be still very rich in ancient traditions.

The Gradual-respond was sung at all Masses in the early Middle Ages, as it is the oldest chant of the Mass. Later it was replaced by an Alleluia in Easter-tide, so that this season has since had two Alleluias. Easter-week itself however has retained the Gradual before the Alleluia. It is a peculiar fact that all the Graduals of this week begin with the same piece, *Haec dies*, and that all their verses are taken from the 117th Psalm. These Graduals accordingly are all connected, and no doubt they formed at first a single chant with several verses, which was performed in full on Easter-Day; later however, when the Mass-responds were reduced to one verse, it was distributed over the days of Easter-week. [1]

The Antiphoner of the Mass in the S. Gall MS. 339 contains 118 Graduals including those later called Tracts. They are distributed over 181 Masses, some of which, *e. g.* the Ember Masses, on account of the unusual number of Lessons, have several Graduals each : others, especially the Masses of the saints, frequently use the same Gradual. 104 of the

---

[1] In early times a copyist wrote for Easter Tuesday the verse *Dicant nunc qui redempti sunt* from ps. 106, an error which appears as early as the books of Monza and Rheinau, and which has survived down to our present books. Only a few books have the original verse from ps. 117 : 'Dicat nunc domus Aaron, quoniam in saeculum misericordia eius,' *e. g.* the *Graduale Compendiense* (see *Patr. Lat.* lxxviij, 678), and a MS. in Tommasi, *l. c.* xij, 91. The mistake is explained by the similarity of the beginning of the verses. The Gradual in *Patr. Lat.* prescribes for Easter day all the verses of ps. 117, which elsewhere are distributed over the whole week.

texts of these Graduals belong to the Psalter, 13 to other books of Holy Scripture; only one is not biblical, the Gradual *Locus iste* of the *Dedicatio ecclesiae.* [1] It is precisely the oldest Masses of the *Temporale* that have a Psalm-gradual, and consequently those of the *Sanctorale*, and those Masses whose text does not belong to the Psalter, must be of later origin. This conclusion follows naturally from the fact that the Gradual-responsory was originally a responsorial psalm. The feast of the Dedication was established in the year 608 as the *Dedicatio S. Mariae ad Martyres* in Rome: [2] now its Gradual *Locus iste* cannot have had several verses and been shortened; and thus again it follows that the abbreviation of the Gradual-psalm took place before 608.

With regard to the Graduals of the Sundays after Pentecost the MSS. offer an interesting variety: in a very few, a set occurs which deviates throughout from that of the S. Gall MS. 339. This difference appears strangely enough as early as in our two MSS. of the 8th century: that of Monza has the order of the Graduals of the S. Gall MS., that of Rheinau the other; the latter is peculiar, in that the texts follow the order of the psalms, as is the case with the Introit. The second is the later plan, and it is due to an attempt to arrange the Graduals like the other chants of these Sundays, which took their texts from the psalms in turn, following their numerical order. [3]

The Gradual-verse almost always comes from the same book of Holy Scripture as the Gradual, a rule which invariably holds good if the source is the Psalter.

THE ALLELUIA

The *Alleluia* is the second piece of chant between the lessons. According to the testimony of S. Jerome [4], a psalm was sung with Alleluia between the lessons in Bethlehem as early as the 4th century: the Alleluia formed the refrain, by the people, to the psalmody of the soloist. In the Greek Church the *Cherubikon*, as it was called, was prescribed for every Mass, even on Good Friday and in Masses for the dead: the joy of the

---

1 The only metrical Gradual text in the MSS. is the distich 'Virgo Dei genitrix, quem totus non capit orbis, In tua se clausit viscera, factus homo,' the verse of the Gradual *Benedicta et venerabilis.*

2 *Liber Pontif.* (*ed.* Duchesne), i, 317.

3 Both sets of Graduals may be found in the Appendix.

4 Morin, *Les véritables origines du chant Grégorien,* p. 48.

Church at the death of the righteous seemed to justify the latter. [1] The singing of *Alleluia* was very popular in the Eastern Churches. The Greeks had their own books with joyous melodies for Alleluia, the *Alleluiaria*, [2] and the Copts, the Egyptian Christians, still sing it for a quarter of an hour at a time. [3]

The Alleluia-chant was introduced into the Roman Mass by Pope Damasus (368—384) at the instance of his liturgical adviser Jerome, in conscious imitation of a feature in the Liturgy of Jerusalem. [4] At first this innovation was confined to Easter Sunday; [5] soon in the 5th century it was sung during the whole season of Easter, and Gregory the Great extended its use to all Sundays and festivals of the Church's year, with the exception of Lent and fast-days. In the above mentioned letter in which he justifies his order about the chanting of the *Kyrie*, he refers to the custom introduced into the Roman Church by Damasus, and also defends his manner of singing the Alleluia *extra Pentecostes* (*i.e.* outside the time from Easter to Pentecost). [6]

On the basis of the testimony of Augustine and Cassiodorus (*cf.* above, p. 33) it has been already suggested as probable that the Alleluia-chant of the pre-Gregorian Mass was a very long protracted melismatic melody. It cannot be stated with any certainty at what point it became the custom to attach one or more psalm-verses to the Alleluia in the manner handed down in the MSS. But as there is not a single Mass in the Gregorian Liturgy containing an Alleluia without a verse, the custom must belong to Gregory's own settlement of the Mass, *i. e.* it cannot be later than Gregory I. At any rate the Alleluia-verses were introduced first by Gregory (†604), for, while the other chants of the Mass, as far as we can trace them back, in text and melody, are the same in all countries of the Roman Liturgy the MSS. vary in a remarkable manner as regards the choice of the verses for the Alleluia. Even in Easter week they are not uniform, and the same discrepancy is also noticeable in the Sundays after Pentecost, which, as we have seen, had no Alleluia until Gregory's day. These Alleluias with their verses are grouped, not with the Introit, Gradual etc. at the several

---

1 Duchesne, *Christian Worship*, 205.

2 Gerbert, *De Cantu.* I, 406.

3 Ortigue, *Dictionnaire du plain-chant*, p. 109.

4 S. Gregory, *Epist.* ix, 12 : 'Ut Alleluia in ecclesia Romana diceretur, de Hierosolymorum ecclesia ex B. Hieronymi traditione, tempore beatae memoriae Damasi traditur tractum' (*Patr. Lat.* lxxvij, 956).

5 Duchesne, *l. c.* 166.   6 *Cf.* above p. 65.

Masses, but stand at the end of the MSS. in an appendix. The text of their verses is also in accord with their late date : for they are taken from the psalms in order, so that the Alleluia for a later Sunday belongs to a psalm which follows later in the order of the Psalter. [1] For other days the choice of the Alleluia was usually left open : thus the Rheinau Gradual has for the Vigil of Christmas, when it falls on a Sunday, the rubric : 'An Alleluia of Advent according to choice.' [2] Fresh Alleluia melodies were composed till late in the Middle Ages, although for other chants of the Mass recourse then was always had to the traditional stock.

This want of uniformity in the Alleluia verses, which is shewn even in the oldest MSS. can only be explained by the fact that the appointment of this chant as a regular constituent part of the Roman Mass by Gregory did not involve the settlement of details. There remained a liberty of selection which still testifies to the later origin of the verses. Accordingly, while the verses to the Introit, Gradual etc. survive in the MSS. as the last remnants of an original psalm, the Alleluia-verses on the contrary are due to a process of accretion. There must have been a reason for adding words to the *Alleluia-jubili*: they were necessitated, no doubt, by the elaborate musical character of the pre-Gregorian Alleluias. The reviser of the Liturgy must have considered these so rich in melismatic beauty that he would not shorten them, but he managed by adding psalm-verses to give them a better liturgical form, without cutting down the luxuriance of the melody.

Even with the verses, and therefore in its less melismatic form, the Alleluia-chant of the Middle Ages gave occasion to the liturgists for exercising their skill in discovering mystical meanings. Amalarius sees in it a foretaste of everlasting bliss: 'The *Jubilatio*, which the *cantors* call *Sequentia*, brings our minds into that state in which we shall no longer need to use words, for one mind will reveal its conceptions to another by the medium of thought alone.' [3] Stephen of Autun follows the same tendency when

---

1 *Cf. Cod. S. Gall.* 339, p. 126, foll.; *Cod. Einsiedl.* 121, p. 343, foll.; & *Cod. Einsiedl.* 133, p. 199, foll.

2 Gerbert, *Monum. vet. lit. Alem.* i, 365. The Gradual of Monza likewise contains no special directions for the Sundays after Pentecost; the choice of the Alleluia was left open even in Easter week. For the Mass of S. Vitalis the MS. says : '*Alleluia quale volueris.*'

3 Amalarius, *De Eccl. Off.* iij, 13 (*Patr. Lat.* cv, 1122) : '*Alleluia quod cantatur per festos dies in recordatione aeternae laetitiae,*' and iij, 16 (*ibid.* 1123): '*Haec iubilatio quam cantores sequentiam vocant, statum illum ad mentem nostram ducit, quando non erit necessaria locutio verborum, sed sola cogitatione mens mente monstrabit, quod retinet*

exceptional. The Gradual of Rheinau adds to the All. ℣. *Pascha nostrum* of Easter Sunday also the ℣. *Epulemur in azymis;* the *Cantatorium* of Monza also to the All. ℣. *Tu es Petrus,* the ℣. *Beatus es Simon.* In *Cod.* 339 of S. Gall the following have two verses : All. ℣. *Laetatus sum* and ℣. *Stantes erant;* All. ℣. *Nimis honorati sunt* and ℣. *Dinumerabo eos;* All. ℣. *Te decet hymnus* and ℣. *Replebimur;* All. ℣. *Venite exultemus* and ℣. *Praeoccupemus.* In *Cod.* 121 of Einsiedeln there are also the All. ℣. *Angelus Domini* and ℣. *Respondens angelus;* All. ℣. *Lauda Hierusalem* and ℣. *Qui posuit;* All. ℣. *In exitu Israel* and ℣. *Facta est Judea;* All. ℣. *Laudate pueri* and ℣. *Sit nomen domini.* Some of these retained their verses throughout the Middle Ages : they are still to be met with in the oldest printed books, *e. g.* in the Graduals of Strassburg (1510) and Basle (1511). The Mass book of the Council of Trent has struck out all second verses, and since then all Alleluias of the Mass have only one verse.

The above-mentioned S. Gall MS. 339 has in all 95 different Alleluia-chants (the *All.* ℣. *Laudate Dominum* comes twice with different notation). The texts of 70 Alleluias come from the Psalter; and of 14 from the other books of Holy Scripture, only 11 are of non-Biblical origin. [1] The lion's share here also falls to the Psalter. Special consideration should be given to the fact that in the oldest MSS. the Alleluias are divided into two groups; one group occurs within the book in such a way that each Alleluia is given after the Gradual of the Mass to which it belongs; the other group stands at the end of the book as an Appendix, and comprises, besides the Alleluia-chants for the Sundays after Pentecost, which again follow the order of the Psalter, [2] some collections of those which might be chosen for the various classes of Saints,—for Apostles, Martyrs, Confessors, Virgins etc. The former group must be the older; the latter gave the

---

1 These are 1. All. ℣. *Veni domine* (Christmas Eve) the first half of which agrees with Habak. ij, 3. The whole may be a translation from the Greek. This is more than probable in the case of 2. All. ℣. *Dies sanctificatus* (Third Mass of Christmas). Others not drawn from the Bible are 3. All. ℣. *In Resurrectione* (Octave of Easter) and 4. All. ℣. *Surrexit altissimus* (Wednesday in Easter-week). 5. All. ℣. *Benedictus es Dei filius* (3rd Sunday after Easter). 6. All. ℣. *Dilexit Andreas* (Feast of S. Andrew, a connexion of the words *Dilexit Andream Dominus* with the phrase which is very frequent in the books of Moses, *in odorem suavitatis.* 7. All. ℣. *Elegit te dominus* suggests Deut. vij, 6 or xiv, 2. S. All. ℣. *Iustus germinabit* is based on Isaiah xxvij, 6 or Hosea xiv, 6. Further 9. All. ℣. *Te martyrum candidatus* is taken from the *Te deum.* 10. All. ℣. *Egregia sponsa* is an independent composition. 11. All. ℣. *Salve crux* (S. Andrew) is the same, or is taken from the *Acta* of the Saint.

2 *Cf.* in the Appendix the series of Alleluias of *Cod.* 339. of S. Gall, etc.

impetus to the formation of the *Commune*, for subsequently not only the Alleluias of each class of Saints, but also the other Mass-chants were thrown together. The very numerous new Alleluias which appeared in the 14th and 15th centuries in the MSS. are chiefly new compositions both in text and melody; they shew the decay of liturgical composition, in their systematic rejection of the Church's official book for prayers and chants—viz. the Bible, and more especially the Psalter : [1] melodically they are entirely confined to those modes which are akin to modern keys.

THE TRACT

On days of mourning and penitence and on Ember Saturdays the Alleluia is replaced by the Tract. 'The *Cantor* ascends the *Ambo* with the *Cantatorium* and sings the Responsory : next follows, according as the season [of the Church's year] directs, the Alleluia or else the Tract;' so says the first *Ordo Romanus*. [2] Alleluia and Tract thus are mutually exclusive. According to the 3rd *Ordo* the Cantor of the Tract (or of the Alleluia) is to be a different person from the Cantor of the Gradual. [3] As far as our knowledge goes, the Tract is always a solo chant, which is interrupted neither by antiphonal nor by responsorial additions, but goes on from beginning to end in one flow. Tommasi connects the name with *tractim*, —in one draught, without interruption. [4] This explanation is supported by Amalarius who distinguishes the Tract from the Gradual-respond by the fact that in the latter the choir answers the soloist, while in the former nobody responds. [5] At any rate the name was given in very early times to the performance of the chant thus designated, which had to be slow, dragging and protracted, corresponding to the penitential character of the day on which it was sung. Bishop Durandus of Mende finds in the fact that the Tract never comes together with the Alleluia (except *ob specialem causam* on Easter Even) a proof that the Tract is more a chant of mourning than the Gradual. [6] According to Hugh of S. Victor, the Tract signifies

---

1 *Cf.* the texts given by W. H. Frere in his Introduction to the *Grad. Sarisb.*

2 *Patr. Lat.* lxxviij, 942.   3 *Ibid.* 979.

4 Tommasi, *l. c.* xij, *praef.* 19. The word *tractim* is also used in the sense of simple recitation, and is then opposed to the modulated chants; thus it is said of a monk Rudulpho in the Belgian Monastery of S. Trudo (12th century) that he 'zealously kept the night and day hours in choir 'et de psalmis *tractim cantandis et cantu dulci aeque modulando.*' Gerbert *De Cantu. I,* 576. *Cod.* 359. of S. Gall has the rubric *Tractus Cantus.*

5 Amalarius, *De Offic.* iij, 12 (*Patr. Lat.* cv, 1121) : 'Hoc differt inter *responsorium,* cui chorus respondit et *tractum,* cui nemo.'

6 Gerbert, *De Cantu. I,* 403.

that 'which expresses sighing and songs of lamentation, the tears of the Saints. It is so named because the Saints *drew forth* sighs and lamentations from the depths of their hearts.' [1]

This explanation does not satisfy the facts; for it has been shewn already that most of the Tracts were really Gradual-responds, and that it was only when the existence of Graduals with more than one verse had been forgotten that they were designated as Tracts, although they long retained the manner of performance characteristic of the Gradual-respond. There is one Tract moreover, *Laudate Dominum*, which contains the very opposite of a lamentation. The real meaning of the word *Tractus* is shown by comparing it with the Greek εἱρμός. [2] The word *Hirmus*, as used by the Greeks of the Middle Ages, means a melody written at the head of a long text, to which its various sections were to be sung,—a kind of typical melody, which was adapted to the various parts of a longer hymn in accordance with definite rules taught in the song-school. It is easy to see how the Latin Tract could acquire this designation if we bear in mind that the melodic material available in all the Tracts is very uniform. All the Tracts belong, as will be shewn in detail in the second part of the INTRODUCTION, either to the 2nd or 8th Ecclesiastical Mode, and by preference use the same melodies. A Greek influence over the Tract may be seen in the fact that, according to a statement in the *Ordines Romani*, [3] on Easter Even the Tract, with the prophetic lessons between which it is inserted, was performed first in Latin and then in Greek.

The Tracts with their verses are among the most prolonged chants of the Mass : in particular the Tr. *Qui habitat in adjutorio* of the first Sunday in Lent recalls the complete psalm of early days. It comprises all the verses of psalm 90 and is the only chant of the Mass which has preserved the whole psalm. The Tr. *Deus, Deus meus, respice* of Palm Sunday comprises the greater part of ps. 21. All the rest are shortened and have only three verses, two, or even one. The length of the Tract is a proof of its great antiquity ; in fact when one considers the close relation in which it stands to the Gradual-respond, one is tempted to believe that the Tract of the Medieval MSS. *exhibits the last remnants of the original Gradual psalm.*

---

1 Hugo of S. Victor, *Spec. Eccl.* 7 (*Patr. Lat.* clxxvij, 359).

2 *Cf.* Christ, *Über die Bedeutung von Hirmos, Troparion und Kanon in der griech. Poesie des Mittelalters* (*Sitzungsber. der Münchener Akademie* 1870, ij, p. 75, foll.). It is important to keep in mind that the name *Tractus* does not appear for the first time in the 9th or 10th century (like that of 'sequence,' which has a similar history), but it already appears in the MSS. of the 8th century, in the Gradual of Monza as well as that of Rheinau.　　　　　3 *Ordo Rom. I.*, 40 (*Patr. Lat.* lxxviij, 955).

Its present melodic form must be that which belonged to all Responsorial psalms before their abbreviation. It is then probable that the Tract melodies are extremely old and venerable monuments of the Chant of the Latin Church, and that they preserve *the melodic forms of the solo-psalmody of the Mass* in the shape in which they were used *up to the 4th and 5th centuries in Italy*, when the solo-singers began to deck them out with richer *melismata* than before, and by this innovation brought on the abbreviation of the psalm.

This suggestion is specially borne out by the fact that far on into the Middle Ages all the texts of the Tract without exception come from the Psalter or the biblical canticles. In *Cod.* 339 of S. Gall out of the 20 chants entitled *Tract* (deducting the 3 Gradual-responds *De necessitatibus, Domine audivi,* and *Domine exaudi*) 17 are psalm-texts (including the Cant. *Sicut cervus* in ps. 41) and the other 3 canticle-texts. When the Gradual-psalm was shortened, the forms of the original Gradual-psalmody were prescribed for penitential seasons only. Our oldest chant-books contain Tracts only for the Sundays from Septuagesima to Palm-Sunday, for Ash Wednesday, the Wednesday, Friday and Saturday of Holy Week, and also for those feasts of Saints which usually fall within this season: thus the Gradual of Monza has for the Feast of S. Valentine Tr. *Desiderium* and of S. Felix Tr. *Beatus vir.* Later it was the custom to sing the Tract also on week days in Lent. However in this case nothing new was composed, but the existing material was made to serve.

THE CANTICLE 'BENEDICTUS ES.'

In the same series with the chants named Tracts is to be included a Canticle which as regards melodic composition, has many analogies with the Tract melodies.

The chant of the Three Children in the fiery furnace certainly belongs to the oldest form of the Latin liturgy. In the Mozarabic liturgy it was an integral constituent part of the Mass; the 4th Council of Toledo [1] was induced to lay particular stress on the obligation to use it on Sundays and Feast-days, and threatened all priests who neglected it with excommunication. The Council issued this direction not only for Spain but also for Gaul. In accordance with this the liturgy of S. Germanus of

---

[1] The Council lays stress on 'Hymnum . . . quem ecclesiae catholica per totum orbem diffusa celebrat.' Gerbert, *De Cantu. I.* 400.

Paris also directs the *Benedictio* after the second lesson, [1] a name which is taken from the frequent recurrence of the word *Benedicite*. Later it was not used so much, and the Mozarabic Mass-book of the Middle Ages prescribes it only occasionally, *e.g.* for the First Sunday in Lent. [2] In the Gallican lectionary it is marked for Christmas Day, after the prophetic lesson, and likewise on Easter Even, [3] on which day Amalarius heard this chant in Tours. [4] In the Roman Mass it is only to be met with on Ember Saturdays, and this practice gradually supplanted the others. [5] In the early Middle Ages it was sung to two different melodies.

THE CREED

To the chants between the lessons from Holy Scripture is added the Creed.

The Niceno-Constantinopolitan [6] Creed first entered the Mass in the East. From the Greek Church it was adopted into the Mozarabic liturgy in 589 by the Spanish bishops assembled in Council at Toledo. [7]

---

1 *Patr. Lat.* lxxij, 91. Duchesne, *Christian Worship*, 195. The word *Benedictio* is also to be so understood in Isidore (*Epist.* 25, 1). 'Ad psalmistam pertinet officium canendi, *dicere benedictiones*, laudes, sacrificium, responsoria et quidquid pertinet ad peritiam canendi.' This has nothing to do with the *Benedicamus Domino*, as Durandus supposes. *Rationale.* ij, 3.

2 Gerbert, *De Cantu* I, 401.   3 *Ibid.*

4 Amalarius, *De Off.* iv, 17. (*Patr. Lat.* cv, 1195).

5 Walafrid Strabo supposes that the Romans sang the hymn of the Three Children only on the 4 days with 12 lessons 'propter multiplicitatem officiorum.' *De Reb. Eccles.* 22 (*Patr. Lat.* cxiv, 947).

6 The Apostles' Creed was probably not used in the Mass, but it certainly was on other liturgical occasions. It is to be found in some MSS., *e.g.* Cod. 381 of *S. Gall, Cod.* 97 of Rheinau, in the Cantonal Library at Zürich, and in English MSS. (*cf. Winchester Troper*, Henry Bradshaw Society, p. 60) in the Greek language, but written in Latin characters and supplied with neums; this shows that it was not simply said like the Mass-Creed, but was sung. In the above-mentioned Rheinau MS. it runs thus (p. 36): 'Pisteuo is theon patera, pantocratora, piitin uranu ke gis. Ke is ison christon, ton yon autu, ton monogeni Kyrion imon. Ton sillisthenta ek pneumatos agiu, genithenta ek marias tis parthenu. Pathonta epi pontiu pilatu, staurothenta, thanonta ke taphenta, katelthonta is ta katotata, triti ti imera anatanta apo ton necron. Anelthonta is tus uranus, katezomenos en dexia theu patros pantodinamu. Er ki then erchomenon krine zontas ki nekrus. Pistheuo is to pneuma to agion, agian ecclesian katholikin, agio kenonian, aphesim amartian sarkos anastasin, zoin euonion, amen.'

7 'Secundum formam orientalium ecclesiarum' says the Council in *Can.* ij, Gerbert, *De Cantu* I, 4, 26,

Here it was precented, not after the Gospel, but after the turning round of the Priest holding the holy Host in his hand, and it was continued by the clergy and all the people. [1] It found an entrance into the Ambrosian Mass, in the old Order of which it is called *Symbolum Dominicale.* Here it stands after the Offertory; the Ambrosian Mass has another chant besides, after the Gospel, which is not found in other Latin liturgies, the *Antiphona post Evangelium.* [2] Beroldus, a Milanese author of the 12th century, describes its performance as follows : 'The Archbishop or Priest precents it, and the choir continues it as far as *Et homo factus est,* from which point the *Magister scholarum* with his boys sing it to the end.' [3] In Gaul and Germany the Creed was likewise known in the Mass, as we learn from the conference which the envoys of Charles the Great held with Leo III in Rome, wherein they appealed for the express permission of the Pope to sing the Creed in the Mass. [4] According to Amalarius, [5] in Gaul all the people took part in chanting the Creed. As regards the Roman Mass, this is evidenced by the 2nd *Ordo Romanus* [6] and by Walafrid Strabo for the time about 800. [7] Shortly after, it seems to have disappeared, until it was definitely incorporated into it under Benedict VIII. The way in which this came about is recorded by an eye-witness, Berno, abbot of the Monastery of Reichenau, [8] who was in Rome in 1014 with the Emperor Henry II. In the second chapter of his book *De quibusdam rebus ad Missam pertinentibus,* in which he sets forth his view of the *Gloria,* he shows that in Rome the Creed did not exist before his time. The Romans, when asked why they did not sing it, answered the Emperor that the Roman Church had never been tainted by heresy, and therefore other churches sooner needed to sing the Creed, such as might have been at times tainted by false belief. The Emperor however urgently besought the Pope to have the Creed sung in the public Mass thenceforth, and the Pope

---

1 Gerbert, *ibid.*

2 Ceriani, *Notitia Liturgiae Ambros. ante saec. med.* XI, (Milan 1895) p. 5.

3 Beroldus, *ed.* Magistretti, (Milan 1894). p. 53.

4 Gerbert, *De Cantu* I, 427.

5 Amalarius, *Ecloga de officio Missae* (*Patr. Lat.* cv, 1323) : 'Postquam Christus locutus est populo suo, fas est, ut dulcius et intentius profiteatur credulitatem suam; sicque convenit populo, post Evangelium intentionem credulitatis suae praeclaro ore proferre.'

6 *Patr. Lat.* lxxviij, 972 : 'post lectum evangelium . . . ab episcopo *Credo in unum Deum* cantatur.'

7 Walafrid Strabo, *De Reb. Eccles.* 22 (*Patr. Lat.* cxiv, 947).

8 *Patr. Lat.* cvlij, 1056. *cf.* above p. 80,

complied with his wishes.   In spite of this, or rather on account of its late introduction, the Creed has always been considered merely as a more decorative part of the Mass.   The 6th Roman *Ordo* leaves it to the Bishop to have a sermon after the Gospel, or, if he does not wish to do this, to start with a loud voice the *Credo in unum Deum*, [1] which is to be continued by the whole choir (the clergy at the altar).   The chanting of the Creed was not a function of the singers, as is shown by the 11th *Ordo*, which prescribes for the Mass of Christmas—'The Pontiff intones the Creed and the *Basilicarii* respond and sing on.   The *Primicerius* and the *Schola* then sing the *Offerenda*.'   The *Basilicarii*, here distinguished from the choir, are the retinue of the Celebrant, who are at the altar. [3]   With this agrees the statement in the exposition of the Mass by Innocent III (13th century),[2] that in the solemn Papal Mass the Creed was not sung by the singers of the choir, but by the sub-deacons at the altar.

As the *Gloria* to the present day does not appear at every Mass, so it is with the Creed.   It is included only in the Masses of Sundays and Feast days.   Like the *Gloria*, it was also sung in Greek, even late into the Middle Ages.   In some MSS. of S. Gall it occurs in Greek, but written in Latin characters, as has been already mentioned.

The melody to which the Creed was sung in the Middle Ages, and which the MSS. have handed down, is a simple syllabic recitative without melodic embellishment.   The same formula of recitative is repeated for most of the verses, so that it was very easy to learn.   Such a style of performance was of course necessary, since it was not the *Schola*, but the whole body of priests assisting at the altar that were bound to sing it.   In the later Middle Ages besides the simple melody there arose others with 'broken notes,' *i.e.* with quicker note-values.   In the strict Orders, *e.g.* among the Carthusians, the old recitative was adhered to: and while for the *Kyrie*, *Gloria*, and the other parts of the *Ordinarium Missae*, the later Middle Ages composed a considerable number of different melodies, for the Creed we find in the MSS., and even in the oldest printed books, very seldom more than one melody, the old recitative.

It seems that towards the end of the Middle Ages in some churches, especially in Germany, the length of the Creed was felt to be burdensome. Some MSS. (*e.g.* the *Cod. S. Gall* 546), as well as printed books, (*e.g.* the Augsburg Gradual printed at Basle in 1511), contained a shortened form

---

1 *Patr. Lat.* lxxviij, 992.
2 *Ibid*, 1033.
3 Innocentius, *De myster. Miss.* II. 52 (*Patr. Lat.* ccxvij, 830).

of music to the Creed side by side with the complete chant. This is remarkable, because it was Germany rather than Italy and France, both at this time and later, that preserved intaćt the Gregorian Chant. In the same way it is strange that such abbreviations should be found in a S. Gall MS. which does not come from outside (like *Cod.* 383 of the same library), but was made to the order of an abbot (Franz Gaisberg) by a member of the monastery, as a record in the MS. informs us. Of the three Creed-melodies comprised in *Cod.* 546, the third simply adds Amen at the words *et homo faćtus est.* The Augsburg Gradual has several shortened Creeds: the first ends like the one at S. Gall just mentioned; the second goes on one verse further, and ends with *passus et sepultus est. Amen*; the third leaves out the whole portion from *crucifixus etiam* to *confiteor.* It is unnecessary to point out that such a proceeding, which moreover went on far into later centuries, bears extremely bad testimony to the liturgical instinćt of that time. It is one of the harbingers of the storms which from the second half of the 16th century onwards were to spring up against the liturgical chant of the Middle Ages.

CHAPTER VI

THE CHANTS OF THE ANAPHORA

After the lessons are ended, the offering of the Sacrifice begins, and with it the Mass proper. After the salutation *Dominus vobiscum*, the celebrant exhorts those present to pray with him, [1] and then begins the ceremonies prescribed for the rite of the Offering. Meanwhile the Choir sings

THE ANTIPHON TO THE OFFERTORY

The chant accompanying the offering is very old: it existed in the first half of the 5th century. S. Augustine, as he himself relates, [2] introduced into the African Church 'the custom of singing hymns out of the book of psalms before the offering of the sacrificial gifts, and during the distribution of the Sacrifice to the people.' It cannot be proved with certainty that Augustine in so doing adopted a Milanese or Roman rite, but it is very probable; on the other hand the absence of the Offertory chant from the Roman Mass for Easter Even [3] shows that the Roman

---

1 It is difficult to say when the prayer introduced by *Oremus* disappeared out of the Mass. Perhaps when the words of the chants first began to be said at the Altar. From that time the celebrant had two texts before him, and may have decided in favour of the later one. But it is remarkable that the *Oremus* remained, although the text of the Offertory following has none of the character of prayer except in a very few cases, as *e. g.* in the Offertory of the Mass for the dead, *Domine Jesu Christe.*

2 A certain Hilarius resisted the innovation, and thus gave Augustine an opportunity for justifying his conduct in a dissertation *(Contra Hilarium)*, which is unfortunately lost ; it certainly contained much valuable information about the history of Ecclesiastical Chant. Augustine, *Retract.* ij, 11 (*Patr. Lat.* xxxij, 634).

3 The ritualists tried to explain this in their usual style: *e.g.* pseudo-Alcuin supposed 'quod autem (on Easter Even) post Evangelium non cantatur *offerenda* et cantores tempore sacrificii silent, ad memoriam reducitur sacrificium seu silentium mulierum' (*Patr. Lat.* lxxviij, 379).

Liturgy did not possess it from the beginning. [1] It was desirable to engage the attention of the faithful by a chant during the offering of the gifts, because the rite of the offering in its original form gave occasion for a disturbing noise. Thus all Latin liturgies from the early Middle Ages onwards have a chant at this place in the Mass, to fill up the time while the people are offering their gifts. In Spain it was called *Offertorium* or *Sacrificium*; [2] the documents of both the Italian liturgies, the Milanese and the Roman, call it *Offerenda* and *Offertorium*, either with or without an indication of the antiphonal method of performance (such as *Antiphona ad Offerendum*, or *ad Offertorium*). In the old Gallican liturgy of S. Germanus of Paris, the chant accompanying the Oblation was called *Sonus* or *Sonum*, [3] and comprised nothing but the *Alleluia*.

The ceremony of the offering by the people was at first universal. It soon disappeared from the Oriental liturgies, but was retained in the Latin ones for a long time. As the *Ordines Romani* show, the people at Rome offered bread and wine, and the clerks and priests as well. Even the officiating Pope had to bring his gift; the singers brought only the water which was mixed with the wine. [4]

Surrounded by bishops and priests, the Pope received the bread, and the Archdeacon the wine. The gifts were thereupon divided into two parts: one was delivered to the Pope and afterwards consecrated. It was possible to judge approximately from the number present how much was necessary for Consecration and Communion, and what remained was specially blessed after the Consecration. The formula for this has been preserved in the Canon of the Mass up to the present time and is even said over the consecrated species, although they need no further blessing. The rite of the Offertory was concluded by the washing of the Celebrant's hands, which also is still to be found in the present Mass.

The melodic character of the Offertory chant was fixed by its liturgical position: like all the chants which accompany ceremonies it was at first a

---

1 Berno of Reichenau has no exact knowledge of the introduction of the Offertory : 'quamvis a prioris populi consuetudine in usum Christianorum venisse dicatur, tamen quis specialiter addiderit, aperte non legimus.' *De quibusdam ad missam pertinentibus*, i. (*Patr. Lat.* cxlij, 1058).

2 Thus Vasaeus, *Chronicon Hisp.:* see *ad. ann.* 717. Gerbert, *De Cantu* I, 431.

3 *Patr. Lat.* lxxij, 92.

4 *Ordo Rom. I.* 13 and 14. (*Patr. Lat.* lxxviij, 943), *cf.* also *Ordo V.* 8, (*ibid* 988). It was retained in France also: Amalarius, *De Offic.* iij, 19 (*Patr. Lat.* cv, 1131): 'Cantores propter instantem necessitatem cantandi non habent licentiam huc illucque discurrendi, ut singuli offerant cum caeteris . . . Populus offert vinum, cantores aquam.'

psalm, which was performed antiphonally by the two halves of the choir. It was necessary to have a chant lasting as long as the rather lengthy offering, and the singers themselves had to offer their gifts; and therefore very soon, and certainly before Gregory the Great, the character of the chant came to be modified. It was found convenient to leave the execution of the verses, not to the choir, but to a soloist. In view of the strong tendency in the Middle Ages for liturgical matters to react on the music, it was very natural that there should accompany this change an enrichment of the melody. Thus from a choir-chant the Offertory [1] became a highly developed solo-chant, like the Gradual and Alleluia; the Gregorian Offertories were richly decked out, and all the art of the soloist was lavished especially on the verses assigned to the soloists. We therefore meet with MSS. which contain Offertory-verses along with the other solo-chants : e.g. the *Cod. S. Gall* 378 and 380, and the *Cod.* of the National Library at Paris, *Fond. Lat.* 1134, 1135. Only the first words are given, as a rule, of the preliminary antiphons to be performed by the choir, together with the cue from which the antiphon was to be repeated after the verses. From the time when the soloists took to singing the Offertory-verses, and the choir sang only the antiphon in between, either completely or in part, the Offertory changed from an antiphonal chant into a *responsorial chant*. But the title *Antiphona* was kept as before.

Besides the solo character of the Offertory verses there is another peculiarity of this chant to be noted. The Offertory-chant is the only one of all the liturgical chants of the Mass and of the Office which occasionally repeats suitable words, or combinations of words, without being directed to do so by the liturgical text of the chant. In all other cases the melody is wedded to the words of the text ordered by the Church, without altering their arrangement, or repeating any part; and thus the liturgical chant grew up and developed in the closest connexion with the liturgical text. The repetition of a word, where the Liturgy does not order it, implies a sort of revolt from it : it denotes the triumph of a subjective conception of the liturgical words. However there is no need to judge the repetitions in the Offertory so severely : they were, it may be said, of a more simple nature, and were demanded by the length of the ceremonies at the offering. The value which the repetition of a word or thought may have, viewed from a purely artistic standpoint, was shown later by the

---

[1] It is the same with the Ambrosian Offertories, the execution of which was the function of the *Magister Scholarum* and his singing boys, according to the ritualist Beroldus (12th century). *Ordo Beroldi* (*ed.* Magistretti), p. 52.

composers of harmonized vocal music, for they made of it one of their most forcible methods of expression. Artistic considerations are not the cause of the repetitions in the old Offertories. This is clear on looking more closely into them. The *Graduale Rhenaugiense* at the end of the Offertory of Christmas Eve, *Tollite portas*, repeats the first thought: *Tollite portas principes vestras et elevamini portae aeternales, et introibit rex gloriae, tollite portas principes vestras.* On Quinquagesima Sunday, the opening sentence *Benedictus es Domine, doce me iustificationes tuas* is sung twice. [1] The repetitions are more numerous in other MSS., *e.g.* in *Cod. S. Gall* 339 : the Offert. *Jubilate Deo* of the 1st Sunday after Epiphany has the opening words *Jubilate Deo omnis terra* twice : the Offert. *Jubilate Deo* of the 2nd Sunday after the Epiphany likewise repeats the opening words *Jubilate Deo universa terra*, and the same part of verses 1 and 2 : the Offert. *Benedictus es Dominus* here and in the Rheinau Gradual does the same in ℣. 3 : the Offert. *Precatus est Moyses* of *Fer. V. post Dom. II. Quadrag.* repeats the opening words *Precatus . . . et dixit*, and does the same in ℣. 3.

It is no doubt possible that these sentences were sung the first time by the soloist as an intonation, and then repeated and continued by the Choir: but there are other repetitions in the same S. Gall MS., which cannot be so explained. ℣. 1 of the Offert. *Domine exaudi* of Wednesday in Holy Week runs : *Ne avertas faciem tuam, ne avertas faciem tuam a me.* ℣. 2 of the Offert. *Domine deus in simplicitate* of the Feast of Dedication runs : *Fecit Salomon solemnitatem in tempore illo, fecit Salomon solemnitatem in tempore illo, et properatus est et apparuit ei Dominus.* ℣. 1 of Offert. *Exultabunt sancti* on the Feast of SS. Basilides, Cirinus, Nabor and Nazarius begins by repeating the words *Cantate domino canticum novum.*

Among the most strange are the repetitions in Offert. *Vir erat* of the 21st Sunday after Pentecost. The ℣. 1 of this runs : *Utinam appenderentur peccata mea, quibus iram merui, quibus iram merui, et calamitas, et calamitas, et calamitas, quam patior haec gravior appareret.* ℣. 2 *Quae est enim, quae est enim, quae est enim fortitudo mea, ut sustineam, aut quis finis meus, ut patienter agam, aut finis meus, ut patienter agam;* and in ℣. 4 : *Quoniam non revertetur oculus meus, ut videam bona,* the first word is even sung three times, and the last three words nine times. Amalarius points to the condition of the the illness of Job, whose groans must have been repeated, as an explanation

---

1 Gerbert, *Monum. vet. lit. Alem.* I, 372, omits the repetition, but it is to be found in the original (*Cod.* XXX. *Rhenaug.* in the Cantonal Library at Zürich).

of this repetition of the words. [1]   For the Offert. *Domine in auxilium* the above mentioned MS. indicates by the word *Domine* the repetition of the first part after the words *auferant me*.

The chronicler Sigebert remarks, at the year 772, that the repetitions were ordered by Pope Hadrian; [2] but this is not very probable.   Not only do they bear the stamp of antiquity, but, more important still, they exist in the Ambrosian chant also, and in precisely the same pieces, *e.g.* in Offert. *Jubilate Domino Deo universa terra* (Sexagesima Sunday) and *Precatus est Moyses* (1st Sunday in Lent). [3]   It is therefore to be concluded that they go back to a very distant age.   Some were sung throughout the Middle Ages, and they are still to be found in pre-Tridentine printed Graduals.   The Tridentine Commission for the reform of the Mass-book struck out most of them : only two Offertories recall the old peculiarity, *Domine in auxilium* and *De profundis clamavi*, for the 16th and 23rd Sundays after Pentecost. [4]

The number of the Offertory-verses was fixed by the length of the offering : two or three is the rule, and there are never more than four. The Rheinau Gradual does not specially mark them, but this is not noteworthy, considering the distinctly rubrical character of the MS. [5] The verses however were known at the date to which the MS. belongs (*c.* 750), as is clear from the repeated words in Offert. *Tollite portas*, which are merely the repetition by the choir after the (unrecorded) verse.   The Offertory verses are often carefully written down in a great number of books,

---

1 *De Off.* iij, 39 (*Patr. Lat.* cv, 1157) : 'In Offertorio non est repetitio verborum in versibus est.   Verba historici continentur in Offertorio, verba Job aegroti et dolentis continentur in versibus.   Aegrotus, cuius anhelitus non est sanus neque fortis, solet verba imperfecta saepius repetere.   Officii auctor, ut effectanter nobis ad memoriam reduceret aegrotantem.   In Offertorio, ut dixi, non sunt verba repetita, quia historicus scribens historiam non aegrotabat.

2 *Patr. Lat.* clx, 147 : 'Hic in Offertoriis et Offertoriorum versibus, quod geminatum est, geminavit.'

3 See the oldest Ambrosian chant-book, of the 12th century, which is published in vols. v. and vj. of *Paléographie Musicale*, in phototype and in modern translation, at vj, clxi and 197.

4 The texts still run : 'Domine, in auxilium meum respice : confundantur et revereantur qui quaerunt animam meam, ut auferant eam : Domine, in auxilium meum respice,' and 'De profundis clamavi ad te, Domine : Domine, exaudi orationem meam ; de profundis clamavi ad te, Domine.'

5 As a rule the Rheinau MS. contains only the texts of the chants, not the melodies, and those only in a shortened form adapted to simple circumstances, even though its Roman origin is unmistakeably shown by the entry of the Stations.

and especially in the S. Gall MSS. [1]   Moreover they are found in the Ambrosian Mass. [2]

If we leave out of sight the responsorial charaᐧter which the Offertory-antiphon, even in the oldest MSS., unmistakeably exhibits, its performance has many points of likeness in detail to that of the Introit-antiphon. The choir began with the first part, and repeated it, either completely or in part, after the verses of the soloist.   In this case also the Pope gave the sign to the singers when to break off. [3]

There are MSS. as early as the 11th century which do not mark the Offertory-verses: from this we must conclude that from that time the offering of the people fell into disuse.   They are wanting in most MSS. after the 12th century, but they were still sung in German Churches in the 13th century, on some feasts even in the 15th and 16th centuries, especially on Christmas day. [4]   Durandus of Mende considers the reason for the omission of the verses to be the need of greater brevity, and the endeavour to make both clergy and people devote themselves more to the prayers. [5]   Ralph of Tongres gives the important information that, since their omission, the Offertory itself was performed more slowly. [6]   The use of the organ to accompany the chant seems to have had an influence in the same direᐧtion; at any rate it is certain that the harmonized music called 'Organum,' which was conneᐧted with a use of the organ, had the effeᐧt of retarding the *tempo* in the performance of the liturgical chant.

Like the repetitions, the verses also were removed from the Tridentine Mass-book.   It is only the Mass for the dead (in which, even at the present time, a kind of offering often takes place), which still recalls the medieval usage by the ℣. *Hostias et preces*, and the repetition after it of the concluding part of the Offertory.

---

1 *E.g.* in *Cod. S. Gall.* 338, 339, 340, 374, 375 (of the 12th century), 376, 378, 380, and 382. Further in *Cod. Einsiedl.* 121 and numerous MSS. of the Paris Bibl. Nat.

2 The Ambrosian Antiphoner of the *Paléographie musicale* has verses to the following Offertories : Off. *Alienigenae* (3rd Sun. in Advent), Off. *Benedixisti* (4th Sun. in Advent), Off. *Confortamini* (5th Sun. in Advent), Off. *Ecce apertum* (Christmas Day) Off. *Stetit angelus* (S. John Ev.), Off. *Visi sunt gressus* (Sun. after Christmas), Off. *Orietur in diebus* (Epiphany), Off. *Scapulis suis* (*Domin. in cap. Quad.*), Off. *Precatus est Moyses* (1st Sun. in Lent), Off. *Haec dicit* (*Domin. de Lazaro*), Off. *Eripe me* (Palm Sunday).   All however have only one verse, except the Off. *Haec dicit*, which has two.

3 *Ordo Rom. II.* 9 (*Patr. Lat.* lxxviij, 973).

4 Two MSS. of the City Library of Trier, of the 13th century, have all the verses still.

5 Durandus, iv, 27.   6 *De can. obs., prop.* 23. Gerbert, *De Cantu* I, 432.

Only about half the Masses of the Church's year have Offertories of their own in the MSS. The *Cod.* 339 of S. Gall has 102 different ones for 203 Masses. Their texts are taken principally from the Psalter (82), some are from other books of Holy Scripture (16); the origin of four is doubtful. [1] In the Sundays after Pentecost we again find texts following numerically the order of the Psalter. [2]

THE SANCTUS

The Greek Liturgy has a double 'Thrice Holy:' in addition to that which corresponds to the *Sanctus* and is usually called *Epinikion* (song of triumph), it has the *Trisagion*, which in the Latin Liturgy is sung in the *Improperia* of Good Friday in Latin and in Greek: *Agios o Theos*, and *Sanctus Deus*, etc. Both occupied an important position in the Liturgy of the first centuries. [3]

In the Latin Liturgy the *Sanctus* forms an immediate continuation of the Preface. According to a notice in the *Liber Pontificalis*, [4] it was added to the Roman Mass by Pope Sixtus I. (*c.* 120). This is not impossible, for prayers like the Preface belong to the primitive elements of the Latin liturgy, and the Latin Mass-Preface always leads into the *Sanctus*. Moreover the further statement of the *Liber Pontificalis*, that the above-mentioned Pope had the *Sanctus* precented by the celebrant, and continued by the whole congregation, certainly describes the original execution of the chant; for the Preface concludes with the summons to those present to raise their voices to the Thrice-Holy, together with the heavenly hosts. In the Gallican Church it was likewise in use from the first, at least at solemn Mass; the council of Vaison (529) ordered it for

---

1 These are Off. *Oratio mea munda* (*S. Lawrence*, probably from his *Acta*), Off. *Protege Domine* (*De exalt. S. Crucis*, probably translated from the Greek), Off. *Domine Jesu Christe (In Agenda mortuorum)* and Off. *Benedictus sit (de S. Trinitate)*.

2 Quite singular, and certainly not of Roman origin, is the custom, noted by Gerbert in an *Ordo* of the monastery of S. Gregory in the Diocese of Basle, of having psalms performed by the clergy after the Offertory and before the Preface, (*e.g.* Pss. 19, 24 and 50), and followed by versicles sung by the people. Gerbert, *De Cantu* I, 439. These versicles were known to Amalarius, but by hearsay only, from which we see that they were not in use everywhere (*Patr. Lat.* cv, 1132).

3 Numerous proofs of this in *Patr. Lat.* lxxviij, 272. The *Apost. Constit.* (viij, 12), order the *Epinikion* to be sung by all the people.

4 'Constituit ut, Missarum actionem sacerdote incipiente, populus hymnum decantaret *Sanctus, Sanctus, Sanctus*,' etc. See *Lib. Pontif.* i, 128.

private Masses also. ¹   It was moreover a congregational chant in Gaul, as is shown by a sermon of S. Caesarius of Arles, who complains bitterly of the bad habit of leaving the church after the Lessons, and asks : 'To whom is the priest to address the *Sursum corda*, and how are all to sing the *Sanctus* congregationally, if they are idling about in the streets, and are absent both in body and spirit ?' ²   In the Gregorian Mass the clergy assisting at the Altar are sometimes the representatives of the congregation : thus the Roman *Ordines* direct that the *Subdiaconi Regionarii, i.e.* the Subdeacons of the different districts who minister to the Pope in the Station-church, should sing the *Sanctus* : when they have finished, the Pope begins the Canon. ³   In Gaul the congregational chanting of the *Sanctus* was not abolished even after the introduction of the Gregorian Liturgy.   The Frankish kings were very well acquainted with the symbolical value of this beautiful practice, and it is urged in various ways in their capitularies. ⁴ In one of these it is ordered that the priest shall not go on with the *Te igitur*, the opening words of the Canon, until the angelic song of praise is quite finished.   The priests were clearly bound to join in singing the *Sanctus*; and this is also attested by an order of Bishop Herardus of Tours in 858. ⁵   At least this obligation of the priest shows a deep understanding of the organic structure of the Sacred Rite.

We still possess the oldest *Sanctus* melody, which is merely the continuation of the Preface melody.   When the choir of singers usurped, in addition to their own, those singing functions which till then had been performed by the congregation, this simple melody seemed too poor; other richer ones were then composed, and the primitive melody was degraded to ordinary days and to Masses for the dead, where it is still sung. ⁶   But the Carthusians even in the 18th century sang the old melody only. ⁷

---

1 Canon 3 : 'Ut in omnibus Missis, seu matutinis seu quadragesimalibus, seu in illis quae pro defunctorum commemoratione fiunt, semper *Sanctus, Sanctus, Sanctus* eo ordine quo ad Missas publicas dicitur, dici debeat.'

2 *Hom.* 12 (*Patr. Lat.* lxxviij, 271).

3 *Ordo I.* 16 (*Patr. Lat.* lxxviij, 945).   The *Ordo* of the Canon Benedict calls them the *Basilicarii* (*Patr. Lat.* lxxviij, 1033).

4 *Capit.* i. 66 ; vj, 170.   5 *Patr. Lat.* lxxviij, 272.

6 In order to convince oneself that the *Sanctus* of ferias and of the Mass for the dead is the continuation of the Preface, one must consult an edition that contains the Gregorian plainsong like the *Liber Gradualis* of Solesmes : in other editions the connexion is often obscured, as they give the *Sanctus* melody at a different pitch to the Preface (*i.e.* a tone lower).   7 Soullier, *Plain-chant,* Tournai, p. 118.

The *Benedictus* was originally, and is still to-day in the mouth of the Celebrant, not an independent piece, but the conclusion of the *Sanctus*. Under the influence of the composers of the later Middle Ages, who often so extended the *Sanctus* in their harmonized Masses that the *Benedictus* could only be sung after the consecration, the singers gradually lost sight of the fact that the *Benedictus* belonged closely to the *Sanctus*. In the 15th and 16th centuries in Rome the *Sanctus* was sung at Solemn Masses no longer in plainsong, but always in harmony; and the custom of singing the *Benedictus* only after the consecration gradually became the rule. [1]

THE AGNUS DEI

The *Agnus Dei* is unknown to the Gelasian Sacramentary, as it is also to the Milanese Order of the Mass; moreover the very ancient Gregorian Mass of the night before Easter, which to-day is said on Easter Even, does not contain it. [2] It is therefore shown to be a later addition to the Latin Mass. The text must have been taken from the *Gloria;* at any rate it was a Greek Pope, Sergius I, (678-701) who naturalized it in Rome. He ordered, so says the *Liber Pontificalis*, that, at the breaking of the Body of the Lord, the *Agnus Dei, qui tollis peccata mundi, miserere nobis* should be sung by the people and clergy. [3] In the Papal Mass, as described

---

1 As however this rule rests on the performance of a harmonized *Sanctus*, and presupposes this, one need not perhaps necessarily take it to mean that the *Benedictus* is to be sung after the consecration in the case of a plainsong *Sanctus* also. The custom accords ill with the common sense principle that the choir should always follow closely the order of the liturgical action; it spoils the connexion between Altar and Choir, for the *Benedictus qui venit* in the mouth of the Priest before the consecration has quite another significance from that which it has in the mouth of the singers after the consecration; to the latter the word *venit* is a perfect, while to the Priest it is a present with a future meaning.

A Mass *Ordo* in *Patr. Lat.* lxxviij, 249 has the rubric that (after the Celebrant has begun *Te igitur*) the assisting deacons and subdeacons should sing the psalms *Exaudiat te Dominus, Ad te Domine levavi, Miserere mei Deus, Qui habitat in adiutorio*, with the verses (*precibus* probably stands for *versibus*); *Salvum fac servum tuum, Desiderium cordis, Vitam petiit a te, Oculi Domini super iustos, Fiat misericordia, Domine exaudi orationem.* As p. 99 points out, these pieces were sung at an earlier date in other Churches. But they were never in general use, and soon disappeared from the Liturgy.

2 A few monastic *Ordines* have the *Agnus Dei* also in this Mass, *e.g.* an *Ordo* of *Einsiedeln* of the 9th century. Gerbert, *De Cantu* I, 455.

3 *Liber Pontif.* (*ed.* Duchesne), I, 376.

by the first Roman *Ordo*, the singers of the *Schola* are entrusted with it, and the assisting Archdeacon gives the sign to begin it. [1] In Gaul the original custom was preserved longer than in Rome, in that all the clergy officiating at the Altar, and sometimes all the people as well, performed the *Agnus*, not the singers only.   Rhabanus Maurus orders it to be sung during the ceremony of the kiss of peace. [2]

It cannot be decided whether the *Agnus Dei* was sung at first as often as the length of the ceremony demanded, or only three times, as directed in all our documents.   The former is probable, for, *e.g.* in the Papal Mass, the ceremony might occupy a considerable time.   At any rate the alteration of the *miserere nobis* to *dona nobis pacem* at the end of the *Agnus Dei* was only carried out later, no doubt with reference to the kiss of peace and the prayer of the Canon following, *Domine Jesu Christe, qui dixisti Apostolis tuis, Pacem relinquo vobis etc.*   In the Lateran Church 'the Mother of all the Churches,' *miserere nobis* is still sung at the third *Agnus*.

Like the melody of the *Sanctus*, that of the *Agnus Dei* was at first a simple recitative melody.   This is still sung at ferial masses and at Masses for the dead.   It can easily be understood that the singers of the Roman *Schola* would not be contented permanently with the simple melody; so they composed other melodies more effective and more ornate.   In a Rheinau manuscript of the 12th century, besides the older melody (*minor*) a richer one (*major*) is mentioned, which was to be sung on high festivals, and on less important festivals at the third *Agnus*. [3]   The *Agnus Dei* translated into Greek and written in Latin characters is found, though rarely, in the MSS., *e.g.* in a Troper of Montauriol of the 11th century. [4]

THE COMMUNION ANTIPHON

Almost all Eastern and Western liturgies, so far as we can follow them, the Apostolic Constitutions (VIII, 13) the liturgy of S. James, the liturgy of S. Cyril of Jerusalem, the Armenian, the Celtic, the Mozarabic,

---

1 *Ordo Rom. I.* 19 (*Patr. Lat.* lxxviij, 946).

2 *De Instit. Cler. I,* 33 (*Patr. Lat.* cvij, 324).   In the Gallican Mass the kiss of peace was given before the Preface and was accompanied by a responsory (Duchesne, *Christian Worship,* 212).   The same was the case also during the fraction of the holy Host, at which point the Ambrosians sang the *Confractorium*.   Later, in the Mozarabic Liturgy, the Creed was said at this place (Duchesne, *ibid.* 220).

3 Gerbert, *l. c.* I, 457.   4 Daux, *Deux Livres Choraux monastiques des Xe et XIe siècles,* (Paris, 1899) p. 103.

the Milanese, and the Roman, prescribe for the communion of the people the chanting of the 33rd psalm, especially v. 8, *Gustate et videte.* [1] It was the unvarying Communion-chant which in all Masses accompanied the administration of the Holy Eucharist. In the African Church the Communion psalmody was introduced at the same time as the Offertory psalm, as we know from the statement of S. Augustine (*cf.* p. 93). In the Mozarabic-Gallican Mass the Communion-chant was called *Trecanum* : [2] in the 7th century it still consisted of verses of ps. 33 with *Gloria Patri.* In Milan the oldest liturgical records call it *Transitorium;* in the Roman Mass it is called *Antiphona ad Communionem.* Many MSS. of Gallican and German origin have a second Communion-chant for the Easter Mass, the celebrated antiphon *Venite populi, e.g. Cod.* 262 of the library of the City of Reims, *Cod. Bohn* of the library of the City of Trier, also the S. Gall MSS. etc. It was sung before the third *Agnus Dei*, as a summons to the reception of the Holy Communion (see the MS. of Reims). [3]

As early as the oldest Roman chant-books the Communion-chant varies for each Mass : the 8th Sunday after Pentecost alone has retained the text *Gustate et videte* in its original position : otherwise all the Masses have other texts. They are always psalm-verses performed alternately with an antiphon, which was repeated, either entirely or partially, after each verse; and thus the Communion with its verses is like the *Antiphona ad Introitum.* The number of the verses was decided by the time occupied with the administration of the Holy Eucharist. In some MSS. up till the 13th century they are specially indicated, *e.g.* in *Cod. Einsiedeln* 121, at the end, *Cod. S. Gall* 381, etc. As at the Introit, so here, there are the verses called *versus ad respondendum*, or *repetendum*, or *prophetales.* The *Cod. Einsiedeln* 121 gives the proper cue of the part of the antiphon to be repeated after each verse. A close study of the texts reveals a noteworthy contrast between the Communion-antiphon and the other Mass-chants of the *Proprium.* For the 201 Masses of the Church's year *Cod. S. Gall* 339 has only 147 different Communions : 54 Masses thus possess none peculiar to themselves. Out of the 147, the texts of 64 are taken from the Psalter, the texts of 80 from other books of Holy Scripture; only 3 are not taken from it. [4] In the case of the other chants, as we

---

1 There are many proofs of this given in *Paléographie Musicale* vj, 22.

2 *Patr. Lat.* lxxij, 94.

3 As to this chant *cf. Paléographie Musicale* v, *Avant-propos*, and Daux, *Deux Livres Choraux*, pp. 137 foll.

4 These are Comm. *Ecce Dominus veniet* (Ember Friday in Advent), *Qui me*

have seen, the Psalter has yielded by far the greater number of texts: here it is in the minority, and in the proportion of exactly 4 to 5. A comparison with the old Gospel capitularies and lectionaries shows that the choice of Communion-texts was confined to the books in which were written the Gospel and Lessons for each day, and especially the Gospel and Lesson of the Mass, although there are some exceptions which perhaps belong to a later arrangement. [1]

For the Sundays after Pentecost the numerical order of the psalms is again followed: the Communion of the first Sunday begins with ps. 9; then follow pss. 12, 16, 17 etc., as may be seen in the Appendix. There are only a few exceptions; but from the 17th Sunday onwards this arrangement is abandoned altogether. Generally the law of the numerical succession of the psalms governs all the chants of the Sundays after Pentecost, at least up to the Sunday mentioned, excepting the old Gradual series. The texts of the week-days of Lent are similarly arranged: they follow the order of the psalms, from the 1st to the 26th. The Sundays and Thursdays interrupt the succession: we shall learn the reason of this later.

As to the relation of the Communion-verse to the antiphon, when taken from a psalm, the same rules hold good as at the Introit; *viz.* if the Communion is the beginning of a psalm, the first verse of the Communion is the one immediately or almost immediately following: if the antiphon is taken from the middle of the psalm, the first Communion-verse is the first verse of the psalm. But if the antiphon is not taken from a psalm, its verses are from the same psalm as those of the Introit. Many MSS. simply give a reference to this: the note *psalmus ut supra* is found in this case. [2] To take a couple of examples: The Comm. *Erubescant* of the Friday before the 2nd Sunday in Lent comes from psalm 6, and forms verse 11 of it. The first Communion-verse runs *Domine ne in furore*, and is the first verse of the psalm. The Comm. of the following day, *Domine Deus meus*, forms the beginning of psalm 7, and the first Communion-verse *Nequando rapiat* follows immediately upon it in the psalm. On the other hand the Comm. *Mitte manum* of Low Sunday comes from S. John xx, 27, and has the verses *Exultate Deo* and *Sumite psalmum*, the opening verses of ps. 80,

---

dignatus est (S. Agatha, probably drawn from her *Acta*) and *Dona eis Domine* (Mass for the dead).

1 *Cf.* the Lectionaries (also called *Comites*) and the *Capitulare Evangeliorum* in *Tommasi, l. c. XII.*

2 *E. g.* in the Gradual printed in *Patr. Lat,* vol. lxxviij.

just like the Introit *Quasi modo geniti*, which is taken from the 2nd chapter of the 1st epistle of S. Peter.

The practice of general communion at the Masses of solemn days must have gone out from the 11th century onward, as from that time the MSS. begin to leave out the verses. Those of the 12th century very seldom have them. As with the other chants, so with the Communion, the original form was preserved longest in Germany: the library of the church of S. Thomas at Leipzig contains a MS. of the 13th century, which gives the Communion-verses for all the days of the Church's year. At that time they were still sung in some parts of Germany, like the Introit-verses and those of the Offertory. From the 14th century onwards they disappeared everywhere; the only Mass which still adds a verse to the Communion-antiphon is the Mass for the dead, the Communion of which, *Lux aeterna*, has the verse *Requiem aeternam;* after it the conclusion of the antiphon, from *cum sanctis*, is repeated.

The execution of the Communion-antiphon was the same as that of the Introit-antiphon. We learn in detail from the Roman *Ordines* that it was started as soon as the celebrant began to administer the Holy Communion. The singers sang the psalm-verses which were necessary, antiphonally with the Subdeacons, in double chorus. When the administration of the Holy Communion was ended, the Pontiff gave the District Subdeacon a sign : he on his part gave the *Prior Scholae* to understand that the *Gloria Patri* was to be sung: there was yet to follow the *Versus ad repetendum*, and, for the last time, the antiphon. [1]

For a long time the Communion-antiphon has been sung after the communion of the priest: at least this is the rule. This has perhaps come about through the fact that the antiphon only very seldom contains any longer any reference to the Holy Communion.

With respect to its musical composition the Communion stands on the same ground as the Introit. They even have, both of them, the same psalm-form.

It only remains now to deal with the lessons of the *Epistle* and *Gospel*, with the *Preface*, the *Pater noster*, and the other prayers which concern the celebrant and his assistants at the Altar,—those liturgical pieces, in fact, for which there arose in the later Middle Ages the not very aptly chosen designation *Accentus*, as opposed to *Concentus*,

---

[1] *Ordo Rom. I.* 20 (*Patr. Lat.* lxxviij, 947), and *Ordo III.* 18 (*ibid* 982).

which was the name given to the melodically developed Antiphons and Responds. However, they interest us here only for their melody, and for this reason the description of them and of the analogous parts of the Office is deferred to the 'Gregorian Scheme.'

In order to enable the reader to get a survey of the music that accompanied the early Medieval Mass, there is appended to this chapter a collection of the variable texts of the chants of the Easter Mass, based upon *Cod. S. Gall* 339 of the 10th century: for the *versus ad repetendum* of the Introit and the Communion *Cod.* 381 (11th century) of the same library has been utilized.

The Chants of the Easter Mass

Antiphona ad Introitum

Ant. Resurrexi et adhuc tecum sum, alleluia: posuisti super me manum tuam, alleluia: mirabilis facta est scientia tua, alleluia, alleluia.

Ps. Domine, probasti me et cognovisti me: tu cognovisti sessionem meam et resurrectionem meam.

Ant. Resurrexi et adhuc, etc.

℣. Gloria Patri et Filio et Spiritui sancto: sicut erat in principio et nunc et semper, et in saecula saeculorum, amen.

Ant. Resurrexi et adhuc, etc.

℣. *ad repet.* Intellexisti cogitationes meas de longe: semitam meam et funiculum meum investigasti.

Ant. Resurrexi et adhuc, etc.

Responsorium Graduale

℟. Haec dies, quam fecit dominus: exultemus et laetemur in ea.

℣. Confitemini domino, quoniam bonus: quoniam in saeculum misericordia eius.

℟. Haec dies, quam fecit, etc.

Alleluia [1]

Alleluia. ℣. Pascha nostrum immolatus est Christus. Alleluia.

℣. Epulemur in azymis sinceritatis et veritatis. Alleluia.

---

1 A manuscript of the 11-12 century (see Tommasi, *l. c.* xij, 89) has the Alleluia ℣. 'Ego dormivi et somnum coepi, et resurrexi, quia dominus suscepit me.'

Antiphona ad Offertorium

Ant. Terra tremuit et quievit, dum resurgeret in iudicio deus, alleluia.

℣. Notus in Iudaea Deus, in Israel magnum nomen eius, alleluia.

Ant. Dum resurgeret, etc. ¹

℣. Et factus est in pace locus eius, et habitatio eius in Sion.

Ant. Dum resurgeret, etc.

℣. Ibi confregit cornu, arcum, scutum, gladium et bellum : illuminans tu mirabiliter a montibus aeternis, alleluia.

Ant. Terra tremuit, etc.

Antiphona ad Communionem

Ant. Pascha nostrum immolatus est Christus, alleluia : itaque epulemur in azymis sinceritatis et veritatis, alleluia, alleluia, alleluia. ²

Ps. Domine probasti me et cognovisti me : tu cognovisti sessionem meam et resurrectionem meam.

Ant. Pascha nostrum, etc.

℣. Gloria Patri et Filio et Spiritui sancto : sicut erat in principio et nunc et semper, et in saecula saeculorum, amen.

Ant. Pascha nostrum, etc.

℣. *ad repet.* Intellexisti cogitationes meas de longe : semitam meam et funiculum meum investigasti.

Ant. Pascha nostrum, etc.

℣. *ad repet.* Expurgate vetus fermentum : ut sitis nova conspersio, sicut estis azymi.

Ant. Pascha nostrum, etc.

℣. *ad repet.* Adducite vitulum saginatum : et occidite et manducemus et epulemur.

Ant. Pascha nostrum, etc.

℣. *ad repet.* Comedite et bibite, amici mei : inebriamini, carissimi.

Ant. Pascha nostrum, etc.

℣. *ad repet.* Quotiens calicem hunc bibetis : mortem domini adnuntiabitis, donec veniat.

Ant. Pascha nostrum, etc.

---

1 The repetition is shown in *Cod. Einsiedeln* 121.

2 *Cod. Einsiedeln* 121 has as first ℣. Confitemini domino, quoniam bonus, quoniam in saeculum misericordia eius : and as the only ℣. *ad repet.* 'Lapidem, quem reprobaverunt aedificantes, hic factus est in caput anguli' (*cf.* the manuscript quite at the end, on p. 422 of the reproduction in *Pal. Mus.* iv).

Antiphona ad Communicandum

Ant. Venite, populi, ad sacrum et immortale mysterium, et libamen agendum : cum timore et fide accedamus; manibus mundis poenitentiae munus communicemus; quoniam Agnus Dei propter nos Patri sacrificium propositum est; ipsum solum adoremus, ipsum glorificemus, cum angelis clamantes alleluia.

CHAPTER VII

A SURVEY OF THE DEVELOPMENT OF THE OFFICE

The oldest constituent part of the Ecclesiastical Hours is formed by the night assemblies, the *Vigils*. The difficulty of coming together at any other time than at night gave rise to them. At first the *Vigil* was only the Vigil of Sunday: [1] especially distinguished was the Vigil of Easter, which clearly was dictated by the idea of spending the moment of the Resurrection in watching. It lasted moreover the whole night, whence came its Greek name παννυχίς. But as a rule the Sunday Vigil normally began after midnight, when the cock began to crow, *i.e.* in the early morning. Nevertheless it was the custom, perhaps in imitation of the Easter Vigil, to spend in prayer the beginning of the night, the time of the setting of the sun, when the lamps were first lit. Hence this hour of prayer was called *Lucernare* (λυχνικόν) or *Hora incensi*. Here we have the primitive form of Evensong, which accordingly in the earliest days represents the beginning of the night Vigil, until S. Benedict made it a day office. In the Syrian Church of the first half of the 4th century a third constituent part of the Vigil was known, a *morning office,* that later called *Laudes.* Thus Evensong, Nocturns (later called *Mattins*) and Lauds are the foundation of the office.

At the Vigils which always preceded the Eucharistic assembly, the Holy Sacrifice of the Mass, the Holy Scriptures were read, prayers were

---

1 Pliny the younger gives early testimony concerning them in his *Epist.* x, 97. 'Quod essent soliti stato die ante lucem (in the night of Saturday and Sunday) convenire. As the Eucharist took place at the close of the nocturnal worship, and this went on into the Sunday, so this day gradually became the day of the Eucharistic celebration, and in the practice of Christians soon replaced the Sabbath as the festival of the week. *Cf.* Cabrol, *La Prière antique* (Paris. 1900), p. 231.

said, and psalms were sung, [1] as at the Jewish hours of prayer, from which the Christians borrowed many rites.

Mass and the celebration of the Vigil in three parts, the liturgical forms of the first centuries, were soon extended from Sundays to the feasts of the Martyrs. On each memorial day of a saint, Mass was preceded by a Vigil : the existence of this *Cœtus antelucanus* may be shewn as early as the middle of the 2nd century. [2] While the Sunday Vigil was held at the usual places of assembly, the Vigil and Mass in memory of a Martyr on the contrary were celebrated at the place of his tomb. [3]

To Sundays and the Feasts of Martyrs there were also added the Station days, the fast days of the week (Wednesday and Friday), which were taken over from the Jewish Church : only in some churches it was the Vigils alone, in others the Mass alone that was celebrated on them. [4]

The further development of the liturgical Hour-service was especially promoted by the reunions of the Ascetics, who from the 4th century onwards flourished everywhere in the East. They kept the Vigil not only on the official days, but daily. Moreover they not only applied themselves to prayer in the evening, after midnight, and in the morning, but they assembled together also at the *third, sixth and ninth hours* for pious exercises. Here also Jewish example must have influenced them, for these hours of prayer were well-known to the Jews; they were besides sanctified by the memory of the chief occurrences of the Passion of our Lord : the *third* hour (9 o'clock in the morning) by His condemnation, the *sixth* (noon) by His crucifixion, and the *ninth* (3 o'clock) by His death. Moreover these hours coincided with the division of the ordinary day. They had already been for a long time honoured by private worship, but henceforward the observance of them became the rule.

Towards the middle of the 4th century the Church allowed the daily vigils, which so far had possessed only a private character, to be observed in the churches of God under the supervision and guidance of the Clergy. This innovation sprang up in Antioch about 350, and soon extended over the Greek orient. The account of the travels of Silvia (*c.* 386) contains

---

1 Tertullian, *De Anima*, 9. Here we may compare what was said in chapter 1 of the chant of the vigils. In them not only the psalms, but the hymns also found their special home.

2 By the letter in which the Christians of Smyrna sent word of the death of S. Polycarp. *Cf.* also Batiffol, *Hist. of the Brev.*, p. 13.

3 *Constitut. Apost.* vj, 17.

4 Batiffol, *l.c.* 14.

a very beautiful description of the ceremonies of the Vigils and of the other Hours of prayer as held in the Church of Jerusalem. Very edifying also are the descriptions of the Fathers, who speak with enthusiam and holy joy of the assemblies at which all the people were present to serve the Lord in prayer and psalmody. [1] S. Basil used to visit, one after the other in the same night, the different churches in which his faithful met together to keep the Vigil: and S. Gregory Nazianzen found it a hardship to depart from Constantinople when he thought of the chanting of the psalms by the whole congregation. [2]

The Ascetics withdrew themselves from the world, and organized themselves in regions undisturbed by its tumult, in order to be better able to lead a life dedicated to prayer and self-denial. They naturally continued the whole system of prayer as it had been so far developed: on the other hand, in the secular churches, only the Vigils seem to have been kept up, so that later, as was said, these observed only the *Cursus nocturnus*, while the monasteries observed the *Cursus diurnus* also. The monastic office was completed later. *Prime* was introduced at Bethlehem when Cassian was living there (390-403). The origin of *Compline* is not quite clear; recent investigations seem to prove that it was already in existence in the second half of the 4th century. [3]

Students are not agreed as to the way in which the office developed in the secular churches of the West. *Evensong*, *Nocturns*, and *Lauds* were known in Gaul in the middle of the 4th century, as Hilary proves. [4] It has already been mentioned that the innovations of S. Ambrose (daily vigils with antiphonal psalmody and hymns) were speedily adopted by nearly all the Latin Churches. [5] For the rest, as in the East, the rites of the secular clergy differed from those of the regular, and occasionally friction took place. [6] Soon not only were the Martyrs venerated, but also

---

1 Compare what has been said in the 1st chapter on Psalmody in general.

2 Gerbert, *De Cantu* I, 128 foll.

3 Vandepitte has pointed out that S. Basil introduced it during his stay in Pontus; see *Rassegna Gregoriana* (Rome, 1903), p. 171.

4 Bäumer *l.c.* 131.

5 *Cf.* pp. 22 and 23. The words of the biographer of S. Ambrose run: 'Cuius celebritatis devotio usque in hodiernum diem non solum in eadem ecclesia (Milan) *verum etiam per omnes paene Occidentis provincias manet.*'

6 The Council of Braga (561) resisted the endeavour to introduce private or monastic practices into the secular churches: 'Ut unus atque idem psallendi ordo in matutinis vel vespertinis officiis teneatur, et non diversae ac privatae neque monasteriorum consuetudines cum ecclesiastica regula sint permixtae' (Batiffol *l.c.* 32). As it is the *ordo*

such holy men as distinguished themselves, not by martyrdom, but by a heroic example of virtues. Thereupon the Saints' days were different of course in different churches, and were in no way universal, with the exception perhaps of a very few old feasts, those of S. Stephen, S. John, S. Peter and S. Paul. The *Natalitia Sanctorum* were confined to the churches where the Saint had suffered martyrdom, or where his relics were preserved. Thus the *Natale* of S. John the Evangelist, that of S. Martin, and that of S. Hilary of Tours, were celebrated in the basilica of S. Martin, S. Peter and S. Paul's day in the basilica named after them; the feast of Christmas in the Cathedral Church. In the monastic office the feasts of the Saints were, it appears, first introduced by the Rule of S Benedict.

In Rome also there were in early times assemblies for prayer independent of the Mass, and first of all the Vigil. [1] It was binding on all the clergy; the people also flocked to it in numbers, so that abuses crept in, which made its retention questionable. [2] Here, as everywhere else, it consisted of psalmody, Scripture-lessons and prayer. Moreover antiphonal singing made its way to Rome after its introduction into Milan. (*cf.* p. 22). For daily Vigils in the Roman Church the first witness we have is the Rule of S. Benedict. But a long time before that there existed *Terce, Sext* and *None* and the prayers at sunset (*Evensong*); up till the end of the 4th century however, in the time of S. Jerome, they seem to have had only a private character, and were not publicly celebrated in Church.

The oldest complete order of the office that lies before us is that in the *Rule of S. Benedict*, which goes back to the year 529 or 530: it gives clear and exact directions as to the Hours of prayer, and their composition. As early as the middle of the 6th century there were Benedictine foundations in the neighbourhood of Rome, at Subiaco, Terracina, and Monte Cassino, where accordingly a complete set of Hours for day and night was observed; [3] this comprised *Vigils, i. e. Mattins* and *Lauds*, then the four lesser Hours of *Prime, Terce, Sext* and *None*, with *Evensong* and *Compline*. About 580 the monks fled to Rome before the Lombards, who

---

psallendi that is in question, the difference of the *consuetudines monasticae* from the *ecclesiasticae* must have reference to the number and distribution of the Psalms; and the explanation which Batiffol gives to the passages appears to go too far.

1 See the 38th Canon of Hippolytus, which Batiffol assigns to the end of the 2nd century. The best German patristic authorities assert it to be considerably later (*e.g.* Bardenhewer and Funk). *Cf.* Bäumer *l.c.* 51.

2 Vigilantius wished it to be abolished on this account, but he was condemned by the Roman Church. *Cf.* Batiffol *l.c.* 42.   3 Bäumer *l.c.* 179.

overran Italy in 568. Here Pope Pelagius (578-590) assigned them a dwelling near the Lateran Church, the parish and cathedral church of the Pope. However it is not impossible that the Benedictines had before this settled down near the Lateran; for Gregory I. in a letter mentions an Abbot Valentinian, a pupil of S. Benedict, who had for many years been at the head of the Lateran Monastery. From that time forward Benedictines were gradually summoned to all the greater churches of Rome, and were entrusted with the celebration of the Office. When the monks of Monte Cassino left Rome and returned to their old monastery, Gregory III. handed over to other monks the Basilica of Constantine near the Lateran, who were 'to keep the day and night-hours as they were observed in the Church of S. Peter.' A monastic foundation in honour of the Apostles Andrew and Bartholomew served similar purposes under Pope Honorius, and was renewed later by Pope Hadrian I. Its inmates, together with the monks of a monastery dedicated to S. Pancratius, had the care of the daily psalmody. [1] In this way it was to be expected that the Roman and Benedictine uses would approximate to one another. These similarities were remarked as early as the 8th century. A distinguished ritualist, Dom Bäumer, defends the view that the Roman Office was in all respects that of S. Benedict, [2] as the Benedictines were throughout the whole of the Middle Ages the pioneers of the Roman liturgy.

However that may be, the external structure of the monastic and of the secular Office was identical throughout the Middle Ages and still is so; both have for a long time been divided into *Mattins* with three *Nocturns*, *Lauds*, *Prime*, *Terce*, *Sext*, *None*, *Evensong* and *Compline*. About 800 *First Evensong* was added, and in consequence the original Evensong of the day became *Second Evensong* and lost much of its liturgical importance.

The order of the prayers, lessons and chants prescribed for the day and night hours of the whole year was called *Cursus*: the name refers especially to the order of the psalms and psalmody, and is therefore the simple equivalent of *Cursus canendi*. In the narrowest sense it was finally used for *Cursus diurnus*, and meant the order of the day hours, Prime, Terce, Sext and None. [3] There must have been a *Cursus* of this kind from the beginning, for as far back as the days of the Synagogue the

---

1 Gerbert, *De Cantu* I, 92. 2 Bäumer *l.c.* 182 foll.
3 *E.g.* in the Antiphoner of Hartker, *Cod.* 390-391 of S. Gall.

choice and succession of the psalms was not left to individuals. As liturgical practices spread after the 4th century, different *Cursus* sprang up in different countries, which were not unlike each other, in Antioch, Alexandria, Constantinople, Milan and Rome, *i. e.* in the centres of the liturgical movement. The Rules of the founders of Orders contain in this respect more or less detailed statements, especially that of S. Benedict. While the monasteries were bound by the same Rule to observe the same *Cursus*, in the secular churches unity of liturgical practices was not so easily attained; but it was the endeavour of the principal Metropolitan Churches, each within its own province, to make the Office uniform. Provincial Synods often issued decrees for this purpose, and also endeavoured to introduce unity in liturgical music, *e. g.* the Synods of Vannes (465), of Agde (506), of Gerunda (517), and of Epaon in Burgundy (517). [1] In the Canons of some of these Synods a uniformity in the *Ordo psallendi* is expressly desired. Of special importance is an enactment of the 4th Council of Toledo, which enjoined the same liturgical practices for the whole of Spain and Southern Gaul. An Order, enforced by authority, was also necessary to regulate the psalmody, together with express rules for the distribution of the Psalms, Antiphons, Responds and other pieces composing the Office. Such an Order is ascribed by Gennadius to the priest Musaeus, of Marseilles, who compiled suitable Lessons, Responds etc. for all the feasts of the year. [2] The forms of *Cursus* which ultimately prevailed were those of S. Benedict for the monastic use, and, for the secular clergy, that observed in the Roman basilicas.

Of great importance were the liturgical movements which resulted in France from the adoption of the Roman rite under Pippin and Charles the Great : they influenced the Roman Office to such an extent, that from the 11th century onward the latter is none other than the Roman-Frankish Office which sprang up in France from the blending of the old Gallican with the Gregorian. We shall return to details of this development, which is especially associated with the names of Alcuin and Amalarius. In the 12th century a simplification of the Office was taken in hand by the Papal Chapel ; and this *Officium Curiae Romanae* or *Capellae papalis* gradually spread over the whole Church, especially after the new order of the Franciscans adopted it. This shortened Office became then the starting

---

1 Gerbert, *De Cantu* I, 184, and Hefele, *History of the Church Councils* III, 16, 76, 105, 107.

2 Gennadius, *De viris illustribus,* 79 (*Patr. Lat.* lviij, 1103).

point of the further development of the Hours of prayer up to the reform of the Council of Trent, and beyond.

In this development of the secular Office little recourse was had to the monastic. This went on in contrast to the former, and still exists, as is well known, side by side with the Roman Office. The difference between the two is even now inconsiderable, and does not concern any single form which is of the essence of the Office. In both cases the responsorial and antiphonal psalmody take the largest place; the hymns have never been able to attain more than a modest position. Almost the only difference consists in the number of Responds and Antiphons [1] (and psalms); in other respects the musical form is the same. The monastic Office in use among the older orders, the Benedictines, Cistercians and Carthusians, has in each of the first two Nocturns six Antiphons and psalms, four lessons and as many Responds; in the third Nocturn it has one Antiphon for all the psalms or canticles, but four lessons and four Responds. The secular Office adopted by the Dominicans, Franciscans etc. has for each of the three Nocturns three Antiphons and psalms, three lessons and Responds. Further, the monastic Evensong has only four Antiphons and psalms, while the secular has five; it is only rarely that five Vesper Antiphons are found in the monastic books, e.g. in the Antiphoner of Hartker (Cod. 390-1 of S. Gall). The examples at the end of the 10th chapter will make these comparisons clear.

According to the idea of its founder, the Office is not intended to be used in private, but sung congregationally in choir. This intention has dictated its structure, and given shape to its formulas. To touch upon only one point: the peculiar alternation of reading and solo-psalmody which fills up a great part of the *Officium Nocturnum* presupposes the reader to be a different person from the singer; if it had been the intention of the founder of the Office to prescribe a form for individual recitation, the Mattins Office would have been differently arranged. But in the same way that the introduction of the Gregorian Order of the Mass had as a result the recitation of the texts of the chants by the celebrant

---

1 The Antiphons and Responds which form the chief part of the Office of the day used later to be called *Historia*, an expression which in its liturgical use refers no doubt to the texts drawn from the historical books of Holy Scripture, the Acts of the Martyrs and other sources. The *Codex Hartkeri*, written about 1000 (*Cod.* 390-1 of S. Gall), already inscribes the title of the Office of the Holy Trinity: 'Incipit historia de S. Trinitate.' Otto von Freisingen praises in his *Elogium Hermanni Contracti* his *Cantus historiales plenarios de S. Georgio etc. Cf.* Schubiger, *Sängerschule von S. Gallen,* p. 84, note 5.

at Low Mass, so the custom arose for the clergy who were not bound to the joint recitation of their service to *say* the parts of the Office which were originally *sung*. This development certainly dates from the time of the 13th century; through the transformation of ecclesiastical life in the later Middle Ages, and with the growth of the work of the secular clergy, it became a necessity and received sanction. But it is very characteristic of the traditional spirit which governs the history of the liturgical forms, that the Church has changed nothing in the structure of the Office. She has given up none of the essential forms of the Office. In its extension she has taken account of the altered circumstances. Accordingly in substance the development of the Office has gone on organically throughout; and since the Breviary of the Council of Trent has established and crowned this development, there need be no fear that another spirit will come into the venerable structure.

CHAPTER VIII

THE DEVELOPMENT OF THE RESPONSORIAL CHANT OF THE OFFICE

The *Cantus responsorius* of the Office has much similarity to that of the Mass; in liturgical position and melodic character both are the same. In only a few particulars has the solo-psalmody in the Office developed differently from that in the Mass, and even then the difference is not so far-reaching as in the case of the antiphonal chants.

It has been shown in this connexion that the responsorial chant has from the first been bound up with the lesson. As this is the case in the Mass, so it has also this liturgical position in the Office; a lesson always precedes it. [1] Moreover as in the Mass the responsorial psalm is the oldest chant, so it is no mere chance that this ancient form of psalmody has the place of honour in that part of the Office which the history of the liturgy indicates as being the oldest, *viz.* the *Nocturns*. None of the other constituent parts of the Office received its form before the later form of the psalmody, the antiphonal, had attracted to itself the bulk of the interest. Therefore the antiphonal chant is almost supreme in the

---

[1] Amalarius after his manner envelopes this circumstance with pious meanings: 'Responsorios sequi lectiones propter disciplinam ecclesiasticam, quae non vult auditores legis tantum, sed factores.' *De ord. Antiph.* 4. (*Patr. Lat.* cv, 1251). Likewise Honorius of Autun: 'Cantor surgit ad responsorium, ut excitet mentes, quae audierunt doctrinam in lectione, surgant ad actiones bonas in operatione.' *Sacram.* 47 (*Patr. Lat.* clxxij, 770). Durandus says very rightly: 'Dicuntur autem antiphonae respectu ad psalmodiam, cui respondent, sicut et responsoria respectu ad historiam' (*i.e.* the Lessons which were originally always taken from Sacred History. Gerbert *De Cantu* I, 507). The old title *Missa* is used for the lessons and prayers connected with the Antiphons and Responds in the Rule of S. Caesarius (*Patr. Lat.* lxvij, 1102), and Aurelian (*ibid.* lxviij, 394). *Cf.* Gerbert, *De Cantu* I, 180.

Officium diurnum, a *Cantus responsorius* is a rarity in it. [1] Thus Vigil and responsorial chant have remained in unbroken connexion from the beginning down to the present day; the Respond is so characteristic of the Nocturns, that wherever there is any sort of reason to surround the Liturgy with especial solemnity, as often happened in old times at the third Nocturn of the chief festivals, an augmented use of the responsorial chant was introduced. Accordingly our oldest MSS. have a great number of Responds in these cases. [2] In days before the *Te Deum* was ordered at the end of the Nocturns, they delighted to lose themselves completely in holy joy, and to let the thoughts pour forth which were suggested by the day. At the corresponding places in the *Officium diurnum* it is to the Antiphons that a like task is allotted.

The melodic form of the *Cantus responsorius* in the Mass is highly developed: all MSS. without exception give to the soloist who ascends the *Ambo* after the lesson a magnificent solo-melody. In the Office also the performer of the Respond is a soloist, and that which he has to sing is a real solo melody. The likeness goes yet deeper. In the Office as well as in the Mass, the Respond of the Vigil originally comprised a whole psalm. All the MSS. of the Office however give now only a shortened form. No doubt the abbreviation was due to the same reasons as were given above (p. 73) in connexion with the Mass-respond. Again the Office-respond also is made up of an introductory chant and a verse. On the other hand Office and Mass-responds are not formed in quite the same manner: in the former case it remained the custom to repeat the first part after the verse; moreover some Responds retained several verses, and finally the verse *Gloria Patri* is habitually added.

The Roman Church until the 9th century preserved the original method of singing and repeating the Respond, in accordance with its own proper character as a responsorial chant, *i. e.* as a solo with a choral-refrain. We learn this from Amalarius, who thus describes the manner of its performance in Rome: the precentor began with the first part, which the choir repeated; hereupon the soloist sang the verse and the choir repeated

---

1 In the MSS. of the Monastic Office Evensong has a Respond after the 4th psalm: *cf.* the tables at the end of Chap. 10. The R̲. *breve* will be treated later on.

2 The *Responsale Gregorianum,* which is printed in *Patr. Lat.* lxxviij from a MS. of Compiègne of the 9th century, has 17 *responsoria* for the third Nocturn of Christmas; the Antiphoner of Hartker (*Cod.* 390-1 of S. Gall) has 10. *Cf.* the tables in Chap. 10. It seems to have been thought well to lengthen the third Nocturn so that Lauds could follow immediately.

for the second time the first part as far as the verse; the soloist added the *Gloria Patri* and the choir repeated its part for the third time, but this time only the second portion of it. Finally the *Cantor* began the Respond again from the beginning, and sang it as far as the verse, whereupon the choir concluded with a last repetition. [1] This manifold repetition of the first part, which thereby became a refrain pure and simple, and the graceful alternation of solo and chorus imprint upon the responsorial chant of the Office the character of charming structural beauty. It is like the clear and distinct edifices of the art of building in their symmetrical proportions.

The repetition of the first part by the choir, of which Amalarius speaks, has up to the present remained the practice in the *Responsoriola*, or *Responsoria brevia*. The instinct for symmetry and beauty of form in the Church's chant had already begun to disappear before the time of Amalarius. Next, the repetition before the verse was left out, and after that, the first part only was intoned by the precentor and continued by the choir. Here we see no doubt an influence of the practice, already provided for in the Rule of S. Benedict *(cap. 4.)*, of the Antiphons being begun by one person, and continued by the choir. It certainly made the twice repeated performance of the first part of the Respond superfluous. This alteration, which was not destructive of the essence of the responsorial form, was not the last. Amalarius remarks that after the *Gloria Patri* the Romans repeated, not the whole of the first part, but only the second half of it. This somewhat disturbed the harmony of the parts. That this incomplete repetition is not part of the original arrangement of the Office-responds may be perceived, as the verse *Gloria Patri* was first added by the Romans in the time of Amalarius, [2] probably in imitation of the antiphonal chant of the Introit and the Communion, which regularly

---

1 Amalarius *De Ordine Antiph. Cap.* 18: 'Non enim sancta Romana et nostra regio uno ordine canunt responsorios et versus. Apud eam praecentor in primo ordine finit responsorium; succentores vero eodem modo respondent. Dein praecentor canit versum; finito versu, succentores vero secundo incipiunt responsorium a capite et usque ad finem perducunt. Dein praecentor canit *Gloriam Patri et Filio et Spiritui Sancto*, quo finito succentores circa mediam partem intrant in responsorium et perducunt usque in finem. Postremo praecentor incipit responsorium a capite et perducit illum usque in finem. Quo finito succentores tertio repetunt responsorium a capite et perducunt illum usque ad finem.' (*Patr. Lat.* cv, 1274).

2 Amalarius *De Ord. Antiph. Cap.* I: 'Priscis temporibus non cantabatur *Gloria* post versum, sed repetebatur responsorium ... *A modernis vero apostolicis* additus est hymnus post versum.' (*Patr. Lat.* cv, 124)

added the Doxology to the verses. This shows the tendency of the originally sharply distinct responsorial and antiphonal forms to approach one another. Since the end of the Middle Ages the Doxology has always been connected with the *final* Responds alone of the *Nocturn*, in contrast to all *Responsoria brevia* outside the Passion Season, in which it is generally omitted. [1] The Gradual-responsory of the Mass is never accompanied by the *Gloria Patri*.

The Roman method of dealing with the refrain after the Doxology was the prevailing one in Gaul about 800 for the repetitions after the other verses also. According to Amalarius [2] the chief difference between the Roman and Frankish method of using the responds lay in this. The second half of the first part received the name *Repetenda*. [3] An example may make the difference clear. The first respond of Christmas Mattins runs : R̄. *Hodie nobis coelorum rex de virgine nasci dignatus est, ut hominem perditum ad coelestia regna revocaret. Gaudet exercitus angelorum, quia salus aeterna humano generi apparuit. V̄. Gloria in excelsis Deo, et in terra pax hominibus bonae voluntatis.*

According to the Roman method, after the V̄. *Gloria in excelsis* the R̄. was repeated from the beginning as far as the V̄.; according to the Frankish method only the second part was repeated, and from the point where it best joined on to the contents of the V̄., *i.e.* from *Gaudet.*

It is noteworthy that the Frankish way of treating the Respond

---

1 In Spain, before the introduction of the Roman Liturgy, instead of *Gloria Patri et Filio* at the end of the Psalms was always sung: *Gloria* et honor *Patri*; this form was made obligatory under threat of excommunication by Spanish conciliar decrees, especially that of Toledo 633 (*Can.* 15): 'In fine psalmorum non sicut a quibusdam huiusque *Gloria Patri* sed *Gloria et honor Patri* dicatur, David propheta dicente : *Afferte Deo gloriam et honorem*, et Joanne Evangelista in Apocalypsi : *Audivi vocem celestis exercitus dicentem : Honor et gloria Deo nostro sedenti* in throno . . . 'Universis igitur ecclesiasticis hanc observantiam damus, quam quisquis praeterierit, communionis iacturam habebit.'

2 Amalarius, *De Ordo Antiph. Prol.* : 'Hinc notandum est necessarium nobis esse, ut alteros versus habeat noster Antiphonarius (the chant-book of the Office) quam Romanus, quoniam altero ordine cantamus responsorios nostros quam Romani. Illi a capite incipiunt responsorium, finito versu, nos versum finitum informamus in responsorium per latera eius, ac sic facimus de duobus unum corpus. Ideo necesse est, ut hos versus quaeramus, quorum sensus cum mediis responsoriorum conveniat, ut fiat unus sensus ex verbis responsorii et verbis versus.' (*Patr. Lat.* cv, 1244). It will presently be shown in the proper connexion that this was one of the striking points in the reform of the Antiphoner which Amalarius himself perceived.

3 This name is formed like *(e. g.)* that of the *Antiphona ad Offerendam.*

prevailed over the old Roman way, and even supplanted it in Rome. Here again it is shown that the Latin liturgy, as established in the Middle Ages, was not exclusively the work of the ruling powers at the centre of the Church, but proceeded from the harmonious common action of various individual churches. The liturgical creative power flourished vigorously outside Rome, and Rome has never refused entrance to non-Roman rites, but rather has given them a trial willingly, and, if they have stood the test, has adopted them herself. The adoption of the Frankish Respond in Rome took place between the time of Amalarius and that of the 11th *Ordo Romanus*,[1] *i.e.* between 840 and 1140. At the very beginning of this *Ordo* the execution of the Respond of the Mattins of the First Sunday in Advent *Aspiciens a longe* is set down as follows:

R7. *Aspiciens a longe, ecce video Dei potentiam venientem, et nebulam totam terram tegentem.* *Ite obviam ei, et dicite:* *Nuntia nobis si tu es ipse* *Qui regnaturus es in populo Israhel.*

℣. 1 *Quique terrigenae et filii hominum, simul in unum dives et pauper: Ite obviam ei et dicite.*

℣. 2 *Qui regis Israhel, intende, qui deducis velut ovem Joseph: Nuntia nobis si tu es ipse.*

℣. 3 *Tollite portas principes vestras, et elevamini portae aeternales, et introibit rex gloriae: Qui regnaturus es in populo Israhel.*

℣. 4 *Gloria Patri et Filio et Spiritui sancto.*

R7. *Aspiciens a longe* up to the ℣. 1 : *Quique terrigenae.*

This is the method described by Amalarius: after the verses the whole Respond is no longer repeated, but only the second half, and it is divided into as many parts as there are verses; after each verse only the corresponding section is repeated. The desire of the Romans for symmetry of form shows itself however again in the repetition of the whole Respond up to the 1st verse after the ℣. *Gloria Patri.* The Respond is thus formed on a clear and symmetrical plan.

The above-mentioned Respond is not the only one which possesses more than one verse. There are also in the same *Ordo* the R7. *Aspiciebam in visu noctis* with the ℣. *Ecce dominator*, ℣. *Potestas eius,*

---

1 This is the already mentioned Ordo of Benedict, Precentor and Canon of S. Peter's, which is dedicated to Cardinal Guido of Castella, who in 1143, as Celestine III, ascended the Papal throne. It is extremely important for the study of the Papal Office in the first half of the 12th century, for its composer desires to explain therein 'qualiter domnus apostolicus, curia sua et tota Romana ecclesia in praecipuis solemnitatibus et quotidianis officiis valeat se regere' (*Patr. Lat.* lxxviij, 1025).

and ℣. *Gloria Patri,* and the ℞. *Missus est Gabriel* with the ℣. *Ave Maria,* ℣. *Dabit ei Dominus* and ℣. *Gloria Patri.* They stand in the same Nocturn, and, so far as the repetitions go, were treated in the same way as the ℞. *Aspiciens.* [1] But it is remarkable that the older MSS. only exceptionally give more than one verse to a Respond. The Antiphoner of Hartker (*Cod. S. Gall* 390-1), written about 1000, has several verses for the ℞. *Aspiciens* and the ℞. *Libera me* only: this last has five. [2] Accordingly it appears that when the Responsorial Psalm of the Office was shortened, a set of verses survived only at the first Respond of the Church's year, in the first Nocturn of the first Sunday in Advent, for the ℞. *Aspiciens* stands in the first place in the MSS. of the Office. Later it was found feasible, in order either to distinguish certain feasts, or to lengthen the Night Office, to add several verses to other Responds. The MSS. of the 12th and 13th centuries are by no means poor in Responds of this kind. MS. 12044 of the Paris National Library, of the 12th century, one of the most valuable of the chant-books of the Office which have been preserved from the Middle Ages to our own time, has them for many feasts. [3] Later, but for a few exceptions, the normal number was again resumed, and the Breviary of the Council of Trent has sanctioned this proportion. But the repetition after the verse or verses was always preserved in the case of the Office Respond, and in this respect it has had a more favourable development than the Gradual Respond in the Mass, which very soon lost the repetition after the verse. The reason for this striking difference lies in the fact that those who had the responsibility of the Office-chant were always clergy, who brought more intelligence to bear on the shape of the liturgical forms and on their organic structure than did the singers who were entrusted with the performance of the chant of

---

1 *Patr. Lat. ibid.* 1027.

2 See the photographic reproduction of this MS. in *Paléographie Musicale,* Series II, vol. I. p. 392.

3 The following are the responds in alphabetical order. ℞. *Agmina sacra* (*fol.* 238, 2 verses), ℞. *Alleluia audivimus* (*fol.* 109, 2 verses), ℞. *Angelus Domini descendit* (*fol.* 99, 2 verses), ℞. *Angelus Domini locutus est* (*fol.* 100, 2 verses), ℞. *Cives apostolorum* (*fol.* 228, 3 verses), ℞. *Cum inducerent* (*fol.* 56, 2 verses), ℞. *Dum staret Abraham* (*fol.* 69, 2 verses), ℞. *Fratres mei* (*fol.* 89, 2 verses), ℞. *Impetum fecerunt* (*fol.* 13, 3 verses), ℞. *Impetum fecerunt* (*fol.* 15, 2 verses), ℞. *In medio ecclesiae* (*fol.* 18, 2 verses), ℞. *Iste est Johannes* (*fol.* 18, 2 verses), ℞. *Mox ut vocem Domini* (*fol.* 216, 2 verses), ℞. *Sanctificamini hodie* (*fol.* 6, 2 verses), ℞. *Solve iubente Deo* (*fol.* 152, 2 verses), ℞. *Tentavit Deus* (*fol.* 69, 2 verses), ℞. *Virgine cum palma* (*fol.* 11, 2 verses). In most of these verses the text or the melody shows that they are later additions,

the Mass from the 13th century onward. These soon became enamoured of harmonized chant music, and in other respects ignored the connexion of the chant with the Liturgy, or suppressed it altogether.

The first evidence that we have of the execution of the Office Respond by more than one soloist in Rome is in the 11th Ordo, the document of the beginning of the 12th century in which we found the same evidence about the Respond of the Mass. It handles in a striking manner the above mentioned three Responds with several verses prescribed for the 1st Sunday in Advent : the first and second singers of the *Schola* are to sing the first ℞., the third and fourth the second, the fifth and sixth the third. It was, no doubt, desirable not to tire the singers with the long Responds. ¹

In the Mass the Cantor of the Respond stood on the steps of the *Ambo*. It was not so in the Office : here he stood in his usual place, as Amalarius ² and his opponent Agobard of Lyons ³ tell us. The others present in the Choir sat during its performance, and only rose at *Gloria Patri*; this is already directed as early as the Rule of S. Benedict for the 3rd or rather the 4th Respond (see *capp.* 9, 11). In the 12th century, on the contrary, the two singers of the above-mentioned Advent Responds both stood before the Altar. ⁴

Amalarius again gives us an interesting insight into the technique of the chant of the Respond. He who had to intone the Respond had to take care, as the melody of the verse usually stood at a higher pitch, not to start the Respond itself too high, so as not to reach an unattainable pitch in the verse ; when on the other hand, the verse was finished, the singer could start the repetition of the Respond at a higher pitch, without regard to the verse. ⁵ There was in general a tendency to sing the Responds at a higher pitch than *e.g.* the Antiphons and Hymns. ⁶ This custom was observed not in France alone : for Bishop Sicardus of Cremona (*c.* 1200) says exactly the same of the boys who sang the Gradual, ⁷ from

---

1 *Patr. Lat.* lxxviij, 1027. The same direction is found in the Antiphoner, the text of which is printed by Tommasi, *l. c.* xj, p. 18.

2 *De ord. Antiph.* (*Patr. Lat.* cv, 1248).

3 *De correct. Antiph.* 7. He explicitly reproaches Amalarius for that he *contra morem nocturni officii ab eminentiori loco pompatice concrepabat* a Christmas Respond (*Patr. Lat.* civ, 332).

4 *Ordo Rom. Benedicti Canonici* (*Patr. Lat.* lxxviij, 1027).

5 *De Eccl. Off.* iij, 11 (*Patr. Lat.* cv, 1120).

6 *Ibid.* iv, 3 (*Patr. Lat.* cv, 1173).

7 Sicardus, *Mitrale. Cf.* Tommasi, *l. c.* xij, p. 12. The statement of Amalarius and

which we see that this practice also existed in the case of the Mass-Responds. It was certainly observed in Rome as well, otherwise Amalańius would certainly have stated the contrary, since he generally tried to bring the observance of his native place into accord with the Roman, and noted any difference between the Roman and the Gallican treatment of the repetition after the verse.

Besides the long lessons of Mattins there were, and still are, shorter ones in the Day Hours. They are also *Capitula*. In the monastic as in the Roman liturgy they are found at Lauds, the Little Hours, Evensong and Compline. A Respond also follows them, but it is a short one, the *Responsoriolum*,[1] also called *Responsorium breve*. The greater Responds of Mattins have the name *Responsorium prolixum* or *modulatum*[2] in contradistinction to it. The *Responsoriola* consist of a couple of short sentences with a melody of syllabic formation, but are otherwise in their execution pure forms of the *Cantus responsorius*. This is especially clear, because the soloist's opening portion is repeated by the Choir before the verse. They have also the *Gloria Patri*, after which the first part is repeated again in its entirety, but, like the *Responsoria prolixa*, they have no *Sicut erat*. The complete doxology belongs to the antiphonal chant only, as is still shewn by the Mass Introit and the Vesper psalmody. The use of the incomplete doxology with the Respond shews that it was a later importation into the chant, unless indeed, as is possible, it was due to melodic considerations.

In the MSS. of the chant-book of the Office (the Antiphoners), besides the Responds arranged according to the course of the Church's year, among the chants allotted to each day, there are introduced at the end some special groups of Responds, *e.g.* the *Historia Regum, Historia de Sapientia, de Job, de Tobia, de Judith, de Esther, de Esdra, de Maccabeis, de Prophetis.* [3] They were sung in the weeks of summer, from the end

---

Sicardus is a proof that far on in the Middle Ages there was no absolute pitch, at least until the introduction of the Organ into the Church, a question which will be dealt with later in the proper connexion.

1 See the Antiphoner of Hartker (*Cod. S. Gall* 390, 391), the Antiphoner of Tommasi *l. c.* xj, 175 and the Statutes of the Order of Sempringham in Ducange, Glossarium, *s. v. Responsorium.*

2 The *Stat. abb. Rivivulp.* of the year 1157 contain the direction: 'Cantor ebdomadarius in loco suo Responsum b. Mariae non breve sed modulatum solus decantabit.' See Ducange, *s. v. Responsorium.*

3 *E.g.* in *Cod. S. Gall.* 390-1, in the Antiphoner printed in *Patr. Lat.* lxxviij, 831, in Tommasi, *l.c.* xj, 115, 128, 136, 139, 140, 141, 144. Also in the second Antiphoner, p. 289.

of July to Advent. The names given refer to the source of the text; they are all taken from the books of the Old Testament.

No explanation has been found for the name given to another series of responds, *Responsoria de auctoritate*, which were sung in the third and fourth weeks after Easter. ¹

---

1 Prescribed under this title in *Cod. S. Gall* 390-391 and the Leipzig manuscript of Regino, which does not however, as supposed, contain Regino's autograph Tonal, but a catalogue of the chants in the order in which they occur in the Office. It is called *Breviarium*, but to-day it would be called *Directorium chori*. The *Responsoria de auctoritate* stand there (*fol.* 91 foll.) and are 14 in number as in the S. Gall MS. 391, p. 54. In addition there is as a 15th Respond *Candidi facti sunt*, with the $\check{V}$. *In omnem terram*. Amalarius (*Patr. Lat.* cv, 1296), has not such a long series. The explanation which he gives for the name explains nothing: 'Propterea iidem praetitulantur 'de auctoritate,' quoniam apostoli, quorum habitus praesentibus responsoriis decantatur, vice Christi auctores extiterunt Judaicae ecclesiae et gentilis.'

CHAPTER IX

THE DEVELOPMENT OF THE ANTIPHONAL CHANT OF THE OFFICE

In the Day-office the Responds have been pushed into the background by the Antiphons; even in the oldest existing books antiphonal psalmody is the rule and responsorial almost the exception. This circumstance may be explained by the fact that the Day Hours in particular are of monastic origin, and that in monasteries attention was specially directed to psalmody in double chorus. Antiphonal singing has grown so closely into this part of the Office that it almost entirely fills it up. If it were taken away from Lauds and the Day Hours, hardly anything would remain.

The antiphonal chant of the Office also has an interesting history to be recorded. It has not remained in its original form, and the contrast between the music of the Office and of the Mass is much sharper here than in the responsorial chant. The Responds of the Mass and of the Office have always kept a certain likeness to one another, in spite of differences; but the development of the antiphonal chant has followed a different line in the Office to that in the Mass. This is due to the difference in the part played by the antiphonal chant in the Mass and in the Office respectively. It has been already shewn in the proper context that the function of all antiphonal chants in the Mass is to accompany something : they form the artistic complement to the ceremonies performed at the Altar, and naturally have to take a subordinate position to these. It is otherwise in the Office. There antiphonal chanting has its own proper purpose, forms the chief consideration, and has no liturgical action to embellish. Secondly, the difference is to be noted in the personages who appear in the Office and in the Mass as liturgical singers. During the whole of the Middle Ages, and ever since, the Office was an obligation laid upon clergy and monks, who, naturally could appreciate to the full the liturgical meaning of the chants, and who from religious conscientiousness did not easily consent to vital changes. But in the Mass, from the end of the Middle Ages onwards, the performance of the prescribed chants rested in the hands of persons in whose minds the artistic and musical element entirely predominated over the liturgical. As early as that time professional singers constantly lost sight of the connexion between the Liturgy and the liturgical chant: consequently, from the time of the rise of harmonized music onwards, the whole history of the chant of the Mass is characterized by the gradual subordination of liturgical considerations to the inclinations of the singer. [1] In the Office the musician never got the upper hand: it was, and it remained, in the faithful charge of persons dedicated to the service of God. Thus the chant of the Office had the advantage of a quieter and steadier development than that of the Mass, especially the antiphonal chant, which from the first had never been the task of the solo singers, but always of the whole congregation.

In the Mass the body which performed the antiphonal chants was the choir expressly appointed for it, and composed of professional singers. The result of this was that antiphonal chanting acquired a more attractive melodic form in the Mass than in the Office, where it always displays great preference for a syllabic style of melody. It is easy to see in the choral parts of the Mass, that the choir to which they are assigned could readily surmount harder tasks. The style of the music is the interesting mixed style made up of syllabic and semi-melismatic melody. This is true at any rate of the psalmodic forms of the Introit and the Communion, which, while rendering the text in the style of a recitative, are not lacking in a certain melodic charm. In the times however to which our oldest plainsong MSS. belong, there was still enough liturgical feeling in the singers to prevent them from going further in this direction than was possible without abandoning the antiphonal character. The antiphonal chants of the Mass never intrude into the province of solo-chant;[2] the border-line which separates the two styles one from another has never been overstepped. And besides, it seems only fitting that antiphonal singing should be more ornamental when it figures in the central act of Christian worship.

---

1 This development was very natural when once the words of the musical parts of the Service came to be said by the celebrant at the Altar; this custom had for its result the loosening of the bond between Altar and choir; thenceforward the choir ceased to perform an important task of its own in the celebration of Mass. I shall return to this point at the proper time.

2 The Offertory alone forms an apparent exception. *Cf.* above p. 95.

In the Office the solo singer had hardly anything to do, except in the Nocturns; elsewhere the service was confined to the alternating of the two choirs, into which the clergy or monks were divided. No one could be prominent in this; all the music was such as to be within the capabilities of every one, even of those who were distinguished neither by beauty of voice nor by skill in singing. This was from the beginning the characteristic of antiphonal psalmody; and in the Office it has never been obliged to part with it. The Antiphons adopt a very simple style of composition; only one or two notes are assigned to a syllable, seldom three. Many Antiphons are entirely syllabic, *e.g.* those for ordinary days which have no festal character. The purpose of the melodies is to prepare for the psalm-tone that follows; they are as it were a prelude to it. [1] In melodic design each conforms to the psalm-tone. The tone is simply such a formula as naturally takes shape when several persons utter the same text at the same time; it is quite unassuming, and attainable by all. It chiefly commands admiration because, though being of a severe and simple style of beauty, always unvarying and attached to all verses of the same psalm, it never becomes tedious or tiresome. The antiphonal psalm-tones of the Office belong to those elemental creations which have lost no freshness or power in their course through the centuries : they are always able to rejoice millions and uplift them to God.

It is noteworthy, and a proof of the mastery which the antiphonal form of melody exercises throughout the Office, that the simple recitative melody comes into use even when one individual performs as representative of all (setting aside of course the solo chants which follow the lessons), as happens for example at the versicles. The Short Respond also, as we have seen, is governed by the antiphonal method. Twice only in each Office does the Antiphon rise to a greater solemnity, viz. in connexion with the *Benedictus* at Lauds and the *Magnificat* at Vespers. Here the style, both of the melody of the Antiphon and of the psalm-tone of the canticle, approaches those of the Introit, and it reaches, especially on feast days, a high level of beauty. These compositions are masterpieces full of power to express the significance of the feast; their melody is remarkable for its

---

1 Amalarius *De Offic.* iv, 7 : 'Antiphona inchoatur ab uno unius chori, et ad *eius symphoniam* psalmus cantatur per duos choros. Ipsa enim (*i.e.* antiphona) coniunguntur simul duo chori' (*Patr. Lat.* cv, 1180). In the 9th chapter of his Exposition of the Benedictine Rule Perez mentions the Antiphons : 'Claves et indices, ad quorum modulationem ac sonum sequens canticum psalmusque alternatim cantatur. Tonus enim totius psalmi ex tono antiphonae sumitur.' Ortigue, *Dictionnaire du plain-chant.* p. 133.

power to express the meaning of the words on Feast-days without sacrificing sublimity and grandeur. Why is it that in this place the chant is raised to a level higher than elsewhere? The key to the answer of this question is again given to us by the Liturgy. These canticles represent the liturgical zenith of the festival. Every catholic knows the sublime ceremonies with which the Officiant accompanies them. As the incense envelopes the Altar and seems to draw everything upward with it, so an elaborate chant bursts forth from the heart of the singer, which mounts still higher than the smoke of the incense, and does honour to the most High. Anyone who has once been present at solemn Vespers even in a poor village church will never forget the impression made on him; even the ordinary man is stirred to enthusiasm when the *Magnificat* is begun by the choir; each one is uplifted, body and soul, in holy joy. Thus it was also in the Middle Ages. The MSS. of the Office indicate plainly the unique position of these Antiphons, when they give them a particular name, *Antiphona ad Canticum, ad Benedictus, ad Magnificat* or *ad Evangelium,* also *in Evangelio.*

The survival in most cases of a whole psalm in conjunction with the Antiphon shews that a more favourable destiny has befallen the Antiphonal music of the Office than that of the Mass, or the whole of the responsorial music. In this respect the original form of the Antiphonal chant has not essentially altered. Some traces however were left in it of the changes which took place, even in the early Middle Ages, with regard to the liturgical chant, and which, as we have seen, specially involved an abbreviation of the words. The relation of the Antiphon to the psalm has shifted somewhat, and the psalmody has changed its character in consequence. Antiphony in its original form required the repetition of the Antiphon after each verse. Perhaps this combination of a shorter and a longer chant has its origin in the practices of the Greek music since the Christian Era; in any case the name *Antiphony* reveals some sort of connexion with Greek music. The repetition after every verse had the effect of lighting up the whole of every psalm with the particular thought expressed in the Antiphon; the Antiphon always recalled the point of view from which on any particular day the psalm was to be regarded; and there was besides a peculiar artistic charm connected with this structure. This archaic practice of repetition must have been long preserved, for it was still in existence when the chant of the Office in the Roman Church was set in order and fixed; and that, as will be shown, was about 600. The relation of the psalmody to the Antiphon which subsisted throughout the Middle Ages, and indeed subsists in modern times, takes for granted this repetition after each verse. In order to link harmoniously the end of the psalm-tone to the beginning of the Antiphons, there were, even for psalm-tones of the same mode, different forms of ending, suitable to the beginning of the Antiphon, called by the name of 'Differences.' As these were utilized at the end of all the verses, and not merely at the end of the last psalm-verse, *i. e.* the *Sicut erat*, the Antiphon must have originally been repeated after each verse. [1] A practice of this kind naturally lengthened the duration of a psalm, and still more that of a whole service. [2] The repetition was given up first of all in the Day Office, as the whole day could not be given up to psalmody alone. This explains the direction of the Rule of S. Benedict (*cf.* p. 24) that the Day Hours are in some cases to be sung without Antiphons. Next they gave up repeating the Antiphon after all the verses at Mattins and Lauds. Traces of the original method of Antiphonal chanting are found in the Office throughout the Middle Ages and down to modern times. Amalarius, in describing the compilation of the ordinary Night Office, mentions six Antiphons which were repeated after each verse by two choirs alternately. [3] On the other hand at a still later date the repetition after each verse was occasionally introduced, if it was wished to lengthen the duration of the Office: the Cluniacs, for example, so treated the Antiphons in the Mattins of S. Martin.[4] Much later still they took to repeating the Antiphon of the canticles at Lauds and Vespers three times over, singing it thus four times altogether,

---

1 The Differences will be discussed in detail later.

2 *Cf.* the remark of Cassian, p. 29 above.

3 Amalarius, *De ord. Antiph.* 3 (*Patr. Lat.* cv, 1251). Contemporary with him is the statement of an anonymous writer to Bishop Batterich of Regensburg (about 814), who gives the reason for the abolition of the repetition of the Antiphon after each verse and censures the liturgical behaviour of the South German clergy: 'Contingit enim me, multa peragendo loca, audisse divina officia inordinate et sine auditus delectatione celebrari. Sunt namque nonnulli, qui tantum ob verecundiam hominum, ne forte ignavi ab ipsis judicentur, intrantes ecclesiam, sine antiphonis cursim et cum omni velocitate, ut citius ad curam carnis exeant peragendam, divinis negligenter assistunt laudibus, cum in mundanis studiosi habentur operibus. Qui nesciunt, quia sancti doctores et eruditores ecclesiae, sancto spiritu et gratia Dei repleti, instituerunt modulationem in antiphonarum vel responsoriorum repetitione honestissimam, quatenus hac dulcedine audientium animus delectatus, ad Dei laudes et amorem caelestis patriae ardentius ascenderetur' (*Patr. Lat.* cxxix, 1 399).

4 See the Life of S. Odo of Cluny by his pupil John. 'Quia eiusdem officii (of S. Martin) antiphonae uti omnibus patet, breves sunt, et eius temporis longiores noctes, volentes officium ad lucem usque protrahere, unamquamque antiphonam per singulos psalmorum versus repetendo canebant.' Tommasi, *l. c.* 66.

before the *Gloria Patri*, and before and after the *Sicut erat*. The name given to this use was *triumphare* or *triumphaliter canere*, which well expresses the triple repetition *(ter fari)*, as also its festal chara&ter.[1] Bishop Durandus of Mende (13th century) already speaks of this pra&tice as an established custom. [2] It was a remnant of the old Antiphonal method. Such customs are an eloquent proof of the pleasure which was felt in artistic liturgical chant.

It sometimes happened that the Antiphon was not simply performed whole by one or both choirs together, but was divided into separate portions, which were then sung in turn by the two choirs alternately. This was called *ad Antiphonam respondere*. [3] An alternation of this kind was customary in the Church of S. Peter at Rome at Epiphany, and on the Feast of S. Peter. The rubric for Mattins of Christmas is especially clear : 'At all Antiphons of the Vigil one choir answers the other, and thus we sing all Antiphons, in the body of the psalm (where necessary) and at the end, after the *Gloria* and the *Sicut erat*.' [4] This division of the Antiphon into several parts was known elsewhere than at Rome : an *Ordinarium Rotomagensis Ecclesiae* [5] dire&ts that the *Magnificat* Antiphon of the 1st Vespers of the Assumption of the Blessed Virgin Mary should be repeated three times (as we have seen, this refers to the repetition before and after the *Gloria* and after the *Sicut erat*). Each time the Antiphon is to be divided into four parts : the right hand choir begins *Ascendit Christus* and sings as far as *et haec est illa;* the left hand choir continues to *in qua gloriosa*, the right again to *quo pia*, the left sings the rest. An alternation in the performance is especially refreshing at the greater Antiphons. [6]

The method of repeating the Antiphon after each verse or group of

---

1 Gerbert, *De Cantu* I, 504.

2 Durandus, *Rationale* 5, 8 : 'Unde mos inolevit, quod in praecipuis festivitatibus antiphona ad *Magnificat* et *Benedictus* ter dicitur, sive toties canendo protelatur.' Gerbert, *ibid.*

3 This phrase has of course nothing to do with *Cantus responsorius*.

4 Tommasi, *l.c.* xj, p. 37, *cf.* also p. 47 for the Epiphany : 'Hodie ad omnes antiphonas respondemus,' and p. 121 : 'In festo S. Petri ad omnes antiphonas vigiliae respondemus.'

5 Tommasi, *l.c.* 62.

6 For an experiment take the Antiphon *Hodie Christus natus est* of the Vespers of Christmas day and sing it in the following way : 1st choir, *hodie Christus apparuit,* 2nd choir, *hodie in terra* to *Archangeli;* 1st choir, *hodie exultant* to *dicentes;* both choirs, *Gloria* to the end.

verses still holds its place at the introductory chant of Mattins. After each division of the psalm *Venite exultemus*, the Antiphon, which is here called *Invitatorium*, is repeated in whole or in part. The same is the case at the 3rd Nocturn of Epiphany, in which the Antiphon *Venite exultemus* is several times repeated in the psalm that follows. Both examples are fundamentally identical, as they have to do with the same psalm (94). [1]

The final outcome of this kind of Antiphonal chanting is the practice of singing the Antiphon before and after the psalm; this prevailed towards the end of the Middle Ages and was formally authorized by the Council of Trent.

A custom, which has completely disappeared from the present liturgy, but which was very popular in the Middle Ages, was to unite a Canticle not with a single Antiphon, but with several, so that a different Antiphon was sung after each verse. This is not to be regarded as the outcome of a liturgical license, such as occasionally broke out at the end of the Middle Ages; we have before us here a form which is connected with the original Antiphonal chanting and is certainly one of its oldest features. The Greek liturgy of the Middle Ages was familiar with a similar practice, [2] and the oldest MSS. contain many examples of it. Further proof of its age is found in the name given to it: it was expressed by the word *Antiphonare* [3]. 'To-day we Antiphon'—this or a similar rubric is found in the MSS. A chant-book of the Office in the Vatican Library, [4] dating from the 10th century, notes at the *Magnificat* of Christmas Vespers the following 5 Antiphons:

> Ant. *Gloria in excelsis Deo*
> *Virgo verbo concepit*
> *Nesciens mater virgo*
> *Nato Domino angelorum*
> *Natus est nobis*

---

1 An interesting rubric concerning the performance of the Antiphon *Venite adoremus* in the above-mentioned Nocturn of Epiphany is found in the valuable Franciscan Breviary (*Cod.* 540 in Ludw. Rosenthal's Catalogue 102): 'Post omnes duos versus psalmi reiteretur antiphona; sed cum venimus ad proprium locum praedictae antiphonae, alte chorus hanc eandem cantat et semper reincipitur a praedicto choro versus psalmi et antiphonae semper altius incipiendo usque ad *Gloria Patri* et *Sicut erat*, et iterum magis altius antiphona cantatur in finem antiphonae.

2 For examples see Tommasi, *l.c.* xj, *praef.* 70.

3 *E.g.* in the Antiphoner of S. Peter's at Rome printed by Tommasi, *l.c.* xj, pp. 21, 36, 41. etc.

4 Gerbert, *De Cantu* I, 503. The same at Lauds and Vespers of Epiphany.

They were inserted in turn between the verses of the *Magnificat*. A MS. of the 11th century has a still more interesting intercalation of Antiphons into the Canticle. The Magnificat of the Vespers of Easter-Even there opens as usual with the Antiphon *Vespere autem Sabbati :* between the 12 verses (including the *Gloria* and *Sicut erat*) 11 other Antiphons are inserted, consisting of shorter sentences ending with Alleluia, which describe the events of the Resurrection with impressive brevity. The Magnificat is thus penetrated with the whole narrative of the Resurrection. It certainly is an interesting method of bringing the Canticle of the Mother of God into harmony with Easter. [1]

Ant. *Vespere autem Sabbati.*	*Ps. Magnificat.*
Et ecce terrae motus.	*Et exultavit.*
Angelus autem Domini.	*Quia respexit.*
Erat autem aspectus.	*Quia fecit mihi.*
Prae timore autem.	*Et misericordia.*
Respondens autem Angelus.	*Fecit potentiam.*
Venite et videte.	*Deposuit potentes.*
Cito euntes dicite.	*Esurientes implevit.*
In Galilaea Jesum.	*Suscepit Israel.*
Nolite expavescere.	*Sicut locutus est.*
Et valde mane.	*Gloria Patri.*
Et dicebant ad invicem.	*Sicut erat.*

There existed also in the Office the *Versus ad repetendum,* with which we have become acquainted at the Introit and Communion in the Mass. Here again it is confined to antiphonal psalmody ; there is no similar verse to a Respond. In its treatment however, and in its relation to what precedes, it is not quite the same in the Office as in the Mass. In the Mass the *Versus ad repetendum* is a kind of compensation for the shortening of the psalm, and is therefore almost always taken from it ; in the Office it is simply an addition for the purpose of emphasizing the character of the Feast. It therefore stands in no relation to the psalm, which is sung complete before it, even though it adopts its melody. It belongs rather to the Antiphon, and, like it, adapts its text to the festival. It is also noteworthy that the *Versus ad repetendum* appears only quite exceptionally in the Office, while the Mass allows it throughout the Church's year. Our oldest MSS. of the chant of the Mass have a verse

---

[1] Tommasi, *l. c. praef.* 87. This manner of performance may be assumed everywhere where several Antiphons are indicated for one Canticle as *e. g.* in the *Responsoriale Gregorianum* of the 9th century. See *Patr. Lat.* lxxviij, 726 foll.

of this kind at each Introit and each Communion, often even several verses. In the MSS. of the Office chant they are more rarely found, and there is never more than one verse added to the psalm. One of the oldest books of the Office chant, the *Antiphonarium Hartkeri* of S. Gall (*Cod.* 390-391), has some for several Antiphons of Saints. [1] The examples here following are taken from the MS. *Cod. Lat.* 12044 of the Paris National Library (12th century). It has for the Mattins of the Conversion of S. Paul (*fol.* 51 foll) the following antiphons with their verses:

Ant. *Saulus adhuc spirans.* Ps. *Caeli enarrant.* ℣. *Paternarum traditionum : amplius aemulator existens.*

Ant. *Ibat igitur Saulus.* Ps. *Benedicam.* ℣. *Et cum iter faceret, contigit ut appropinquaret Damasco.*

Ant. *Et subito circumfulsit.* Ps. *Eructavit.* ℣. *Audivit autem vocem dicentem sibi : Saule, Saule, quid me persequeris ?*

Ant. *Saule, Saule, quid me.* Ps. *Omnes gentes.* ℣. *Sed surge et ingredere civitatem : et dicetur tibi quid te oporteat facere.*

Ant. *Viri autem qui comitabantur.* Ps. *Exaudi.* ℣. *Saulus autem cadens in terram : apertisque oculis nihil videbat.*

Ant. *Paulus autem.* Ps. *Exaudi Deus.* ℣. *Viri autem qui comitabantur cum eo : stabant stupefacti.*

It is evident from their relation to the Antiphons that the verses are in this case a later addition. The Antiphons follow the line of the Acts of the Apostles (*cap.* 9); the verses on the contrary not only contain superfluous repetitions, but also reverse the order of the events. [2]

Such verses also appear at the Antiphons of the Canticles. This fact is easily explained by the solemn ceremonies which are performed during them (the censing the Altar, the Clergy or the Monks) often demanding a prolonged chant. In this case too the verse always stands in logical connexion with the Antiphon. In Rome, for example, in the 12th century to the Antiphon *Spiritus sanctus in te descendet* (Lauds of 1st Sunday in Advent) was added after the *Benedictus* the verse *Et ingressus angelus ad eam dixit.* Clearly at this point the Antiphon *Spiritus sanctus* [3] was

---

1 Cf. *Cod.* 390, 391 of S. Gall (I quote from the phototype edition of the *Paléographie Musicale*, series II, vol. I) pp. 284, foll., where all the Antiphons of the Office of S. Paul have their verses, and pp. 289 foll. the Antiphons of the 1st Vespers and Mattins of S. Lawrence.

2 *Cod.* 12044 contains at ff. 124 foll. such ℣ ℣. for the Lauds Antiphons *de S. Trinitate*, at ff. 154 foll. for the Nocturn Antiphons of the Commem. of S. Paul, and also of the feast of S. Laurence (f. 172).

3 *E.g.* in the Antiphoner of S. Peter's. Tommasi, *l. c.* 21. *Cf.* also p. 261.

repeated. A Venetian Antiphoner of 1489 has a similar verse on the feast of S. Paul after the *Magnificat.* [1]

In liturgical writings and chant-books from the 12th century onwards we first make the acquaintance of another means of lengthening the Antiphons to the canticle when necessary. To the last syllable of the Antiphon there was simply attached a long *melisma*, the so-called *Pneuma.* This practice, which was not general, but was retained in places till the 16th century, reveals the gradual decay of the feeling for alternation in liturgy and chant. *Melismata* hinder choral singing and the true antiphonal chant. When in the early days Antiphons were ornamented with *melismata*, it was understood that thenceforward they were given over to the soloists, as has been shown in dealing with the Offertory of the Mass. It is important to bear in mind that the melismatic Antiphons of the Office formed no part of its original arrangement, but were a later and inconsequent addition. In the Responds the *melismata* play an integral part; they are plentifully used especially in the last Responds of each Nocturn. The Antiphons with the *jubilus* on the last syllable seem to have been especially popular in Germany and France : a synod of Worms of 1316 speaks of them as an accustomed practice. [2] But there were not wanting judicious voices which were raised against it : various French synods of the 16th century tried to abolish it and to free the Office from this parasite, *e.g.* those of Cambrai (1565) and Besançon (1581). [3]

At the chanting of the Antiphons and the psalms connected with them the two choirs of clergy and monks, as now, stood facing one another, not turned to the Altar. [4] The Antiphon was begun in monasteries, according to the direction of the Rule of S. Benedict, by the monks in turn, beginning with the Abbot (*cf.* above p. 23). In the secular

---

1 Tommasi, *l. c. praef.* 64. Judging from the standpoint of the present day one would certainly have to call such additions to the official constituent parts of the liturgy unliturgical. But a judgment of this sort would not be very just to the character of the medieval liturgy. At that time the liturgical forms with their vigorous life and flow were far removed from the torpidity which was an inevitable result of the liturgical centralization of the 16th century.

2 'Quotiescunque matutinae dicuntur cum tribus vel novem lectionibus, finalis iubilus, qui dici *consuevit* in fine antiphonarum, obmittatur.' Gerbert, *De Cantu* I, 338.

3 The Synod of Besançon in particular speaks strongly against these additions, but then adds with reference to the legitimate *melismata* contained in the old books : 'Qui pneumatis ritum contemnunt, ipsi turpiter desipiunt,' a sentence which forcibly refutes the view upheld by prejudiced writers that an abbreviation of the richer chants was desired in the 16th century. *Cf.* Gerbert, *De Cantu* I, 506, and II, 184.

4 Durandus, *Rationale* 5, 2, 30. Tommasi, *l. c.* 69.

churches, in which even the Antiphonal chant was more and more handed
over to the choir of singers, we learn from Amalarius, [1] that the first
Antiphon was intoned by the first singer of one choir, the second by the
first of the second choir. The whole choir continued the Antiphon to
the end; and then came the psalm.

The texts of the Antiphons belong either to Holy Scripture or to the
oldest Christian literature, the *Acta Martyrum* and the *Vitae Sanctorum*. [2]
The former consist of the word *Alleluia*, or are taken from the psalm or
canticle which follows, or else from some other part of the Bible. It is
natural that the Alleluiatic Antiphons should especially fit the Office of
the season of Easter, and it is so provided as early as in the Benedictine
Rule (chap. 15). [3] A special class of Antiphons comprises those which
are formed from the words of the psalm or the canticle which follows.
They are not to be placed in the same class with the Alleluiatic or with
the other Antiphons: they seem to have their origin in the psalmody *in
directum*. In this case too an indication was needed of the pitch of the

---

1 *De Off.* iv, 7 (*Patr. Lat.* cv, 1180). On the other hand the view of Tommasi
that the Antiphon was sung twice before the psalm, once by each of the choirs, does not
seem to me tenable, even if there were such a custom in the Mozarabic liturgy. There
the Antiphon at Prime for instance runs throughout the whole year thus: 'Praevenerunt
oculi mei, Deus, ad te diluculo, ut meditarer eloquia tua.' It was repeated, and
thereupon followed the Mozarabic Doxology ℣. *Gloria et honor*, again the antiphon
Praevenerunt, and lastly the Psalms.

2 Gevaert (*Melopée antique dans le chant de l'Eglise Latine*, pp. 189 foll.) puts
forward a chronology of the Antiphons which is instructive because of many interesting
observations bearing on the history of the Office. It is however open to objections.
The occurrence of an Antiphon in a document does not justify the conclusion that they
did not exist before.

3 In the oldest MSS. Septuagesima Sunday is still 'Alleluiatic.' The 9th century
Antiphoner printed by Migne (*Patr. Lat.* lxxviij, 747) has a large number of Alleluias
provided for the Antiphons of Mattins. When the Sunday was merged in the season of
penance, the Alleluia was thenceforth sung only on the day before, but for that reason
so much the oftener. The 11th *Ordo Romanus* of the first half of the 12th century has
the rubric: 'Sabbato Septuagesimae ad vesperum tacetur Alleluia.' *Patr. Lat.* lxxviij, 1037.
In the later Middle Ages the cessation of Alleluia gave occasion for remarkable liturgical
uses. At Toul for example in the 15th century the Alleluia was 'buried' the day before
Septuagesima. The Statutes of the Church of the 15th century say: 'Sabbato
Septuagesimae in nona conveniunt pueri chori feriati in magno vestiario, et ibi ordinent
sepulturam *Alleluia*. Et expedito uno *Benedicamus* procedant cum crucibus, tortiis,
aqua benedicta et incenso, portantesque glebam ad modum funeris, transeant per chorum
et vadant per claustrum ululantes usque ad locum, ubi sepelitur: ibi aspersa aqua et dato
incenso ab eorum altero redeant eodem itinere.' For a yet stranger practice *cf.* Ortigue,
Dictionnaire du Plain chant. 107.

psalm-tone, which could then follow on with the first or another verse of the psalm or canticle. Within the psalm and at the end no antiphonal repetition needed then to be inserted. This recalls the practice still prescribed at Sunday Vespers for starting the *Dixit Dominus* where the Antiphon and the first psalm-verse are one and the same. In this case there is good evidence of the derivation of the custom from the psalmody *in directum*. The melody of the words *Dixit Dominus* serving as intonation of the Antiphon is in fact nothing but the beginning of the oldest form of the 7th tone. Thus the psalm has, properly speaking, an Antiphon at the end only, and none at the beginning, and is a *cantus in directum*. The Antiphoner of S. Peter's in Tommasi contains several similar examples *e.g.* [1]

Ant. *Confitebor tibi Domine in toto corde meo.* Ps. *In consilio.*

Ant. *Miserere mei Deus.* Ps. *Secundum.*

Ant. *Credidi propter quod locutus sum.* Ps. *Ego autem.*

The Antiphon-texts taken from the Acts of the Martyrs or the Lives of the old Roman Saints form the latest constituent part of the medieval collection of Antiphons.

In even the oldest MSS. of the Office there is a series of Antiphons which prove to be paraphrases of Canticles,—of the *Cant. trium puerorum* '*Benedicite omnia opera*,' of the *Cant. Zachariae* '*Benedictus Dominus Deus Israel*,' and of the *Magnificat;* they are accordingly called *Antiphonae de prophetia Zachariae* and *de Hymno S. Mariae.* They are given in a MS. as early as the 9th century (the *Responsale Gregorianum* in *Patr. Lat.* lxxviij, 839). These expansions of the texts of the Canticles are interesting memorials of the pleasure which was taken in the Liturgy in the Middle Ages. I here subjoin the *Antiphonae de Cantico S. Mariae* as contained in *Cod. S. Gall* 390, p. 230.

Ant. *Magnificat anima mea Dominum.*

Magnificat anima mea Dominum et sanctum nomen eius.

Magnificat anima mea Dominum.

Magnificet te semper anima mea, Deus meus.

Magnificamus te, Domine, quia fecisti nobiscum magnalia, sicut locutus es.

Magnificamus Christum Regem Dominum, quia superbos humiliat et exaltat humiles.

Exsultat spiritus meus in Domino Deo salutari meo.

---

[1] Tommasi, *l. c.* xj, p. 52.

In Deo salutari meo exsultavit spiritus meus.

Exsultavit spiritus meus in Deo salutari meo.

Quia respexit Deus humilitatem meam, beatam me dicent omnes generationes.

Respexisti humilitatem meam, Domine, Deus meus.

Respexit Dominus humilitatem meam et fecit in me magna, quia potens est.

Quia fecit mihi Dominus magna, quia potens est et sanctum nomen eius.

Fecit mihi Deus meus magna, quia potens est.

Sanctum est nomen tuum, Domine, a progenie in progenies.

Misericordia Dei et sanctum nomen eius super timentes eum.

A progenie in progenies misericordia Domini super timentes eum.

Fecit Dominus potentiam in brachio suo et exaltavit humiles.

Fac Deus potentiam in brachio tuo, et exalta humiles.

Deposuit potentes, sanctos persequentes, et exaltavit humiles, Christum confitentes.

Exalta Domine humiles, sicut locutus es.

Esurientes replevit bonis Dominus, et potentes divites dimisit inanes.

Suscepit Israhel puerum suum, recordatus Dominus misericordiae suae.

Suscepit Deus Israhel puerum suum, sicut locutus est Abraham et semini eius, et exaltavit humiles usque in saeculum.

Sicut locutus es ad patres nostros, Domine recordare misericordiae tuae.

Ad patres nostros Dominus locutus est a progenie in progenies.

Abraham et semen eius usque in saeculum magnificat Dominum.

A few more kinds of Antiphons are here enumerated, which have been provided with special names in the MSS. and by ritualists. I mean the Antiphons *de cruce*, the *Antiphonae majores*, and a series of alleluiatic Antiphons which were not so originally. The Antiphons *de cruce* or *ad crucem* are found only in the monastic and the Milanese Offices, and refer to the Commemoration of the Holy Cross, which is peculiar to these Offices : *cf.* the Lauds of Christmas Day in *Cod. S. Gall* 390, in the tables at the end of the next Chapter. The *Antiphonae majores* are the Antiphons sung at Vespers and also at Lauds on the last days before Christmas, which all begin with O, and on that account are called also the O-Antiphons. Their number varies : the oldest known Office MS., the *Responsale Gregorianum* of Compiègne, [1] of the 9th century, has 9 of them, the S. Gall Antiphoner of Hartker of the 10th century (*Cod.* 390 S. Gall) has 12, a Roman Antiphoner of the 12th century (edited by Tommasi) has 7. According to Amalarius [2] they were sung at *Magnificat*, at Vespers; the last named Roman Antiphoner prescribes them for *Benedictus* at Lauds. Lastly, of Alleluiatic Antiphons, which were originally used with other texts, there is a fair number: as we shall return to them in the SECOND PART, only one example is here given to explain the peculiarity of these Antiphons. *Cod.* 12044 of the National Library at Paris has the melody of the Antiphon *Angelus autem Domini* twice; once with the well-known text with which it is still associated to-day, and afterwards with a tenfold Alleluia; the adaptation to the latter text is carried out syllable for syllable: instead of the four syllables *Angelus au* the four syllables *Alleluia* are sung, and so on.

When Antiphons were provided for the lesser Day Hours (which were originally said *in directum, i.e.* without Antiphons) they were almost always taken from other parts of the Office, especially Lauds; consequently many MSS. give no Antiphons at all for these Hours, or else one Antiphon was made to suffice for the whole Hour, even when it comprised many psalms. It appears that at Lauds also several psalms were sung under one Antiphon, and in many Offices of the season of Easter the whole set of psalms had for Antiphon only the word *Alleluia*, otherwise it was the rule, particularly in the oldest part of the Office, the Nocturns, that each psalm should have its own Antiphon.

It is interesting to recall the distribution of the psalms among the Hours of the Office. The three *Nocturns* make use of the series Ps. 1-108 with a few exceptions; Ps. 109-147 belong almost exclusively to *Vespers*. The psalms which are not taken up by either of these two series are distributed over the remaining parts of the Office; so that *Lauds* claim psalms 5, 39, 42, 50, 62, 64, 66, 80, 91, 92, 99, 142, 148, 149, and 150, *Prime*, Ps. 21-25, 53, 117 and part of 118, *Terce, Sext* and *None* the remaining parts of Ps. 118, and finally *Compline* Ps. 4, 30, 90 and 135. The Nocturn and Vesper psalms follow straight on in numerical order from the beginning; on the contrary those of Lauds, Compline, and (in part) those of Prime are selected with reference to the character of the Hour concerned. Thus Lauds refers to the dawn, or to the Resurrection of our Lord which took place in the early morning. Nocturns and

---

1 Printed in *Patr. Lat.* vol. lxxviij.
2 *Patr. Lat.* cv, 1264.

Vespers were arranged at the same time and after the same principles, the first two thirds of the Psalter being allotted to the former and the remaining third to the latter. The arrangement of the psalms at Lauds resembles that of Prime, while the three lesser Hours, Terce, Sext and None, fall into a group by themselves. This distribution of the psalms is now observed only on ferial days: on the greater Feasts of our Lord, and of the Saints, the numerical succession is abandoned in the Nocturn and Vesper group, and such psalms of the two groups are chosen as appear to be especially suited to the feast. This is not the case at Terce, Sext, None and Compline, which are invariably composed of the same psalms throughout the ecclesiastical year. These arrangements, carried out from such different points of view, disclose some hidden interesting facts about the development of the Office in general. [1]

The custom of calling chants which have no psalm or psalm-verse, Antiphons is of comparatively late date. Perhaps the *commemoratio* or 'Memorial' led to it. In old times the memorial of a feast was kept, not by the complete Office belonging to it, but by a Respond, an Antiphon with the ℣. *Gloria Patri* and *Sicut erat*, and the saying of a collect. It thus comprised a specimen of each of the forms which made up the constituent parts of an Office. [2] In the case of the Antiphonal psalm the only existing part left is the Doxology. When this also is left out the last stage of the development of the Antiphonal chant has been reached, in other words its complete dissolution has taken place. A mere piece of chant survives without any distinctive structure. The best known examples of this are the four Antiphons in praise of the Blessed Virgin, with which for a long time the Office has concluded: *Alma Redemptoris mater, Ave Regina coelorum, Regina coeli laetare*, and *Salve Regina*. Originally however they were joined to psalms, and thus were Antiphons proper. The Antiphoner of S. Gall 390, 391, in the parts written by Hartker and therefore belonging to the 10th century, has as yet none of these chants: on p. 10 of *Cod.* 390 are the Antiphons *Alma Redemptoris mater* and *Salve Regina* (with three verses)[3] in the Office of

---

1 On the distribution of the psalms in the Middle Ages *cf.* Brambach, *Psalterium* (*Sammlung bibliothekwissenschaftlicher Arbeiten, ed.* Dziatzko, part I, p. 15), and Cabrol, *Livre de la prière antique*, p. 18 foll.

2 John of Avranches, *De Eccl. Off.* See Tommasi *l. c.* ix, *Isagoge liturg.* xiij, 22.

3 It is also a Respond and runs with the verses: 'Salve Regina misericordia . . . O clemens, O dulcis, O pia Maria. ℣. 1: Virgo clemens, virgo pia, virgo dulcis, O Maria, exaudi preces omnium ad te pie clamantium. ℣. 2: Virgo, mater ecclesiae, aeternae porta gloriae, ora pro nobis omnibus, qui tui memoriam agimus. ℣. 3: Gloriosa Dei mater,

the Annunciation of the Blessed Virgin Mary, in writings and neums of the 13th century. The Paris MS. 12044 of the 12th century gives the Ant. *Alma redemptoris* (*fol.* 177) at Sext of the Assumption of the Blessed Virgin Mary, the Ant. *Ave Regina* at None of the same day. In the Antiphoner of S. Peter's at Rome of the 12th century, published by Tommasi, the *Regina coeli* stands as an Antiphon of the Octave of Easter. [1] These Antiphons were deprived of their connexion with psalm or psalm-verse when they were placed at the end of the *Horae Diurnae*, as Gregory IX ordered in the case of the *Salve Regina* in 1239. [2] But there are chants of this kind without psalm or psalm-verse in MSS. as early as the 10th century; *e.g.* at the end of *Cod. S. Gall* 339 there stands a large number of Antiphons for the *Litania major*, *Ad postulandam pluviam*, *Pro serenitate*, *Ad deducendas reliquias etc:* likewise in *Cod. Einsiedl.* 121 at the end. The name 'Antiphon' only attaches to these chants in an improper sense, as is shown by their texts: they nearly all have the form of a prayer. [3]

If we glance over the devious path along which the development of Antiphonal chanting has gone from the 4th century till recent times, it shows itself to be in all essentials a retrogression from a rich and artistic form to simplicity. The repetition of the Antiphon after each verse of the psalm, such as was customary in the earliest times of antiphonal chanting, created a structure of great aesthetic importance, which is somewhat on a parallel with the modern form of the *Rondo*. This structure became still more interesting when not merely one Antiphon but several alternated with the verses of a psalm or canticle; in this case, by securing a real connexion in the Antiphons, care was taken that the whole unit, the psalm and its Antiphons, did not fall to pieces. As we have seen, many *Antiphonae ad Evangelium* are memorials of this stage of Antiphonal chanting. Since both forms of Antiphony protracted the service of the monks and clergy to a great length, abbreviation naturally suggested itself, at least at the ordinary performance of the Office. The result was that

---

cuius natus est et Pater, esto nobis refugium apud Patrem et Filium.' One can see from their rhythmic form (with rhymes) that these Verses are not part of the original. Until recent times Hermann Contract has been looked upon as the composer of the *Salve Regina*: wrongly as Fr. Gabriel Meier proved at the Catholic congress of Savants at München in 1900. See the *Acts* of the Congress, p. 160.

   1 Tommasi, *l. c.* xi, p. 100.

   2 Bäumer, *Breviersgesch.* 261 and 353.

   3 Thus an *Antiphona in tempore mortali* runs: 'Libera, Domine, populum tuum de manu mortis et plebem istam protegat dextera tua, ut viventes benedicamus te Domine.' *Cod. Einsiedl.* 121, p. 405.

in the end the Antiphon was sung only before and after the psalm, no longer during it. This new kind of antiphonal chanting, which is not wanting in artistic effect (we recognize it in the type ABA), was found to be so suitable that it has held the field in the Middle Ages as well as in modern times as the normal form of antiphonal chanting in the Office. The custom of only intoning the Antiphon before the psalm, and not singing it entire till after the psalm, comes from a time when the aesthetic structure of a liturgical whole was no longer well understood, and quite disregards the fact that the simple intonation before the psalm often gives no logical sense at all. [1] A final stage led the antiphonal chant to a state of complete dissolution, wherein a simple chant without any psalmodic melody is called Antiphon. None of the constituent elements of the antiphonal chant, neither the alternate chanting nor the connexion with a psalm or psalm-verse, exists here any longer : no further modification of the antiphonal chant in this direction was possible. It was fortunate for the structure of the Office that this form only occurred in a few cases, which form an exception.

---

[1] It has never contented the liturgical student : 'What is the use,' says Tommasi, (*l.c.*xij, 5), 'of such fragmentary phrases, the words of which give no complete sense, and the melody of which does not clearly indicate the mode of the Antiphon according to which the psalm is to be sung ?' At the Introit of the Mass the Antiphon is still sung complete before it is time for the psalm-verse, both on ordinary days and festivals. It sounds inartistic when the Antiphon after the verse is replaced by organ-playing, for then every trace of antiphonal chant has disappeared ; and it is to be wished that with a growing feeling for liturgical beauty this concession may cease to be adopted. The form ABA which, as has been shown, forms the basis both of the Alleluia and the early medieval Gradual-respond, is one of those types which serve to restore organic connexion and comprehensive unity : according to it the Creator made the body of man, in which harmonious parts are grouped symmetrically round a centre. In the liturgical chant, if it be a work of art (as it was in the Middle Ages), repetition has ample justification. It is superfluous to expound it (to do so would betray an ignorance of the fundamental laws of aesthetics) for it governs all musical forms.

CHAPTER X

THE DEVELOPMENT OF THE OFFICE HYMNS

A new era of Greek hymnology began in the 7th century. Its chief figure is Romanus, who lived probably in the first half of the 8th century. [1] He worked in Emesa, Berytus, and finally Byzantium. His most famous composition was a Christmas hymn which was performed with much pomp, not only in church but also at the Imperial table, up to the 12th century. His poems mark the final transformation of the classic metre, which had already taken place in the older Syrian hymnody, and the method of scansion by quantity was almost entirely given up. Before and after him other distinguished composers of hymns were Anastasius of Sinai, Sergius the Patriarch of Constantinople, (who later joined the Monothelites, and whose poem in honour of the Mother of God is still solemnly sung in the Greek liturgy), also Sophronius, Patriarch of Jerusalem (†638), two Cretan Archbishops named Andreas in the 8th century, S. John of Damascus of the same date, etc. As a result of the Iconoclastic controversy in the 8th and 9th centuries, much that was very ancient was banished from the liturgical books of the Greeks; and it cannot always be decided what compositions are due to the Fathers of

---

[1] He lived under one of the two Emperors who bore the name Anastasius. The first reigned 491-518, the second 713-716. Accordingly he is placed in the first part of either the 6th or the 8th century. Latterly the 8th century seems to have been the alternative fixed upon. See Krummbacher in the *Abhand. der Bayer. Akad. der Wissenschaft* 1899, vol. II, pp. 1 foll. It would add support to this hypothesis, if the 'Romanus' mentioned by authors at S. Gall proved to be not a Roman singer (which is very improbable) but the personification of the influence of Byzantine singers appearing at S. Gall from the 8th century onward.

Greek Hymnody. The Greek monasteries in Italy have maintained the old traditions better than those of the East. [1]

The Latin Church also had plenty of gifted composers of hymns, who took S. Ambrose and his immediate successors as their model. In the first half of the 5th century there flourished Sedulius, [2] author of the hymns *A solus ortus cardine* (Christmas) and *Hostis* now *Crudelis Herodes Deum* (Epiphany); Claudius Mamertus (†473) is spoken of as the author of the hymns *Pange lingua gloriosi lauream certaminis* and *Lustra sex qui jam peregit.* Pope Gelasius (†496) also belongs to this list; for the *Liber Pontificalis* says of him, that he composed hymns after the pattern of Bishop Ambrose. [3] The hymn on S. Peter and S. Paul was written by Elpis, who is said to have been the wife of Boethius. In the Mozarabic Breviary there are to be found hymns by Ennodius, Bishop of Pavia (†521). In the Roman are some of Venantius Fortunatus, Bishop of Poitiers (†c. 600); the most famous of them are *Vexilla regis prodeunt* (Passiontide), *Quem terra, pontus aethera* (now *sidera*), *O gloriosa domina* (now *virginum*, both of these *de S. Maria*), and *O redemptor, sume carmen* (sung at the consecration of holy oil on Maundy Thursday). To Pope Gregory I. are ascribed *Primo dierum omnium, Nocte surgentes vigilemus omnes* (Sunday Mattins), *Ecce jam noctis tenuatur umbra* (Lauds), *Lucis creator optime* (Vespers), *Audi benigne conditor* (Lent), and *Conditor* (now *Creator*) *alme siderum* (Advent). [4]

In the 7th century hymns were composed for the Spanish Office by John, Bishop of Saragossa (†631), Isidore of Seville (†c. 635), Conantius Bishop of Palencia (†639), Eugenius II of Toledo (†658) and Julian of Toledo (†690). In the 8th century there flourished the Venerable Bede (†735) the English Theologian, Paul Warnefrid (†c. 797) famed as the composer of the *Ut queant laxis* (S. John Baptist), and others. The hymn *Veni creator spiritus* is by an improbable tradition ascribed to Charlemagne. [5] Theodulf of Orleans (Bishop in 788) is the composer of *Gloria, laus et honor* (Palm Sunday procession). Somewhat later is Rhabanus Maurus, Archbishop of Mainz who died in 856.

The hymns soon won for themselves great popularity, so that they threatened to throw into the shade the older constituent parts of the Office.

1 Bäumer in the *Kirchenlexikon*, vol. VI, art. 'Hymnus.'

2 We have already spoken of his *Carmen paschale* on *p.* 61. *Cf.* also the last chapter of this book.

3 *Lib. Pont.* I, 255.   4 *Patr. Lat.* lxxviij, 849.

5 Chevalier, *Poésie liturgique au moyen âge*, p. 89.

Many of them were more expressive of the subjective feelings of their composers than of correct Church doctrine : and thus they met with much opposition, as being forms of prayer and chant not drawn from Holy Scripture. This hostility found expression at the Council of Braga (563), and the hymns were rejected on the ground of the decree of the Council of Laodicea (middle of the 4th century), which allowed nothing but the text of Holy Scripture[1] to be used in the liturgy. Other Church councils were more favourable to the hymns, *e.g.* those of Agde (506) and Tours (567), the latter, it is to be observed, four years after the decision of Braga. But the movement hostile to the hymns seems to have found even more important supporters in Spain, for once again in 633 the Council of Toledo took the opportunity of speaking out energetically on behalf of the hymns and of threatening their opponents with excommunication. In answer to the objection that they are not contained in the Canon of Holy Scripture, the Fathers of the Council pointed out that by the same reasoning *Gloria Patri*, *Gloria in excelsis*, and many of the lessons would have to be abolished. [2]

When once introduced into the Milanese liturgy by the father of Latin hymnody, the hymns became a popular constituent part of the Office wherever there was a liturgical connexion with Milan, and especially in Gaul and Spain. The direction of the Rule of S. Benedict (*cap.* 9), which orders a hymn for each Hour, was very favourable to their extension, as were the similar directions in the rules of Aurelian and Caesarius. We cannot exactly determine when hymns found an entrance into the Roman Church, *i.e.* into the Offices of the secular clergy, for the monks were much earlier bound to the use of them by their Rule. When Popes like Gelasius and Gregory I. composed hymns, one would imagine that they made provision for their liturgical use. Moreover the Church of England was acquainted with hymns as early as the 7th century, [3] and this suggests their use in the Roman Office of the 7th century ; for in its liturgical practices the English Church stood in more direct and often in more thorough accord with Rome than others. On the other hand we know from Amalarius [4] that the Roman Office in the first half of the 9th century admitted no hymns : moreover they are not mentioned in the

---

1 *Cf.* above p. 38.

2 Bäumer, *Breviergeschichte*, 327, Gerbert, *Vet. Lit. Alem.* II, 828.

3 Aldhelm, Bishop of Sherborne (†709), in a poem in praise of the king's daughter Bugge, who had erected a Church, mentions the chanting of hymns, psalms, and responds (*Patr. Lat.* lxxxix, 290).   4 Gerbert, *Vet. Lit. Alem.* II, 828.

Ordo of Benedict, Canon of S. Peter's (first half of the 12th century). [1]
From this we must conclude that the Office of the secular clergy in Rome,
in contrast to that of other Latin churches, invariably consisted of psalmody,
reading and prayer only: and when Rhabanus Maurus (middle of the 9th
century) declares hymns to be in use in all the Churches of the West,[2] the
Roman is to be excepted. The Office of the papal chapel however, which
took shape from the second half of the 12th century onward, and through
its adoption by the Franciscans in the 13th century became of such
decisive importance in the further development of the Breviary, gave to
the hymns that position which they have possessed uncontested since the
end of the Middle Ages. [3] From this it would appear that they penetrated
into the Roman Church in the second half of the 12th century. On the
other hand it is argued that the *Breviarium Curiae Romanae* can scarcely
have introduced the hymns; any enrichment and extension of the Office
is quite contrary to the tendency of this Breviary, which aimed throughout
at abridgement. So on this account we must place the adoption of the
hymns by Rome at a somewhat earlier date. The oldest existing Roman
Office books which have admitted the hymns do not put them together
with the Antiphons and Responds on the respective days to which they
belong, but at the end of the book, in an appendix. [4] Even down to the
present time the Roman Breviary has no hymn for the last days of Holy
Week nor for Easter-week: in the latter place there is sung instead the
Respond *Haec dies*. [5] The Breviaries of Lyons and of Vienne until recent
times had scarcely any hymns. [6]

---

1 *Patr. Lat.* lxxviij, 1025 foll.

2 *De Instit. Cler. II*, 49: 'cuius celebritatis (of the hymns) devotio dehinc per
totius occidentis ecclesias observatur' (*Patr. Lat.* cvij, 362).

3 See the *Breviarium sec. consuet. Curiae Romanae* belonging to the 3rd decade of
the 13th century, in the possession of the bookseller Ludw. Rosenthal (*Cat.*102,No. 540).

4 The second part of this 'Introduction' will give the melodies of the above-
mentioned Franciscan Breviary.

5 This Respond must have originally been a simple Versicle with a Response,
like many others in the Office. But in very early times it was usual to sing it as a
Responsorium prolixum, and it was all the easier to do this as the Mass of the day had
the same text for the Gradual. The melody used at the Mass was thus simply taken
over for use at the Office. Accordingly the Antiphoner of Hartker (*Cod.* 391 of S. Gall,
p. 38) writes expressly R̃. G. *Haec dies*—that is *Responsorium graduale*—and not, as
in the case of the other Office Responds, simply R̃. The *Ordo* of the Roman Canon
Benedict (12th century) says: 'Versus *Haec dies quem fecit Dominus* cantatur sicut
graduale' (*Patr. Lat.* lxxviij 1042).

6 Gerbert, *De Cantu* I, 253. Walafrid Strabo in his *De Reb. Eccl.* 25 (*Patr. Lat.*

Ambrose's hymns, unlike the verses of the classic poets, were restricted to the style of popular poetry. Its chief form, the *Versus Saturninus*, had dominated the oldest poetry of the Romans, but after the 3rd century B. C. it had to give way before the Greek metres that invaded Rome; and from that time forward it was used only in the popular poetry. It has the form

$$\smile \acute{\_} \smile \acute{\_} \smile \acute{\_} \smile \parallel \acute{\_} \smile \acute{\_} \smile \acute{\_} \smile \acute{\_}$$

when treated from the point of view of *quantity* or

$$. \; \prime \; . \; \prime \; . \; \prime \; . \parallel \prime \; . \; \prime \; . \; \prime \; . \; \prime \; .$$

when treated as a verse with a rhythm depending upon *accent*. [1] In the first case it consists of alternating short and long syllables; in the second case of alternating unaccented and accented syllables. The *caesura* in the middle divides it into two half-verses of opposite character : the first is a combination of *iambics*, the second a combination of *trochees*. Accordingly the Latin hymn writers were especially fond of iambic or trochaic metres. By adding one syllable to the first part of the Saturnine verse an iambic dipody is obtained, and we have the metre used by S. Ambrose :

$$. \; \prime \; . \; \prime \; . \; \prime \; . \; \prime$$
Aeterne rerum conditor

From the second half of the Saturnine verse there developed the trochaic counterpart of the iambic dimeter :

$$\prime \; . \; \prime \; . \; \prime \; .$$
Ave maris stella

Iambic and trochaic tripods and tetrapods are also found. Even when hymns were outwardly based on an exact imitation of classical models, metrical licenses penetrated to them, derived from popular poetry. In the Ambrosian hymn *Conditor alme siderum* we have :—

$$. \; \prime \; . \; \prime \; . \; \prime \; . \; \prime$$
Castus amor salvus erit

---

cxiv, 956), tells us the interesting fact that in some countries hymns were also sung during Low Mass *(Missa privata)*; the Patriarch Paulinus of Friuli introduced this use. Walafrid adds that this very worthy man could not have introduced this practice without strong reason. *Cf.* Gerbert, *De Cantu* I, 355.

[1] Philologists are not agreed upon this question. *Cf.* Gleditsch, *Metrik* in Ivan Müller's *Handbuch der klass. Altertumswissenschaft.*

where short syllables with an accent take the position and function of long ones. Perhaps such things as these came in when the Latin poets became acquainted with the rhythmic accented poetry of the Orientals. It would be difficult to decide with certainty how much was due to the Latin popular poetry and how much to this new conception of verse. But whether the one or the other view be taken, the result is the same, namely a gradual assimilation of the *quantitative* poetry, in which the stress goes with the long syllables, to the *rhythmic*, which takes account of the raising and lowering of the voice, of accented and unaccented syllables. Throughout the Middle Ages the metrical and antique, and the unmetrical, rhythmic forms of poetry go on side by side. The latter is characterized by the Venerable Bede as follows: 'Rhythm is an arrangement of words which is harmonious and pleasing to the ear, and depends not on metrical considerations, but on the number of syllables, according to the custom of popular poetry : but even in rhythm the artistic disposition of them *(ratio)* will also be found.' [1] We recognize the combination of both conceptions of verse in later hymns, such as *e. g. Sacris solemniis juncta sint gaudia,* where the more antique versification and the rhythmic arrangement of syllables peaceably alternate one with the other. Rhyme also, which forms a kind of punctuation for the ear, begins now gradually to gain ground. The same hymn is instructive in this respect : but the beginnings of it are already traceable in some hymns of Ambrose, where, again in imitation of popular poetry, lines occasionally end alike : thus we have in the hymn *Intende qui regis Israel,*

> *Veni Redemptor gentium,*
> *Ostende partum virginis,*
> *Miretur omne saeculum,*
> *Talis decet partus Deum.*
>
> *Non ex virili semine,*
> *Sed mystico spiramine etc.*

The ancient avoidance of the hiatus disappears. The ancients evaded it by elision, but it offers no difficulty to the singer. On the contrary, the vowels form the musical element in language, that which enables language by its sound to enter into union with singing, for one cannot sing consonants : consequently a succession of vowels is far from being unmusical. The musical languages of the South are thus especially full of vowels undivided by consonants, and in Italian even the diphthongs are separated. In singing, the hiatus gives no trouble at all, but elision

---

1 *Patr. Lat.* x, 173.

and contraction do.   Some hymns, following the model of Old Testament canticles, are constructed alphabetically, the first strophe beginning with A, the second with B, etc : as *e. g.* the hymn *A solis ortus cardine*, whose second strophe begins with *Beatus auctor saeculi*, the third with *Castae parentis viscera*, the fourth with *Domus pudici pectoris*, and so on.

Most of the hymns used in the Middle Ages are formed, like those of Ambrose, of stanzas of four *iambic dimeters*.   As a specimen of *iambic trimeters* it is usual to cite the verses of the hymn of S. Peter and S. Paul, *Aurea luce et decore roseo.*

Trochaic formation is also not uncommon : the verse consists either of three trochees, as in the hymn *Ave maris stella*, which has a stanza consisting of four such lines, or of four, as in the hymn *Stabat mater dolorosa* : here the stanza consists of three lines, in the last of which one syllable is wanting (a catalectic conclusion).   In the hymn *Pange lingua gloriosi praelium certaminis* each line is composed of eight trochees : each is catalectic and three form one stanza.

Other hymns are written in the sapphic measure, consisting of three eleven-syllable sapphic lines, and one five-syllable adonic line, as *Nocte surgentes vigilemus omnes*, *Christe sanctorum decus angelorum*, and *Ut queant laxis resonare fibris.*

The hymns *Inventor rutili dux bone luminis* and *Sanctorum meritis inclyta gaudia* are composed of asclepiads and glyconics.

There are also instances of the distich made up of a hexameter and a pentameter : *Salve festa dies, toto venerabilis aevo*, and *Gloria, laus et honor tibi sit, rex Christe redemptor.*

The hymn-melodies, as we know, were originally quite simple and popular. [1]   But as in the course of the Middle Ages the tendency made itself increasingly felt to exclude the congregation from singing in church, and to leave the music entirely to the singers who were employed for that purpose, there was less and less reason for keeping entirely to the old syllabic form of melody.   The singers naturally aimed at having melodies which were musically interesting and effective for the hymns, especially on feast days. [2]   As a matter of fact the hymn melodies of the Office in

---

1 The hymns in the Roman ferial Office were still syllabic at the beginning of the 14th century : 'unicam atque facilem habent notam,' says Ralph of Tongres, *Propos.* 13 (in Gerbert, *De Cantu* I, 510), and this is entirely corroborated by our own MSS.

2 Ulric, *De. Ant. Cluniac. Consuet.* II, 25, says of the Easter hymn that it was as simple as those of ordinary days; he wished therefore for a richer melody.   Gerbert, *l. c.* I, 511.

our oldest MSS. are not all syllabic ; there are among them forms as fully developed melodically as those in use to-day. This holds good especially in the case of the hymns which appear in the pre-eminent, most exalted part of the services, the Mass, like the hymn *Pange lingua gloriosi*, as used on Good Friday. This melody, even in the oldest MSS., is of an ornate style, and far in advance of the syllabic method of composition : here the metrical considerations proper to the verses are to some extent obscured, and the laws of musical rhythm take their place.

Almost all the Office hymns of the Middle Ages are written either in metrical or in rhythmical form. But there are in the background signs of an older kind, whose structure, like that of the psalms and the other relics of Semitic poetry, rests rather on a law of parallelism between the parts. Among these may be classed the short Doxology, *Gloria Patri*, which is attached to the last verse of a psalm (the great Doxology *Gloria in excelsis*, as we have seen, figures among the chants of the Mass) ; also the *Te decet laus* of the Benedictine Office (p. 37). But the chief representative of this series is the so-called Ambrosian Hymn of praise, the *Te Deum*, which is mentioned as early as the rule of S. Benedict. The question as to the origin of this composite hymn, and of its original form, has not as yet been solved. The structure of the melody, as handed down in very old MSS. of the Office, seems to point out that the part beginning *Aeterna fac* is of later origin : the first part is referable to the time when only Christian Martyrs received liturgical veneration ; at any rate they alone are mentioned besides the Apostles and Prophets, and there is no mention of the Confessors who distinguished themselves by heroic virtues without actually laying down their lives for divine truth.

The *Te Deum* belongs to the fixed plan of the monastic Office, and is given in the MSS. from the oldest chant-books of the Office onwards, from the Antiphoner of Bangor, [1] written towards the end of the 7th century, down to the present day. In Rome its use was in the time of Amalarius (9th century) still limited to the birthdays of the Popes, and it was not a regular item of the Office. [2] In the middle of the 12th century however it was in almost daily use in Rome, as we learn from the 11th *Ordo* of Benedict, Canon of S. Peter's. [3] It was sung like an antiphonal

---

[1] Preserved in a MS. of the *Ambrosiana* at Milan, and printed by Muratori in the 4th vol. of the *Anecdota Ambrosiana* (1713), and recently phototyped as vol. 4 of the publications of the *Henry Bradshaw Society* (1893).

[2] *Patr. Lat.* cv, 1246.

[3] *Patr. Lat.* lxxviij, 1027.

psalm, verse and verse about, by the two halves of the choir, [1] a method of performance which was the natural result of its structure, and to which the melody was adapted. The verses from *Per singulos dies* onwards were sung rather louder than the preceding ones, as Durandus tells us. [2] Its most frequent position was the conclusion of the third Nocturn on Sundays and festivals : it was so popular there that it even supplanted the third Respond. [3] Moreover it soon became the hymn for general use in public and solemn thanksgiving, and for this purpose took the place of the *Gloria in excelsis*. To-day it is familiar to the clergy as part of the Office, and to the people as an inspiring song of praise to the grace of God.

The structure of the Office, monastic as well as secular, may be studied in the following tables, in which there are given the musical portions of the Christmas Office. The authorities used for the monastic Office are the Hartker Antiphoner (*Cod.* 390 S. Gall of the 10th century), and *Cod.* 12044 of the Paris National Library of the 12th century; for the secular Office, the *Responsale* of Compiègne of the 9th century, (printed by Migne in *Patr. Lat.* lxxviij), the Antiphoner of S. Peter's at Rome of the 12th century (printed by Tommasi and quoted from Galliciolli's edition of the works of Gregory the Great, vol. xi), [4] and a MS. of the beginning of the 13th century in the possession of the bookseller Ludw. Rosenthal at Münich, containing a Franciscan Breviary *secundum consuetudinem Curiae Romanae*. It will not be difficult by a comparison of these five MSS. to form an adequate idea of the difference between these two Offices, and also of the variations which are to be found in MSS. of the same Office. [5] The tables will place the fact beyond all doubt that in the Middle Ages the music of the Office was not nearly so uniform as the music of the Mass.

---

1 It is thus prescribed in the *Hirschau Constitutions*. Gerbert, *De Cantu* I, 488.
2 Gerbert, *Ibid.*
3 Ralph of Tongres, *Prop.* 12, Gerbert, *l.c.* 512. *Cf.* also the MSS. of the Secular Office of the 12th and 13th centuries, from which the Christmas Office printed at the end of this chapter is taken.
4 This Antiphoner has two Offices for the Feast of Christmas. In the tables the second only is utilized, as it corresponds more closely with those of other books.
5 Even the verses of the Responds vary in MSS.

In particular, special attention is called to the fact that neither the monastic Office of the 10th century, nor the secular Office of the 9th, nor even that of the 12th century, knows anything of Hymns : they are first noted in the Paris MS. of the 12th and the Rosenthal MS. of the 13th century. The monastic Vespers makes a Respond precede the Antiphon to the *Magnificat* and it is a *Responsorium prolixum* (the present Benedictine Breviary has a R̠. *breve*) ; the MS. of Hartker, though of monastic origin, has five vesper Antiphons.

THE CHANTS OF THE OFFICE AT CHRISTMAS

AD PRIMAS VESPERAS

A. OFFICIUM MONASTICUM

Cod. Hartkeri (10. saec.)	*Cod. Paris. 12044 (12. saec.)*
ANT. Scitote quia prope est.	ANT. Levate capita vestra.
Rex pacificus magnificatus est.	Scitote quia prope est.
Magnificatus est rex pacificus.	Completi sunt dies.
Orietur sicut sol.	Ecce completa sunt omnia.
Levate capita vestra.	RESP. Judaea et Hierusalem. ℣. Constantes estote.
RESP.[1] Sanctificamini, filii Israhel. ℣. Ecce dominus.	℣. Gloria Patri.
IN EVANGELIO	HYMN. Veni redemptor gentium.
ANT. Dum ortus fuerit.	℣. Tecum principium. ℟. In die virtutis.
AD CRUCEM	IN EVANGELIO
ANT. O Hierusalem civitas.	ANT. Bethlem, non es minima.
Ave Maria.	

1 A later hand has marked between the lines the ℟. *Judaea et Hierusalem*, with the ℣. *Constantes* and the Ant. *Cum erat desponsata.*

B. OFFICIUM SAECULARE

Responsale Gregorianum (9 saec.)	*Antiphonarium Tommasi (12 saec.)*	*Brev. Curiae Romanae (13 saec.)*
ANT.[1] Judaea et Hierusalem. Hodie scietis, quia veniet. Crastina die delebitur. Exspectetur sicut pluvia. Crastina die erit vobis. ℣. Tanquam sponsus. ℟. Dominus procedens.	ANT. Judaea et Hierusalem. Crastina erit. Hodie scietis, quia. Crastina die delebitur. Magnificatus est. ℣. Hodie scietis. ℟. Et mane videbitis.	ANT. Rex pacificus. Magnificatus est. Completi sunt. Scitote, quia prope est. Levate capita vestra.
		HYMN. Christe redemptor omnium. ℣. Crastina die. ℟. Et regnabit.
IN EVANGELIO	IN EVANGELIO	IN EVANGELIO
ANT. Dum ortus fuerit.	ANT. Dum ortus fuerit.	ANT. Dum ortus fuerit.

1 The MS. gives no Antiphons of its own for this Vespers, because they were all taken from Lauds of the Vigil of Christmas.

INVITATORIUM ET IN PRIMO NOCTURNO

A. OFFICIUM MONASTICUM

INVITATORIUM

	Cod. Hartker.	*Cod. Paris.*
ANT.	Christus natus est nobis.	Christus natus est nobis.
	Ps. Venite exultemus.	Ps. Venite exultemus.
HYMN.		Christe redemptor omnium.

IN PRIMO NOCTURNO

	Cod. Hartker.	*Cod. Paris.*
ANT.	Dominus dixit ad me.	Dominus dixit ad me.
	Tanquam sponsus dominus.	Tanquam sponsus.
	Elevamini, portae aeternales.	Natus est nobis hodie.
	Diffusa est gratia.	Diffusa est gratia.
	Rex omnis terrae Deus.	Verbum caro factum est.
	Suscepimus Deus.	Suscepimus Deus.
RESP.	Hodie nobis caelorum rex.	Hodie caelorum rex.
	℣. Gloria in excelsis.	℣. Gloria in excelsis.
	Hodie nobis de caelo.	Hodie nobis de caelo.
	℣. Gloria in excelsis.	℣. Gloria in excelsis.
	O regem caeli.	O magnum mysterium.
	℣. Domine audivi.	℣. Domine audivi.
	Descendit de caelis.	Quem vidistis.
	℣. Tanquam sponsus. ℣. Gloria patri.	℣. Dicite quidnam.
	℣. Tanquam sponsus.	

B. OFFICIUM SAECULARE

INVITATORIUM

Responsale Gregorianum	Antiphonarium Tommasi	Breviarium Curiae Romanae
ANT. Christus natus est nobis. Ps. Venite exultemus.	ANT. Christus natus est nobis. Ps. Venite exultemus.	ANT. Christus natus est nobis. Ps. Venite exultemus. HYMN. Christe redemptor.

IN PRIMO NOCTURNO

Responsale Gregorianum	Antiphonarium Tommasi	Breviarium Curiae Romanae
ANT. Dominus dixit ad me. Tanquam sponsus. Diffusa est gratia. ℣. Tanquam sponsus.	ANT. Dominus dixit ad me. Tanquam sponsus. Diffusa est gratia. ℣. Tanquam sponsus. ℟. De thalamo suo.	ANT. Dominus dixit ad me. Tanquam sponsus. Diffusa est gratia. ℣. Tanquam sponsus. ℟. Dominus procedens.
RESP. Hodie nobis caelorum rex. ℣. Gloria in excelsis. Hodie nobis de caelo. ℣. Gloria in excelsis. Descendit de caelo. ℣. Tanquam sponsus.	RESP. O regem caeli. ℣. Domine audivi. Hic est dies. ℣. Natus est nobis. Sancta et immaculata. ℣. Benedicta tu.	RESP. Hodie nobis caelorum. ℣. Gloria in excelsis. Hodie nobis de caelo. ℣. Hodie illuxit. Quem vidistis. ℣. Dicite quidnam.

IN SECUNDO NOCTURNO

A. OFFICIUM MONASTICUM

Cod. Hartker.

ANT. Orietur diebus domini.
Veritas de terra.
Homo natus est.
Ipse invocabit me.
Laetentur caeli.
Notum fecit dominus.

RESP. Quem vidistis.
℣. Dicite quidnam.
O magnum mysterium.
℣. Domine audivi.
Beata Dei genitrix.
℣. Ave Maria.
Sancta et immaculata.
℣. Benedicta tu.

Cod. Paris.

ANT. Orietur diebus domini.
Veritas de terra.
Ipse invocabit.
Laetentur caeli.
Beatus venter.
Notum fecit.

RESP. Beata viscera.
℣. Dies sanctificatus.
Sancta et immaculata.
℣. Benedicta tu.
Beata Dei genitrix.
℣. Beata quae.
Ecce agnus Dei.
℣. Hoc est testimonium.

B. OFFICIUM SAECULARE

Responsale Gregorianum	*Antiphonarium Tommasi*	*Breviarium Curiae Romanae*
ANT. Suscepimus Deus. Orietur in diebus. Veritas de terra.	**ANT.** Suscepimus Deus. Orietur in diebus. Veritas de terra. ℣. Natus est nobis. ℞. Qui est Christus.	**ANT.** Suscepimus Deus. Orietur in diebus. Veritas de terra. ℣. Speciosus forma. ℞. Diffusa est.
RESP. Quem vidistis. ℣. Natus est nobis. O magnum mysterium. ℣. Domine, audivi. Beata Dei genitrix. ℣. Ave Maria.	**RESP.** Congratulamini mihi. ℣. Castae parentis. Continet in gremio ℣. Virgo Dei genitrix. Ecce agnus Dei. ℣. Hoc est testimonium.	**RESP.** O magnum mysterium. ℣. Ave Maria. Beata Dei genitrix. ℣. Beata quae. Sancta et immaculata. ℣. Benedicta tu.

IN TERTIO NOCTURNO [1]

A. OFFICIUM MONASTICUM

Cod. Hartker.	*Cod. Paris.*
ANT In principio et ante saecula. Verbum caro factum est. Natus est nobis hodie.	ANT. Parvulus filius.
RESP. Beata viscera. ℣. Ave Maria. Congratulamini mihi. ℣. Castae parentis. Beata et venerabilis. ℣. Domine audivi. Verbum caro factum est. ℣. Puer natus. Ecce agnus Dei. ℣. Hoc est testimonium. Benedictus qui venit. ℣. Lapidem. Hic qui advenit. ℣. Ecce advenit. Continet in gremio. ℣. Maternis vehitur. Confirmatum est cor. ℣. Domus pudici. Nesciens mater virgo. ℣. Ave Maria.	RESP. Congratulamini mihi. ℣. Beatam me. Verbum caro factum. ℣. In principio erat. Descendit de caelo. ℣. Tanquam sponsus. [2]
Te Deum laudamus. Interrogatio : Quid regna poli. Responsio : Nunc puerum.	Te Deum laudamus.

1 *Cod. Hartker* gives the title : 'Super III Cantica : *Cod. Paris*: 'ad Cantica.'

2 To this is attached a *Prose* which is here omitted, because it did not originally belong to the Office.

B. OFFICIUM SAECULARE

Responsale Gregorianum	Antiphonarium Tommasi	Breviarium Curiae Romanae
ANT. Ipse invocabit me. Laetentur caeli. Notum fecit dominus.	ANT. Ipse invocabit me. Laetentur caeli. Notum fecit dominus. ℣. Verbum caro. ℟. Et habitavit.	ANT. Ipse invocabit me. Laetentur caeli. Notum fecit. ℣. Ipse invocabit. ℟. Pater meus.
RESP. Sancta et immaculata. ℣. Benedicta tu. Beata viscera Mariae. ℣. Ave Maria. Ecce agnus Dei. ℣. Hoc est testimonium. Benedictus qui venit. ℣. Lapidem quem. Congratulamini mihi. ℣. Beatam. ℣. Castae parentis. Beata et venerabilis. ℣. Domine audivi. Continet in gremio. ℣. Virgo Dei genitrix. Confirmatum est. ℣. Domus pudici. Nesciens mater. ℣. Ave Maria. ℣. Beata viscera. ℣. Domine audivi. O regem caeli. ℣. Tanquam sponsus. In patre manet. ℣. Ipsum genuisti. Te laudant angeli. ℣. Omnia per ipsum. Verbum caro factum est. ℣. Hodie saeculorum. Hodie dominus ex utero. ℣. Natus est nobis. Hic est dies. ℣. Ecce advenit. Hic qui advenit. ℣. Et factus est. Ecce advenit dominator.	RESP. Verbum caro factum est. ℣. Gloria in excelsis. Benedictus qui venit. ℣. A domino. Te Deum.[1]	RESP. Beata viscera. ℣. Dies sanctificatus. Verbum caro. ℣. Omnia per ipsum. Te Deum.

1 The *Te Deum* is not indeed indicated here, but is necessitated by the lack of a Respond.

IN MATUTINIS LAUDIBUS

A. OFFICIUM MONASTICUM

Cod. Hartker.

ANT. Quem vidistis.
Genuit puerpera.
Angelus ad pastores.
Facta est cum angelo.
Parvulus filius.

IN EVANGELIO
ANT. Gloria in excelsis.

AD CRUCEM.
ANT. Hodie Christus natus est.
Pastores dicite.

Cod. Paris.

ANT. Quem vidistis.
Genuit puerpera.
Angelus ad pastores.
Facta est cum angelo.
Nato domino angelorum.

RESP. Benedictus qui venit.
$\check{V}$. Lapidem.

HYMN. A solis ortus cardine.
$\check{V}$. Verbum caro.
R̲. Et habitavit.

IN EVANGELIO
ANT. Gloria in excelsis.

B. OFFICIUM SAECULARE

Responsale Gregorianum	*Antiphonarium Tommasi*	*Breviarium Curiae Romanae*
ANT. Quem vidistis.	ANT. Quem vidistis.	ANT. Quem vidistis.
Genuit puerpera.	Genuit puerpera.	Genuit puerpera.
Facta est cum angelo.	Ecce advenit dominator.	Angelus ad pastores.
Angelus ad pastores.	Angelus ad pastores.	Facta est cum angelo.
Parvulus filius.	Facta est cum angelo.	Parvulus filius.
℣. Benedictus qui venit.	℣. Puer natus est.	HYMN. A solis ortus cardine.
	℟. Filius datus est.	℣. Notum fecit dominus, alleluia.
		℟. Salutare suum, alleluia.
IN EVANGELIO	IN EVANGELIO	
ANT. Gloria in excelsis.	ANT. Gloria in excelsis.	AD BENEDICTUS
Ecce advenit dominator.	Parvulus filius.	ANT. Gloria in excelsis.
Dum medium silentium.	Puer natus est nobis.	
Virgo verbo concepit.	Verbum caro factum est.	
Nesciens mater virgo.	Natus est nobis.	
Beatus venter.	Christum natum positum.	
Verbum caro factum est.	Pastores dicite.	
Natus est nobis hodie.		
Virgo Dei genitrix.		
Ecce de quo Joannes.		
Beata mater.		

PER HORAS

A. OFFICIUM MONASTICUM

Cod. Hartker. [1]

ANT. Lux orta est.
Virgo hodie fidelis.
Hodie natus est nobis.
Gaudeamus omnes fideles.

Cod. Paris.

ANT. Lux orta est.
Hodie intacta virgo.
Gaudeamus omnes fideles.
Virgo hodie fidelis.
℣. Puer natus est.
℟. Et filius.

B. OFFICIUM SAECULARE

Antiphonarium Tommasi

Breviarium Curiae Romanae

AD PRIMAM
℟. Christe fili Dei vivi.
℣. Qui natus.

AD TERTIAM
℟. Verbum caro.

AD SEXTAM
℟. Notum fecit.

AD NONAM
℟. Viderunt omnes.

Responsale Gregorianum [2]

AD TERTIAM
℟. Verbum caro. ℣. Et habitavit.
℣. Ipse invocavit.

AD SEXTAM
℟. Notum fecit. ℣. Salutare.
℣. Verbum caro.

AD NONAM
℟. Revelabitur gloria. ℣. Et videbit.
℣. Notum fecit.

1 *Cod. Hartker* gives the title: *Ad cursus.* 2 *Responsale Gregorianum* has neither Prime nor Compline. The portions given for the other *Horae* are all *Responsoria brevia* like those of the *Breviarium Curiae Romanae.* The Antiphons were chosen from those of Lauds, and therefore the Antiphoner of Tommasi does not give them either.

AD SECUNDAS VESPERAS

A. OFFICIUM MONASTICUM

Cod. Hartker.

ANT. Tecum principium.
Redemptionem misit.
Exortum est.
Apud dominum.
De fructu.

RESP. Verbum caro.
℣. Puer natus.

IN EVANGELIO
ANT. Hodie intacta virgo.

Cod. Paris.

ANT. Tecum principium.
Redemptionem misit.
Exortum est.
Apud dominum.

RESP. Virgine cum palna.
℣. Haec tua Christe.
℣. Gloria Patri.
(per hebdom.) Verbum
caro factum.
℣. Et vidimus.
℣. Gloria Patri.

IN EVANGELIO
ANT. Hodie Christus natus est.

B. OFFICIUM SAECULARE

Responsale Gregorianum	*Antiphonarium Tommasi*	*Breviarium Curiae Romanae*
ANT. Tecum principium. Redemptionem. Exortum est. Apud dominum. De fructu. ℣. Verbum caro.	The same. ℣. Notum fecit. ℟. Salutare.	The same. HYMN. Christe redemptor omnium. ℣. Notum fecit. ℟. Salutare.
IN EVANGELIO ANT. Lux orta est. Virgo hodie fidelis. Gaudeamus omnes fideles. Hodie Christus natus est. Hodie intacta. Magnum nomen domini.	IN EVANGELIO ANT. Gloria in excelsis. Virgo hodie fidelis.	IN EVANGELIO ANT. Hodie Christus natus est.

CHAPTER XI

THE SETTLEMENT OF THE ROMAN LITURGY AND ROMAN CHANT BY GREGORY THE GREAT (†604)

The development of the Roman liturgy, and the music belonging to it, up to the close of the Middle Ages, which has been described in detail in the foregoing chapters, though manifold in character is in no way an extensive transformation; it is only the adaptation of an already existing organism to new circumstances and requirements. It presupposes the existence of a liturgical and musical Order which remains in all essential points unchanged, and it is always concerned only with the several parts of this Order, not with the structure to which the different forms belong. Now that the complete results of medieval activity in the matter of Church music lie spread out before us and we have learnt to recognize the characteristics of the musical forms as well as their correspondence with the rites that compose the liturgy, we can approach the question, Who was the builder of this huge structure, who started this movement which has been developing these thousand years?

In general, the impulse towards liturgical directions in Rome proceeded for the most part from the Popes. We are told that Pope Hormisdas (514-523) instructed his clergy in the psalms. [1] We are not told whether this statement is to be interpreted as referring to psalmody as well, and its authenticity cannot be verified. We have only one further document concerning the action of the Popes in the matter of Church music in the 5th and 6th centuries; it is the anonymous narrative of a Frankish monk who stayed in Rome and collected information on the

---

1 *Liber Pontif.* I, 269 (*ed.* Duchesne): 'Clerum composuit et psalmis erudiv it.'

state of the liturgy and liturgical chant. [1] He expresses himself only in general terms and uses almost the same words about all the Popes of whom he speaks; so he and his informants can have had scarcely more than a vague knowledge of past events. For this reason it is advisable to accept his narrative only so far as it is supported by other documents.

He states that 'the holy Pope Damasus with the support of S. Jerome introduced the liturgical Order of Jerusalem into the Roman Church.' It is an ancient tradition that Pope Damasus (366-384) turned his attention to the Roman liturgy. No less an authority than Pope Gregory the Great, as we have seen, testifies that the *Alleluia* was added to the Roman Mass by Damasus at the instance of his liturgical adviser Jerome. From his sojourn in Bethlehem Jerome was familiar with the liturgical practices of the East. Equally well known is the revision of the text of Holy Scripture by Jerome at Damasus' request, which the latter authorised for official use shortly before his death in 383. As was remarked on page 22, it is possible that the Council in Rome in 382, at which several Eastern Bishops were present, made the Romans acquainted with antiphonal psalmody. If this hypothesis be correct, then the pontificate of Damasus marks the beginning of the glorious history of the Roman Church music. Some ritualists have even asserted that Damasus regulated the whole of the Roman liturgy, [2] just as the first organization of the Milanese liturgy is attributed to Ambrose, and the Greek to Basil.

'After him,' says the anonymous monk, 'Pope Leo (440-461) arranged the chant for the Church's year, and composed important liturgical works. Anyone who refused to accept and honour them all, without exception, was excommunicated.' These statements, so far as the music is concerned, cannot be corroborated, as there is no other document upon the subject extant.

'Next Pope Gelasius (492-496) in like manner composed music for the whole ecclesiastical year, besides canonical (liturgical) writings, after an assemblage of a great many priests at the see of the holy Apostle Peter.' This assembly of clergy in Rome under the presidency of the Pope must be meant for the Council of Damasus. Nothing else is recorded of the activity of Gelasius in regard to ecclesiastical chant, but the Liturgy is indebted to him for considerable augmentation. At least the Sacramentary

---

1 *Anonymus de prandiis monachorum, qualiter monasteriis in Romana ecclesia constitutis est consuetudo* (*Patr. Lat.* cxxxvij, 1347); *cf.* Batiffol, *Bréviaire*, 349.

2 So Probst. *Die ält. Röm. Sacramentarien und Ordines* (Münster 1892), p. 82, and Bäumer, *Geschichte des Breviers*, 139.

in use in Rome and Gaul before the introduction of the Gregorian liturgy is named after him. [1] It is not impossible that some sort of organization of Church music accompanied his arrangement of the Mass. There certainly existed in Italy, and in Spain and Gaul as well, before the reforms of Gregory, a liturgical chant which was supplanted by the Gregorian Reform, just as was the case with the Gelasian Sacramentary.

Further, our author mentions Popes Symmachus (498-514), John (523-526) and Boniface (530-532): each of them, he says, arranged a course of chant for the whole year (*cantus annalis* or *cantilena anni circuli*). But in view of their short term of Office one can scarcely believe that these Popes were directly occupied with Church music.

Gregory the Great is mentioned as the last Pope but one, and to him 'a famous chant for the whole ecclesiastical year' is ascribed; Martin is the last Pope mentioned. In conclusion the author names several abbots as having been composers of a *cantus annalis*, viz. Catalenus, Maurianus and Virbonus. Of the two first we are told that they were abbots of S. Peter's. This is worthy of note, for it was from the cloisters at S. Peter's that the Gregorian Choir-school was recruited by preference.

The pith of the Frankish monk's narrative is, perhaps, that the Popes from Damasus to Martin greatly assisted the development of the Roman liturgy, and that, when the main lines of the Mass and Office were set in order, the papal singers also arranged and settled the music of the Church. This development continued for more than two centuries and a half. It would be a gain to discover more about the date of these abbots of S. Peter's. If they were contemporary with Gregory, this statement would harmonize with the tradition which ascribes the arrangement of the Roman ecclesiastical chant to this Pope.

This tradition concerns one of the most important sides of the history of Plainsong, and it requires detailed treatment.

A. THE GREGORIAN TRADITION

There is a tradition more than a thousand years old, which ascribes to Gregory I, who was Pope 590-604, the order of Mass and Divine Service with the chant belonging to it, which in the course of the Middle Ages from the 7th century onwards supplanted all others, and is, in all essentials, the one accepted to-day. It is usually expressed by such designations

---

1 Probst. *l. c.* p. 143 foll.

as 'Gregorian Sacramentary,' one which was very often used in the Middle Ages, and '*Officium Gregorianum*,' but more especially '*Antiphonarium S. Gregorii, i.e.* the whole collection of liturgical music, and 'Gregorian chant.' Thus, according to tradition, the groundwork of the whole Roman liturgy of the present day goes back to Gregory I.

During the whole of the Middle Ages no one doubted this tradition. Pierre Gussanville was the first to do so in 1675. [1] Half a century later Georg von Eckhart [2] (1729) thought it referred to Gregory II. (715-731). In our time the question has been treated afresh, in a sense unfavourable to the tradition, by Gevaert, who pronounces it in favour of Gregory II or III. (731-741). His work [3] excited interest and caused others to step forward with the results of their inquiries, such as Morin, [4] Cagin, [5] Brambach, [6] and Frere. [7] Gevaert finding himself unsupported by a single competent investigator, returned to the subject in 1895. [8] It has now had sufficient light thrown upon it from all sides, and may be considered for the present as settled. Gevaert has re-awakened a marked interest in a period of the history of plainsong that was hitherto obscure : the result has been to strengthen the tradition, so that it has now taken the rank of an historical fact, according to the conclusion reached by Belgian, French, German and English investigators.

The authors of the Middle Ages, such as S. Aldhelm (†709), Pope Hadrian I. (772-795), Alcuin [9] and many others, testify that Pope Gregory

---

1 Gussanville edited the works of Gregory in 1675. On his attitude towards the Gregorian tradition *cf.* Tommasi, *l. c.* xi, *praef.* 11.

2 *De rebus Franciae orientalis* (Würzburg, 1729), p. 718.

3 *Les origines du chant liturgique de l'Eglise Latine*, Ghent, 1890.

4 *Les véritables origines du chant Grégorien* 1890 (*Revue Bénédictine*, Maredsous, afterwards published as an independent work there in the same year).

5 *Un mot sur l'Antiphonale Missarum*, Solesmes, 1890.

6 *Gregorianisch*. Leipzig, 1895 (2nd edition 1901). See also an interesting treatise, discussing the whole question with logical exactness, *De origine cantus Gregoriani Theses xx* in the *Kathol. Kirchensänger* (Freiburg in Breisgau, 1896), No. 7.

7 In the Introduction to the *Graduale Sarisburiense* of the Plainsong and Medieval Music Society, 1894.

8 *La Mélopée antique dans le chant de l'Eglise Latine*, Ghent, 1895.

9 (*Patr. Lat.* ci, 266 foll.) Pope Hadrian's witness has reference to the Gregorian Sacramentary : 'Sed et sancta et apostolica ecclesia ab ipso sancto *Gregorio Papa ordinem missarum, solemnitatum, orationum suscipiens* etc (*Patr. Lat.* xcviij, 1252). A generation earlier Egbert, Archbishop of York (732-766), says in his *Institutio Catholica:* 'Nos autem in ecclesia Anglorum idem primi mensis jejunium, ut noster didasculus Gregorius in suo Antiphonario et *Missali libro* per Paedagogum nostrum

.edited the Sacramentary : and for this reason the Mass-books introduced into France under Pipin and Charles the Great are called Gregorian Sacramentaries to distinguish them from the earlier Gelasian books.

Gregory's Order of the Mass was not concerned with Low Masses, the *Missae Peculiares*, which continued to rest as they had previously done, even in Rome, on the Gelasian Sacramentary. It consisted, for convenience sake, of three separate parts : *Proprium de Tempore*, *Proprium de Sanctis*, and the *Missae & Orationes communes*. These three books Gregory combined into one for the purpose of the Roman Stational Masses. [1] The *Sacramentarium Gregorianum* was consequently compiled for the stational services, and was originally suited only to them; it was only later on that it was revised in Gaul to suit non-Roman conditions. This stational service was the general official service in Rome, and was solemnly celebrated in some Basilica or other church duly selected and announced beforehand. The other churches of the city were represented at it by their delegates. The people used to assemble in a different church, and, after a short prayer, went in solemn procession with singing and prayers to the church of the Station in order to be present at the Mass of the Pope or his deputy. [2] Gregory made new arrangements for this rite, and compiled the Masses necessary for the stational services from the Gelasian and also perhaps from new sources.

The Office also owes its arrangement to the same Pope, according to a well-attested tradition. Amalarius (1st half of the 9th century) who, having been on the spot, was personally familiar with the Roman use, calls Gregory 'the pre-eminent regulator of the clerical Office.' He ascribes to him the organization of the psalmody of the Office. [3] His contemporary,

---

Augustinum transmisit ordinatum et rescriptum' etc. (*Patr. Lat.* lxxix, 441). The tradition that Gregory I. was the composer of the Mass-book was specially current in England because it was he who sent Augustine with forty monks for the evangelization of England, and gave him the necessary liturgical books. As we have already seen, Gregory shews in his own writings that he effected changes in the Mass in regard to the *Kyrie* and *Alleluia*. These points formed part of his arrangement of the Mass : but his defence dealt only with these details because it was on account of them that he was attacked.

1 Johannes Diaconus, *Vita Gregorii* II, 17 (*Patr. Lat.* lxxv, 94). 2 *Cf.* above, p. 66.

3 Mabillon, *Vetera Analecta* (Paris 1723), 93. Morin, *l. c.* 18 : 'quorum Gregorius inter caetera quibus provexit ecclesiam, clericalis officii maximus enituit institutor.' And later : 'Necdum tamen tum temporis (S. Benedicti) totus ordo psallentium in Psalterio et Antiphonario ad liquidum in ordinem redactum fuerat, quod postea Gregorius Papa . . . studiosissime ordinavit institutione S. Spiritus.' And again : 'nec vituperandi sunt, sed potius laudandi, qui gregorianum tenent morem.

Hildemar, bears witness to the existence of this tradition in North Italy. ¹
The oldest MSS. of the Office bear the name of this Pope at the beginning.²
Finally, it is agreed that the rich collection of melodies which forms the
bulk of the Roman Office book was certainly extant about 600: it therefore
follows that the order of the Office itself cannot be later than Gregory I.
Some alterations were carried out later; but just as we still possess the
Missal and Breviary of the Council of Trent in spite of the festivals which
have since been introduced, so the medieval Roman Office is Gregorian.

The medieval Mass and Offices are very richly endowed with chant;
according to the tradition, S. Gregory did not *compose the melodies of the
Mass and Offices*, but either *arranged them himself or had them arranged*.
This tradition is not at all improbable, for an arrangement of the Church
music was the necessary result of the liturgical measures of the Pope.
The Gregorian Sacramentary and chant-book mutually control one
another. The liturgical Order was incomplete without the chant, for
then, as now, there were no solemn Masses or Offices without chant.
Moreover, in the Middle Ages the liturgical singers stood in a much
more intimate relation to the Altar than in later times. High and Low
Masses are distinguished from one another to-day only by fuller provision
of ceremonies and music; in both the minister is bound to say the words
of the chants, and it makes no difference whether or not a choir sings them
also; moreover the same thing applies to the parts sung at the Altar by
others than the celebrant, such as the Gospel etc. It was otherwise in
the Middle Ages. Then the sung parts had their place only in the Solemn
Mass (Low Mass had originally no Introits, no Offertory etc.); moreover
they belonged to the choir alone, and the Sacramentary contained none
of them, neither the chorus nor the solo parts; all listened to the latter,
even the celebrant, so that the action was interrupted for the time. The
medieval choir possessed liturgical functions, and that in no small degree :
in a certain sense the celebrant and choir shared in the celebration, for
each had his own task, which belonged to him and was not to be performed
by the other. In these days the choir no longer has its special liturgical
work : it is rather an adjunct to the celebration than an integral part of it.
The part rendered by the singers at the Altar is to a certain extent non-
essential, since the celebrant must always say the words of the chants himself.

---

1 Hildemar (c. 840), who spent the greater part of his life in Milan and Brescia,
says in his exposition of the Benedictine Rule : 'Maxime cum b. Gregorius, qui dicitur
Romanum officium fecisse, regulam Benedicti laudavit.' Morin, *l. c.* p. 14.

2 *E. g.* the one printed in *Patr. Lat.* lxxviij, the S. Gall Antiphoner of Hartker
(*Cod.* 390-391), and others. *Cf.* also Bäumer, *Breviergeschichte*, pp. 203 foll.

From this intimate relation between Altar and Choir we can understand that the reform of the Liturgy involved a reform of the liturgical chant; and even apart from the witness of the writers, one would be almost compelled to derive the arrangement of the chant from that of the Liturgy. [1] Thus the Gregorian tradition is well supported by internal and external evidence. The best known external testimony is the statement of John the Deacon, who wrote the life of Gregory the Great about 870. His account, which was intended for liturgical lessons in the Office, [2] says that Gregory compiled the *Cento Antiphonarius*, and founded or reorganized the *Schola Cantorum*, the celebrated Song-school in Rome, endowing it with two houses. At the time of John many memorials were preserved of his active connexion with the *Schola*, especially his authentic Antiphoner, his own copy of the book of chant. Gevaert rejects the witness of John the Deacon as unworthy of credit, because it was written nearly 300 years after Gregory's death. It is true that the biographer of Gregory relates an anecdote about the fate of Gregorian chant in Germany, France and England, in the interest of the Roman singers : but in this he was the victim of the singers to whom he went for information. In other respects his work gives quite another impression. [3] He says himself that he obtained the particulars of the Saint's life from the papal archives by order of John VIII (872-882), to

---

1 This connexion of Sacramentary and Antiphoner was especially emphasized by Brambach in his papers in the *Kath. Kirchensänger*. Gevaert, at the very beginning of the discussion aroused by him, dealt with this connexion,—which is not favourable to his view of the origin of the Music,—as though it were of secondary importance. It is not easy to say when the custom arose for the Celebrant to recite the text of the musical parts at Low Mass. It is certainly connected with the adoption of the Gregorian Mass-book for the *Missa privata* and with the compilation of the *Missale plenarium*. In the *Constitutions* of William of Hirschau (11th century) it is prescribed in the 86th chapter:—'De missa privata, quomodo sit cantanda, i.e. legenda : inde missam incipiens totum cantum, qui ad eum pertinet, pro edicto patrum nostrorum magis legit in directum, quam audeat cantare' (*Patr. Lat.* cl, 1015). The term *cantare* is very generally used also of the *Missa privata*. Gerbert, *De Cantu* I, 355.

2 *Vita S. Gregorii Magni*, II, 6 (*Patr. Lat.* lxxv, 90) : 'Deinde in domo Domini, more sapientissimi Salomonis, propter musicae compunctionem dulcedinis, Antiphonarium centonem,*cantorum studiosissimus*, nimis utiliter compilavit. *Scholam* quoque *cantorum*, quae hactenus eiusdem institutionibus in sancta Romana ecclesia modulatur, constituit: eique cum nonnullis praediis duo habitacula, scilicet alterum sub gradibus basilicae beati Petri apostoli, alterum vero sub Lateranensis patriarchii domibus fabricavit, ubi usque hodie lectus eius, in quo recubans modulabatur, et flagellum ipsius, quo pueris minabatur, veneratione congrua cum authentico Antiphonario reservatur.'

3 Brambach, *Gregorianisch.* p. 14 foll.

whom it was dedicated, and that he always adhered to that as his authority. John the Deacon is no exaggerator; at any rate it is clear from his story that about the year 870 the Roman *Schola Cantorum* dated its existence back to Gregory I. and ascribed the editing of the chant-book to him as well. If the biographer of Gregory were the only one to tell us of this, it might be said that John merely repeated legends. But there are earlier witnesses to the work of this Pope, and John the Deacon invented nothing. Pope Leo IV. (847-855) in a letter to the Abbot Honoratus, who held office near Rome, speaks of the Gregorian origin of the chant as beyond all question. He blames the Abbot because he did not accept the chant which had originated from Pope Gregory and was sung almost everywhere, and also because he did not follow the rites established by Gregory in other liturgical matters. In this letter [1] the tradition of the Apostolic See is laid down; and the Pope in the person of Leo IV. threatened anyone who rejected it with excommunication. [2] This testimony alone would suffice to prove the historical character of the tradition to any but obstinate critics.

In the first half of the 9th century the Gregorian tradition is attested by Walafrid Strabo (807-849), who mentions Gregory's liturgical and musical reforms in the same breath, [3] and by his contemporary Amalarius,

---

1 See Morin, *l. c.* p. 10, whose excellent and conclusive statement I follow in all particulars. The Pope's words run thus: 'Res una valde incredibilis auribus nostris insonuit . . . id est cum dulcedinem Gregoriani carminis, cum sua quam in ecclesia traditione canendi legendique ordinavit et tradidit, in tantum perosam habeatis, ut in omnibus in huiusmodi ratione non tantum ab hac proxima sede, sed et ab omni pene occidentali ecclesia . . . dissentiatis. Quae cunctae ecclesiae cum tanta aviditate et amore arduo praedictam traditionem Gregorii acceperunt . . . Qui plane sanctissimus papa Gregorius . . . edidit et sonum iam dictum . . . Idcirco sub excommunicationis interpositione praecipimus, ut nequaquam aliter quam et S. Papa Gregorius tradidit et nos tenemus, in lectione et modulatione peragatis.' This is, as far as I know, the first time that the expression *Carmen Gregorianum* (Gregorian Chant) is used: it is interesting that it should come from the mouth of a Pope.

2 Probst, *Die ältesten Röm. Sacramentarien und Ordines.* p. 302.

3 'Traditur denique beatum Gregorianum, sicut ordinationem missarum et consecrationem, ita etiam cantilenae disciplinam maxima ex parte in eam, quae hactenus quasi decentissima observatur, dispositionem perduxisse, sicut et in capite Antiphonarii commemoratur' (*Patr. Lat.* cxiv, 948). This note refers to the chants of the Mass; there is a second referring to those of the Office: 'Ordinem autem cantilenae diurnis seu nocturnis horis dicendae beatus Gregorius plenaria creditur ordinatione distribuisse' (*Patr. Lat.* cxiv, 956). This also Gevaert tries to invalidate (by laying stress on the words *traditur* and *creditur*) on the ground that it depends only upon a legend. But then Gregory's reform of the Mass must be in like case, for the word *traditur* refers to

who actively forwarded Gregory's work. [1] To the 8th century belongs
Pope Hadrian I. (772-795), who, in a prologue to the Gradual, which was
written to be sung before Mass on the 1st Sunday in Advent, ascribes the
origin of the chant-book to a *Praesul Gregorius*. [2] From the first half
of the 8th century comes the testimony of Egbert, Archbishop of York
(732-766), who speaks of the *Liber Antiphonarius* which Pope Gregory
gave to Augustine when he sent him forth to christianize England. [3]

The strongest testimony to the Gregorian tradition belongs to the
7th century, at the beginning of which Gregory I. died. The Venerable
Bede, the historian of the English Church, born *c.* 670, who was in an
unique position for setting forth the historical facts accurately and truth-
fully, mentions two men *not hitherto noticed, but worthy of a decisive place in
the controversy*, men who were concerned with ecclesiastical chant, and of
whom one was adorned with the honour of episcopacy. Bede praises
Putta, Bishop of Rochester, who died in 688, for his knowledge of *the
Roman Chant which he had learnt from the pupils of S. Gregory*. [4] The
Gregory here mentioned can of course be no other than Gregory I., for

---

it also. Besides, how would it be possible to acquire any knowledge of history at all,
if everything were to be regarded as fable which is handed down'?

1 *Cf.* above, p. 170. Oddly enough, in many of the MSS. of his works everything
which attests the Gregorian origin of the Roman liturgy and music has been suppressed
by those who opposed Amalarius as the man who always and everywhere furthered the
Roman use, *i. e.* by the Lyons School of Agobard and Florus, which was unwilling to
give up its older customs. Only a few MSS. have the unshortened text.

2 A prologue of this kind appears in five forms of varying length. The shortest is

    'Gregorius praesul meritis et nomine dignus,
      Unde genus ducit, summum conscendit honorem ;
      Renovavit monumenta patrum priorum : tunc
      Composuit hunc libellum musicae artis
      Scholae cantorum anni circuli : Ad te levavi' etc.

This form is probably that of Hadrian. But all five begin with the two lines *Gregorius
praesul* and *Unde genus ducit* : the last in particular suits Gregory I. alone : one of his
ancestors was the Pope Felix, to whom Gregory himself refers (*Dialog.* iv, 16) : he thus
enters upon a kind of family inheritance, 'Unde genus ducit, summum conscendit honorem.'
Gevaert at first thought that the superintendence of the editing of the chant-book of the
Mass was the work of the Syrian Pope, Gregory III. († 741). But this is impossible, for
one cannot suppose that Hadrian, who became Pope in 772 and was alive under
Gregory III., had a piece sung which praised Gregory I. as the author of a work which
he must have known proceeded from Gregory III.

3 In the passage of his *De Institutione Catholica* quoted above (p. 169). Gevaert
gets rid of this passage by declaring it to be an interpolation.

4 Beda, *Hist. Eccl.* iv, 2, at the end : 'Maxime autem modulandi in Ecclesia more
Romanorum, quem a discipulis b. Papae Gregorii didicerat, peritum' (*Patr. Lat.* xcv, 175).

Gregory II. did not ascend the throne till long after Putta's death (715) Under Bishop Acca of Hexham, who died in 709, a singer named Maban was employed, who 'had been instructed by the successors of the pupils of S. Gregory in Kent.' [1]   This notice also makes it impossible to ascribe the ordering of the Roman ecclesiastical chant to any other Gregory than the first, and, together with what has been already quoted, forms an argument not hitherto properly appreciated, but all the more important, both for the existence of the Gregorian tradition in the 7th century, as well as for its truth.   Moreover Gregory's liturgical reform concerned the Church at Rome only: he had no intention of providing an order to serve for the whole Church.   Uniformity with regard to the Liturgy and Church music was not attempted until the time of the Carolingians, and then it was not the Popes who took the lead in it, but civil rulers, Pipin and Charles the Great.   In Italy, even in the neighbourhood of Rome, the older chant survived.   Only by degrees did that of Gregory prevail in Italy, as we see from the writings of Leo IV.   It is natural that the oldest proofs of the organizing activity of Gregory in the province of the Liturgy and Church music should come from English and Frankish sources.   The Anglo-Saxons became acquainted with his reforms in his lifetime, and the Franks under Pipin and Charles.

It is far from true that Gregory's zeal for Church music is only attested by his biographers who wrote in the 2nd half of the 9th century: on the contrary, it is attested wherever it could have been known: the writings of the Venerable Bede in particular take us back even to the century of the death of Gregory I.   Therefore it is no exaggeration to assert, that few historical facts are confirmed by such important and direct proofs as S. Gregory's activity in the matter of Church music.

These quotations do not represent the whole proof of Gregory's work: it contains in itself unequivocal evidence of its origin.

B.   The 'Antiphonarius Cento'

This is the phrase used by John the Deacon to denote the book of chant which had come down from Gregory.   'Antiphoner' denotes generally a book of Church music, for the Antiphons occupy the principal part of it. *Cento* is a Low-Latin word, meaning 'patch-work,' 'combination' or

---

1 *Ib.* xcv, 270: 'Qui a successoribus discipulorum b. Gregorii Papae in Cantia fuerat cantandi sonos edoctus.'

'compilation.' Consequently *Antiphonarius Cento* means a book of Church chant compiled and put together from various sources Such an expression from the lips of John the Deacon is very striking. If he were indeed an exaggerator or a mere frivolous retailer of legends which had been foisted on him, one would expect that he would at least declare Pope Gregory to be the composer of the ecclesiastical chant. But he does not do this : he gives his hero much slighter praise when he only says of him that he collected the chants into a *Cento* ; he says nothing of his having been the actual composer of them himself. This vouches for the truth of the report which he had derived from the tradition of the Roman singers.

But it is a significant circumstance that the Gregorian Antiphoner is actually a *Cento*. It is not one complete work governed from beginning to end by one idea, but a compilation in which one can still recognize the different *strata*, resting one above another. This may be proved by the analysis of our oldest Manuscripts.

The 'authentic Antiphoner' of which John the Deacon speaks has not yet been discovered. Our oldest MSS. of the liturgical chant with musical signs date from the 9th century. For the Mass-book indeed we have MSS. of the 8th century. One comes from the Monastery of Rheinau and is now in the Cantonal Library at Zürich. [1] Another is the Gradual

---

1 The Rheinau Gradual occupies the first 13 leaves of *Cod.* xxx of the Zürich Cantonal Library. It begins with the *verso* of the first leaf; unhappily there is a gap after leaf 12. Leaf 12 concludes with the opening of the Gradual *Protector noster aspice Deus* of the 12th Sunday after Trinity, and leaf 13 begins with the words *templi habens thuribulum* of the Offertory of the *Dedicatio S. Michaelis*. Thus the texts of the Offertory and Communion of the 12th Sunday, and all the texts of the 13th, 14th, 15th, 16th and 17th Sundays after Trinity, including the Introit, Gradual and the beginning of the Offertory of the feast of S. Michael, are missing : besides, probably, the texts of the Ember days of September. After leaf 13 also at least one leaf is missing, as leaf 13 *verso* concludes with the opening of the All. *Qui sanat* of the 23rd Sunday after Trinity. If the MS. is compared with others of the oldest Chant-books, it is easy to see that it represents an abbreviation of a Roman original. Only a couple of feasts of Saints figure in it ; all the others are left out. I have compared the original with the reproduction by Gerbert in *Monumenta liturg. Aleman.* I, 362 foll., and can correct the following errors. (a) In the Offert. *Benedictus es Domine* (Quinquagesima) the opening passage *Benedictus es Domine, doce me iustificationes tuas* stands twice. Gerbert (*l.c.* p. 372) has printed it only once, probably because he supposed it to be an error of the writer, who certainly is not always very careful. (b) Gerbert (p. 376) gives no psalm-verse to the Intr. *Oculi mei* (3rd Sunday in Lent), but in the MS. may be clearly read *Psalm. Ad te Domine.* (c) In the $\stackrel{.}{\text{V}}$. *Liberator meus* of the Gradual *Eripe me Domine* (5th Sunday

of Monza, but it only contains the solos during Mass, and is consequently a *Cantatorium*. ¹ Strangely enough neither of these MSS. has notes, but only the text; still we cannot conclude from this that liturgical notation was not yet known. But though we are not in possession of the 'authentic Antiphoner' of Gregory, we are none the less in a position to reconstruct it from the oldest MSS. which have come down to us, by taking away all that was added to the Liturgy after Gregory's time. A task of this kind can be accomplished on historical lines if we may assume that the Gregorian chant was not substantially altered before the 9th century, the time of our oldest noted MSS. This however is shewn to be true by the writings quoted of Pope Leo IV., who by his papal authority assigned the chant then current in Rome to Gregory I. This excludes the possibility of any important change in the 7th and 8th centuries. Consequently the books which have been preserved to us of the 9th century give us the chant of S. Gregory.

As regards the music of the Mass, W. H. Frere has undertaken a reconstruction of the Gregorian Chant-book from a MS. of the British Museum of the beginning of the 13th century. ² It is very instructive to investigate the text of the Gregorian nucleus which remains over when the demonstrably later additions have been taken away. As the chants of the *Ordinarium Missae* have developed differently from the variable ones of the *Proprium*, and were not originally entrusted to the choir, we must not expect to find them in the oldest MSS. Nor are they in Gregory's Antiphoner. Moreover the *Temporale*—which we now

---

in Lent) the MS. has not the words *iracundis: ab insurgentibus*, which Gerbert prints (p. 379). (d) At Wednesday in Holy Week, after the Intr. *In nomine Domini*, Gerbert gives ℣ *seu psalmus;* in the MS. there is only ℣. (e) The psalm-verse opening *Domine probasti me* to the Easter Introit Gerbert has printed in small type (p. 383), like the additions from the 12th century Gradual of S. Blasien, from which he filled up gaps in his edition of the Rheinau MS. But they stand in *Grad. Rhenaug.* (f) In the Intr. *Jubilate Deo omnis terra* (3rd Sunday after Easter) Gerbert has omitted the words *date gloriam laudi eius, alleluia* before the two last Alleluias. (g) The Intr. *Factus est Dominus* (2nd Sunday after Pentecost) concludes in the MS. with *salvum me fecit, quoniam voluit me*, not as in Gerbert, *salvum me fac propter misericordiam tuam.* (h) In the Gradual *Fuit homo missus a Deo* (Vigil of S. John the Baptist) the verse begins, as in all MSS., with *Ut testimonium*, not with *Hic venit* as Gerbert gives (p. 390), in accordance with the later revision.

1 Printed by Tommasi, *l.c.* xij, p. 214.

2 In the Introduction to the *Graduale Sarisburiense.* Mr. Frere's treatise is one which it is a great pleasure to study, and gives an insight into a number of very important questions concerning the history of the Liturgy and of the liturgical chant.

call the *Proprium de Tempore*,—and the *Sanctorale*—now the *Proprium de Sanctis*—were combined. Each Saint's-day stood at the place in the book assigned to it according to the course of the Church's year—*i. e.* among the Festivals of our Lord. Only since the 12th century have the Saints'-days been separated from the *Temporale* and put together as a special section. And even still the Missals and Graduals testify, as do the corresponding books for the Office, that these were originally combined, for the separation is not carried out strictly. The feasts of S. Stephen, S. John the Evangelist and the Holy Innocents are in the *Proprium de Tempore*, but all the other Saints-days are in the *Proprium de Sanctis*. Moreover in A.D. 600 there was no *Commune Sanctorum*; the chants were specially indicated for each festival, or written out again entire, even though they had appeared already in the earlier part of the book. In the 12th century the constant repetition of the same texts and melodies led to the creation of the *Commune*; the chants for the various classes of Saints,—Apostles, Martyrs, Confessors etc.,—were written together, so that for each individual feast of one of these classes nothing but a reference to the *Commune* was necessary, unless indeed it possessed special chants of its own. [1]

The Gregorian Chant-book of the Mass was thus all in one piece, and the music was arranged for the course of the Church's year, just like the S. Gall MS. 339, from which the text of the music given in the Appendix of this book is taken.

The *Cento*-character of the Gregorian Chant-book of the Mass becomes apparent as soon as the text is subjected to a closer inspection. The oldest constituent part of the book comprises the feasts in honour of the events of the Gospel history and of the earliest Roman Saints. For

---

[1] The vigil-Mass of the Apostles was originally the vigil-Mass of S. John Evangelist : for the Mass of the day pieces were taken from the Masses of SS. Simon and Jude, and SS. Peter and Paul. The chants for the Masses of the Evangelists come from the Mass of S. Matthew with the exception of the Gradual. The *Commune unius Martyris* is chiefly compiled from the vigil-Mass of S. John Baptist, the Masses of SS. Vincent, Valentine, Vitalis, George and Gorgonius. The *Commune plurimorum Martyrum* is derived from the Masses of the Holy Innocents, SS. Felix and Adauctus, Fabian and Sebastian, Hippolytus, Cyriacus, John and Paul, Gervasius and Protasius, Nereus and Achilles, perhaps also from those of SS. Cyrinus, Processus and Martinianus, Marcellinus and Petrus, Timotheus and Symphorianus. The *Commune unius Confessoris et Pontificis* comes especially from the Masses of SS. Silvester, Marcellus and Sixtus; the *Commune unius Confessoris et Abbatis* from the Mass of S. Eusebius; and finally the *Commune Virginum* from the Masses of the B. V. M. on Jan. 1st, and of SS. Pudentiana, Sabina, Agnes and Cecilia. The tables in the Appendix of this book contain all the material requisite for testing this explanation of the origin of the *Commune*.

these texts are chosen from the Scriptures, especially from the Psalms which directly allude to the feast. See the texts for Easter and Whitsuntide, Christmas, the feasts of SS. Peter and Paul, and S. John Baptist. Feasts of non-Roman origin have the texts of the Church from which they come : for instance the Introit *Gaudeamus omnes* for the feast of S. Agatha is taken from the Sicilian Church, in which the *cultus* of the Martyr originated. [1] If the feast comes from the Greek Church, it has chants of which the texts are translated from the Greek (*cf.* p. 45). The want of uniformity in the arrangement of the texts is striking if we compare the different kinds of chants with one another. For some Masses the texts are all taken from the same source : *e.g.* the texts of the Mass of the B. V. M. on Jan 1st are from Psalm 44, those of the first Sunday in Lent from Psalm 90; but these are exceptional. The rule is that the words of one and the same Mass are of varying origin.

If we summarize the results of investigations made as to the origin of the texts of the Mass in *Cod.* 339, the following table is obtained :

THE MASS CHANTS IN THE CODEX OF S. GALL NO. 339

	From the Psalter	From other books of the Bible	Non-Biblical	Total
Introits	102	41	6	149
Graduals	104	13	1	118
Alleluias	70	14	11	95
Tracts	17	3	—	20
Offertories	82	16	4	102
Communions	64	80	3	147
Total	439	167	25	631

Out of the 631 chants of the Mass, the texts of 606 are taken from Holy Scripture and of 439 from the Psalter. Thus even in the Middle Ages the Bible remained the liturgical Chant-book, and this title is especially appropriate to the Psalter in particular. The number of texts taken from outside sources is relatively inconsiderable. The preponderance of Holy Scripture increases, if we disregard the Masses introduced for the first

---

1 Perhaps this text also is a translation from the Greek. *Cf.* above, p. 61.

time after Gregory's death : *e.g.* the Mass of the Holy Trinity, which dates from the 9th century, and that of the Dedication. The latter Mass is the only one in which the text of the Gradual is not biblical ; and thus we have the interesting result that in the book of chant, as it came from the hand of Gregory, *all the more ancient solos of the Mass, Graduals as well as Tracts, without exception had biblical texts.* Up to the time of Gregory the liturgical soloists had only the Bible in their hands. This fact not only attests the relationship which has been already asserted between the Gradual and the Tract, but it proves also,—what is of importance to us,—that the choice of the texts of the solos in the Mass was made according to one system and in compliance with an established tradition. Thus in the Gregorian *Cento Antiphonarius* the solo Graduals and Tracts form a special self-contained group.

Essentially different from this class are the remaining sets of Mass-chants. They are chosen from other points of view. As was explained in detail and shown by the above table, the non-biblical words are here more numerous : moreover books of the Bible other than the Psalter come more to the front. [1] If we compare the Graduals and Introits together we find that they are compiled on different principles. The oldest feasts have Psalm-Graduals, but Introits from other books of Holy Scripture. The order of the Introits and Graduals is thus not of the same date : that of the latter is certainly older than that of the former. For the Communions the majority of the words are taken from other biblical books than the Psalms : we have seen that the Gospels of the Mass influenced the choice of the texts of the Communions. No other class of the Mass-chants was influenced by such a consideration, and thus the Communion-texts form another *stratum* in the *Cento Antiphonarius*. No reference is made to the Gradual and the other chants of the Mass, not even to the Offertory, and so we are compelled to assume that the different chants of one and the same Mass are not all contemporary, but that the various classes of chant were fixed at different times. As the knowledge of liturgical history progresses, no doubt much more light will be thrown in detail on the superimposed *strata* of the Gregorian Chant-book. Specially noticeable is the arrangement of the texts according to the numerical order of the Psalms. This represents the latest work done upon the Chant-book. Examine the Communions of the week days of Lent. [2] Beginning with Ash Wednesday their texts are taken from Psalms 1 to 26 : exceptions are

---

1 For the following statement compare the tables in the Appendix of this book.
2 *Cf.* Cagin, *Un mot sur l'Antiphonale Missarum*, p. 14 foll.

made by the Saturday before the 1st Sunday in Lent, which is passed over, and the Thursdays. The latter interrupt the course, which jumps from Wednesday to Friday. Moreover instead of Psalms 12, 16, 17, 20 and 21 there stand texts taken from the Gospels of the days in question. It is clear that the system following the order of the Psalms was already in existence when the Thursdays received their Masses. As this happened under Gregory II. (715-731), it follows that that system and the whole Order of the Mass to which it belongs was earlier than his time. Moreover these Communions form a separate *stratum* in the Gregorian *Cento*, for their arrangement follows laws which are disregarded in the text of the other chants of the Mass. An arrangement of this kind on a larger scale appears in the text of the Sundays after Pentecost, from the 1st to the 17th, not merely in the Introits where the plan is carried out without exception, but also in the Offertories and Communions, where occasionally texts from other books of the Bible interrupt the order of the Psalms. After the 17th Sunday this arrangement is quite abandoned, and one is led to the conclusion that these two groups of Sundays did not receive their texts at the same time. The first however, which was doubtless the later in date, was already incorporated in the Chant-book when the Thursdays in Lent received their Masses under Gregory II, for it provided them with the greatest number of their chants.

The sets of Graduals for the Sundays after Pentecost are peculiar: there is one which follows the arrangement of the bulk of the Chant-book; and there is another which joins on to the arrangement which prevails in the Introit, Offertory and Communion of the same day. The latter series must be a later re-arrangement, made in order to bring the whole set of chants for the Sundays after Pentecost into the system that follows the numerical order of the Psalms. It never won its place; all MSS. except two follow the older series. But the existence of a cycle of Graduals which is not constructed like the other sets of Mass-chants again proves that the chants for the Sundays after Pentecost were not originally fixed at the same time : again we have two *strata* different in design and therefore not contemporary.

Thus the *Cento* character of the Gregorian Chant-book of the Mass is proved beyond doubt by a comparison of its constituent parts. John the Deacon was quite right when he called it a compilation. It is difficult to say for certain how many generations have worked at it. Side by side with later parts, which are distinguished by a systematic observance of definite principles of arrangement, we may see older parts, the arrangement of which is certainly lost in the remote 4th and 5th centuries. But everything added in course of time to the original plan was kept : when the plan of the Church's year had reached an almost settled state, men shrank from insisting on a strained unity which could not be attained without great inconveniences; it was preferable to retain the newly acquired arrangements side by side, partly even to combine them. Thus the book of the chant which passed together with the Gregorian Mass-book, into England, France and Germany, is no new creation, not even a new arrangement; if it were so, many of its features would have been altered; it is a collection and compilation of many interesting varieties—a *Cento*.

We have seen that the settlement of the chants preserved in it belongs neither to Gregory III. nor Gregory II. : it was previous to the pontificate of these two Popes. Gevaert, driven from his original position, now ascribes the organization of Church chant to the Greek Popes of the 7th century : Sergius I. (687-701), Benedict II. (684-685), Leo II. (682-683), and Agatho (678-681). [1] He relies on the statement of the *Liber Pontificalis*, according to which these Popes were brought up in the Roman Song-school and became duly qualified singers. However, it will not do to ascribe such a work to Popes who possessed the See of Peter for a short time only, and were confronted by other important tasks; besides, the *Liber Pontificalis* only expresses itself in general terms, and also gives us to understand that in the second half of the 7th century the liturgical chant was already set in order : otherwise it could not have been taught systematically. This new hypothesis however is proved to be untenable. The investigations of Morin and Frere have demonstrated that the newly-established feasts of the 7th century have hardly any melodies of their own : they make use of already existing ones, even when they have their own new texts. [2] This does not show that no one was able any longer to compose new melodies, for at a still later date the Office was enriched with many new settings. The reason can only be, that the book of the music of the Mass was a complete book, and that it would have seemed unwise or presumptuous to add to it. [3] Since the great festivals of the B. V. M. [4] were introduced under Sergius I. viz : the Annunciation, Assumption and Nativity; besides the Exaltation of Holy Cross and the Procession of Candlemas, one or other of their pieces of chant must have originated with him, or at least

---

1 Gevaert, *Mélopée antique*, Introduction p. 12 foll.

2 For proofs see Morin, *l.c.* 49 foll. and 73 note, Frere, *l.c.* p. 20 foll.

3 The only Mass with its own melodies which dates from the 7th century is that of the Dedication : but it is only four years later than Gregory (608).   4 The feast of the Purification is older and is cited in the Gradual of Monza as *Nativ. Simeonis.*

must have been composed at his request, if he had been the special promoter or organizer of the ecclesiastical chant. But the opposite is the case: all the chants of the Masses mentioned are taken from older Masses, viz. those of Advent and older feasts of virgins and martyrs. Again, the Procession of Candlemas offers us the remarkable spectacle of a simple adoption of a Greek text and melodies by the Roman Church. [1] Any organization of Church music under Sergius I. would have included these processions as well. But they stand in the Roman Chant-book solitary and like strangers. The text is half Latin and half Greek. The melody is unlike the others of Latin origin, as is specially noticeable in its tonality, which is entirely different from the Gregorian. This contrast as regards mode between the Greek chants adopted in Rome under Sergius I. and the remaining chants of the Antiphoner of the Mass would be quite inexplicable on the supposition that some sort of regulation of ecclesiastical chants had taken place under this Pope: both kinds of chants would then have been handled after the same fashion. [2] Consequently the organization of the liturgical chant must be older than Sergius I.: nothing remains but to place it in the time of Gregory I.

This is supported by another argument. If we open an old Gradual to-day, we find that many texts appear with two different readings. In the Mass of the first Sunday in Advent the Introit-verse begins thus: 'Vias tuas Domine *demonstra mihi;*' whereas the Gradual begins 'Vias tuas Domine *notas fac mihi.*' Whence comes this difference? The former version is that of the *Vulgate*, and the latter that of the *Itala*. The psalm-verses of the Introits and Communions, as also the *Versus ad repetendum*, are indicated only by their first words in most Chant-books of the Mass, and are not written out in full; [3] they were sung to the eight psalm-tones which were familiar to everyone, and there existed definite rules for the adapta-

---

1 *Cf.* above, p. 45. A few chants of the Palm Sunday Procession also belong to this class, *e.g.* the R̲̃. *Collegerunt.*

2 By this fact a bright light is thrown on the question of the antiquity of the *Octoechos*, the system of the four authentic and four plagal modes. As the establishment of the liturgical melody in Rome cannot have been carried out under Sergius I, as little also can the *Octoechos* have penetrated to Rome first in his time. Its Greek origin is beyond all doubt. But as its treatment in the Greek pieces first imported into Rome in the 7th century is quite different from the older Latin ones, we must conclude that it was developed differently in the two Churches. The most natural explanation is this: that it was connected with the Antiphonal chant at the beginning, then transferred to the responsorial, but differently developed by the Latins and the Greeks.

3 Thus *e.g.* in *Cod.* 339 S. Gall., *Cod* 121 Einsiedeln and others.

tion of words to music, which every Church singer knew by heart and had learnt to use by daily experience. The text of the psalm-verses required for this choral psalmody was taken from the Psalters; but since the time of Gregory these contained the Vulgate version. [1] As early as the first half of the 7th century, Isidore of Seville says that the version of S. Jerome was better than the earlier one and was therefore already in use in all the churches. It is otherwise with the musical parts of the Mass which had melodies of their own, and were therefore written out in full from the beginning, *i.e.* the Antiphons of the Introit, the Offertory and the Communion, and the solos. They follow the version of the *Itala*. [2] It therefore follows that the compilation of these chants cannot have been carried out later than Gregory, or else the version of the Vulgate would have been chosen for them too.

We can express ourselves more concisely in relation to the Office, for in this case the conditions are generally simpler, and no difference of opinion exists in the main among investigators. The settlement of the chant of the Office for the Roman Church cannot have taken place after Gregory's time,—even Gevaert has proved that convincingly, [3] by an investigation of the melodic forms of the Antiphons like that which Morin and Frere have applied to the Mass-chants. Still more frequently than in the chants of the Mass, one notices the use of the same melody, even for different texts, in the Antiphons of the Office. The reason of these repetitions is without doubt the necessity of enabling those who had no particular musical talent to take an active part in the chant of the Office. For the same reason, while the responsorial psalmody sometimes apportioned different melodies to single verses of the same psalm (*e.g.* the Tracts of the Mass), the verses of antiphonally sung Psalms on the contrary are always without exception provided with the same simple form. When this was arranged for music all the verses of the same psalm followed the same form. But this consideration also extended to the Antiphons, as the present Chant-book of the Office

---

1 Morin p. 37.

2 The question ought to be investigated more thoroughly, as it is of great importance for the chronology of the Mass chants.

3 *Mélopée antique* etc. p 172 foll. Gevaert's theory of modes however lies under grave doubts, especially the unjustifiable connexion with the secular music (*Citharodie*), and the untenable explanation of the ancient high, low and normal forms, which he desires to discover in the music of the Antiphons. That he wrongly explains the ancient expressions, σύντονος and ἀνειμένος, Dechevrens has proved in his *Etudes de science musicale* I, p. 426 foll.

demonstrates by numerous examples. [1] Many a monk or clerk, who would have found a difficulty in intoning a new and unfamiliar Antiphon, was glad to be able to sing a melody which he knew well. Thus the frequent use of the same melody considerably facilitated the prescribed execution of the Office. The number of Antiphon melodies is therefore very small in proportion to the number of texts.

For the chronology also of the Antiphons, Gevaert has utilised these Antiphon forms, and on the whole with complete success. [2] Next, he has established that Antiphons whose text belongs to the Psalter are distinguished by the great simplicity of their melodies: their compass is small, while the formation of the melodies is chiefly syllabic and unadorned, without modulations into other modes. On the other hand, those texts in particular which are taken from the prophetic books are set to splendid melodies, full of fire and interesting characterization, which bring out the meaning of the words.

Of special importance is Gevaert's proof that the texts of the Antiphons which were lastly incorporated in the Office, viz. those from the *Acta Martyrum*, have not a single melody of their own: they all adopt melodies which had been set to older texts. It therefore follows that the Office-music was settled when the texts were extracted from the *Acta Martyrum*. According to Gevaert this happened shortly after Gregory I: he inferred this from an utterance of Gregory I. declaring that, apart from Eusebius' account of the Martyrs, he possessed nothing but a list of names in a book. But it is unquestionable that the *Acta Martyrum* were appropriated for liturgical purposes in the 5th and 6th centuries in Rome, [3] and, even if Gregory's remark had the meaning which Gevaert gives it, nothing follows from it as to the practice of the church singers. The Rule of Stephen and Paul forbids Antiphons with their melodies to be sung which are not contained in the Canonical Scriptures: this prohibition presupposes that such Antiphons were in existence and were sung in the 6th century; only in the monasteries they were more conservative than in the secular churches.

---

1 Gevaert explains these repetitions as being the effect of the old Greek *Nomos*, but we do not rightly know what the proper form of this was. It was a musical form of many parts, which may perhaps be compared with the *Sonata* or *Suite*, but in no case with the Antiphon. I suspect that Gevaert arrived at this opinion through the meaning of the word—'Rule', or 'Law.'

2 Unfortunately the sources which Gevaert uses for his statement of the changes in the Antiphons are mostly very obscure, and he places printed books on the same level as the MSS.

3 Bäumer, *Breviergeschichte*, 266 foll.

Consequently it is certain that about 600 the composition of Antiphons came to an end, and thus the comparative study of the chants of the Office as well as of the Mass leads in the same manner to the result that about that time *the same arrangement of Church chant was current in Rome which is the groundwork of the medieval and also of the present liturgical music.*

The Gregorian tradition is proved by this to be a historical fact. External testimony—the statements of men who had direct dealings with it—as well as more internal testimony, taken from the Chant-books, prove it to be correct. Gregory I. is the organizer of the liturgical chant in the West, and it is properly called 'The Gregorian Chant.'

Let us try to summarize briefly Gregory's musical reform. The decree of the year 595, by which the office of the soloist was handed over to the subdeacon or to those of minor orders, seems intended to correct abuses, and not to favour the singers. The same tendency shows itself in the rubrics of the Gregorian Sacramentary, directing the Pontiff to give the sign to the *Schola* when to stop at the Introit and Communion; as also in the abbreviation of the Mass Respond sanctioned by Gregory, because it took from the singers the possibility of prolonging the Mass beyond reasonable limits. To the same context belongs the union of the *Alleluia-jubilus* with a verse, as it is highly probable that this also goes back to Gregory. Gregory may have shortened the *jubilus*. Although he took care that the soloists should be moderate in their share of the public worship, he did not radically alter the old and hallowed forms of the Mass-chant, but preferred to unite the old chants still more closely to the Liturgy by linking them with liturgical words. [1] At any rate, in Gregory's reform there is an unmistakeable leaning towards severity with the singers, which quite agrees with the portrait which history draws of this great man. Much light is thrown upon the intentions of the man who composed the Liturgy which still prevails to-day by his action with regard to it. Having to decide whether to re-introduce the whole responsorial psalm, as it

---

[1] It has at all times been the principle of the Church not simply to abolish practices which, though justifiable in their existence, might give occasion for abuses in their performance, but so to regulate them that the abuses disappeared. Thus, in spite of all opposition, it has permitted hymns not taken from Holy Scripture; thus it has honoured melismatic chant and given it a permanent abode in the Liturgy. Accordingly musicians, who in 1600 altered the *Alleluia* chants according to their subjective taste, acted neither in the spirit of the Church nor in that of the Roman liturgy; they perverted many compositions which were reckoned among the most artistic works of the Middle Ages into disconnected forms without order or symmetry, satisfactory neither to musicians nor to people of taste.

was originally, without very rich melodies, or to content himself with a single Gradual-verse, leaving untouched the florid solo passages with which the singers had ornamented it, he chose the latter course; thereby he decided in favour of the *shortening of the liturgical text*, but not of the melody, and incorporated it thus into his liturgical arrangement. Sternly anxious for the dignity of the service, and rejecting all abuses, Gregory had a wonderful feeling for the artistic structure of the whole Liturgy : he put every part in its right place, and moulded it as it best answered his purpose, but he did not fail to appreciate the beauty of a rich display of the musical art. In Gregory's liturgical arrangement the music is subordinated absolutely to the sacred action.) The chants of the choir are merely hymns of accompaniment, during which the action proceeds. It is this that is supreme. On that account a melodic setting is provided which is always unobtrusive and always remains modestly in the background. It is meant to raise the soul of the Christian to heaven, so that he may be the better able to follow what is taking place at the Altar. Quite different is the liturgical situation of the solos. Nothing goes forward in the Gregorian Mass while they are being sung ; they do not accompany, but have their own proper place; the Pontiff and all the clergy officiating at the Altar listen. Here the chant is placed on quite a different footing. The singer need not withold his skill in consideration of the action,—on the contrary he is given time and opportunity to display it—the chant itself becomes the action. The author of the Liturgy has given the soloist the definite right to sing as a soloist must sing, if his rendering is to match the splendour and sublimity of the liturgical ceremonies, and if the intention is to have a soloist sing in contrast to the choir. Thus in Gregory's Order of the Mass the chant is perfectly adapted to the end in view, and all is arranged to suit the liturgical theme and its surroundings. [1]

Were the melodies which, from the 7th century onward, spread gradually into all countries of the Latin Church, new compositions, or only artistic rearrangements of existing older ones? The latter supposition is the more probable one ; it does not exclude the possibility that the papal

---

[1] How paltry in form does all later Church music seem from the point of view of the Liturgy ! During a florid Kyrie now-a-days, who thinks of what the priest is saying at the Altar in the name of the Church? who thinks at the Offertory of the sublime proceed-ings? Does it not often seem as if the priest at the Altar had to provide the liturgical accompaniment to the beautiful music? One cannot think without regret of the unhappy circumstances which have broken the bond between the Liturgy and art. And what an unnatural thing it is to put chorus melodies into the mouth of a soloist, as the modern choir-books do !

singers, or even Gregory himself, desired new compositions. As the reform of the Liturgy of the Mass by Gregory was not a new arrangement which replaced the former rites, so we must say the same of the arrangement of the chant. Before Gregory's time there were papal singers in Rome; in fact the transformation of the responsorial music of the Mass which took place between 450 and 550 (*cf.* pp. 74 foll.) demanded a system of solo singing in the Mass which we must regard as a preparatory stage to Gregory's reform. This latter was chiefly confined to shaping the existing forms to suit a single point of view. We are led to this opinion by considering the important differences of style which characterise the Chant-book of the Mass, as well as of the Office, from beginning to end. With all its variety of expression, the melodic treatment of each Introit is essentially the same: it may be distinguished at the first glance from that of a Gradual, as well as that of a Communion from that of an Offertory. *This distinction of the different styles of chant* is so constant and so marked that it cannot be accounted for merely by the contrast between antiphonal and responsorial chant; we shall do best to regard it as the result of the Gregorian reform. It is all the more worthy of admiration because, as we have seen, the texts selected for the music are not everywhere so uniform, but, as in a true *Cento*, the different kinds of disposition are combined with one another. Their melodic treatment is carried out with a care and unity of method which puts the *Cento*-character of the book quite in the background, and even causes it to be forgotten. This is one of the most splendid aesthetic characteristics of the Gregorian Chant-book; not only is it arranged on the most adequate plan, but it compels our admiration as a work of genius, for its perfect conformity to artistic laws. [1]

With the means of investigation which exist to-day one cannot definitely decide if there were written liturgical melodies before Gregory. It is not impossible, and an important ritualist has pronounced in favour of this theory. [2] It is only from imperfect acquaintance with liturgical history that the supposition could ever have arisen that the Roman singers of the 9th century were the first to introduce the rich melodies of the music of the Mass. The forms of chant differing from the Roman-Gregorian, which survived long after Gregory's death in Upper Italy and

---

[1] The havoc which the modern plainsong publications since the 17th century have made of this work, from the Medicean Gradual in 1614 and 1615 onwards, belongs to the history of artistic vandalism. Of style in particular there is nothing left; liturgical and musical ignorance and wilfulness reign supreme.

[2] Carus, *i.e.* Tommasi, in the *Prefatio* of his *Antiphonarium et Responsale*, pp. 44 foll.

Spain, [1] and which in any case are of not later date than that, constantly present forms even more melismatic. Everything shows that the chant which preceded Gregory's reform was not essentially different from that which is preserved in Milan under the name of Ambrosian. A chronicler of the Monastery of Monte Cassino [2] states that it was at the direct command of Pope Stephen IX. (1057-1058) that the convent exchanged the 'Ambrosian chant' for the Gregorian. Here the pre-Gregorian chant is simply called 'Ambrosian.' This view is on the whole true, as is shown by a comparison of the numerous chants which are common to both liturgies. Involuntarily the thought arises that the Gregorian form has resulted from a remodelling of the Ambrosian, and has been in many cases an exceedingly clever abbreviation. [3]

C. THE GREGORIAN SCHOLA CANTORUM

According to John the Deacon the Roman *Schola Cantorum* traces its foundation back to Gregory I. He gave it property to defray the expense of its maintenance, and also two houses, one near S. Peter's, and the other near the Church of the Lateran.

In the Middle Ages teaching depended much more on instruction by word of mouth than it does to-day; teaching by means of books had not the same importance. The existence of musical instruction is a particularly interesting circumstance. For reasons which we shall presently learn, musical instruction went on the assumption that the pupils must have learnt the melody by heart. Certainly there was a written copy,

---

1 *Cf.* the Ambrosian Antiphoner of the British Museum, *Cod. Add.* 34209 of the 12th century (published in *Paléographie musicale* V and VI), and the few MSS. of the Mozarabic chant, *e. g.* in the Spanish Abbey of Silos: from one of these (of the 11th century) the *Paléographie musicale* has published some Antiphons (vol. I, pl. II).

2 Gerbert, *De Cantu* I, 255.

3 *Cf.* the Ambrosian and Gregorian setting of the Gradual *A summo caelo* (British Museum, *Cod. Add.* 34209, p. 7, and *Cod.* 339, S. Gall, p. 6), and the Off. *Benedixisti* with the ℣. *Ostende nobis* (pp. 21 and 4 respectively) and many others. The comparative study of the Gregorian and Ambrosian melismatic chants is very instructive. The latter are of an astonishing length, confused in structure, and without melodic accent; the former are models of design, and are works of an extremely symmetrical and highly artistic construction.

but this was something quite different from a modern noted book from which one simply reads off the melodies. This modern method first came into existence in the 13th century at the earliest. A MS. with the melodies noted was intended for the director of the choir as a help when conducting with the hand, which he moved up and down according to the course of the melody, and when practising the chants; the soloist also had his own book—the *Liber Cantatorius*, as the book of solos for the Mass was called.

Consequently the institution of a song-school was more of a necessity in the Middle Ages than now. Each church had to be provided with a staff of liturgical singers. In Rome there was already an establishment of this sort before the time of Gregory. It was he who strengthened it, definitely organized it, and gave it an assured position.

We might suppose that the musical part of Gregory's reform was the work of his song-school : in that case he regulated the forms of prayer and the ceremonies, and left the arrangement and composition of the melodies to the singers of the *Schola*, which he had founded in order that they might select and execute the chants necessary and complementary to his Order. He then gave their work his recognition and approval. The papal singers, then, were not actually in error later on, in ascribing to their organizer the musical side of the liturgical reform also; for *quod quis per alium fecit, ipse fecisse dicitur*. One cannot go a step further from the tradition without contradicting the established fact that the chants of the Mass, like those of the Office, were already existing in collected form about 600. If we accept this supposition, the last doubt which can be entertained as to the Gregorian tradition disappears. Equally do the objections disappear which have been derived from the fact that in the oldest accounts of Gregory his musical activity is not noticed, and from the decretal of 595 which forbade the Deacon to fill the office of chief singer at the Mass, and entrusted it to the subdeacon or to the minor orders. But neither objection is sufficiently justified to make this supposition a necessity. It represents the utmost that can be conceded to the opponents of the tradition. Nothing prevents us from maintaining that Gregory took a direct part in the arrangement of the music. In particular we cannot so lightly disregard the letter of Pope Leo IV. to the Abbot Honoratus, in which the Pope pronounces with his whole authority in favour of Gregory's authorship of the melodies, without setting down the Pope as deceiving or deceived. The papal singers are said to have introduced and spread the legend : then we must ask, for what purpose ? were not the liturgical chants quite as worthy of honour when the singers set them in order and the Pope sealed their work with his authority? why ascribe to him something to which he laid no claim?

The powerful impulse which Church music received from Gregory in Rome was in full operation throughout the whole of the 7th and 8th centuries. The *Schola Cantorum* in a short time acquired an unforeseen importance. In every country it proved itself to be the powerful promoter of all efforts towards the introduction of the Roman liturgy. Its influence is shown by the fact that most of the Popes of the 7th century were closely connected with it, or came directly from it. The singing boys from whom it was recruited came chiefly from orphanages (*orphanotrophia*); it was therefore called *Orphanotrophium* itself. [1] In the boarding-house which was connected with it, the boys were instructed not only in singing, but also in everything else which was then taught in schools.

Pope Honorius I. [2] (625-638) was an enthusiastic friend of Church music; also Vitalian (657-672), to whom a later tradition, unconfirmed by any older note, attributes a reorganization of Church music. [3] His successor Adeodatus (672-676) had been a chorister in the seminary, and as such had taken part in the music of the day- and night-hours. [4] Leo II. (682-683) was an excellent singer and well versed in psalmody. [5] Of Benedict II. (684-685) the same is reported. [6] Of Greek descent (like Leo II.) was Sergius I. (687-701) who came to Rome under Adeodatus and was admitted among the Roman clergy. On account of his beautiful

---

1 *Liber diurnus* of the Popes (*Patr. Lat.* cv, 116). With this may be compared the 9th *Ordo Rom. I*: 'In qualicunque schola reperti fuerint pueri bene psallentes, tolluntur inde et nutriuntur in schola cantorum et postea fiunt cubicularii' (*Patr. Lat.* lxxviij, 1003). Here we may remember that in the 17th and 18th centuries also the Italian Song-schools often sprang from orphanages and were called '*Conservatori*' from them. The Gregorian *Schola Cantorum* was thus the first Conservatorium.

2 *Liber Pontif.* I, 326: 'Divino in carmine pollens.'

3 Gerbert, *De Cantu* II, 41. Ekkehart even speaks of *Cantores Vitaliani* who performed in the presence of the Pope a chant of his own, viz. of Vitalian (Ekkehart, *Vita Notkeri Balbuli* II, 12). Ought we to connect this with the three MSS. which deviate somewhat from the Gregorian tradition, Vatican No. 5319, and Archives of S. Peter, Nos. F 22 and B 79 (*Paléographie musicale* II, 5)?

4 *Lib. Pontif.* I, 346.

5 *Ibid.* 359: 'Cantilena ac psalmodia praecipuus et in earum sensibus subtilissima exercitatione limatus.' A later tradition, which also found a place in the Roman Breviary, has made of it a complete reorganization of the chant: 'psalmodiam composuit hymnosque ad meliorem concentum redegit, artem exercitatione confirmans.' Found as early as Platina (Gerbert, *De Cantu* II, 41).

6 *Lib. Pont.* I, 363.

voice and his zeal he was made Head of the *Schola*, and gradually climbed to the highest spiritual dignity. [1] Sergius II. (844-847) also began his career as a chorister in the *Schola Cantorum*, to which Pope Leo III. admitted him. Here 'he took part in the general instruction, and learnt the mellifluous *Cantilenae*,' wherein he soon excelled all his fellow-pupils. When he became Pope, he had the buildings in which the *Schola* lived restored from their foundations, as they were in need of repair. [2] From Gregory's establishment there proceeded also Gregory II., Stephen II. and Paul I.

The chief persons of the *Schola Cantorum* were, first the director and leader of the whole, the *Prior Scholae*, also called the *Primicerius*; then the *Secundicerius*, the *Tertius*, and the *Quartus Scholae* who was also called *Archiparaphonista*, because he had under him the singing boys, the *Paraphonistæ*. Besides the boys there were also seven subdeacons. [3] All the lower Roman clergy were subordinate to the *Primicerius*, and for this reason he was a very important personage. According to Hugo Victorinus [4] the rights of the *Primicerius* were extremely extensive: he had the supervision of all the ceremonies, as far as chanting and reading were concerned, and looked after the moral conduct of the clerks. Indeed he played an important part in the choice of a Pope, and subscribed the nomination decree. For example, that by which Calixtus II. in 1119 was chosen, has, immediately after the subscription of the last Cardinal deacon, *Primicerius Scholae cantorum laudo et confirmo*. [5] Until the departure of the Pope to Avignon, the papal *Schola Cantorum* remained true to its Gregorian tradition. In Avignon the singers became acquainted with the recent novelty, measured music, and from this time onwards the papal choir turned into the paths of innovation. Its further activity does not concern the history of the liturgical chant.

We have already spoken in the 4th chapter of some of the duties of the Roman singers. Some others may be added here, which are also enjoined in the Roman books of ceremonial. While the Pontiff was vesting in the Sacristy, it was the duty of the *Primicerius* and the *Secundicerius* to help him: in particular they had to see that the different vestments sat properly. The *subdiaconus regionarius*, the subdeacon of

---

1 *Ib.* 371.

2 *Lib. Pont.* II, 86 and 92.

3 Tommasi, *l. c.* xij, 4.

4 Gerbert, *De Cantu* I, 307.

5 *Ibid.* 295.

the church in which the station was celebrated, then opened the doors of the sacristy, summoned the *Schola*, and inquired of the *Archiparaphonista*, who was to sing the *Responsorium*. The information received was delivered to the Pope in the sacristy, and he gave his consent thereto. When this consent was once given, no change in the person of the soloist was allowed. The *Archiparaphonista* himself was responsible for the observance of the command, and was threatened with excommunication if any other sang the solo than the one who had been announced to the Pope before Mass. When the Pope gave the sign to the deacon standing before him, the latter went into the Church and ordered the candles to be lit. The *Archiparaphonista* for his part betook himself to the *Schola* assembled in the presbytery, and bade them place themselves in readiness for singing. The singers then went to the Altar, and placed themselves in two rows [1] before it in the Choir, within the allotted place which was surrounded by a marble enclosure. [2] At the back stood the boys in two rows. This was the time for the *Prior Scholae* to intone the Antiphon of the Introit. At the same moment the Pope with his retinue left the sacristy. [3] The singers (with the exception of the boys) wore during Mass a long linen alb, and over it a *planeta* or *casula* which they threw back over both arms as soon as the Introit was begun, so that it folded in over the breast from outwards. [4] When the Pontiff had once reached the Altar, they might begin a new chant only when he signed to them; the same rule also held good for the Bishop's Mass. [5] The soloist used to lay aside his *planeta* before ascending the *Ambo*—the one who sang the *Responsorium* as well as the singer of the *Alleluia*. The same order

---

1 In the Byzantine Church also it was the rule for the singers to place themselves in two choirs; in the Greek Chant-books they are called the Right and the Left Choir. Each of these had at their head one Precentor, the *Domesticos* (a term which, from the relation of the Cathedral of Byzantium to the Court, was about the equivalent of 'Court-singer'). Over both was placed the *Domesticos Protopsaltes*, the leader of the whole, who had his place in the middle, between the two choirs. He intoned the Antiphons, whereupon the two choirs, each directed by its *Domesticos*, continued alternately with one another. Gerbert, *De Cantu* I, 291.

2 There is still such an enclosure to be seen in the Church of S. Clemente in Rome: other Churches still have traces of it, *e.g.* the Cathedral Church of Ravenna.

3 *Ordo Rom. I.* 6 foll. (*Patr. Lat.* lxxviij, 940 foll.).

4 Of course we must here understand the old Roman *planeta*, the wide, circular garment, closed all round like the present *cappa*. The *Ordo II.* 3 says : 'Subdiaconi de schola levant planetas cum sinu' (*Patr. Lat.* lxxviij. 969).

5 The 6th *Ordo*, which describes the Bishop's Mass, says, §5 : 'Sine cuius (*i. e.* episcopi) insinuatione cantorem nihil canere licebit' (*Patr. Lat.* lxxviij, 991).

applied to the readers. [1]   Only the one who read the Gospel placed himself on the highest step of the *Ambo* : the other readers and the singers always stood on a lower step. [2]

The singing of the Antiphons of the Office was always executed by the *cantores clerici*, the seven subdeacons : the *Primicerius* intoned the first Antiphon, the *Secundicerius* the second, and so on, with the exception of some Antiphons *ad Evangelium* on Easter-day which the deacons had to sing.   In the oldest service-books it is always the *Primicerius* or *cantor* who intones the Antiphon, never the Pontiff or Officiant.   Doubtless the two choirs sang these intonations chanting in turn.   On feast-days, however, the *Primicerius* was always the first to precent, at least in Rome. [3]

Later, the Roman singers attributed directly to Gregory the *composition* of the melodies, an idea which also spread outside Rome.   It does not quite correspond with the historical order of things, but it is conceivable.   The Antiphoner of Hartker, the monk of S. Gall, contains on one of its first pages the following figurative representation.   On his throne sits the holy Pope, and dictates to a scribe those melodies with which the Holy Spirit in the form of a dove inspires him. [4]   Another MS. introduces the Introit of the 1st Sunday in Advent with the following text to a melody : *Sanctissimus namque Gregorius, cum preces effunderet ad Dominum, ut musicum tonum ei desuper in carminibus dedisset, tunc descendit Spiritus Sanctus super eum in specie columbae et illustravit cor eius, et sic demum exorsus est canere, ita dicendo : Ad te levavi.* [5]

---

1 Amalarius, *De Off. div.* iij, 15 (*Patr. Lat.* cv, 1122).

2 *Ordo Rom. VI.* 5 (*Patr. Lat.* lxxviij, 991).

3 Tommasi, *l. c.* xi, 67.

4 *Cf.* the reproduction of the whole MS. in *Paléographie musicale*, series II, vol. I. The same representation is also in Gerbert, *De Cantu* I (before p. 1), and Lambillotte, *Antiphonaire de S. Gall, pl.* 1.

5 A MS. of the 10th or 11th century at Verona (Gerbert, *De Cantu* II, 2).   The MSS. which introduce the Introit of the 1st Sunday in Advent by this or a similar prologue (*cf.* above, p. 174) are not uncommon.   Of such MSS. as I have examined on the spot, I may mention the Gradual of the Paris National Library, *Nouv. acquis.* 1235, and the Gradual of the City Library of Chartres, 520.   In the 2nd volume of the 'INTRODUCTION' I shall print the melodies in question from these MSS.   In the 1st edition of the *Liber Gradualis* of Dom Pothier (Tournai 1883) the prologue quoted in the text is given with neums.   A certain priest named John, in a MS. of the 11th century at Monte Cassino, made a complete romance out of Gregory's work, which can be read in Gerbert, *De Cantu* II, 2.

CHAPTER XII

THE SPREAD OF THE GREGORIAN CHANT

As Gregory's reform of the Mass was regulated with a view to the Roman Stations, so the organization of ecclesiastical chant which sprang from it was primarily intended for Roman needs, *i.e.* for the Papal Chapel. Circumstances however made this the basis of the entire development, not only of this particular section of divine worship, but of Western Music in general.

Copies of the authentic Antiphoner must have reached Southern Italy in Gregory's time. Other places did not accept the new order so quickly. From the writings of Leo IV. we see that about 850, 250 years after Gregory's death, the pre-Gregorian chant was still in use in the neighbourhood of Rome; even the monastery of Monte Cassino, we are told, would not give up the Ambrosian chant without a direct command from the Pope.

The Milanese Church strenuously opposed all attempts to rob it of its chant: people and clergy clung with wonderful tenacity to their old rites and music. The patriotism of the Milanese chroniclers has drawn the veil of legend over the real occurrences that took place, so that it is impossible now to state the facts historically. Landulfus, an author of the second half of the 11th century, relates that Charles the Great wished by every means to exterminate the Milanese tradition. All the books that he could obtain were burnt or done away with: only with great trouble could Bishop Eugenius preserve the old Liturgy and its music for the city of Milan itself. But a miracle is recorded, to confirm the Milanese claim. On the Altar of S. Peter, so he says, there were laid both the books, the Ambrosian and the Gregorian, to await a decision from above; they both opened simultaneously of themselves; and this was considered to be a confirmation of their equal authority. The attempts of the legate of Pope

Nicholas II. and of Peter Damian (1059) had no better result. Four centuries later, in 1440, Pope Eugenius IV. tried through Cardinal Branda di Castiglione to move the Milanese to give up their special liturgy, but without result. The Cardinal so aroused the rage of the people that he was obliged to take flight in order to save his life. Pope Alexander VI. sanctioned the privilege of a special liturgy for the Milanese in 1497. But even so they could not yet enjoy their possession undisturbed. In the time of San Carlo Borromeo a Spanish vice-governor made himself a tool of the party hostile to the Milanese, and it was only with difficulty that the great Bishop preserved the tradition of his church. Above all, he vindicated the Roman origin of its liturgy. [1] Since then the Ambrosian liturgy with its accompanying chant has had no other attacks to withstand in Milan; it still flourishes in unimpaired strength, and is, in its main features, a worthy memorial of ancient times.

It would be strange if the Ambrosian chant had not been damaged through these assaults. Unfortunately, in the later Middle Ages many alterations were made in it; while it was also much affected by the influence of the Roman-Gregorian chant. From France also it occasionally adopted a melody. In the 12th century the Canons of the Cathedral of Milan are said to have combined French melodies with the Ambrosian; but this is a great exaggeration. An Ambrosian Antiphoner of the 13th century which Gerbert consulted has one single melody only with the superscription *Francigena* and some musical notation, viz. the Alleluia *Et lilium convallium*. [2] About the year 1280 the Milanese Breviary was enriched by the Arch-priest O(b)ricus Scacabarozus with various new offices, the texts and melodies of which were due to him: *e.g.* for the festivals of SS. Nazarius, Marcellinus, Peter, Mauritius, Anna, Sophia and others. [3] It is remarkable too that the Ambrosian Office was able to gain ground outside Milan. For some time it was used in Capua. [4] Still later, at a time when the Gregorian had already prevailed in all lands of the Latin liturgy, in the 12th century, two Ratisbon clergy, Paul von Bernried and his nephew Gebhard, approached Martin,

---

1 Guéranger, *Institutions liturgiques* I, 189 foll.

2 Gerbert, *De Cantu* I, 257. Perhaps the piece referred to was not a melody merely, but a harmonized composition : it may be proved that Italy was much visited in the second half of the 13th century by wandering musicians from the north, so that measures had to be taken to get rid of them. At that time France was the home of the *Musica mensurata.*

3 Muratori, *Antiqu. Med. Aev.* iv, 953.

4 Gerbert, *l. c.* I, 254.

the treasurer of Milan Cathedral, in order to ask for an *Antiphonarium cum notulis*. In the monastery of S. Ambrose at Prague in the 12th century, not only the Office but also the Mass was celebrated according to the Ambrosian rite at the instance of its founder, the Emperor Charles V; and in the diocese of Augsburg the Ambrosian and Roman liturgies were combined until the year 1584. [1]

Outside the district occupied by the Milanese liturgy the Roman chant reigned without a rival. The accessibility of the Roman *Schola Cantorum* facilitated its maintenance and proper efficiency; and when in the course of the 7th and 8th centuries we see teachers of the chant coming at different times to the north-west and north of Europe from Gregory's establishment, in order to make distant nations acquainted with the Roman chant, we can all the more easily see that in Italy too the liturgical chant spread very naturally from the same centre. The monasteries and Cathedral churches were bound to bestow the utmost care upon the correct performance of this important part of the Liturgy. On the whole, the development of ecclesiastical chant in Italy seems to have proceeded quietly, and there is not much information about it. The organization of the papal *Schola Cantorum* formed a model for similar establishments in monasteries and Cathedral churches. Thus we hear of a Neapolitan Bishop Athanasius (9th century) who established for himself schools of lectors and cantors. [2] The Chief Singer of each church had everywhere the same papal authority as the *Primicerius*. In a diploma issued by Otto III. the *Primicerius* of Arezzo has precedence immediately after the Archdeacon. Mention is made of a Cantor called John, who flourished in Florence in the 10th century, and in the following century of another Cantor named Rogo; nothing more is said about them. [3] One centre of the study of liturgical music was the monastery of Monte Cassino, where the traditions of S. Benedict and S. Gregory entered into a pleasing alliance. This is attested by the extant MSS. there, which are among the most precious which we possess to-day. A certain John, who probably lived in the 11th century (at least the admirable handwriting is of that date), left behind him some instructive remarks upon the way in which the teachers of singing used to conduct the choirs. Here, as in the *Schola Cantorum*,

---

1 The See of Augsburg originally belonged to the province of Milan, and from the beginning the Ambrosian rite and chant must have prevailed there. *Cf.* Hoeynck, *Geschichte der Liturgie des Bistums Augsburg,* pp. 11 foll., Bäumer, *Breviergeschichte,* 243.

2 Gerbert, *l. c.* I, 296.

3 Gerbert, *l. c.* I, 298.

the singers were seven in number: they placed themselves in two rows of three each; the *Magister* stood in the midst between them, vested in alb and cope. In his left hand he held a pastoral staff as a sign of his dignity, with the right hand he conducted, moving it up and down according to the character of the music, so that he, as it were, drew the melody in the air. His movements were followed by the other singers step by step. From this manner of conducting he was also called *Chironomica* (χειρονομικός). Before the beginning of the melody he used to give the pitch by first singing an ascending and a descending scale of five notes (clearly corresponding to the required mode). The name *Chironomica*, as well as the mode of conducting, is of Greek origin; and the seven enigmatical names, such as *Tricanos*, *Cuphos* etc., by which perhaps the notes of the octave were each designated, [1] point in the same direction. This manner of conducting is the one that was generally employed in the Middle Ages for the liturgical chants: there is evidence of its use also at Milan and S. Gall. [2]

The duties of the *Cantor*, by which name the chief singer was denoted in Italy and elsewhere, was fixed by definite rules, which give us an instructive insight into the arrangement of the church-service in the Italian Church of the 9th and succeeding centuries. With his assistant, the *Succentor*, he led all the chanting in church. Everywhere for the Mass a special choir was provided, which was composed, like the *Schola* in Rome, of monks or secular clergy, and boys. The Office on the other hand was performed by all together. Following the custom which had existed since the 4th century, the monks were placed, like the clergy, in two divisions, on the right and left of the Altar. The *Cantor* stood on the right, the *Succentor* on the left side. Both had to take care that the singers standing below them were always on the alert, that no mistakes might be made in the performance of the Antiphons, Responds, Psalms and Hymns, and, if such were made, that all might quickly get on to the right track again.

Further, the *Armarius*, who was originally practically a librarian, came to have a number of duties relating to the due performance of the Office; they are exactly prescribed in the monastic constitutions. Those of the monastery of Farfa, which were drawn up by Abbot Guido (*c.* 1093), contain the following rules on this subject. On Saturday the Order of the Services for the whole of the next week shall be fixed; a boy is to write the first words of the Responds on a slate; the *Cantor* then appoints those who

---

1 Gerbert, *l. c.* I, 320. prints the passage from the MS.
2 Kienle, in the *Vierteljahrschrift für Musikwissenschaft*, 1885, 158 foll.

are to precent the Alleluia and Respond of the Mass, and the *Armarius* those who are to read the Epistle and Gospel, and the Lessons during the Office and at meal-times. On special feasts the *Armarius* can appoint, in the place of the brother tabled as *Cantor* for the week, someone else more capable, and above all a good singer for the Invitatory. Further, he has to choose the books which are read aloud at meal-times; also to examine the chief singers and readers to see if they understand their duties; to keep all the books in proper condition, to bind them, and make corrections when necessary. In the absence of the Abbot he is to take his place in precenting the *Antiphonae ex Evangelio.* Lastly, it is his duty together with the *Cantor* to put all the books in readiness, and replace them after service. [1]

Information about the *Gallican liturgy* is scarce. It has much in common with the Milanese and Spanish; but a recent investigator [2] has put forward the opinion that the non-Roman liturgies are fundamentally identical, mere branches of the same liturgical order, of which Milan is to be regarded as the centre. However this may be, there were rites established in Gaul before the adoption of the Gregorian liturgy, and liturgical music closely connected with them. The Gallican practice has been already on several previous occasions compared with the Roman. The Order of the Mass of S. Germanus of Paris (†576) presupposes a complete order of liturgical chant; Venantius Fortunatus mentions the zealous activity of the great Bishop with regard to the psalmody of the whole community; Cæsarius of Arles was also a great promoter of this practice (*cf.* above, p. 8). In Gaul they appear to have taken a great delight in the performance of psalmody by boys; thus Gregory of Tours relates that Archbishop Nisier of Lyons kept the boys at psalmody in their early years, and that Bishop Quintain of Clermont had a boy, whose beautiful voice he had admired in a monastery, brought to him to grace the psalmody in his Cathedral. [3] Moreover Church-music was highly appreciated at the court of the Sovereign. Gregory of Tours [4] relates that Chilperic, the ruler of the Franks, composed hymns, but they were not considered to be of any particular poetical merit, as he had no knowledge of metre, and put long syllables for short, and short for long. At the baptism of his son he summoned the bishops from all parts of the kingdom, and

---

1 Guido, *Disciplina Farfensis, cap.* 28 (*Patr. Lat.* cl, 1271).
2 Duchesne, *Christian Worship.* pp. 86 foll. *Cf.* above, pp. 48 foll.
3 Gregory of Tours, *Vitae patrum* 4 (*Patr. Lat.* lxxj, 1022).
4 Gregory of Tours, *Histor. Franc.* 5, 45 (*Patr. Lat.* lxxj, 361).

made them bring their best singers with them to grace the festive occasion. During the banquet they had to take turns in displaying their skill in the execution of solos (Responds). [1]

The forms of the Gallican chant were the same as those of the chant of other churches, viz. responsorial and antiphonal, not to mention the hymns. There is no evidence as to how it was performed in detail. The result of the introduction of the Roman liturgy under Pippin and Charlemagne was that the Gallican books became scarce. It must have had strongly pronounced peculiarities as contrasted with the Roman. Walafrid Strabo declares that in the Gallican Church enthusiastic and clever musicians were not wanting, and that many of their compositions had been combined with the Roman Office since its adoption ; also that it was easy to identify these Gallican melodies, as they differed much from the Roman in text and melody. [2] As we shall see, the Roman melodies were difficult for Gallican singers, especially on account of the number of embellishments and refinements of execution : hence we may conclude that the Gallican chant was free from such things, and was simpler than the Roman.

The Gallican liturgy showed no such capacity for resistance as the Milanese. It disappeared, suppressed by the policy of the Frankish rulers, or rather, as will be shown below, it became combined with the newly-adopted Roman-Gregorian liturgy.

The Spanish liturgy, [3] side by side with its original elements which were probably common to the old Latin liturgy, had in the early Middle Ages, after the immigration of the Goths, adopted many practices from them. The Gothic compositions were often modelled on various Byzantine-Greek originals; this fact may be explained by the sojourn of various important Spanish Bishops in Byzantium, *e. g.* John of Gerona, and Leander (about 580). As the result of the conversion of the Arian Goths, towards which Leander made specially praiseworthy efforts, it was found necessary to strengthen the Gothic element still more, in order not to alienate the new converts. This stage of the Gothic liturgy was defined

---

1 It is related of King Dagobert that he was so charmed with the chanting of a nun named Nantildis that he wanted to have her for a wife (See Ambros, *Musikgesch.* II. 104). Nantildis was certainly one of his wives, but the idea that she had been a nun was an error which arose from the incorrect reading *monasterio* for *ministerio* in the Chronicle of Fredegar, 50 (*Patr. Lat.* lxxj, 643).

2 *De Reb. Eccles.* 25 (*Patr. Lat.* civ, 956).

3 Bäumer, *Breviergeschichte*, 243.

by Isidore of Seville (c. 560-636) at the council of Toledo in 633, in which the likeness of the Spanish liturgy to that of Southern Gaul was brought out. About the middle of the 7th century S. Ildephonsus of Toledo, who also is said to have composed Church music himself, introduced some improvements; as also S. Julian (†728). Since the rule of the Moors in Spain this Liturgy has received the name *Mozarabic*. At the end of the 8th century the movement had already begun which led to the adoption of the reforms of Gregory the Great, and many foreign elements seem to have crept into the Mozarabic liturgy. In spite of the opposition of the people, the Roman model triumphed in the 11th century; this was especially owing to the efforts of Pope Gregory VII, who was actively supported by King Alfonso of Castille. Since then the Roman liturgy and chant have prevailed throughout Spain, with the exception of some churches in Toledo and Valladolid, to which the Popes gave the privilege of retaining their ancient liturgies. Lastly, to the 11th century belongs the well-known Geraldus, Archbishop of Braga, who was at first *Primicerius* and teacher of chant in the monastery of Micy near Orleans, and afterwards, at the request of Archbishop Bernard of Toledo, gave instruction in Church music to the choir of that Church. [1]

The country which became acquainted with the Roman chant in the life-time of Gregory I. is that of the *Anglo-Saxons*. The spread of Christianity there is his greatest work next to the liturgical reform. It is well known that he had a special affection for this nation. In the year 596 he sent the Benedictine Abbot Augustine to England with forty companions. [2] They went to meet King Ethelbert of Kent in procession with sacred chant, and announced to him their joyful news. [3] Later on, Augustine received more helpers, among whom Bede mentions Mellitus, Justus, Paulinus and Rufinianus. Gregory provided them with everything necessary for the rites and ceremonies of divine service—with sacred vessels and ornaments, altar cloths etc., as well as manuscripts. [4] If the Pope was so much concerned to secure the reverent celebration of the service, it is certain that among the 'many manuscripts' there were those which contained the liturgical chant. Consequently the first copies of the Gregorian Antiphoner came to England.

---

1 Gerbert, *De Cantu* II, 28.

2 Ven. Bede, *Hist. Eccles.* i, 23 (*Patr. Lat.* xcv, 52).

3 *Ibid.* 25. They sang the Antiphon *Deprecamur te, Domine, in omni misericordia tua, ut auferatur furor tuus et ira tua a civitate ista, et de domo sancta tua, quoniam peccavimus, alleluia.* 4 *Ibid.* 29.

The kingdom of Kent became the centre of missionary activity. Here churches sprang up; and Augustine, now Bishop of Canterbury, planted the liturgical order of Rome on the ground newly won to Christendom. The Church music also was ordered after the Roman pattern. It was not enough to provide for the Office which was to be said in so many newly founded monasteries, but the solemn Mass in like manner required musical organization; it was also a matter of importance to make an impression on those who were to be converted, by the beauty of the services and ceremonies. Among Augustine's companions there doubtless were some who were able to execute the solos during Mass, and to teach a choir to render the choral music. As a teacher of church-chant a certain James is mentioned with praise, who was first deacon and precentor at Canterbury, and in 633 was appointed by Paulinus as his successor in ruling the Church at York. With his excellent knowledge of Church music, he soon became a highly valued teacher of ecclesiastical melodies; and, as Bede thinks necessary to relate explicitly, he taught them just as it was customary in Rome. [1] Thus the Gregorian chant took root in Northumbria also. In the year 669 Pope Vitalian sent Theodore to England as Archbishop of Canterbury, and with him as companion the priest Hadrian: it is noted of both, that they were highly experienced in all secular and ecclesiastical learning, and instructed many therein. From this time liturgical music received a special impetus in all churches, and in the North also, (particularly after Wilfrid, a northerner, became Bishop of York), under the skilful direction of Eddi Stephen, who, like James, had studied music at Canterbury. [2] An Anglo-Saxon named Aeonan gave him help in his musical tuition. Another teacher of chant was Putta, who was raised by Wilfrid to the episcopal See of Rochester which had been vacant for some time; he also gave his instruction in church chant according to the Roman use, as Bede informs us. [3]

An enthusiastic lover of Church music at this same time was Benedict Biscop. Sprung, like Wilfrid, from a highly-respected Anglo-Saxon family, he had stayed a long time abroad, and had become familiar in Rome with the liturgy of the papal church as well as with its chant. An important feature in the development of the Roman liturgy and chant in England was the sending, on his initiative, of John the *Archicantor* of the papal chapel and Abbot of S. Martin, by Pope Agatho (678-682). [4] When

---

1 Bede, *l. c. Cap.* 20.

2 Bede, *l. c.* IV, i (*Patr. Lat.* xcv, 175).

3 *Ibid.* IV, i. 174.   4 *Ibid.* IV, i. 199.

Rome agreed to send this personage, who was certainly one not easily to be spared, to the newly converted land for a considerable time, it is more than ever clear what interest was taken in the endeavours of the English clergy to conneét themselves with the Roman church in everything which concerned the Liturgy and liturgical chant. The labours of John were richly blessed, and justified the hopes that had been formed about his mission in Rome. He taught his pupils in the monastery of Wearmouth to sing and recite the '*Ordo* and *Ritus*' and whatever was appointed for the festivals of the Church's year as celebrated in the church of S. Peter at Rome. Pupils came from all quarters, and they made use of the two years sojourn of the Roman master to render themselves proficient in all that concerned Church music. In 680 John returned to Rome, and was able to give a glowing account of the success of his mission. We shall often again come across the direét teaching of Church music to the non-Italian nations by members of the papal song-school : from the very beginning this was considered by the Gregorian singers to be one of their most important tasks. They remained faithful to this duty of theirs up to the 9th century, when the Schools of Music springing up everywhere were strong enough themselves to spread the Roman chant.

Acca, the successor of Wilfrid, trod in the footsteps of his great predecessor. Having himself a great love and much knowledge of Church music, he summoned the singer Maban from Kent, [1] which was still its head quarters, in order, as it would appear, to freshen up the tradition, which had fallen into disuse about 700. He kept him with him for twelve years, a time which more than sufficed to restore the chant to its original splendour. Moreover, in the basilica which the Anglo-Saxon princess Bugge had built, there resounded antiphons, psalms, responds and hymns, as her contemporary Aldhelm (†709) relates. [2]

In the following century this development was completed by the Council of Cloveshoe in 747, in which the Fathers determined, among other things, that in all churches the liturgical chant should be carefully studied, and of course according to the Chant-book which had been sent from Rome. [3] About 885 legend says that King Alfred summoned to

---

1 *Ib.* IV, i. 270. *Cf.* above, p. 201.   2 *Patr. Lat.* lxxxix, 289.

3 'Ut uno eodemque modo dominicae dispensationis in carne sacrosanétae festivitates, in omnibus ad eas rite competentibus rebus, *i. e.* in baptismi officio, in missarum celebratione, in cantilenae modo celebrentur, iuxta exemplum videlicet quod scriptum de Romana habemus ecclesia. Item, ut per gyrum totius anni natalitiae sanétorum uno eodem die iuxta martyrologium eiusdem Romanae ecclesiae cum sua sibi conveniente psalmodia seu cantilena venerentur' (*Can.* 13). Further : 'Ut septem

Oxford a celebrated Frankish teacher of music named John, and conferred on him a professorship of Church music at the newly-founded university. His companion Grimbald also was said to be celebrated as an excellent Cantor. The English singers kept up their connexion with their Frankish colleagues. In the year 946 at the instance of the Abbot Ethelwold some monks of Corbie came to England as teachers of Church chant; towards the end of the 11th century there flourished Osbern and Goscelin, whom Bishop Herman of Salisbury brought to England with him, and who did valuable work in numerous secular and monastic churches. [1] About this same period John Cotton wrote his treatise, a work of great importance in the history of medieval music. [2]

As in Rome the position of the foremost papal singer had in course of time become very honourable and important, so in England also had the office of Cantor in the monasteries and Cathedral churches gradually become influential. It is related of many of the distinguished priests who appear in the later history of the English church, that they were Cantors; the following are mentioned as Cantors of merit: Simeon, one of the first historians of England, John of Canterbury the mathematician, the learned Wulfstan of Winchester, Thomas Walsingham the historian, William Somerset, and others. Of one Cantor, Eadred by name, it is related that the use of his voice was denied him for six years before his death; only in church was it restored to him. [3]

| The time of working and planting had lasted for a century and a half; from 750 onwards the Liturgy and liturgical chant in England had continued in a quiet and steady course. The numerous monasteries which covered the country faithfully guarded the rites and music which had been entrusted to them. [4] Then the tradition was temporarily disturbed. Thurstan of Caen, the abbot appointed to the monastery of Glastonbury

canonicae orationum diei ac noctis horae diligenti cura cum psalmodia et cantilena sibimet convenienti observentur, et ut eandem monasterialis psalmodiae parilitatem ubique sectentur, nihilque quod communis usus non admittit praesumant cantare aut legere, sed tantum quod ex sacrarum scripturarum auctoritate descendit et quod Romanae ecclesiae consuetudo permittit, cantent vel legant' (*Can.* 15). Gerbert, *De Cantu* I, 262.

1 Gerbert, *De Cantu* I, 282.   2 Published in the 2nd vol. of Gerbert's *Scriptores.*
3 Gerbert, *De Cantu* I, 299.
4 Of great importance with regard to the history of the Liturgy and chant in the English monasteries in the 11th century are the decrees issued for the Benedictine monasteries of his Church by Lanfranc, Archbishop of Canterbury (1089). The first part deserves special attention, as it treats (in ten sections) of the Liturgy of the whole Church-year, and gives exact information as to the pieces of chant (*Patr. Lat.* cl, 446 foll.).

by William the Conqueror, who was in other respects also not a pattern abbot, attempted about the middle of the 11th century to suppress the Roman chant in favour of a new and very different kind, attributed to William, monk of Fécamp. [1] The monks offered him such opposition that he was obliged to give up his project. We have no information as to the character of this new chant; it may have depended on a novel manner of execution connected with the *Organum*. The same kind of innovation is also ascribed to William of Dijon. [2]

The zealous study of the liturgical chant together with the strongly pronounced musical talent of the Anglo-Saxons bore rich fruit. Outside the churches, in the monasteries and at the palaces of ecclesiastical dignitaries the national music seems to have enjoyed great esteem; and this sometimes caused friction between the two kinds. [3] These facts are of great importance in musical history, as the art of part-singing gradually grew up through the blending of secular music (in many respects founded on an instrumental basis) with the Church chant. The art of part-singing owes its existence primarily to certain practices of instrumentalists : but the liturgical chant soon lent its best resources, and thus invested it with new forms, so that it gradually spread over the whole of the West, where the ground was in many ways prepared for it.

Through the ecclesiastical disturbances in the 16th century the Gregorian chant died out in the country which had first received it from Rome.[4]

The Popes did not think of pressing the Roman chant upon churches which already possessed adequate melodies for their liturgical use; this is clear from the way in which it was introduced into the country of the Franks. Here it was the secular rulers who urged the introduction of the Roman chant in order to unite their subjects by the links of the same Liturgy. Roman liturgy and Roman chant entered France under Pippin (751-768), the founder of the Carolingian dynasty. The opportunity came for the project when Pippin in 753 sent Bishop Chrodegang of Metz with an embassy to Rome, which in the following year resulted in the journey

---

1 Lebœuf, *Traité historique et pratique du chant ecclesiastique* (1741), p. 71.

2 Gerbert, *De Cantu* I, 262.

3 To this connexion belongs the remark of William of Malmesbury, that Thomas, Archbishop of York, banished effeminate music from his Church and restored music of a strong and serious character. Gerbert, *De Cantu* I, 283. *Cf.* also Nagel, *Geschichte der Musik in England* I, pp. 15 foll.

4 In our own day the liturgical and artistic value of the Gregorian chant has again been recognized in England; in particular in a striking manner by the Anglicans, who frequently sing the old melodies to English words.

of Pope Stephen II. to France. This Pope, as we know, crowned Pippin and his sons Charles and Carloman in S. Denys, and demanded of them protection from the Lombards. The contrast between the rites and melodies of the Roman and Frankish clergy who were in the retinues of Pippin and the Pope was brought into strong relief at the festivities which were given in honour of the latter. Pippin resolved to put an end to it, and, after negociations with the Pope, the Romans began to instruct the Franks in Roman rites and chant. [1] Pippin on his part left nothing undone to forward the introduction of the Roman chant : he was supported in particular by Bishop Chrodegang of Metz, who after travelling to Rome was profoundly interested in the Roman rites and chants. He introduced them into his church, [2] and in the year 762 issued special orders with a view to their propagation, from which it is evident that he thoroughly understood the Church music. [3] A teacher of music, who had been instructed in Rome, was entrusted with the arrangement and direction of a song-school at Metz. It seems that Pippin's efforts were not immediately followed by the desired result, for after the death of Pope Stephen he turned to his successor with a request for singers. Pope Paul I. recognized the importance of the opportunity and sent to Pippin Chant-books, an *Antiphonale* and a *Responsale*. Thus the first Gregorian books reached France. In order that their contents might not remain a dead letter, the Pope commissioned a Roman teacher of chant named Simeon to organize a school of music in Rouen, where Remigius (or Remedius) Pippin's brother was bishop, after the pattern of the one at Rome, just as a century earlier Pope Agatho had ordered one of the foremost singers of the Gregorian school to do in the land of the Anglo-Saxons. But Simeon, who was vice-principal of the Roman school, was soon obliged to return to Rome on account of the death of the principal, George, in order to occupy his position in accordance with the regulations. Pippin informed the Pope of the plans which Remigius had made, with the result that some of the members who had already profited by Simeon's instructions in Rouen betook themselves to Rome and finished their education in the *Schola Cantorum*. [4] On their return home they became the teachers of their nation, and contributed greatly to the strengthening

---

1 Walafrid Strabo, *De Rebus Eccl.* 25 (*Patr. Lat.* cxiv, 956).

2 *Patr. Lat.* xcv, 705.

3 His *Regula Canonicorum* is in *Patr. Lat.* lxxxix : chapters 50 and 51 deal with Church music.

4 The answer of the Pope is given in *Patr. Lat.* xcviij, 200.

of the new *régime*. The song-school at Metz attained to great fame in Pippin's life-time: the chanting at Chrodegang's cathedral was esteemed equal in beauty to that of the *Schola Cantorum*. Pupils came even from England, attracted by the splendour of the services, *e.g.* Sigulf, who learned the liturgical customs in Rome, but the Church music in Metz. [1]

Even more than Pippin did his successor Charles the Great strive for the union of all Christians of the Latin Church by means of the same Liturgy and the same chant. Under his father many of the bishops had held aloof, but his numerous and energetic measures could not fail to have their effect. A number of synods and decrees were concerned with the compulsory introduction of the *Cantilena Romana* and the Roman liturgy. The collection of his Capitularies contains a decree of 789, addressed to all the clergy of his empire, [2] ordering them all to learn perfectly the *Cantus Romanus*, and to perform the Nocturnal Office and the *Gradale* in the appointed manner, in accordance with the decree of his father, who had abolished the Gallican chant for the sake of conformity with the Apostolic See and the unity of the whole Church. Accordingly there are minute directions given in the same Capitulary: *e.g.* in *No. 70* the Bishops are to take care that the psalms are sung in a reverent manner, with a pause at the division of the verse, that the *Gloria Patri* is added at the end, and that the priests sing the threefold *Sanctus* (in the Mass); according to *No. 72*, if mistakes have crept in, the priests are to correct the psalms and chants scrupulously. One Capitulary, of 802, [3] which bears upon the examination of the clergy, expressly mentions that they are to be examined in psalmody and in the Day- and Night-Office according to the Roman use. [4] The synod of Aachen in 803 again enjoined on the bishops the obligation to perform the Office with their clergy *sicut psallit ecclesia Romana*, and added that they ought to erect *Scholæ Cantorum* at suitable places. The royal envoys who travelled over the whole kingdom on Charles' behalf to keep a watch on the observance of his commands, received special instructions respecting the execution of his measures about Church chant. [5] From all this it is evident that Charles tried resolutely and energetically to accomplish his cherished idea. In his

---

1 See the Life of Alcuin, the predecessor of Sigulf as abbot of Ferrières, in Jaffé, *Monum. Alcuin*, p. 16.

2 The *Capit.* of Charles in *Monum. Germ.* I, 61.

3 *Ibid.* I, 110.

4 *Schannat und Harzheim* I, 378.

5 In the *Capit.* of Charles I, 131.

Court-school at Aachen the chant was carefully studied: the Anglo-Saxon Alcuin, Charles' friend and liturgical adviser, had drawn up for its use, in his encyclopædic school-book, the elements of his theory of music, [1] viz. the doctrine of the four authentic and the four plagal modes. Alcuin had been well acquainted with it from his youth, which he had passed in the monastery at York. It was taught, together with the Roman Office, in the country of the Anglo-Saxons. One Sulpicius is celebrated as the teacher of music at this Palatine school. [2] In certain disputable questions about the antiphonal chant it soon took a solid position, and Aurelian of Réomé, a theorist of the 2nd half of the 9th century, could speak in this connexion of a tradition of the *Schola Palatina*. The same author pronounces this school to be an imitation of the Roman. [3]

Among the bishops who energetically responded to Charles' encouragement, Haito of Basle may also be mentioned (814-827); he insisted that each of his priests should possess an Antiphoner of his own, and was also anxious for the purity of the liturgical tradition, as is evident from his Capitularies. [4]

---

1 In Gerbert's *Scriptores*, vol. i.

2 In Alcuin's Poem 221 :

> 'Candida Sulpicius post se trahit agmina lector;
> Hos regat et doceat certis ne accentibus errent.
> Instituit pueros Idithun modulamine sacro,
> Utque sonos dulces decantent voce sonora,
> Quos pedibus, numeris, rhythmo stat musica, discant.'

Gerbert, *De Cantu* I, 277. A monk of S. Gall who describes the life of the Emperor (*Patr. Lat.* xcviij, 1376) relates some interesting anecdotes about the part taken by Charles in the organization of the service. As often as his business and his health allowed it, the Emperor was present at Mass as well as the Day and Night Office. All had to be prepared to execute the lessons of the day : Charles used to specify with his finger or with a staff the one whom he wished to hear. When the one chosen had sung enough, Charles gave him to understand by coughing that he was to stop. As may be imagined, all waited anxiously for this sign ; no one would have dared to go on singing, even if the passage was not ended. How it befell the poor clerk who once approached too near the Choir and then had to sing too, well or badly, although he understood nothing about it, may be read in Ambros, *Musikgesch.* II, 106.

3 His *Musica Disciplina*, a work of great importance as regards the knowledge of Church music in the time of the Carolingians, is printed in the *Scriptores* of Gerbert, vol. i. In chapter 11 he says that the *Palatini* attributed the Antiphon *O Sapientia* to the first ecclesiastical mode on account of its high pitch, though it had formerly been attributed to the second. *Cf.* also chap. 7.

4 These are in the *Monumenta Germaniae* with the Capitularies of Charles the Great, vol. i, 363 and 365.

The abolition of the Gallican rites and chant did not make such rapid progress as Charles wished: this was due, not solely to the tenacity with which ancient customs are preserved, and the opposition which everything new encounters. The Roman liturgical books demanded a state of things quite different from that in France, and some alterations were needed to adapt to Frankish customs the rites and chants which were created for the solemn offices of the Pope. This adaptation to simpler liturgical conditions proved a source of continual discord, each bishop endeavouring to effect it in a different way; and instead of unity a diversity threatened to appear, which imperilled all reform. To remedy this, Charles had the Roman Sacramentary altered for the Franks by his liturgical adviser Alcuin; [1] he also took steps for the preservation of the Roman melodies, by procuring on several occasions both singers and copies of the Gregorian Antiphoner from Rome. No new Chant-book was to be taken into use until it had been compared with that model, and been found to agree with it.

These statements as to the care of the Emperor for the purity of the Roman chant are mingled with legendary details. [2] But all agree in recognizing how near the integrity of the tradition lay to his heart, and how in every case he used the right means to keep the liturgical chant in harmony with the Roman practice. The movement often led to strife between the Roman and the Frankish singers. It is easy to understand that the Gauls did not allow themselves to be deprived of their accustomed melodies without protest; besides, the teachers from Rome, proud as they were of their skill, often neglected the moderation and prudence which are indispensable for such a task. If John the Deacon belittled as much as he could the capabilities of the Gauls and Germans, and said all sorts of rude things about them, [3] a monk of S. Gall was justified in complaining

---

1 So the *Micrologus De Eccles. Observ.* 60 (*Patr. Lat.* clj, 1020). No doubt Alcuin, who had acquired an accurate knowledge of the Roman liturgy and chant in his native country, was not without a share in the reform of the chant.

2 *E.g.* John the Deacon in his biography of Gregory I. *Patr. Lat.* lxxv, 90 foll., and the S. Gall biographers of Charles the Great. *Patr. Lat.* xcviij, 1377.

3 *Patr. Lat.* lxxv, 90: 'Huius modulationis dulcedinem inter alias Europae gentes Germani seu Galli discere crebroque rediscere insignite potuerunt, incorruptam vero tam levitate animi, quia non nulla de proprio Gregorianis cantibus miscuerunt, quam feritate quoque naturali, servare minime potuerunt. Alpina siquidem corpora, vocum suarum tonitruis altisone perstrepantia, *susceptae modulationis dulcedinem proprie non resultant*, quia bibuli gutturis barbara feritas, dum *inflexionibus et repercussionibus mitem nititur edere cantilenam*, naturali quodam fragore, quasi plaustra per gradus

of the undue self-exaltation of the Romans. [1]   At S. Gall and Metz the schools of music had shown that the abilities of the Teutons and Gauls were not at such a low level; and in no country have the Gregorian melodies met with such maltreatment as at a later period in Italy.   On the other hand, there is a story told by the monk of S. Gall who wrote the life of Charles the Great, of twelve Roman singers, who being envious of the renown of the Gauls agreed each to teach a different method of singing, and received in consequence from Charles the penalty of publicly asking pardon of the insulted Franks. [2]   Charles took pains to secure the true method as soon as he noticed variations : that is the kernel of the account given by John the Deacon, who dismisses the quarrel between Romans and Franks with the emphatic words which he puts into the mouth of Charles : 'Thus will we also return to the unpolluted sources.' [3]

In the time of Pippin and Charles there occurred an event which powerfully influenced the development of medieval music, viz. *the acquaintance of the Frankish musicians with those of Byzantium.*   In the year 757 Byzantine musicians appeared at Pippin's Court, and on the part of their Sovereign presented him with an organ.   In Byzantium this instrument, which had formerly existed solely for the purposes of profane music, had penetrated into the Church, and thenceforward it obtained a new position.   In Charles' day a yet larger instrument came to Aachen, and the S. Gall biographer of the Emperor records amazing things about it.   Of course there were also players belonging to these organs, who gave instruction in the use of the new instrument.   The above-mentioned anonymous writer relates what is probably a fable, when he says that Charles once listened to the Mattins chants of the Greeks in the Cathedral of Aachen, and, enraptured by what he heard, immediately had them translated into Latin.   The narrative of Aurelian of Réomé [4] may be similarly characterized, which recounts that when some singers asserted

---

confuse sonantia rigidas voces iactat, sicque audientium animos, quos mulcere debuerat, exasperando magis ac obstrependo conturbat.'

1 *Cod. S. Gall.* 578, p. 54 : 'ecce jactantiam Romanis consuetam in Teutones et Gallos.'   2 *Patr. Lat.* xcviij, 1577.

3 *Patr. Lat.* lxxv, 91: 'Carolus noster patricius, rex Francorum, dissonantia Romani et Gallicani cantus Romae offensus, cum Gallorum procacitas cantum a nostratibus quibusdam naeniis argumentaretur esse corruptum, nostrique e diverso authenticum antiphonarium probabiliter ostentarent, interrogasse fertur, quis inter rivum et fontem limpidiorem aquam conservare soleret? Respondentibus fontem, prudenter adjecit : Ergo et nos, qui de rivo corruptam usque hactenus bibimus, ad perennis fontis necesse est fluenta principalia recurramus.'   4 Gerbert, *Scriptores* I, 41.

that all the Antiphons could not be included in the eight modes, Charles caused four more to be instituted. It is a fact however that from this time forward we meet at every step with Greek, and therefore Byzantine, expressions among the Frankish musicians. The practice of music was also indebted to the new influence for some important suggestions.

The adoption of the Roman liturgy in the empire of the Carolingians was accomplished, not by the disappearance of the rites which had hitherto obtained, and their being replaced by the Gregorian, but rather through a blending of Roman and Frankish elements, the result of which was the medieval Roman-Frankish liturgy. This process occupied the 8th and 9th centuries, and was completed in the 10th century. We have already heard of Alcuin's transformation of the Gregorian Sacramentary. But that was not all. The Roman Office was still more conformed to the new circumstances, in fact the new liturgical work was almost exclusively concerned with this.

The Chant-book of the Mass underwent no alteration in the melodies during the whole of the Middle Ages; a book of the 15th century contains the same music as the MSS. of the 9th and 10th; moreover the secular clergy and the monks used the same book and the same chants. But as to the Office there was no such agreement; here there were differences, not in the general structure but in certain details. The bishops of the individual churches naturally exercised a certain influence over its formation: nearly every church had its own Office and its own Antiphoner, although they were fundamentally the same everywhere, including the melodies. This state of affairs lasted, as is well known, until the Council of Trent.

Amalarius, a pupil of Alcuin, inherited from his teacher the love of liturgical studies, and adopted all his ideas. [1] He worked mainly in Metz, where, as we know, liturgical activity and Roman chant had stood in high honour ever since the time of Chrodegang. The chief work of his which comes under our consideration has the title *De Ordine Antiphonarii*. [2] It is preceded by a prologue which describes the object of the work. In

---

1 On Amalarius of Metz, *cf.* Mönchemeier, Paderborn 1893, in the *Kirchenge-schichtlichen Studien* of Knöpfler, Schrörs and Sdralek. The most recent investigations of Dr. Marx ('Archbishop Amalarius of Trèves,' in the *Jahresbericht der Gesellschaft für nützliche Forschungen*, Trèves 1899) have proved, in agreement with G. Morin (*Revue Bénédictine* 1899, p. 419 foll.) and against Mönchemeier, that the Amalarius of Metz and Trèves are one and the same person.

2 *Patr. Lat.* cv, 1243 foll.

the course of his liturgical studies he had had numerous opportunities of observing the defects and irregularities of the Office-books, and he endeavoured to bring them as far as possible into agreement with the Roman original. With the permission of the Emperor Louis the Pious he undertook a journey to Rome to Pope Gregory IV. in 831 or 832, in order to study the Roman use at its source. He begged the Pope to give him an Antiphoner for the Church of Metz. But the Pope explained to him that the last which he had to dispose of had been given to the Abbot Wala of Corbie, who had lately stayed in Rome : all the other copies he needed himself. In the meantime Amalarius was able to get instruction in the peculiarities of the Roman rites and music from Archdeacon Theodore, whom the Pope had pointed out as able to give him every information. On his return to Metz he began to search for the Antiphoner of Wala, and discovered it in the monastery of Corbie. It consisted of four volumes, three of which contained the *Officium Nocturnum* and the fourth one the *Diurnum*. On comparing it with his own, he noticed with astonishment sundry variations from the Roman use, such as had been introduced by Chrodegang into the Church of Metz. Many Antiphons and Responds which stood in the new books were missing in the old Roman ones, and *vice versa*. A note in one of the volumes of the Antiphoner of Wala, *Hoc opus summus reparat Pontifex domnus Adrianus sibi memoriale per saecla*, gave him the key to the puzzle. While in Metz they had faithfully gone on using the Roman use since Chrodegang's time, some revision of the office had been undertaken in Rome under Pope Hadrian (772-795). Thus there did not exist, as he had at first supposed, a Roman Office which was unalterable, and for all time a conspicuous example for other churches. In order then to have something serviceable for the Church of Metz which did not differ too much from the Roman Office of the time, there was nothing left for Amalarius but to compile a new Antiphoner. He took many things from the new Roman Antiphoner of Wala, others from the old Roman one of Metz, and added some himself, amongst other things Antiphons and Responds which had been previously taught by Alcuin in Tours, and some for the local feasts of Metz. His book *De Ordine Antiphonarii* contains the details of these proceedings of his.

Amalarius paid especial attention to the text of the Verse of the Respond. In this he was assisted by a priest named Helisachar, who had been the Chancellor of Louis the Pious, and later received the revenues of the monastery of S. Maximian near Trèves. We have already spoken of the difference between the Gallican method of singing the Responds and that which prevailed in Rome, and was also prevalent in the Antiphoner of Wala. According to the Gallican use, after the Verse, the Respond was not repeated in full, but only the second half of it; consequently there were at times pieces fitted to one another without any logical connexion. Amalarius made a point of having only such verses as had a logical connexion with the second half of the Respond: but to secure this he proceeded in as conservative a manner as possible. [1] The work of Amalarius met with violent opposition at Lyons. Here Bishop Leitrad († 816) had introduced the Roman liturgy and set up a song-school. [2] His successor was Agobard, who was pronounced to have forfeited his office by contentions about the government in France. In 835 Amalarius was appointed administrator of the bishopric, and endeavoured, as such, to procure the introduction of his liturgical reforms into Lyons also. But a powerful antagonist arose in Florus, a highly respected master in Lyons. Agobard, after his return to the See of Lyons, contended with all his might against Amalarius. He wrote a refutation of the *De Ordine Antiphonarii*, the treatise which went with the Antiphoner of Amalarius,—under the title *De Correctione Antiphonarii*. [3] This treatise also formed the introduction to an Antiphoner which Agobard had caused to be compiled according to his own ideas. He found especial fault with that of Amalarius because it contained texts which were not derived from Holy Scripture. He had everything of that kind removed from the Antiphoner of Lyons, setting aside the rule which had been almost universal in the Church since the 4th century, by which non-biblical texts might be permitted for liturgical use. Many texts of the Antiphoner came from the Acts of the Martyrs, others were original compositions, or paraphrases of biblical texts. Thus a number of ancient Roman texts of the chant

---

1 The above-mentioned theorist, Aurelian of Réomé, also insists that the sense should not suffer at the repetitions of the Responds, and proposes that in certain circumstances the text should be slightly altered, in order that the verse may be fitted on without loss of sense to the ℟. He gives, among other examples, the ℟. *Veni Domine et noli tardare*, with ℣. *A solis ortu et occasu, ab aquilone et mari*, and says that in the part of the ℟. to be repeated after this ℣. *Et revoca dispersos in terram suam*, the *Et* should be omitted (Gerbert, *Scriptores*, I, 45).

2 In a letter to Charles the Great, Leitrad writes: 'In Lugdunensi ecclesia est ordo psallendi instauratus, ut iuxta vires nostras secundum sacri palatii ritum omni ex parte agi videatur, quidquid ad divinum exsolvendum officium ordo exposcit. Nam habeo scholas cantorum, ex quibus plerique ita sunt eruditi, ut alios etiam erudire possint' (*Patr. Lat.* xcix, 871).

3 *Patr. Lat.* civ, 330 foll.

were sacrificed to the one sided counter-reform of Agobard. He and Florus succeeded in bringing Amalarius before an ecclesiastical court and getting him condemned. [1]

In spite of all opposition the compilation of Amalarius gained for itself the esteem not only of the Church of Metz, but of most of the Churches of the Empire of the Franks. The reformers of the liturgical chant among the Cistercians in the 12th century and the Premonstratensians made use of it. [2] Even in Rome the Gallican method of singing the Responds was adopted. In fact the work of Amalarius became the general basis of the rich and interesting Roman-Gallican liturgy, which after a thousand years is still able to justify its existence. [3]

The melodic form of the Office-chants remained untouched by the reform of Amalarius. Neither in his writings nor in those of his opponent is there a syllable said of the melodies being in any way affected by Amalarius' alterations of the text. Had this been the case, Agobard and Florus would not have spared their abuse. The work of Amalarius was especially concerned with the texts of the Verse of the Respond, and for the execution of this there were fixed chant-formulas, so composed that they could be adapted to any text.

The Metz song-school, the eldest daughter of the Roman *Schola Cantorum* in the kingdom of the Franks, remained, even after Charles' death, the most influential among her numerous sisters. It was held in high esteem until the 12th century, and was always regarded as the faithful guardian of the Roman chant. [4] In the 10th century its most famous

---

1 Mönchemeier, *l. c.* In consequence of this controversy it is to be observed that, under the influence of the liturgists of Lyons, all the passages in the writings of Amalarius which call Gregory the Great the organizer of the Office have been suppressed. See Morin *l. c.* p. 23.

2 Bäumer, *Breviergeschichte* 283. We shall speak later of the Cistercian reform of the liturgical chant, and of that effected by the Dominicans.

3 A comparison of the Antiphoner of Trèves (*ed.* Hermesdorff 1864) with the *Ordines Romani* proves conclusively that the former contains much that is primitive Roman. *Cf. e.g.* above, p. 65.

4 In the 9th century the Metz chant held this position, and had the reputation of being far superior to all the other Churches in France and Germany, as John the Deacon expressly intimates: 'Denique usque hodie quantum Romano cantu Metensis cedit, tantum Metensi ecclesiae cedere Gallicanarum ecclesiarum Germanarumque cantus, ab his, qui meram veritatem diligunt, comprobatur' (*Patr. Lat.* lxxv, 91). This remark of Gregory's biographer has a polemical ring, and is directed against a tendency to belittle the merits of the Metz song-school in favour of another, which can only be S. Gall. This view is confirmed by the anonymous biographer of Charles the Great, who also

leader was Rotlandus; associated with him was Bernacer, a deacon and precentor of the Church of S. Saviour. [1] In the early years of the 11th century the bishopric of Metz was held by Theoger, who had been a Benedictine at Hirschau and at S. George in the Black Forest. He too was a great lover of Church music, and wrote a work upon it which has come down to us. [2]

When it seemed necessary, synods again enforced a due attention to Church-chant in the schools, *e.g.* the third Council of Valencia. [3] On the whole, the Frankish song-schools reached their prime in the 10th and 11th centuries. A monastery at Argenteuil near Paris was celebrated chiefly in consequence of the teaching of the Deacon Addalaldus (9th century). [4] In Paris itself Remigius of Auxerre (end of 9th century), who left behind him a tract on Greek rhythm, [5] taught dialectic and music. His teachers were Hericus, a pupil of Rhabanus Maurus, and Haymo of Halberstadt, who in their turn had received instruction from the singers who came from Rome to France, or from their first pupils. [6] The most famous pupil of Remigius was Odo, the first Abbot of Cluny, who enjoyed a great reputation as a singer and composer. His setting of the antiphons of the Office of S. Martin is spoken of as his most important work, and these are classed with the most beautiful parts of the Roman Office. Hymns on S. Julian, S. Mary Magdalene and others are ascribed to him. He died in 942. [7] There were highly esteemed song-schools at Toul, Dijon, Cambrai, Chartres and Nevers. In the latter town there laboured Hucbald

---

wrote towards the end of the 9th century; according to him, throughout the regions of France in which Latin was spoken, in place of the term *Ecclesiastica Cantilena* the term *Cantilena Metensis* was used (*Patr. Lat.* xcviij, 1378). (*Vita Carol.* I, 11). This evidence is all the more above suspicion as it comes from a monk of S. Gall. It seems in fact that the activity of the Song-school of Metz has hitherto been greatly underrated.

1 Mabillon, *Acta SS. Ord. Bened. V. saec.* 372 foll.

2 Printed in the *Scriptores* of Gerbert, vol. II.

3 The Council decreed in its 18th Canon: 'Ut de scholis quam divinae quam humanae litterarum nec non et ecclesiasticae cantilenae iuxta exemplar praedecessorum nostrorum aliquid inter nos tractetur, et, si fieri potest, statuatur atque ordinetur, quia ex huius studii longa intermissione pleraque ecclesiarum Dei loca et ignorantia fidei et totius scientiae inopia invasit.' Gerbert, *De Cantu* I, 243.

4 *Histoire littéraire Franc.* V. 249.

5 Printed in Gerbert, *Scriptores*, vol. I.

6 Lebœuf, *Traité historique et pratique sur le chant ecclésiastique.* Paris 1741, p. 8, note.

7 Sigebert, *De Script. Eccl.* c. 124 (*Patr. Lat.* clx, 573). *Cf.* also Gerbert, *De Cantu* I, 280, and II, 34. His biographer (Mabillon, *Acta SS. Ord. Bened. V saec.* p. 153)

(about 930). The cathedral school of Chartres [1] enjoyed a high reputation under Bishop Fulbert (11th century) and his pupil Arnold, who was also active as a composer, and to whom pupils flocked from afar. [2] At Dijon there was a musical instructor named William, whom we have already mentioned as the reputed author of certain novelties in the Chant, (others are ascribed to William of Fécamp), which however did not succeed in establishing themselves permanently anywhere. [3]

As the performance of the Office was deemed by the monks to be their chief duty, there were consequently similar establishments of greater or less extent in all monasteries. Efforts were made everywhere to beautify the services, and the music-master of the monastery, *i.e.* the Cantor, laid great stress on the correct and artistic performances of his singers. Church chant and, with it, the theoretical rules of music were taught as prescribed parts of the school instruction: together with arithmetic, geometry and astronomy, music formed the *Quadrivium*. A superb choir of boys was the pride of a monastery or of a secular Church of that time, as the richly developed melodies of the Responds and Alleluias were thought to be especially suited to boys' voices. It was not unusual for the psalmody in a monastery to be performed by a hundred monks and boys. [4] In Italy and England the Cantor became an important personage, and the monastic and other constitutions describe his rights and duties in detail. [5] His office soon became an honorary position, as was shewn by the title *Archicantor*. Conspicuous musical knowledge was no longer necessary for it. The post became the preliminary step to that of Abbot or Bishop. Aurelian of Réomé dedicated his musical work to the *Archicantor* Bernard, whom he calls his future Archbishop. In Metz the

---

gives the following account of the reasons which led to the composition of the Antiphons of S. Martin. The Antiphons at Mattins being too short to fill up the winter night, they at first resorted to repeating the Antiphon after each verse of the Psalms. This lasted too long for the monks, and at their repeated request Odo composed longer Antiphons. The *Dialogus de Musica* (Gerbert, *Scriptores* II) is undoubtedly genuine.

1 On the cathedral school of Chartres we now possess a model work by Clerval, *L'ancienne Maitrise de Notre-Dame de Chartres*. Paris. 1899.

2 Lebœuf, *Traité historique et pratique*. p. 24.

3 He is called *Psalmorum concentus distinguens*, and is said to have embellished them *dulcissimo melodimate*. Gerbert, *De Cantu* II, 30.

4 Angilbert, the friend of Charles the Great, organized for the monastery of S. Riquier a school and a college for one hundred boys, who were to be divided into three sections, to aid the psalmody of the monks, so that each time one hundred monks and thirty-four boys sang together. *Monum. German. Script.* XV, 178.

5 Gerbert, *De Cantu* I, 303 foll.

Roman title *Primicerius* was retained. In course of time this officer also became a high ecclesiastical dignitary. In one of the grants made to the Church of Metz his name stands before that of the Dean and the *Chorepiscopus*.[1] The latter seems to have exercised to some extent the same functions in the secular churches as the *Armarius* in the monasteries. He is mentioned as early as in the Capitularies of Charles the Great. The decrees of the Council of Cologne in 1260 call him the leader of the singers; in the Church of Trèves also he was an important personage.[2] The supervision of all the Offices was his duty. In France the *Armarius* was the representative of the Abbot in the monastery; according to a Cluniac *Ordo* of the 11th century, not only did he sing over a melody to the Abbot when it was his duty to start it, but if the Abbot were absent, he himself had to sing his Antiphons and Responds. Like the *Chorepiscopus* in the Cathedral, he had to supervise all the services in the monastic churches; and so he was the immediate superior of the actual musical leader to whom the technical execution of the Church music was entrusted.[3]

The services in nunneries were ordered in the same way: the chief singer, called *Cantorissa* or *Cantrix*, superintended the performance of the Offices and instructed the nuns in reading and singing.[4]

The care which was given to the orderly performance of the ceremonies makes it easy to understand that here and there, through studying the artistic and finished execution of the music, the severe simplicity which the monastic rule seemed to desiderate was neglected, and that occasionally an importance was attached to these things which was out of harmony with monastic observances. Thus the Cistercians later on reproached the Cluniac Order for using artistic means of enhancing the flexibility and beauty of the voice. They also considered many of the melodies in the newly introduced Offices of these monks to be licentious and contrary to their Rule.[5] Such opinions may be explained by the general line of the Cistercians, who wished to revive the original monastic severity. Some monasteries thought so much of the beautiful execution of the prescribed chants that they refused to accept novices who were not skilful in Church music, as is shewn by Abbot Peter of Andern.[6]

---

1 *Ibid*, 306.
2 Gerbert, *De Cantu*, I, 298.
3 *Ibid*, 309.
4 Ducange, *Glossarium*, *s. v.* 'Cantrix.'
5 Gerbert, *Ib.* 318.
6 *Ibid.* 284.

The 9th, 10th and 11th centuries were the best period of the Liturgy and its chant.   The churches vied with one another in the splendour and embellishment of their services, and the faithful flocked in numbers to the liturgical gatherings. | Even secular rulers did not think it beneath their dignity to take part in them, and to show an active interest in all that concerned the Liturgy; though the tradition which ascribes to Charles the Great the text and melody of the hymn *Veni Creator Spiritus* is not probable, [1] nor that which credits Charles the Bald with composing an Office in honour of the Holy Winding-sheet.   An enthusiastic admirer of the Liturgy was King Robert (†1031): whenever he was not hindered by pressing business he took part in the Canonical Hours.   He was a composer of liturgical music of the most varied kinds,—hymns, antiphons and responds.   Among the best known ones are the R̆. *Cornelius centurio* in honour of S. Peter, [2] the R̆. *Judaea et Jerusalem*, [3] which was formerly sung at the first Vespers of Christmas, and especially the R̆. *O constantia martyrum*. [4]   Even the Sequence *Veni sancte Spiritus*, which was probably composed by Innocent III., was ascribed to him, [5] as also the Notkerian Sequence *Sancti Spiritus adsit nobis gratia*.   In later times (under Louis IV.) Count Fulke of Anjou distinguished himself by his enthusiasm for the Liturgy: he used to sing the Office with the clergy, in clerical attire, and is said to have been the composer of twelve Responds in honour of S. Peter. [6]

---

1 The melody of this hymn was first connected with the Ambrosian Easter hymn *Hic est dies verus Dei*, and was afterwards transferred to the Pentecostal hymn.   It is still to be found with both texts in some later MSS., *e. g. Cod.* B. V. 23 of the City Library of Basle, of the 15th century.

2 Published in the *Processionale Monasticum*, Solesmes, p. 125.   Robert is said to have brought it as an offering to Rome on S. Peter's day, and Pope Sylvester, his former teacher, thereupon directed it to be used.   *Cf.* Bäumer, *Breviergeschichte*, p. 290.

3 *Processionale Monasticum*, p. 25.

4 Likewise the R̆R̆. *Solem institiae* (*Process. Monast.* 185), *Stirps Jesse* (*ib.* 186), *Ad nutum Domini* (*ib.* 187) in honour of the B. V. Mary.   They each consist of three Hexameters.

5 Lebœuf, *Traité historique et pratique*, p. 17.

6 *Processionale Monasticum*, p. 195.

CHAPTER XIII

THE SEQUENCES

Of the numerous monastic foundations flourishing in the Frankish and German regions which strove as though in rivalry for the *Cantilena Romana*, that of S. Gall deserves a more detailed account, because it was the centre from which new forms of Church chant proceeded. [1]

Ekkehard IV., the historian of the monastery of S. Gall, speaks of two Roman teachers of chant, Petrus and Romanus, whom Pope Hadrian in 790 sent to the Emperor Charles the Great, at his wish, with copies of the authentic Antiphoner. They did not both arrive at their destination. Romanus, being taken ill on the way across the Alps, was obliged to break his journey at S. Gall, while Petrus went on to Metz. With the Emperor's permission, Romanus remained with the hospitable monks and instructed them in the Roman chant. The song-school founded by him at S. Gall was organized entirely on the Roman pattern, and the Antiphoner which he brought with him from Rome enjoyed the same reverence as the authentic one at Rome. It was kept near the altar of S. Peter, and consulted whenever necessary. [2]

The monastery of S. Gall unquestionably depended on Rome for its chant, (apart from the Office, which was monastic,) as did all other churches and monasteries of the Gregorian-Roman rite. All the most ancient MSS. of the mass-chants clearly shew themselves, by their arrangement and

---

1 On the S. Gall song-school *cf.* the work of Schubiger, which is very important considering its date, but not critically enough arranged : *Die Sängerschule von S. Gallen*, Einsiedeln, 1858. Also the *Paléographie musicale*, I, 57, 70.

2 Ekkehard IV, *Casus S. Galli*, 47, (edition of Meyer von Knonau, p. 170.)

their feasts, to be of Roman origin, and S. Gall is no exception. On the other hand, Ekkehard's account of the direct reception of the Roman chant, and the founding of the S. Gall song-school, from Rome is not credible. In this respect he followed a tradition which obscured the real circumstances in order to confer lustre on the monastery. [1]   At any rate the anonymous author of S. Gall about 150 years later, who in 883 [2] wrote the biography of Charles the Great, [3] represents the circumstances with essential differences, thus.   When Charles noticed that the singers sent from Rome did not fulfil the hopes set on them, he sent two of his own singers to Rome for instruction.   On their return, one remained at Charles' court and the other was ordered to Metz.   The former, named Petrus, then laboured for some time at S. Gall at Charles' bidding, and taught the Roman chant from an authentic Antiphoner.   Here the second singer is not named at all, and, in contrast to Ekkehard, the founding of the S. Gall school is traced back to a Frankish singer, Petrus.   This account certainly deserves more credit than that of Ekkehard, and thus the *Cantor* Petrus, in spite of his suspicious name, [4] may be an historical personage.   The singer Romanus on the other hand rests upon too late a testimony to be placed in the same rank as Petrus.   The S. Gall song-school itself was regarded as a daughter of that of Metz.   There, ever since the time of Chrodegang, the use of the Roman chant had flourished; and if one has to trace back the S. Gall school to another non-Roman one, no other can enter into competition with that of Metz.   But it need not follow from this that the later school took the tradition of the older one as its guiding principle in everything.   There were manifold influences which affected the musical history of the S. Gall monastery.   But the number of artists was far greater on the foundation of S. Gall than in any other monastery.

In the first place Ekkehard mentions Marcellus. [5]   He flourished about 860.   In him there united for a common work the two countries

---

1 All investigators agree that the statements of Ekkehard are to be greatly mistrusted. See *e.g.* Wattenbach, *Deutschlands Geschichtsquellen*, p. 365.

2 *Cf.* Wattenbach, *Deutschlands Geschichtsquellen*, (5th ed.) I, 177.

3 Monachus Sangallensis, *De Carolo Magno* I, 10 (*Patr. Lat.* xcviij).

4 Meyer von Knonau *l.c.* declares the names Petrus and Romanus to be fictitious : these names, were intended to give support to the tradition that S. Gall received its chant direct from Rome, and it was certainly easy to invent them. Bäumer, *Breviergeschichte* 239, also considers them to have been invented.

5 Ekkehard, *Casus*. 33.

which were the first to learn the Roman chant, the islands lying to the north-west of the continent of Europe, and the kingdom of the Franks and Germans. An Irishman by birth, he had been in Rome and had been able to add to his knowledge of the Gregorian chant in its native place. With his uncle Marcus he then repaired to S. Gall, where he found a field of work corresponding to his inclinations, so that he remained there. It is not without importance that the oldest known artist of S. Gall is of Irish origin. A fact which more than anything else demonstrates the important influence of the Anglo-Irish musical customs over the practice of the rising German monastery, is the unmistakeable similarity of the notation in the oldest German plainsong MSS. and the English. The oldest S. Gall MSS. have the same graceful, well-rounded, delicate neum-forms as the English; in fact one of the oldest MSS. of Franco-German origin, if not the oldest, the so-called autograph of the Tonarius of Regino of Prüm in the Leipzig City-Library, is written entirely in Anglo-Irish neums. [1] The monks from the Island kingdom who christianized Germany certainly taught in the monasteries founded by them no other order of liturgy and chant than the one which was current among them. The foundation of S. Gall, in all that concerns Church chant, stands in close relation to the English and Irish Churches.

Side by side with Marcellus, and equal to him in ability, we find a master named Iso. He died in 871, after a long and laborious career. Among their pupils mention may be made of Hartmann, Waltram and Salomon; but the threefold constellation of Notker, Tutilo and Ratpert outshone the rest.

Notker, surnamed Balbulus, the Stammerer, was of noble family, and came to S. Gall about 840, where he died at a great age in 912, revered by all. He is called the creator of the Sequence-form. We learn its origin from a letter which he is said to have sent, at the same time as his collection of Sequences, to a friend of the S. Gall monastery, the Chancellor of Louis the Fat, Luitward of Vercelli. [2] The letter mentions certain *longissimae melodiae* which offered almost insurmountable difficulties to the memory. As a young man Notker used to meditate over some means of overcoming this difficulty by providing words. He was encouraged in this idea by the Antiphoner of a monk who had fled to S. Gall (about 860) from the monastery of Jumièges near Rouen, when it

---

1 The second part of the 'INTRODUCTION', Freiburg, 1905, has at p. 91 a reproduction of a page of this MS. in phototype.

2 *Cf. e.g. Cod.* S. Gall 381 ; *Cod.* Einsiedeln 121, and others. Printed in Gerbert *De Cantu* I, 412, note.

was destroyed by the Normans. In this book some verses were 'set to the *Sequentiæ*. [1] The Latin musicians, as we already know (p. 83) used *Sequentia* as a technical term for Alleluia-*jubili*: it was some of these then that were provided with words in the Antiphoner of Jumièges. But Notker found little satisfaction in them, as they were full of mistakes. He then set to work, following them as his model, and provided other *jubili* with words : hence the origin of the Sequences *Laudes Deo concinat orbis* and *Coluber Adae deceptor*. Thereupon his teacher Iso suggested to him that it was best that only one note should go to each syllable. The new experiments likewise met with the approval of his other teacher, Marcellus, who at once had them performed by the choir-boys. As the other monks did not fail to approve also, he worked on and gradually completed his whole collection.

Whether this account really hails from Notker, and deserves the credit hitherto given to it, we need not inquire here ; in any case it is incomplete. It is true that the MSS. of Notker's Sequence-books mention many Alleluia-*jubili* among the melodies thus transformed into Sequences. But it is important to notice that most of them are much more lengthy than the Alleluia-*jubili* found in the Chant-books of the Mass, including those of S. Gall : many Sequences have hardly anything in common with the *jubili* of the Mass but the title or first phrases. [2] The latter are seldom so extremely long, not longer than *e.g.* the neums of many Gradual-responds of the Mass. The description 'longissimae melodiæ' however exactly suits the *jubili* which are written in the MSS. along side of the texts of the Sequences. Consequently the Alleluia-*jubili* of the Chant-books of the Mass cannot, or cannot alone, have provided the material for Notker's Sequences. The MSS. above-mentioned point to the existence of other melodies also, which do not appear in any Mass-book ; such as served to introduce the Sequences, and were called *Frigdola*, *Graeca* and *Hypo-diaconissa*; sometimes these names are written in Greek characters. Others have Latin names which may be translations from the Greek, such as *Virgo plorans*, and *Puella turbata*; other melodies again are called *Organa*, *Nostra tuba* and *Symphonia*, names which point to instrumental music.

---

1 'Aliqui versus ad sequentias erant modulati.' The *jubili* were also called *neumae*: *e.g.* in Ekkehard himself: 'Jubilus i. e. neuma quem quidam in organis jubilant.' Also Hugo Cardinalis, *In explic. missae*, 11 : 'Alleluia repetitur cum neuma . . . Significatur autem per sequentias idem ac per neuma.'

2 *Cf. Cod.* S. Gall 376, 378, 379, 380, 381 and 382; and *Cod.* Einsiedeln 121. I have looked carefully through the Sequences of the Einsiedeln MS. with a view to this.

Metensis major and *minor* probably originate from Metz; and this is not remarkable, since the school of S. Gall was founded from Metz, and Notker kept up a connexion with the Church there, for he composed four hymns on S. Stephen for Ruodbert, the Archbishop of Metz. [1] One melody, called *Romana*, is generally attributed to the singer Romanus. But the greater number of these *longissimae melodiae* in the Notkerian MSS. bear simply the title of Alleluia-*jubili*; they are 23 in number.

Among the melodies used by Notker for his Sequences there are no doubt to be found Greek (Byzantine) melodies. Other facts show beyond all doubt that the monastery of S. Gall was not unconnected with the Byzantines. We meet with the Byzantine names of the modes *Nonannoeane*, *Noeagis* [2] and others in the S. Gall MSS., e g. *Cod.* 390 and 391, and others. One of the oldest writings on organ music, a tract called *De mensura fistularum organicarum*, [3] was probably written by Notker Labeo of S. Gall, about the year 1000. Now it was the musicians sent to the Frankish court under Pippin and Charles the Great who were the means of making France and Germany acquainted with the organ. They certainly gave the impulse to many innovations which occupied the musicians from the 9th century onwards: they were the fathers of the *Organum*, and also of the Sequences and Tropes. Even the name Sequence is Byzantine: it is only the translation of the Greek ἀκολουθία, which is a technical term among the Middle-Greek musicians. [4] Such a derivation of a Latin name from a Greek one is also justified by the fact that the Tropes, which sprang up at the same time at S. Gall, also took their name from Byzantine music. *Sequentia* is the name in the first place for the *longissimae melodiae*, and, later, for the new liturgical chant-form evolved from them.

The collection of the *longissimae melodiae* which gave Notker his first idea of the Sequence-form is still existing in the S. Gall MS. 484, written throughout in Latin neums. It contains, among other things, a number of greatly prolonged Alleluia-*jubili* which are provided only with the

---

1 Schubiger. *Sängerschule.* p. 55.

2 R. Schlecht has for the first time thrown light on these names, (which in the Middle Ages had already ceased to be properly understood by the theorists), in the *Choralvereinsbeilagen zur Cäcilia.* Trèves. 1876.

3 In Gerbert's *Scriptores* vol. i.

4 *Cf.* Christ, in the *Sitzungsberichten der Münchener Akademie der Wissenschaften.* 1870. II, p. 89. On the explanation of Michael Praetorius (*Syntagma musicum* I, 46) who connects the name with the announcement of the Gospel which follows (*Sequentia Sancti Evangelii etc.*), it is unnecessary to waste a single word.

vowels of the word *Alleluia*. It is thus an *Alleluiarium*. [1] The MS. bears all the signs of a foreign origin. The melodies are written from the bottom to the top, so that the singer must begin from the left hand end of the lowest line upwards. Their formation is shewn by an F, which divides them into periods composed of various neums. [2] It is remarkable that almost every period, except the first and last, is repeated. A comparison of the oldest Sequence MSS. at S. Gall and Einsiedeln shews that all are derived from *Cod.* 484; the same melodies stand in the former with text, and in the latter without text.

A peculiarity of the oldest MSS. of Notker's Sequence-book is that the Alleluia-melody which served as the original is written on the margin, at the side of each verse, so that the number of the notes indicated by the notation (neums) corresponds exactly with the number of syllables of the verse belonging to it. When the Sequence was performed, the Alleluia-melody written in the margin was to be split up into its component parts in such a way that one note should fall to every syllable of the text. Sometimes the syllables of the Sequence-verses are also each provided with their respective signs, so that the melody is recorded twice, once in the margin, as an Alleluia-melody with the notes grouped, and a second time with the notes written separately in single signs above the text. [3] A similar method of noting the whole melody in the margin is to be found in the Byzantine hymn MSS : in many of these the text of the hymn is preceded by a short indication of the melody as it is to be sung, while in others the melody is set out in full as a *Hirmos*. [4]

As regards their structure, Notker's Sequences fall into two groups : one bears a certain likeness to the Latin hymns in its preference for strophic formation; the other is marked by a lack of that symmetrical formation in its parts. Most of the Sequences belong to the former group : they may be recognized at once by their range. The latter class is represented by only comparatively few examples, which are all remarkable for their small

---

1 *Cf.* above p. 81, Schubiger *l. c.* 41 is the best to consult on the MS.

2 This F has been supposed, following Schubiger, to be an indication of *Finis* (end), but wrongly : we have here a Greek symbol which has its foundation in a practice, not yet thoroughly investigated, of Greek music. It is significant that the papyrus of the Archduke Rainer, described in 1892 by Wessely, which has preserved for us a fragment of the Orestes of Euripides, contains a similar kind of symbol. *Cf.* on this point Car. Janus. *Musici Scriptores Graeci*, 427 foll., and Crusius in the *Philologus*. 1893.

3 *Cf. Cod.* Einsiedeln 121, p. 578, Sequence *Ecce solemnis diei.*

4 Dom Pitra, *Analecta sacra* I, 202, 218, 273 and others. See also his *Prolegomena*, p. 54.

compass. A couple of examples of each of the two types will make the difference clear. I have taken them from the 10th century Einsiedeln MS. 121 of Notker's *Liber Hymnorum.*

TYPE A

is represented by four Sequences: the first is based upon the Alleluia ÿ. *Laetatus sum* of the 2nd Sunday in Advent; but it has only the first notes in common with its melody: it is at p. 508 in *Cod.* 121. The corresponding strophes are placed together and identified by numerals such as 2 and 2a: the figures after the verses refer to the number of syllables. '

IN DEDICATIONE ECCLESIAE

Laetatus sum

1	Psallat ecclesia mater illibata	12			
	et virgo sine ruga honorem	10			
	huius ecclesiae	6			
2	Haec domus aulae coelestis	8	2a	In laude regis coelorum	8
	probatur particeps	6		et ceremoniis	6
3	Et lumine continuo aemulans	11	3a	Et corpora in gremio con-	
	civitatem sine tenebris	9		fovens	11
				animarum, quae in coelo vivunt	10
4	Quam dextra protegat Dei	8	4a	Ad laudes ipsius dici.	8

---

1 For the right understanding of the structure of the Sequence, it is of great importance to retain the division into verses and parts of verses which is so strictly carried out in the oldest MSS. The writer of the MS. never deviates from it, except where the verse is too long to be contained in a single line. The notation in the margin, which is always the same for the two corresponding verse-groups, puts the proper division beyond all doubt in this respect. Hitherto no one has laid proper stress on these points; some have allowed themselves to be misled by late MSS. like the Brander MS (*Cod.* S. Gall 546 of the 16th century), used by Schubiger and others after him. As in Greek hymns three unaccented syllables often fall between two accents, the same may be noted in the Sequences, and therefore in the following tables I have assumed secondary accents only at the end of verses, since a conclusion with two unaccented syllables is inadmissible.

5 Hic novam prolem gratia par- turit [1] 11		5a Angeli cives visitant hic suos 11	
foecunda spiritu sancto,	8	et corpus sumitur Jesu,	8
6 Fugiunt universa	7	6a Pereunt peccatricis	7
corpori nocua	6	animae crimina	6
7 Hic vox laetitiae personat	9	7a Hic pax et gaudia redundant 9	

8 Hac domo Trinitatis laus   8
et gloria semper resultant.   9

The following Sequence (p. 442 of *Cod.* 121) is based upon the melody *Romana*:

In Nativ. S. Joannis Evangelistae

Romana

1 Johannes Jesu Christo   7
multum dilecte virgo   7

2 Tu eius amore carnalem	9	2a In navi parentem liquisti	9
3 Tu leve coniugis pectus	8	3a Ut eius pectoris sacra	8
respuisti Messiam secutus	10	meruisses fluenta potare	10
4 Tuque in terra positus gloriam 11		4a Quae solum sanctis in vita	
		creditur	11
conspexisti filii Dei	9	contuenda esse perenni	9
5 Te Christus in cruce trium-		5a Ut virgo virginem servares	9
phans	9		
matri suae dedit custodem	9	atque curam suppeditares	9
6 Tu te carcere flagrisque	8	6a Idem mortuos suscitas	8
fractus testimonio	7	inque Jesu nomine	7
pro Christi es gavisus.	7	venenum forte vincis	7
7 Tibi summus tacitum	7	7a Tu nos omnes precibus	7
caeteris verbum suum	7	sedulis apud Deum	7
pater revelat	5	semper commenda	5

8 Johannes Christi care. 7

Upon the Alleluia-verse of Christmas, *Dies sanctificatus*, there has been composed the following Sequence, which always stands first in the MSS. of Notker's book (*Cod.* 121, page 437).

---

[1] In the MS. the line ends with 'gratia' because the space is filled up: but the word 'parturit' belongs to the same line, as is shown by a comparison with the parallel strophe; this is also evident from the point which the scribe has placed after the word.

In Nativitate Domini

Dies sanctificatus

1 Natus ante saecula 7	1a Per quem fit machina 6
Dei filius 5	coeli ac terrae 5
invisibilis, interminus. 9	maris ac in his degentium 9
2 Per quem dies et horae labant, 9	2a Quem angeli in arce poli 9
et se iterum reciprocant. 9	voce consona semper canunt. 9
3 Hic corpus assumpserat 7	3a Hoc praesens diecula 7
fragile sine labe 7	loquitur perlucida 7
originalis criminis 8	adaucta longitudine 8
de carne Mariae virginis, 9	quod sol verus radio sui 9
quo primi parentis culpam 8	luminis vetustas mundi 8
Evaeque lasciviam tergeret. 10	depulerit genitus tenebras. 10
4 Nec nox vacat novi sideris 9	4a Nec gregum magistris defuit 9
luce, quod magorum oculos 9	lumen, quos perstrinxit claritas 9
terruit scios. 5	militum Dei. 5
5 Gaude Dei genitrix 7	5a Christe patris unice 7
quam circumstant obstetricum 8	qui humana nostri causa 8
vice concinentes 6	formam assumpsisti, 6
angeli gloriam Dei. 8	refove supplices tuos. 8
6 Et quorum participem te 8	6a Et ipsos divinitatis 8
fore dignatus es Jesu 8	tuae participes Deus 8
dignanter eorum 6	facere digneris 6
suscipe preces 5	unice Dei. 5

In Ascensione Domini

Dominus in Syna

(*Cod.* Einsiedeln 121, p. 576.)

1 Christus hunc diem jocundum 8
cunctis concedat esse Christianis 11
amatoribus suis. 7

2 Christe, Jesu, fili Dei mediator 12	2a Officiis te angeli atque nubes 12
naturae nostrae ac divinae. 9	stipant ad patrem reversurum. 9
3 Terras Deus visitasti 8	3a Sed quid mirum? cum lactanti 8
aeternus aeterna 6	adhuc stella tibi 6
novus homo transvolans. 7	serviret et angeli. 7

4 Tu hodie terrestribus rem no-   4a Te hominem non fictum le-
       vam et dulcem 14   vando   10
     dedisti domine   6   super sidereas   6
     sperandi coelestia.   7   metas regum domine.   7
5 Quanta gaudia tuos   7   5a Quis dedisti cernere   7
     replent apostolos.   6   te coelos pergere.   6
6 Quem hilares in coelis tibi   9   6a In humeris portanti diu   9
     occurrunt novi ordines   8   dispersum a lupis gregem unum, 10

7 Quem Christe, bone pastor,   7
tu dignare custodire.   8

Type B

As already remarked, the number of Notker's Sequences which belong to this type is very small, not exceeding more than half a dozen; among them are:

2ND SUNDAY AFTER EASTER (P. 480). 3RD SUNDAY AFTER EASTER (P. 481).

In te domine speravi   *Qui timent*

1 Laus tibi sit, o fidelis Deus.   10   1 En regnator coelestium et ter-
2 Qui nunquam confundis in te   8   renorum.   13
     confidentes, sed eos   7   2 Victor fortis infernalium reg-
     magis glorificas.   6   norum.   12
3 Tu propugnaculum adversus   3 In sede sibimet digna sedens   10
             hostiles 12   rector angelorum.   6
     incursatus et insidias.   9   4 Humanos labores indulgens
4 Pastor noster, disruptor laquei, 10   miseratur 13
             eorum, qui timent   6
5 Tu conservas, qui timent te   8

             potestatis ipsius natum.   9
     valde magna dulcedine,   8   5 Idcirco mundus omnis plaudat   9
     Deus indulgens.   5

             iubilet, canat exsultans   8
             cunctorum saeclorum rectori.   9

Both Sequences consist of five strophes : others are somewhat longer ;
e. g. the following :

4TH SUNDAY AFTER EASTER (P. 482).—*Exultate Deo*

1	Laeta mente canamus Deo nostro.	11
2	Qui defectam peccatis	7
	semper novat ecclesiam.	8
3	Et eam pallidulam	7
	de radio veri solis illuminat.	12
4	Et terrae de Mesraim	7
	eduxit fornacibus ignitis.	10
5	Quique in omni tribulatione	11
	eam exaudit.	5
6	Insuper coelesti nutrit pane	10
	et cultum docet suum.	7
7	Quin de petra melle dulci	8
	eam adimplet.	5

The division into several parts, consisting of one or more verses, is
common to all the Sequences of Notker : this division is indicated above
by capital letters corresponding to the original method. The first form is
more regular in structure than the second : it connects every two sections
of the Sequence with one another by an equal number of syllables, and
above all by the identity of the melody ;[1] in this manner there arise
strophes of one or more lines. Occasional exceptions occur : *e. g.* in the
Sequence *Christus hunc diem* a line of 14 syllables corresponds, in one
case, with one of 10 ; in another, one of 8 with one of 10 syllables (strophes
4 and 4a, and 6 and 6a). In this case the range of the melody is of course
different.[2] As may be seen from the same Sequence (*cf.* strophes 2, 3,
2a and 3a), the parallel strophes do not always follow each other
immediately, but are sometimes separated by others, two pairs of strophes
being intermingled. Usually the Sequence begins and ends with an
independent strophe of greater or less length, and furnished with a melody

---

[1] Durandus of Mende especially brings forward this peculiarity of the Sequence
structure in contrast to the other Mass-chants : 'Versus sequentiarum bini et bini sub
eodem cantu canuntur, quod contingit, quia ut plurimum bini et bini per rithmos sub
paribus syllabis componuntur.' Gerbert, *De Cantu* I, 403. note A.

[2] *Cf.* the melody in Schubiger, *l. c.*, example 21. *Cod.* Einsiedeln 121 agrees
throughout with this.

of its own: it thus stands out from the symmetrical order of the whole. In the second type of Sequence the whole poem is also divided into strophes: but they do not correspond, either in their length, or in the number of syllables in the lines, or in the melody: we have here a form which as regards its external structure differs little from prose.

It is noticeable, and a characteristic that distinguishes Sequences from Hymns, that it is always two strophes only that have the same length, number of lines, and melody; longer and shorter pairs of strophes alternate with one another. Moreover the various lines of the same strophe are not of equal length. But the Sequences are especially distinguished from the hymns by the absence of anything like prosody or quantity. Here we have *rhythmical poetry* of a distinct stamp. No regard is paid to the length or shortness of syllables: this is clearly shewn by the fact that, even in the corresponding verses of the parallel strophes, the first time a short and the next time a long syllable occurs in the same place. The accents on the words (*arsis*) are never bound to a fixed place, even if the number of the unaccented syllables between two accented ones is never greater than three. The endeavour to form identically parallel lines is unmistakable here, though it is not quite realised. Only the number of the syllables and accents is the same in almost all the parallel lines.

This peculiar structure is a result of the Alleluiatic melodies, upon which the Sequences were modelled. Every melodic group became a line, which was longer or shorter in accordance with the varying length of the group: if a repetition of a group took place in the melody, a parallel line was the result, and where that was not so, the poetical form developed with the loose structure of the second Sequence type.

It is unnecessary to point out further that in Notker's Sequences there is no connexion with hymn-poetry as it developed in the Latin Church from the time of Ambrose: on the contrary, hymnody does not possess a single form which might have served as a model for them. They cannot have grown up on Latin soil; they are nothing else than *Byzantine Hymn-poetry* which has been transplanted. The previous arguments have made this probable; it becomes evident, if we compare Notker's Sequences with the Greek hymns published by Pitra. [1] The similarity of

---

[1] Pitra. *Analecta. Cf.* above p. 224 note 2. There is nothing to contradict the supposition that direct translations from the Greek appear in many of Notker's Sequences. For example the ὕμνος ἀκάθιστος of the Byzantine liturgy is to be found in the Zürich MS. from S. Gall, *c.* 78. *Cf.* Winterfeld. *Zeitschrift für deutsches Altertum. Berlin,* 1903, p. 81.

the structure of the whole and of the respective parts is unmistakable. Thus not in the melody alone, but also in the text, the Sequences shew that they belong to the latest and most important influences of the Middle-Greek Church music upon the Latin. It is this principally that gives them their position in musical history. Their undeniable descent from the Byzantine music justifies one in mistrusting Notker's letter to Luitward. Perhaps even the name *Romanus*, which emerges in the later S. Gall tradition subsequent to the 10th century, is nothing but the personification of the Byzantine influence at S. Gall. At any rate the chief representative of the second period of Greek hymnody is a 'Romanus.' When at S. Gall the real origin began to be forgotten, and the foundation of the song-school was traced directly back to Rome, it was natural to point to the name which was still in obscure remembrance from the end of the 8th century as a witness to the novel legend; possibly it gave the impulse to it. If this supposition be correct, we must recognize a Byzantine composition in the Alleluia-melody called 'Romana,' which served as a theme for Sequences.

The structure of the Sequences shews the way in which they were performed. Either there were two choirs to perform the parallel strophes, alternating with one another, or else all joined in singing the Sequence through from beginning to end. The former manner of performance prevailed in the Sequences of Type A, the latter in those of Type B. Durandus of Mende has this last in his mind when he says: 'The Sequence is sung by the whole choir together, to symbolize the harmony of love.' [1]   In the case of the longer Sequences of the first type, the introduction and conclusion were sung by all, and in their case there is frequent mention of united singing; but the pairs of strophes were sung alternately. Boys also took part in it, and their clear voices, alternating or uniting with those of the men, gave the chant great brilliancy and freshness. [2]

The melodies exhibit a taste for imposing and sonorous strains, boldness in melodic development, the frequent occurrence of wide intervals, and an extended compass, such as was made possible by the use of boys. In consequence the Sequences often extend to a pitch which men's voices cannot reach. All such features are foreign to the older liturgical chants of the Latin Church, especially to the choral chants. It is usual for them to glide along on quieter and more even lines, without

---

[1] *Rationale* iv, 22.   [2] *Cf.* upon this Bartsch, *Sequenzen*, 19 foll.

any sign of musical pretensions : they are altogether indifferent to mere outward splendour, and are content to render the liturgical words in such a manner as to produce a sense of fervour and devotion in the heart of a pious Christian. One might sing them alone without any audience, and yet find that they lost nothing in expression and beauty. It is quite otherwise with the Sequences : if they are to fulfil their purpose, they must resound in a church where the faithful are assembled : they are like a herald, who with bold and energetic voice proclaims the truths of Christianity to the people.

The syllabic form of melody must have made an impression of its own, for from the beginning it differentiated the Sequence from the antiphonal and responsorial chants of the Mass. It is quite the exception for Notker to abandon his rule and provide one syllable with two notes. [1] The idea of Iso, *Singuli motus cantilenae singulas syllabas debent habere*, is obviously traceable to the Byzantine hymnody. As there is constant mention in the oldest Sequences of the *Organum*, which was known to the Franks and Germans only through the Byzantines, there is ample reason for supposing that the Sequences were from the very first accompanied by the organ. Slowness in performance was the necessary consequence; the oldest authors, when speaking of the *Organum*, lay particular stress upon the slowness (*morositas*) of its execution. The syllabic form of melody fits in very well with this; it might even have been the cause of it. But it was exactly this peculiar connexion between words and music that made the Sequences approximate to the popular method of singing, and thus led to their popularity and their wide extension. Regarded from this point of view the Sequences were a sort of *reaction of the Folk-song against the sublime art of the Church ;* and this circumstance adds a special importance to the stage of Medieval musical development which was introduced by them.

Among the composers of the Middle Ages Notker is the first of whom we have more than general knowledge. The picture of him which Ekkehard, the historian of the S. Gall Monastery, gives us, is an attractive one. In spite of the defect in his speech—he stammered—he was a highly educated man, with a facile power of artistic creation. Many of his poems and songs owe their origin to some accidental circumstance.

---

1 Examples of it are scarce in proportion to the antiquity of the MSS. referred to, *e.g. Cod.* Einsiedeln 121, which on pp. 578 foll. provides the Sequence *Ecce solemnis diei* with neums in the margin and single signs above the text, *i. e.* with a *virga* and a *punctum* ; occasionally also with the *cephalicus*, the liquescent equivalent of the *virga*.

It was while watching the building of a bridge over a deep abyss that he thought of the danger of death to which mankind is perpetually exposed, and composed his wonderful *Media vita in morte sumus.* [1] It quickly spread, and became an ecclesiastical folk-song: even miraculous powers were ascribed to it, and it was believed to be a protection from death, sickness, and all kinds of evil. [2] An Easter antiphon of his was also famous,—*Cum rex gloriae Christus.*

But it was Notker's Sequences that won the greatest veneration, and the invention of them was unhesitatingly ascribed to divine inspiration. They are said to have received the approval of ecclesiastical authority during his lifetime. [3] When in 1215 Abbot Ulrich of S. Gall was in Rome, transacting some imperial business with Pope Innocent, the Sequence *Sancti spiritus adsit nobis gratia* made such an impression on the Pope, that he expressed his astonishment that so pious a man as its author must be should not yet have been canonized. At the beginning of the 16th century Pope Julius II. included the inventor of the Sequence-form among the beatified.

It cannot be decided with certainty which Sequences are due to Notker, as those of other artists were soon added to his, and the two sections were not kept separate in MSS. which were intended for practical use. It appears that Notker composed Sequences for all the more important days of the Church's year; at any rate the MSS. of the *Liber Hymnorum Notkeri* begin with a Sequence for Christmas and then go through the ecclesiastical year. [4]

Notker's Sequences soon passed beyond the walls of the monastery

---

1 May not the *Media vita* also have been suggested by a Greek original? The exclamations *Sancte Deus, Sancte fortis* remind one of the Greek portions of the Good Friday *Improperia.*

2 When in the year 1263 the Archbishop of Trèves appointed a certain William to be Abbot of the monastery of S. Matthias against the will of the monks, they prostrated themselves on the ground and said the *Media vita* and other prayers, and thus hoped to get protection from the Abbot who was being forced upon them (Gerbert, *De Cantu* I, 561). The Council of Cologne in 1316 forbade the *Media vita* to be sung against anyone without the bishop's permission. It was soon translated into German and sung everywhere; and in our own day Notker's pious song is known as *Mitten in dem Leben sind wir vom Tot umfangen.*

3 From Pope Nicholas (†867). See Ekkehard, *Vita B. Notker, Cap.* 4.

4 *Cf.* Schubiger *l.c.* 45 foll.; Bartsch *l.c.* 6 foll.; Wilmans, *Zeitschrift für deutsches Altertum* XV, 267 foll.; Chevalier, *Poésie liturgique au moyen âge, Histoire et rhythme*, pp. 96 foll., and the very meritorious work of J. Werner, Notker's *Sequenzen* (Aarau, 1901), where the whole question is dealt with in a most thorough and able manner.

of S. Gall, and in a short time found their way into the German churches. Numerous copies of his *Liber Hymnorum* were made. The structure of the melodies, as it approximated to the popular manner of singing, won all hearts, and the Sequences became the most popular part of the Mass music. To the ordinary singers the novel poetic form seemed to be *prose*; consequently it was given the name of Prose, [1] and this was retained even when it assumed a new form. It was in France especially that the name *Prosa* was customary, while in Germany *Sequentia* was always used.

Within and without S. Gall there rose up imitators of Notker, with the result that there were several Sequences for the same feast. They were so much appreciated that it became the custom in many monasteries for the *Cantor* on feast days to ask the Abbot in chapter which Sequence was to be sung. As they supplied the place of the Alleluia-*jubilus*, this was not repeated after the Alleluia-verse, if a Sequence followed. [2]

Of the two Sequence-types, the one which was more permanently suitable and was generally adopted by the early writers was the first. In it, for example, Wipo composed his magnificent Easter Sequence *Victimae paschali*. Wipo was chaplain at the Court of Conrad II. and his son Henry III.; he flourished therefore in the first half of the 11th century. In his Sequences he dispensed with an independent concluding phrase, but on the other hand he preserved the introductory one : he also inclined to the occasional use of rhyme. In its original form the above-mentioned Sequence runs thus :

1 Victimae paschali laudes   8
immolent Christiani.   7

2 Agnus redemit oves,	7	2a Mors et vita duello	7
Christus innocens Patri	7	conflixere mirando,	7
reconciliavit	6	dux vitae mortuus	6
peccatores.	4	regnat vivus.	4
3 Dic nobis, Maria,	6	3a Angelicos testes,	6
quid vidisti in via.	7	sudarium et vestes.	7
4 Sepulcrum Christi viventis,	8	4a Surrexit Christus, spes mea,	8

---

1 The Constitutions of William of Hirschau say : 'pro signo prosae, quam quidam sequentiam vocant' (*Patr. Lat.* cl, 951). Accordingly he considers the name *Prosa* to be the original one.

2 Durandus of Mende says : 'quando autem dicitur sequentia, non dicitur pneuma post *Alleluia*' (Gerbert *De Cantu* I, 408).

et gloriam vidi	6	praecedet suos [1] in	6
resurgentis.	4	Galilaeam.	4
5 Credendum est magis soli	8	5a Scimus Christum surrexisse	8
Mariae veraci,	6	a mortuis vere,	6
quam Judaeorum	5	tu nobis, victor	5
turbae fallaci.	5	rex, miserere.	5

This Sequence attained as great a celebrity as Notker's *Media vita.* Sung with enthusiasm as early as the 12th century, this song of triumph penetrated into Italy, where it is found in many of the old missals; it found a place in the Mysteries, the plays which brought the sacred history before the eyes of the people on Easter-day. Translated into German as *Christus ist erstanden*, it has had a glorious history, reaching down to the present time. Numerous imitations were composed in honour of the Blessed Virgin and other saints, with which the favourite and triumphant melody of Wipo could be used. [2]

There flourished at the same time other poets and composers of Sequences, who all continued in the road marked out by Notker; and together with him they occupy the first period of Sequence-poetry. Moreover the melodies used by Notker were continually set to new texts. In a south German Monastery there laboured the Monk Heinrich, who was the composer of the Sequence *Ave praeclara maris stella.* [3] This also was sung for many generations in praise of the Mother of God, and finally as a German carol. A pupil of his was Godeschalk, of whom only a few Sequences are preserved. [4] From the S. Gall school there came also Berno of Reichenau (†1048), who was well versed in all scientific studies, and remarkable alike as a Church composer and as a theorist. Hermann Contract, who, like Berno, was brought up at S. Gall, and was afterwards a most fruitful worker at Reichenau, also belongs to this class. All these artists who centre round Notker are of German descent; the scene of the first development of the Sequence is principally Alemania.

If the central point of the new form in its first period, which comprises the 10th and 11th centuries, lies in the creations of Notker and his

---

1 At the revision of the Missal by the Council of Trent *suos* was altered to *vos* and the whole of the 5th strophe cut out, probably in order not to destroy the joyful character of the whole by the mention of the *Judaeorum turba fallax*. But the Sequence-form has suffered in consequence, as the last strophe 5a has no longer any corresponding member. The words *Amen, Alleluia* were also added.

2 I have printed two of them in the *Gregoriusblatt*, Aachen, 1896, Nos. 11 foll.

3 Schubiger *l.c.* p. 88.

4 Schubiger. *l. c.* p. 89.

followers, the situation changes with the 12th century. The Sequence was then transferred from the German soil upon which it sprung into other lands. First it passed to France, thence to Italy, Spain and England : it assumed thereby new forms which were not excluded even in Germany. This *second period* of Sequence-poetry and composition may be distinguished by a gradual divergence from Notker and the Byzantine type, and an approximation to the Latin hymn-form. The Byzantine hymn-strophes, as transplanted by Notker on to Latin soil, must have seemed strange to the poets of France and other countries which did not come directly under middle-Greek influence; it was only natural that under their hand the new form should become quite Latinized, that is to say, should approximate more to the hymn,—the only poetical form of liturgical poetry with which they were acquainted.

It is certain that long before the appearance of the great poet who first struck out in the new direction, the Sequences of the old type were known in France, chiefly in the monastery of S. Martial at Limoges. This development may perhaps be connected with the early attempts made in the monastery of Jumièges before Notker, if the statement on the subject in the letter of Notker to Luitward be a correct one. But the Notker of the second period is the Parisian canon *Adam of S. Victor*. [1] Of the facts of his life little is known; he is said to have come from Brittany and to have died in 1192; it is only certain that he flourished in the 2nd half of the 12th century. According to the universal testimony of good judges, Adam was one of the greatest poets of the Middle Ages. His Sequences are in fact worthy of admiration for the freedom and facility with which he treats the verses, for the clearness and significance of the ideas, and for the wealth of symbolic imagery contained in them.

Adam of S. Victor does not follow a fixed type in the external structure of his Sequences any more than Notker; on the contrary there is to be oberved in them a development which occupied the whole of the brief second period of Sequences, which departed from the Notkerian type and gradually passed into the hymn-form. The external structure of the following Sequence reminds one of Notker's :

---

1 *Cf.* Léon Gautier. *Oeuvres poétiques d'Adam de S. Victor*, Paris, 1894, 3rd ed. Dreves, *Analecta Hymn.* vol. vij, and *Stimmen aus Maria Laach*, 1885, vol. 29. There has lately been published by Welter at Paris a careful critical edition by Misset and Aubry of Adam's proses both in text and music (1900); in this the melodies were published for the first time. The music has however not yet been fully investigated : there remains in particular the very interesting question of the tonality and rhythm of the Sequences to be dealt with.

Feria II. post Pascha

1 Ecce dies celebris,
   lux succedit tenebris,
   morti resurrectio.

2 Laetis cedant tristia,
   cum sit maior gloria
   quam prima confusio.

2a Umbram fugat veritas,
    vetustatem novitas,
    luctum consolatio.

3 Pascha novum colite,
   quod praeit in capite,
   membra sperent singula.

3a Pascha novum Christus est.
    qui pro nobis passus est,
    agnus sine macula.

4 Hosti, qui nos circuit,
   praedam Christus eruit,
   quod Samson praecinuit,
   dum leonem lacerat.

4a David fortis viribus
    a leonis unguibus
    et ab ursi faucibus
    gregem patris liberat.

5 Quod in morte plures stravit,
   Samson Christum figuravit,
   cuius mors victoria.

5a Samson dictus sol eorum,
    Christus lux est electorum,
    quos illustrat gratia.

6 Jam de sacro crucis vecte
   botrus fluit in dilectae
   penetral ecclesiae.

6a Jam calcato torculari,
    musto gaudent ebriari
    gentium primitiae.

7 Saccus scissus et pertusus
   in regales transit usus,
   saccus fit soccus gloriae,
   caro victrix miseriae.

7a Quia regem peremerunt
    rei regnum perdiderunt,
    sed non deletur penitus
    Cain in signum positus.

8 Reprobatus et abiectus
   lapis iste, nunc electus
   in tropheum stat erectus
   et in caput anguli.

8a Culpam delens, non naturam
    novam creat creaturam,
    tenens in se ligaturam
    utriusque populi.

9 Capiti sit gloria
  Membrisque concordia.

In this poem the connexion of the second Sequence-period with the first is strikingly brought out. Like most of Notker's Sequences, it consists of parallel strophes, with independent introductory and concluding phrases. There the likeness ceases : in the nature of the superstructure Adam is intrinsically different from Notker : although the different pairs of strophes are not always of the same length, yet there is an unmistakeable tendency not to make them too dissimilar. In our Sequence, apart from the introductory and concluding phrases, three-lined and four-lined strophes are found in equilibrium. With Notker a lively alternation is the rule, in the second period it is the exception; and further development leads to the complete correspondence of all pairs of strophes, so far as the number and form of the lines is concerned. Thereupon the introductory and concluding phrases had to disappear, for they were out of harmony with a structure which formed all the strophes of the poem of equal length. As a matter of fact, with Adam they are rather rare, and almost the exception.

An important contrast between these and the older Sequences is found in the construction of the lines. Rhythmical poetry has here reached its complete development. Notker had already set aside all considerations of prosody and quantity, and the tonic accent had become supreme. Adam goes yet a step further, and arranges the succession of the accents of the words. The laws by which *arsis* and *thesis* follow one another may be briefly summarized thus : a word of one syllable may be accented or not, as it happens; a word of two syllables is always accented on the first; a word of several, on the penultimate when it is long, and on the antepenultimate when the penultimate is short. Further, when necessary, secondary accents are regularly placed on every other syllable. Thus, as a rule, verbal accents are separated by only one syllable; exceptions to this are chiefly to be found in the brief final lines of the strophes : *e.g.* strophe 2 :

quam prima confusio.

But as a rule the binary rhythm predominates. The rule as to the number of the syllables is carried out, if possible, even more strictly than by Notker. The most characteristic point however of the new Sequence-form is *Rhyme*. Practically non-existent in Notker's compositions, it governs the form of the Sequence in the whole of its further development. It is remarkable that it appears simultaneously in the most varied forms, so that one is forced to recognize a definite transition from the Sequences of Notker to those of Adam ; for the skilful use of this artistic device can only be the result of much preliminary investigation and study. Even intermediate rhymes are not uncommon in Adam. The *caesura* yet remains to be mentioned; it appears in lines of 8 syllables and upwards. Lines of 8 and 10 syllables have it after the fourth unaccented syllable, the uncommon 12 syllable lines after the sixth accented syllable. The number of syllables in the line is 4, 6, 7, 8, 10 and 12; verses of 5, 9 and 11 syllables do not appear in Adam's genuine Sequences. This also is a point of contrast with the Sequences of Notker. The lines are combined by strophes with admirable variety, and thus bring out the art of rhyme.

The structure for which Adam [1] finally abandoned Notker's model, forms all strophes of the poem in the same way. Thus the Sequence completely appropriated the form of Latin hymnody. A very beautiful example of this style, noteworthy alike for its form and its contents, is the following:

DE S. TRINITATE [2]

1 Profitentes unitatem
  veneremur trinitatem
  pari reverentia.

1a Tres personas asserentes
  personali differentes
  a se differentia.

2 Hae dicuntur relative,
  cum sint unum substantive
  non tria principia.

2a Sive dicas tres vel tria,
  simplex tamen est usia,
  non triplex essentia.

3 Simplex esse, simplex posse,
  simplex velle, simplex nosse,
  cuncta sunt simplicia.

3a Non unius, quam duarum
  sive trium personarum
  minor efficacia.

4 Pater, proles, sacrum flamen,
  Deus unus, sed hi tamen
  habent quaedam propria.

4a Una virtus, unum numen,
  unus splendor, unum lumen,
  hoc una, quod alia.

5 Patri proles est aequalis,
  nec hoc tollit personalis
  amborum distinctio.

5a Patri compar filioque
  spiritalis ab utroque
  procedit connexio.

6 Non humana ratione
  capi possunt hae personae
  nec harum discretio.

6a Non hic ordo temporalis,
  non hic situs aut localis
  rerum circumscriptio.

7 Nil in deo praeter Deum,
  nulla causa praeter eum,
  qui creat causalia.

7a Effectiva vel formalis
  causa Deus et finalis,
  sed nunquam materia.

8 Digne loqui de personis
  vim transcendit rationis
  excedit ingenia.

8a Quid sit gigni, quid processus,
  me nescire sum professus,
  sed fide non dubia.

9 Qui sic credit, non festinet,
  et a via non declinet
  insolenter regia.

9a Servet fidem, formet mores,
  nec attendat ad errores
  quod damnat ecclesia.

---

1 The number of Adam's Sequences has formed the subject of some controversy. Léon Gautier accepts 103 as genuine. Misset rejects 52 of them : most of the remaining 51 must be genuine. More precision than this can hardly be attained.

2 Misset and Aubry, p. 195. *Les mélodies*, p. 271.

10 Nos in fide gloriemur,
    nos in una modulemur
    fidei constantia.

10a Trinae sit laus unitati,
    sit et simplae trinitati
    coaeterna gloria.

So far, it has not been made clear from what source the melodies come which appear with Adam's Sequences in the MSS. At any rate the Sequence has in this stage completely emancipated itself from the Alleluia-chant. Curiously enough, the same melody often appears over again in several Sequences, and at times the melodies are extraordinarily alike. [1] Many melodic harshnesses, especially a certain preference for passages containing the *tritone*, lead one to suppose that they originated in France. There may be popular melodies among them. At an early date it was proposed to provide Adam's poems with new melodies which would be more pleasing and offer more variety. [2] But the syllabic form of the melody and the same musical treatment of the parallel strophes always remained a characteristic of the Sequence.

Adam's compositions soon penetrated into most of the French churches; they are also to be met with in German books: [3] like Notker he found imitators. His Sequence of the Holy Cross *Laudes crucis attollamus* inspired Thomas Aquinas, who was entrusted by Urban IV. (1264) with the compilation of the Office of Corpus Christi, with the composition of *Lauda Sion Salvatorem*. They both have the same melody. The exquisite Pentecostal Sequence *Veni Sanɕte Spiritus* is said to have been composed by Pope Innocent III. [4]

The Sequence-form, as transformed by Adam, has a still more popular

---

1 On this *cf.* Misset and Aubry, pp. 119 foll.

2 Ambr. Kienle in the *Kirchenlexikon*, 2nd ed. *sub* 'Sequences.'

3 Chevalier (*Poésie liturg. au moyen âge*) has on p. 107 a long list of churches which contained Adam's Sequences in their Service-books.

4 I have found an interesting imitation of this for the feast of S. Katharine in *Cod. Lat. nouv. acquis.* 1235 of the Paris National Library, written in a hand of the 14th or 15th century (*fol.* 245, v):

    Veni sanɕte Spiritus, Katherinae celitus, invitatus merito,
    Veni splendor numinis, Katherinae virginis, mentem replens subito.
    Consolator optime, doɕtor disertissime, Katherinam instruens.
    In labore gratiam, in verbis prudentiam, Katherinae tribuens.
    O lux beatissima, per quem fit gratissima, huius vita virginis.
    Pulchra nobilissima, et magistra maxima, supra vires hominis,
    Lavit viros sordidos et rigavit aridos aqua sapientiae.
    Fleɕti fecit rigidos et reduxit devios ad viam iustitiae
    Sapientes graeciae Christi subdens gratiae artium pericia.
    Haec pro nobis hodie sit patrona veniae in celesti gloria. Amen.

character than that of Notker : no wonder then that it soon passed into a song-form. To this stage belongs the *Dies irae* of Thomas of Celano, who flourished in 1220-1249. At that time the Black Death was raging in Europe, warning men to contemplate the terrors of the Day of Judgement. The poet portrays them in a moving way up to the point at which the soul commends itself to the Divine mercy. Some old books give the following introductory strophes : [1]

1a Cogita, anima fidelis,
    Ad quid respondere velis
    Christo venturo de cœlis.

1b Cum deposcet rationem
    Ob boni omissionem,
    Ob mali commissionem.

2a Dies illa, dies irae,
    Quam conamur praevenire
    Obviamque Deo ire.

2b Seria contritione,
    Gratiae apprehensione,
    Vitae emendatione.

But these may be only a later addition. This is certainly the case with the two last lines of the present text, beginning *Pie Jesu*, which are more in keeping with the liturgical use of the Sequence, and apparently replace the older concluding strophe :

    Consors, ut beatitatis
    Vivam cum justificatis
    In aevum aeternitatis.

The *Stabat mater dolorosa* also, the great masterpiece of Jacobus de Benedictis (Jacopone da Todi, † 1306), belongs to this series, together with its counterpart, *Stabat mater speciosa*. Compositions of this kind show that all remembrance of the connexion of the Sequence with the Alleluia-*jubilus* had completely disappeared. As on days of penitence and mourning, especially in Lent, the Alleluia was banished from the Mass, so also there was at first, at least for these days, no Sequence either.[2] It was only when the Sequence had become quite independent, and had received the character of a chant which clothed the subject of the day in poetical form, that it was possible to call poems like the *Dies irae* and *Stabat mater* Sequences. [3]

---

1 *Cf.* Raymund Schlecht in the *Choralvereinsbeilagen zur Cäcilia*, Trèves, 1874, No. 10.

2 In the 12th century a special papal permission was still needed in order to sing a Sequence after Septuagesima Sunday, as the abbot of S. Blasien was told with regard to the Purification, Annunciation, and the Feast of S. Blaise. Gerbert, *De Cantu* I, 409.

3 The connexion between the later Sequence and the hymn proper is made clear by the remarkable appearance of one and the same text both as Sequence and as hymn: the first 10 strophes of the Sequence *Stabat mater* are also used as a hymn (*In fest. Sept. Dolor.* B. V. M.).

It is easy to understand that the Sequences soon became naturalized, particularly in the secular churches. In the monasteries they were more conservative : the Cistercians and Carthusians, for example, would have none of the innovation. It was only with great difficulty that S. Odilo, Abbot of Cluny, succeeded in getting his monastery to open its doors even to the Pentecostal Sequence *Sancti Spiritus adsit nobis gratia*, and 100 years later Sequences were still sung there only on the highest festivals. [1] The Missals and Graduals of the secular churches however were rich in Sequences from the 13th century onwards. Probably Italy is the only country in which they failed to appeal to popular taste. The *Missale completum secundum consuetudinem Romanae curiae* (Milan, 1481) has only 5 Sequences : *Victimae paschali* for Easter, *Veni sancte Spiritus* and *Sancti Spiritus nobis adsit gratia* for Pentecost, *Lauda Sion* for Corpus Christi, and *Trinitas una, Deitas summa* for Trinity Sunday. A *Missale Romanum* of 1504 has also the Sequence *Dies irae*. [2] They are frequent in Spanish books, but are principally found in Germany, France and England. It was in these countries that they had been preserved the longest, and in which they entranced the people with their attractive melodies. Up to the middle of the 16th century the books often exhibit a superabundance of Sequences. A Gradual of Basle of 1511 has 44 of them. It was natural, in such circumstances, that compositions of doubtful merit not unfrequently found their way into the churches. At the time of the Tridentine reform, the recent date of the Sequences was taken into account, and to prevent the original good seed from being over-run by the new tares, they were all banished from the Mass-book except the existing five. [3]

In musical history the Sequences are important, in that they gave an impulse to the development of the German ecclesiastical folk-songs. They became the most popular element of the liturgical chant : many of them were translated into the language of the people, and helped to augment the treasury of spiritual songs with which Germany is so richly endowed.

---

1 Gerbert, *De Cantu* I, 411.

2 Hoeynck, *Geschichte der Liturgie des Bistums*, Augsburg, 1889, p. 58.

3 An extremely large number of Sequences from medieval MSS. and older printed books are published in the admirable collection of Dreves and Blume, *Analecta hymnica medii aevi*. Older collections are in Mone and Kehrein. W. J. Weale and Misset are now publishing Sequences in their periodical, *Analecta liturgica* (Paris. H. Welter).

CHAPTER XIV

THE TROPES

The overflowing piety, for which the official forms of the liturgical chant in some measure failed to suffice, called the Tropes also into existence. Like the Sequences they are fundamentally connected with the methods of the Byzantine musicians. Τρόπος is a word frequently used in Greek music. In ancient times, and later, it was a name for the *Tonoi*, the scales (each comprising two minor octaves) which were formed by transposing the diatonic scale to the pitch of each semitone of the octave. In the Middle Ages the word had yet other meanings: it had been generally used for certain melismatic formulas[1] used in musical instruction to exemplify the characteristics of the modes. The man to whom the S. Gall historian ascribes the invention of the tropes is Tutilo. Little is known of his life, but it is certain that he was a contemporary of Notker. The historical documents depict him as an universal genius: he was as famous as a painter, an architect, and a clever worker in gold, as he was as a musician. His talents procured him numerous invitations to undertake the decoration of other churches. He equally understood how to handle musical instruments, and he often had to instruct the sons of eminent families in the use of them. He died about 915, somewhat later than Notker.

The tropes, or '*Festivae laudes*,'[2] as they were called by the Romans, who did not grasp their connexion with Greek music, may be described as introductions, insertions, or additions to the liturgical chant. The result is always an extension of the original text, and often also of the

---

1 As shown on p. 30. Even Cassian was acquainted with the word in this sense.

2 According to a Paris MS. See Lebœuf, *Traité historique*, p. 104. *Cf.* Gerbert, *De Cantu* I, 341.

original melody. The origin of the tropes is unmistakeable when the text of these insertions is examined. Until far on into the 12th century they abound in Greek words, the whole manner of expression betraying an Eastern origin, being sometimes dramatic, always profuse in types and symbolical images, and differing greatly from the precise Latin style. It is significant to find that the MS. 484 of the monastic Library of S. Gall, which is so important for the early history of the Sequences, has a number of such melismatic interpolations, melodic passages without words being inserted into the existing chants: this is the original form of the S. Gall tropes, and thus it is clear why these new forms were given the name of tropes. The same MS. however also contains many tropes which were already provided with words. Not content with adding occasional sentences of this kind to already existing chants, they went further, and we find Tutilo composing tropes which are so protracted in text and melody that thenceforward the original chant looked like an interpolation. One of Tutilo's most famous tropes is the following extension 'of the Christmas Introit *Puer natus est*: [1]

Hodie cantandus est nobis puer, quem gignebat ineffabiliter ante tempora Pater, et eundem sub tempore generavit inclita Mater. *Interrogatio*: Quis est iste puer, quem tam magnis praeconiis dignum vociferatis? dicite nobis, ut collaudatores esse possimus. *Responsio*: Hic enim est, quem praesagus et electus symmista (hymnista) Dei ad terras venturum praevidens longe ante praenotavit sicque praedixit: *Puer natus est nobis* absque nascentium ordine procreatus de virgine sine viri semine. *Nobis* (with a longer *melisma*) *Et filius datus est nobis.* Qui nos filios sui parentis adoptivos fecit carnem sumens, quos et nominat fratres. *Cuius imperium super humerum eius.* Deus, quod pater suo misso in mundum nato et incarnato semper suum dat secundum carnem. *Et vocabitur nomen eius* nomen, quod exstat omne super nomen, quod supernae tremunt potestates, terra et inferus quem adorant et trepidant, *Magni consilii angelus.* Ps. *Cantate domino canticum novum, quia mirabilia fecit,* miro modo, cum de Virginis utero ut homo processerat, et ut Deus imperitat. *Gloria Patri et Filio et Spiritui sancto. Sicut erat in principio et nunc et semper, et in saecula saeculorum. Amen.* Alleluia. Laus tibi Christe, qui hodie cum magna luce descendisti. Dicite eia, Alleluia.

These additions to the Introit *Puer natus est* are all drawn from the

---

1 *Cod.* S. Gall 484 pp. 13 foll. *Cf.* the tropes of the *Ordinarium Missae* in the appendix of the *Graduale Sarisburiense* (Plainsong and Medieval Music Society, 1894) taken by W. H. Frere from an English MS. of the 15th century.

group of ideas suggested by the feast, and interpret it. Their obvious purpose is to give as much richness and dignity to the liturgical acts as possible. According to the testimony of Ekkehard there are other tropes attributed to Tutilo: he intercalated Offertory-melodies also in the same way.

A second kind of trope, which also goes back to Tutilo, resembles the Sequences, and is often like them called *Prosa*, or, when of lesser extent, *Prosula*. As Notker had developed from the Alleluia-*jubili* a new and independent creation by adding words to them, Tutilo treated other melismatic passages of the Church music in the same way, so that all the melismatic notes were distributed syllabically over the text. In particular, the *melisma* on the last syllable of the word *Kyrie*, and similar ones in the Graduals and Offertory-verses also, were thus transformed. But unlike the Sequence, which developed on independent lines and became a separate entity, existing side by side with the other chants of the Mass, this kind of trope always remained attached to the piece which contained the *melisma* on which the trope was founded: it thus continued to be an insertion in the liturgical text. A widely extended and much imitated example of Tutilo is the following Kyrie-trope: [1]

Cunctipotens genitor Deus, omnicreator *eleison*.
Fons et origo boni pie luxque perennis *eleison*.
Salvificet pietas tua nos bone rector *eleison*.
Christe Dei forma virtus patrisque sophia *eleison*.
Christe patris splendor orbis lapsi reparator *eleison*.
Ne tua damnemur Jesu factura benigne *eleison*.
Amborum sacrum spiramen nexus amorque *eleison*.
Procedens fomes vitae fons purificans nos *eleison*.
Purgator culpae, veniae largitor optime, offensas dele, sancto nos
munere reple *eleison*. [2]

The compositions of Tutilo are distinguished from the other chants of the Church by a strongly marked individuality: any musician of even moderate attainments could identify them from among others. It would seem that he accompanied them with stringed instruments (the *Rota*). [3]

---

1 *Cod.* 484, pp. 21 foll.

2 The last sentence in the melody contains a repetition according to the scheme A A B and is therefore the longer text.

3 Ekkehard has the important words: 'Quia per rotam, qua potentior ipse erat, neumata inventa dulciora sunt, ut apparet in *Hodie cantatus* and *Omnium virtutum gemmis.*' He adds a statement that Tutilo presented these tropes to Charles the Fat as an addition to the *Offertorium* composed by him, and at his desire composed others.

The tropes of Tutilo accorded with the spirit of the age, as is proved by the many imitations that arose in S. Gall and other churches, especially monastic ones, up till the 13th century and later. S. Gall MSS. with tropes are numerous; and they are also to be met with in MSS. of other parts of Germany; but they seem to have been most popular in French monasteries and secular churches.

In time they inundated all the chants of the Mass and of the Office like a flood; only in the case of the *Creed* is no mention made of tropes: clearly no one dared to lay hands on the hallowed form of the Confession of the Faith. [1] In general, the development of the new form ran a course corresponding to that of the Sequences; the first tropes, those of Tutilo and his immediate successors, are written in prose, though occasionally a hexameter is to be met with. From the second half of the 11th century onwards, tropes appear which make a liberal use of rhyme, and from that time they are mostly written in metrical forms, especially in iambic and trochaic verses. The earlier tropes are mere interpolations of the liturgical text; the later ones developed into independent poems which, appearing side by side with the prescribed forms, obscure them and force them into the background. In the first period it is the chants of the Mass that are troped by preference, in the second it is chiefly those of the Office.

The number of the tropes is legion, especially those of the *Ordinarium Missae*; together with the Sequences they belong to the most interesting and characteristic productions of the pious gladness and sacred poetry of the Middle Ages. It is to be regretted that they have not hitherto found an intelligent appreciation, either on their melodic or on their liturgical side. [2] We must be content to give here a few examples of each of the troped liturgical chants.

---

[1] The tropes have been declared, and with considerable reason, to be an infringement of the established laws of the liturgical chant. A judgement of this kind however rests upon a more modern conception of the Liturgy. In the Middle Ages the sentiment of the inviolability of liturgical uses was as yet little developed; the liturgical forms were living and elastic enough to bear additions. From purely external reasons of convenience, long before the rise of tropes, the musical texts underwent much abbreviation. Moreover the connexion of the faithful with the Liturgy was a closer one than it is to-day; they lived in it, so to speak. We have become colder, and the fire of enthusiasm, which was formerly kindled by the Liturgy, and acted as a stimulus to fresh developments, has unfortunately died out.

[2] Léon Gautier in his *Histoire de la Poésie liturgique au moyen âge* (I Paris 1886) gives a very welcome collection of materials from many MSS. of tropes: he does not enter upon melodic questions. Ad. Reiner has published the tropes, Proses and Preface-

Tropes to the Chants of the Mass

Introitus de Epiphania, from Cod. Rhenaug. 97 of the Zürich Cantonal Library, pp. 6 foll.

Forma speciosissimus, manuque potentissimus, ex davidis origine natus Maria Virgine, ecclesiae sponsus, illuminator gentium, baptismatis sacrator, orbis redemptor *Ecce advenit* Jhesus quem regem gentium cum muneribus mysticis Hierosolimam requirunt dicentes : ubi est, qui natus est *Dominator.* Vidimus stellam eius in oriente et agnovimus regem regum natum esse. *Et regnum* cui soli debetur honor, gloria, laus et iubilatio. *Et potestas.*

Aliter

Hodie clarissimam secuti stellam magi munera deferunt ad Christi cunabula, de quo prophetae venturo praedixerant. *Ecce advenit.* Olim promissus ac cupitus patribus venerandis. *Dominator.* Laxare vincula, strictum quibus humanum detinebatur genus. *Et regnum.* Regnum, quod nullo defectu corrumpi umquam possit minui perpetim. *Et potestas.* Quae sedes per Christi nobis humanam innotuit appparitionem. *Amen.* De manu eos scilicet fortissimorum hostium liberando. [1]

Kyrie eleison with tropes from the same MS., pp. 27 foll.

Kyrieleison.	Ineffabilis et interminabilis, immense et omnipotens.
Kyrieleison.	Cui omne genu flectitur coelestium, terrestrium et infernorum.
Kyrieleison.	Tu factor noster nos, opus tuum, facturam tuam, ne deseras.
Christeleison.	Qui dives cum esses, pro nobis pauper factus es.
Christeleison.	Et pro nobis te ipsum dederas, in tantum nos dilexeras.
Christeleison.	Quos tam sacrosancto redemeras pretio, alteri, Christe, ne dederis.
Kyrieleison.	Fons et origo et consummatio omnis boni, spiritus alme.
Kyrieleison.	Aequalis patri filioque maiestate et aeternitate.
Kyrieleison.	Without trope.

From the same MS.

Kyrieleison.	O pater piissime, Deus nobis miserere.
Kyrieleison.	Libera nos a malis omnibus, supreme genitor.

chants of solemn High Mass in the Middle Ages from some Paris MSS. (Luxemburg, 1884). There are some details respecting the tropes in Daux (2 *livres choraux monastiques des* Xe *et* XIe *Siècles,* Paris 1899, pp. 41 foll). The Introduction to Frere's *Winchester Troper* (Henry Bradshaw Society) is very good. In the second part of the present 'INTRODUCTION' the melodic character of the tropes will be dealt with.

[1] The same MS. has three more tropes for the same Introit.

Kyrieleison.	In tuo nos famulatu conserva, Deus magne et clementissime.
Christeleison.	Christe Jesu, fili Dei, factor orbis atque redemptor.
Christeleison.	Tu nos redimere dignatus es, tu nos semper custodias.
Christeleison.	Qui es venturus mundum iudicare, de poenis nos libera gehennae amarae.
Kyrieleison.	O sancte Spiritus, alme Deus, tuam nobis gratiam clementer infunde.
Kyrieleison.	Sancta trinitas, Deus omnipotens, gloria, laus et honor tibi sit nunc et per cuncta saecula.
Kyrieleison.	Without trope.

From the same MS.

Kyrieleison.	Pater infantium.
Kyrieleison.	Refectio lactantium.
Kyrieleison.	Consolatio pupillorum.
Christeleison.	Imago genitoris.
Christeleison.	Abolitio facinoris.
Christeleison.	Restauratio plasmatis.
Kyrieleison.	Fomes caritatis.
Kyrieleison.	Plenitudo probitatis.
Kyrieleison.	Without trope.

In the Cathedral of Nevers, after the Kyrie in the third Mass of Christmas, the following *Antiphona ad episcopum* was sung (*Cod. Lat. nouv. acquis.* 1235 of the Paris National Library, *f.* 185.) [1]

Ant. Cives superni hodie suam simul et nostram nuntiant mundo festivatem, gloriam Deo resonantes omnes.

The MS. continues: Pontifex dicat:

Gloria in excelsis Deo. Et in terra pax hominibus bonae voluntatis. Pax sempiterna, Christus, illuxit, gloria tibi, pater excelse. *Laudamus te.* Hymnum canentes hodie, quem terris angeli fuderunt Christo nascente. *Benedicimus te.* Natus est nobis hodie salvator in trinitate semper colendus. *Adoramus te.* Quem vagientem inter angusti antra praesepis angelorum coetus laudat exultans. *Glorificamus te. Gratias agimus tibi propter magnam gloriam tuam. Domine Deus, rex coelestis, Deus pater omnipotens.* Ultro mortali hodie indutum carne precemur. *Domine, fili unigenite, Jesu Christe. Domine Deus, agnus Dei, filius patris.* Cuius a

---

1 This MS., which I hope some day to be able to publish, contains a troped *Gloria* for almost all the festival Masses. The tropes of the Gloria in *Cod. Rhenaug.* 97 are shorter.

sede lux benedicta caliginoso orbi refulsit. *Qui tollis peccata mundi, miserere nobis. Qui tollis peccata mundi, suscipe deprecationem nostram.* O ineffabilis rex et admirabilis, ex virgine matre hodie prodisti mundoque subvenisti. *Qui sedes ad dexteram patris, miserere nobis. Quoniam tu solus sanctus, tu solus dominus, tu solus altissimus.* Regnum tuum solidum. Jesu Christe altissime. Per te obtinere mereamur veniam Nunc et semper, sine fine et sine termino Qui cum patre semperque regnas Simul et per infinita saeculorum saecula. *Jesu Christe. Cum sancto Spiritu in gloria Dei patris. Amen.*

In judging of tropes of the *Ordinarium Missae*, one must not forget that the texts of the *Kyrie, Gloria etc.* contain no direct reference to the character of the feast of the day, this being expressed in the varying texts of the *Proprium*. In that case then, if liturgical scruples were once overcome, insertions in the text were a means of colouring all the texts of the Mass with the idea suggested by the feast; the unity which was thus obtained and the harmony which prevailed when all the musical texts were directed to one point, were features of real aesthetic importance. Even up to the 16th century it was usual to sing at the end of the *Gloria* in the Masses of the Mother of God '*Quoniam tu solus sanctus* Mariam sanctificans, *Tu solus Dominus* Mariam gubernans, *Tu solus altissimus* Mariam coronans.' Other considerations gave rise to an interpolation which is also found in many MSS. and early printed books: in the *Gloria* the invocation *Domine Deus, rex coelestis, Deus pater omnipotens* is followed by a similar prayer to God the Son: *Domine Deus, Agnus Dei, filius patris.* Here an invocation of the Holy Ghost was also thought necessary, and a trope was therefore added: *Spiritus et alme orphanorum paraclite.*

It is strange that even the Lessons from Holy Scripture were furnished with additions: but tropes of this kind were rare, although in France they gained considerable importance, through being composed in the vernacular, and chanted facing the people. Such *Farciturae* or *Farsiae*, as they were called, were for the most part only translations of the Epistle, and were especially popular for the Masses of Christmas and the following days. [1]

The *Gradual* used not to be troped, in spite of the melismatic nature of its melody, but the *Alleluia* was; and the *jubilus* before the Verse as well as the melismatic passages in the Verse itself were resolved into their

---

[1] There are examples of troped epistles in Gerbert, *De Cantu* I, 391 and Gautier, *Les Tropes*, 151 foll. Some tropes of this kind will be given later from a MS. of the City Library of Chartres.

constituent notes, and provided with words.   We give two examples : [1]

From Cod. Lat. 1338 of the Paris National Library.

Alleluia.   Laudetur omnis tibi caterva a cunctis, potens qui condidisti coelorum astra et regnas per saecula.   *Dicite gentibus, quia dominus regnavit a ligno.*   *Dicite* coniuncti et psallite *in gentibus, quia* magna domini clementia, suis respiciens ovibus *regnavit* omnia et ïmperavit *a ligno,* proprio suo filio crucifixo, qui surrexit et sedet in throno, deconculcato Zabulo.

From Cod. Lat. 1118 of the same Library.

Alleluia.   *Vox exultationis et salutis* et laetae jucunditatis, aeternae iuventutis.   In tabernaculis justorum pax, lux, iucundaque laetitia.   Gaudentes laetentur omnes.   Jubilant iuvenes, senes, sedulo, dulcibus cantibus, in habitationibus, *in tabernaculis justorum.*

Even the repetition of the Alleluia after the Verse was prolonged by an intercalation.   From all points of the authorized musical text tropes burst forth and overran the old forms.   Even in places where the Gregorian Order of the Mass had assigned no chant, the pleasure of singing found an outlet.   The passage of the Deacon to the *Ambo* whence he sang the Gospel was accompanied with chant.   The oldest example [2] of it hails from Hartmann, a monk of S. Gall : it consists of five double strophes of four lines each : the first two of these may be given here :

From Cod. S. Gall 381, pp. 22 foll.

Versus Hartmanni ante Evangelium cum legatur canendi :

Sacrata libri dogmata	Mundemus omnes corpora
Portantur evangelici	Sensusque cordis simplici
Cunctis stupenda gentibus	Purgantes conscientia
Et praeferenda laudibus. Sacrata.	Verba pensemus mystica. Cunctis.

The habit of not troping the Creed may be traced to the absence of any melismatic formation in its melody, and still more to the fact that there was a reluctance to add anything to the Church's Confession of Faith, as has already been indicated.

Tropes to the Offertory of the third Mass of Christmas *(from Cod. Lat. Paris. nouv. acquis. 1235, f. 186).*

Tui sunt celi.   E coelo rex domine per saecula futurus, ut omnem iudices orbem.   *Et plenitudinem.*   Portio nostra, Christi, de sacra virgine

---

1 Gautier *l. c.* 153.   2 Similar poems, *ibid.* 158,

natus, salva nos, qui per habitum servi evacuasti iussa tyranni. *Praeparatio.* Tui sunt celi et tua est terra, dicite filii eya.

To the Offertory of Easter *(from the same MS. f. 210.)*

Ab increpatione et ira furoris domini *Terra tremuit.* Monumenta aperta sunt et multa corpora sanctorum surrexerunt *Dum resurgeret* Christus iudicaturus et vivos et mortuos, quando venerit *In iudicio Deus.* Christo resurgente a mortuis, venite adoremus eum omnes una voce proclamantes, *alleluia.*

These tropes, like the *Hodie cantandus est* of Tutilo, form in text and melody an extension of the original chant : a verse is prefixed like a prologue, others are inserted after the stops by way of final additions. Further, Tutilo's second type, the one which is illustrated in the Kyrie, was also applied to the Offertory. The second verse of the Offertory *Jubilate* of the second Sunday after Epiphany concludes with the words *veritas eius.* The syllable—*tas* is provided with a very long *melisma.* Words were added to this, so that it then ran thus : [1]

From Cod. Lat. Paris 9449, fol. 20 :

Laudate nomen eius, quoniam suavis est dominus, in aeternum misericordia eius et usque in saeculum saeculi *Veritas* istam salvando turmam benigne regat, sola sua misericordia interveniente, soluta pessima hostis catena, quam conterat nobis pietas *eius.*

Tropes of the Sanctus *(from Cod. S. Gall 383, pp. 145 foll.)* [2]

Sanctus Deus pater, cuius providentia
      Bene condita reguntur omnia.
Sanctus Filius patris coaeternus
      Semperque cum eo per omnia laudandus.
Sanctus Spiritus utrius connexio,
      Fidelium salus, vita et consolatio.
Dominus Deus. Pleni sunt. Verbo cuius existunt omnia.
                Coelum, pontus, tellus, aethera.
Benedictus qui venit.

From the same MS.

Sanctus Sanctorum exultatio
Sanctus Sanctorum benedictio.
Sanctus Sanctorum consolatio.

---

1 Gautier *l.c.* 162.   2 For others see Gautier *l.c.* 162.

Dominus Deus Sabaoth. Pleni sunt coeli et terra. Quem decet laus, salus et honor.

Gloria tua, hosanna in excelsis. Quem dulci iubilo sanctorum concinit ordo.

Benedictus qui venit.

From the same MS.

Sanctus Alme Deus, genitoris honor pie saecula salvans.

Sanctus Justorum virtus, decor integritatis eisdem.

Sanctus Spiritus omne replens, cui consors coelica psallit.

Dominus Deus. Te chorus hic resonat, celebrat et ovanter honorat.

Benedictus qui venit. Summa salus, pax vera, Deus, tibi rex jubilamus.

Tropes to the Agnus Dei *(from the same MS.)* [1]

Agnus Dei. Deus deorum, creator omnium, rex angelorum. Mortis destructor, vitae reparator, mundi redemptor. Inferni vastator, paradisi reparator, perennis salvator.

Agnus Dei.

From the same MS. (evidently intended for feasts of the B. V. M.) :

Agnus Dei. Christe, theos agye, salvator orbis, nate Mariae.

Agnus Dei. Unica spes veniae, via vitae, nate Mariae.

Agnus Dei. Pacis primiciae, patris hostia, nate Mariae.

From the same MS.

Agnus dei. Indomitos arce, subiectis rex pie parce.

Agnus dei. Audi clamantes, exaudi digna rogantes.

Agnus dei. Sintque tibi curiae, qui flent sua crimina pure.

Tropes to the Communion of Epiphany *(from Cod. Rhenaug. 97 of the Cantonal Library at Zürich) :*

Nato novo principe
Viso novo sydere
Urbe magi regia
Ipsum vadunt quaerere. *Vidimus.*

From the same MS.

Quae est ista tam clara solemnitas, fratres dilecti, in hac puer de virgine natus stella duce est gentibus revelatus, quae et dicebant : *Vidimus.*

Even the last sung text of the Mass, the *Ite missa est,* was not left unaltered.

---

1 Others in Gautier *l. c.* 163.

From Cod. S. Gall 378. p. 392.

Ite sine dolo et lite. Pax vobiscum. *Missa est.*
Deo semper agite in corde gloriam et *gratias.*

TROPES TO THE CHANTS OF THE OFFICE

If the chants of the Office are not so much interwoven with tropes as those of the Mass, the reason must be sought for in the simpler melodical structure of most of the Office music. The Antiphons and psalms, which occupy a great part of the Office, were all of such a simple sort of melody that no one thought of making them more syllabic than they were by means of interpolations. Such an attempt was only made in the case of the Responds of the Nocturns and a few other pieces : here the singers could not refrain from introducing tropes. Nevertheless their number even in the Responds is comparatively small.

Gautier mentions a troped *Deus in adiutorium* (*l.c.* 166). Among the Responds of the Office of Mattins, that of Christmas, *Descendit de coelis*, deserves especial mention. It is as follows:

Descendit de coelis missus ab arce patris, introivit per aurem virginis in regionem nostram, indutus stola purpurea, et exivit per auream portam, lux et decus universae fabricae mundi. ℣. Tanquam sponsus dominus procedens de thalamo suo. ℣. Gloria Patri et Filio et Spiritui sancto. ℣. Sicut erat in principio et nunc et semper, et in saecula saeculorum, amen. ℣. Tanquam sponsus dominus procedens de thalamo suo.

After the Verses the conclusion of the Respond was repeated from *Et exivit* onwards. In these repetitions various very long *melismata* were provided to be used on the syllable *fa* of the last word but one, *fabricae.* They certainly did not belong to the Respond originally, as they were used only at the repetitions of the word *fabricae* after the Verses ; and the corresponding passage in the Respond does not differ at all in style from what is usual in Responds. But they are to be found as early as in our oldest MSS.: *e.g.* in Hartker's Antiphoner of the 10th century, *Cod.* S. Gall 390. p. 46. Indeed Amalarius [1] has a symbolical meaning

---

1 Amalarius, *De Ord. Antiph. c.* 18 (*Patr. Lat.* 105, 1274): 'Eo neumate monstrant (*sc.* cantores) difficultatem magnam inesse in schola cantorum verbis explicare, quomodo idem, qui natus est hodierna die ex Maria Virgine, fabricasset mundum et ornasset, et quomodo ipse sit lux et decus universae fabricae mundi. Eadem sententia est in versu *Tanquam sponsus.* Impossibile est, apud scholam cantorum de ordine processionis Christi de utero virginis narrare, quae comparatur sponso procedenti de thalamo.'

for them.   Later MSS. from the 12th century onwards add words to the *melismata.   E. g.* MS. 12044 of the Paris National Library (the Antiphoner of S. Maur des Fossés of the 12th century) *fol.* 8 foll. has

The first time :

Familiam custodi, Christe, tuam, quam natus alma de Maria redemisti morte tua, ut cognoscant te conditorem [1] *Fabricae mundi.*

The second time :

Fac Deus munda corpora nostra et animas die ista, ut tua protecti dextra collaudemus auctorem *Fabricae mundi.*

The third time :

Facinora nostra relaxari mundi domina,
Petimus mente devota David regis prolem inclitam,
Virgo quem casta saeclo Maria protulit summi patris gratia.
Cuius ortus salvat omnes cuncta per saecula.
Et die hac nobis jugiter faveat atque omni *Fabricae mundi.*

Each of the three pieces called Proses leads into the words *Fabricae mundi,* which are thereupon sung as in the Respond itself, not as in the elaborate setting.

Moreover in the same Respond the first syllable of the ℣. *Tanquam* contains a *melisma,* which is however not so prolonged : it also was troped, and runs in the same MS. thus :

> Tanta nunc resultent gaudia,
> Quia Christus natus est in terra
> Coaequalis Patri in gloria
> De sancta Maria.

The same MS. contains another complete series of interesting tropes. They always reveal their connexion with the Respond from which they spring, by leading into its concluding words.   The ℟. *Confirmatum est,* which belongs, like the ℟. *Descendit,* to the third Nocturn of the Christmas Office, shews the sort of expedient to which recourse was had when the Respond itself did not offer the melodic material for an interpolation. It concludes before the ℣. with the words *et hominem.*   To the ℣. *Domus pudici pectoris* is annexed the following Prose, which is a trope of the long *melisma* in the Alleluia ℣. *Senex puerum* in the Mass of the Purification :

---

[1] The word 'conditorem' is omitted in the MS. : I have supplied it from *Cod. Paris. nouv. acquis.* 1235 *f.* 243.   A few other errors of the writer have been corrected from the same MS.

Et honore virginali integro permanente filium generavit,
Quae superno paranympho credula ac de tanto nuntio laeta dixit:
Fiat, ut prolem deicam virgo et mater proferam *et hominem.*

The R̄. *Gaude, Maria virgo* is in like manner connected with the prose *Inviolata nos iuva,* set to the same music to which a rather later hand wrote the well-known Prose *Inviolata, integra et casta,* [1] so that the same melody has two different texts:

Cod. Paris Lat. 12044 f. 57. In Purificatione B. M. V.

R̄. Gaude, Maria virgo, cunctas haereses tu sola interemisti, quae Gabrielis archangeli dictis credidisti, dum virgo Deum et hominem genuisti et post partum virgo inviolata permansisti. V̄. Gabrielem archangelum scimus divinitus te esse affatum, uterum tuum de Spiritu sancto credimus impregnatum; erubescat iudaeus infelix, qui dicit Christum ex Joseph semine esse natum. Dum Virgo. V̄. Gloria Patri. R̄. Gaude Maria.

After this follows the *Prosa*:

Inviolata nos iuva gratia sancta tua,
Mundo gaudia quae protulisti Maria,
Nempe benigna atque gloriosa,
Solve delicta orbis permaxima,
Mater innupta precata deduc nostra,
Christo tollenti crimina mundi cuncta,
Per te, o regina, percipiat regna
Plebs devota coelestia
Quae beata atque benedicta *permansisti.*

Inviolata, integra et casta es, Maria,
Quae es effecta fulgida coeli porta,
O virgo sola Christi carissima,
Suscipe pia nostra precamina,
Quae nunc flagitant devota corda, ora,
Nostra pura pectora sint et corpora,
Tua per precamina dulcissima
Nobis concedas veniam per saecula,
O benigna, quae sola inviolata *permansisti.*

Tropes to other chants of the Office are, as has been shown, exceptional. The S. Gall MS. 383 (p. 17) tropes the *Te Deum,* and that in a way which recalls the expansions of the *Gloria.* As in the latter an invocation of the Holy Ghost was inserted after that of God the Father and God the Son, so there was felt to be lacking after the words of the *Te Deum* 'Te martyrum candidatus' [2] a reference to the other classes of

---

1 Both Sequences end their lines with the vowel *a*, a custom not at all uncommon, which is a reminder that the Sequences are indebted for their origin to the *melismata* on the last syllable of the word *Alleluia.*

2 This trope is taken from a MS. which came from Italy to S. Gall. The harmonized portions which make up its last section, which have hitherto escaped the

Saints, the Confessors and Virgins, and therefore the following verse was added:

> Te concinit confessorum sacerdotalis ministerii puritas,
> Te integritas virginum ac continentium adornat puritas,
> Te sanctorum simul omnium iocunde collaudat unanimis caritas.

Occasionally in some monasteries they troped the *Deus in adjutorium* at the beginning of the Hours, the *Tu autem Domine* at the end of the Lessons, besides the *Magnificat* and the Antiphons of S. Mary.[1] Here is an example of a troped *Benedicamus Domino* of Christmas:

From Cod. Lat. Paris, nouv. acquis. 1235 f. 244.

Mirabile mysterium,	Usiae gigas geminae
Deus creator omnium	Assumpto Deus homine
Per incorruptam virginem	Alvo conceptus feminae
Nostrum suscepit hominem,	Non ex virili semine
Et nata mater patre est,	Natus est rex ab homine,
Qui natus matre pater est.	Jesus est dictus nomine.
Credit Eva diabolo,	De spinis uva legitur,
Maria credit angelo,	De stella lux exoritur,
Per illam mors introivit,	De petra fons elicitur,
Per istam vita rediit,	De virga flos egreditur,
Perdiderat haec condita,	De monte lapis lapsus est,
Haec restauravit perdita.	De lapide mons factus est.
Cedrus alta de libano	Qui fuit, erit et qui est,
Sub nostrae vallis hysopo,	Qui loquebatur, praesens est,
Cum visitavit Jericho	Nobiscum est rex Israel,
Cypressus fit ex platano	Qui dicitur Emmanuel.
Cinnamomum ex balsamo	Nos ergo multifarias
Benedicamus domino.	*Deo* dicamus *gratias.*

It is clear that a further development of tropes of this kind within the bounds of the authorized Liturgy was impossible: they threatened to overwhelm it, and, in order to save it, the only course left was to remove them altogether. Just as in Germany, though the Sequences did not call the sacred folk-song into being, yet they vigorously promoted its growth,

---

notice of investigators, lead us more especially to this conclusion. Gautier (*Les Tropes*, p. 170) therefore is not justified in saying that the Te Deum was troped only at *S. Gall*, and only in the first period of the tropes, for *Cod.* S. Gall 383 belongs to the 13th century. The trope given by Gautier is a prologue to the *Te Deum*.

1 For examples see Gautier *l. c.* pp. 166, 169 foll.

so in France from the rhymed tropes there grew up new compositions, spiritual songs of various kinds, which were also performed in the churches. [1]

These new songs, which had no longer any connexion with the liturgical text, were the delight of those vagabond clerks and 'ne'er-do-weel' students who were everywhere ready to sing for gain their tropes and other songs which were often far from blameless, against whom the Church had to take many precautions. Those of the clergy who held a high view of the importance of the Liturgy, and, above all, numerous provincial councils, opposed these disorders most energetically, and from the 13th century onwards this kind of trope disappears from the Liturgy. But the older harmless and beautiful kind of interpolation, which connected the liturgical text more closely with the character of the feast, was still retained during the centuries following. In the pre-Tridentine Graduals we often come across a troped *Gloria* or *Sanctus*, etc. The tropes were longest preserved in the Church of Lyons, which was especially distinguished for its attachment to old traditions. In the middle of the 18th century many of the chants of the *Ordinarium Missae* were still sung there with interpolations, as is shewn by a book printed in 1765. [2]

To return to S. Gall. There were other men of note who increased and extended the renown of the German monastery. Besides Notker and Tutilo, mention has already been made of Ratpert, their contemporary. His activity was confined to narrower limits, within the walls of the monastery. He created no new form, but we have several celebrated chants of his; *e.g.* a processional litany *Ardua spes mundi*, a litany frequently sung at the Baptisms of Easter and Pentecost, *Rex sanctorum Angelorum*, and a Communion chant *Laudes omnipotens*. A German hymn on S. Gall was also attributed to him. [3]

About the same time S. Gall was the abode of Hartmann, Ekkehard I, and Notker Physicus, who were famed as composers. [4] Notker Labeo

---

1 In this connexion mention should be made also of the liturgical plays and mysteries which sometimes appear in MSS. in company with the tropes. Thus *Cod. Lat. nouv. acquis.* 1235 of the Paris National Library contains on *fol.* 198 a piece to be sung after the Communion of Epiphany in which the three Wise Men of the East appear in turn, besides a Messenger and Chorus. Unfortunately many of the parts are indicated only by the first words. I hope to publish elsewhere this highly interesting 'mystery.' At Freiburg in Switzerland a similar one was preserved up till the 19th century, only much more prolonged. It was to be performed partly in church and partly outside.

2 Bohn, in the *Cäcilia*, Trèves, 1877.   3 Schubiger, *l.c.* 36 foll.

4 Notker Physicus composed a chant, *Rector aeterni*, which was treasured in the

is also mentioned as an author [1] and Ekkehard IV as an excellent singer.

Since Schubiger has sketched the musical history of the monastery in the time of its chief success, we can see almost throughout its musical tradition an exact imitation of the Roman *Schola Cantorum*. Ekkehard IV, who traced back the foundation of the S. Gall Song-school directly to Rome, also tells of an authentic Antiphoner, which, like Gregory's original one at Rome, was venerated as an undisputed standard of Church music. In the time of Hartmann (†924) it was still at S. Gall, and this monk made it his chief task to teach the chants as given in the authentic Antiphoner. Godeschalk and Cunibert are famous as praiseworthy copiers of this Chant-book. It is certainly incontestable that the S. Gall MSS. of liturgical chant are among the most ancient and valuable which have been preserved to our time.

There is still in existence to-day at S. Gall an Antiphoner of Godeschalk, besides one written by Hartker, a pious penitent who was a voluntary recluse there.[2] In the *Cod.* 359, of which Lambillotte published a facsimile in 1851, it was believed that the original MS. of Romanus had been discovered, or at least a contemporary copy of it. But Ekkehard's account of this affair is suspicious. Above all, the much-quoted anonymous S. Gall biographer of Charles the Great establishes the very important fact that the S. Gall chant of his time was strikingly different from the Roman. [3] There is no reason to refer this statement to the Office only, in which respect individual churches differed from one another; in any case it must somewhat lessen the enthusiasm felt for the S. Gall MSS. They are remarkable for a number of new signs quite unknown to the Italian and French traditions, so that the inference can hardly be avoided that the Roman melodies were connected at S. Gall with elements originally foreign to them, which show a more complicated rhythm and mode of execution than the other MSS. It is practically certain that these elements are of Greek origin; the most important sign is the horizontal stroke, which was already in early times the sign for rhythmical

---

Middle Ages and has been preserved in actual use down to our own day. Latterly the melody has been sung to the hymn *Vita sanctorum* of the Trèves Breviary.

1 To him we owe the oldest tract on music in the German language, printed in Gerbert, *Scriptores*, I, 96.

2 It is the often-quoted MS. 390-391, which has now appeared in a magnificent new phototype edition in the *Paléographie musicale*, series II.

3 'Nimiam dissimilitudinem nostrae et Romanorum cantilenae' (*Patr. Lat.* xcviij, 1377). Attention was for the first time drawn to this passage by Bäumer, *Brevierge-schichte*, 233 foll.

lengthening. The same signs are found as early as in *Cod.* 484, in which we have already seen traces of Byzantine influence; they thus made their appearance at the time when the middle-Greek hymn-poetry was adopted at S. Gall. In the discussion of the liturgical notation and the MS. memorials of the *Cantilena Romana* more will be said on these points.

The establishment of the Song-schools in the Middle Ages was due not to accident, but to necessity. The medieval notation was certainly not intended to give all that we expect to-day from a notation : it rather presupposed a strong oral tradition. In the early centuries at least, the liturgical chant could only be handed on by being impressed upon the memory of a competent choir. It is also remarkable that the Song-schools lost their importance from the very moment that the musical staff was adopted, which led to a more satisfactory notation. About the year 1100 they had completed their task. The tradition of the liturgical chant thenceforward rested on other foundations.

Not only at S. Gall, but in all the monastic foundations in Germany throughout the 10th and following centuries, did the Liturgy and the Roman chant flourish. Many of them were in direct communication with S. Gall and thankfully accepted the great artistic gifts of the monks there. Reichenau was the centre of musical achievement : it was here that Berno and Hermann Contract lived and laboured. At Hirschau also, where the Abbot William wrote a detailed work on music, at S. George and many other monasteries, and finally in the secular churches, they vied with one another in love for the Liturgy and the liturgical chant. Everything was regulated by precise rules, and so we see little sign of the introduction of innovations in Church music. [1] As in Italy and the region west of the Rhine, so in Germany also, after the Roman liturgy had once been adopted, the chant belonging to it was faithfully maintained, until a dangerous enemy to the *Cantilena Romana* arose in the *Musica mensurata*. This originated in the North, and not only drove the old chant from the Sanctuary and superseded it, but also gradually transformed the relationship between the Altar and the choir. Finally the chant which had grown out of the Liturgy fell a prey, first in its method of execution, and then in its melodic and rhythmical essence, to the theories and principles of the new art.

---

[1] Towards the end of the 11th century Bishop Benno of Meissen reformed the Church music in his diocese according to the model of the Church of Hildesheim : 'regularem canendi modum restituit fecitque, ut concinne et eleganter divina officia decantarentur.' AA : SS. Bolland. III, *June* 16.

CHAPTER XV

OFFICES IN METRICAL FORM

In spite of their overwhelming number, the Sequences and Tropes were really only an external decoration to the Liturgy of the Middle Ages, which affected its structure and nature but slightly. The reforms of the Cistercians and Dominicans affected the liturgical chant also, only to a smaller extent, far less in fact than has generally been supposed, and the liturgical work of the Franciscans entailed no change in the music. Thus the history of the liturgical chant ran its course uninterruptedly till the end of the Middle Ages. This is true especially of the chants of the Mass. The elements common to all MSS. which formed the contents of the Gregorian Antiphoner of the Mass underwent only a few unimportant alterations. Some feasts disappeared and some others were added; the melodies however of the former were not lost, but were retained in use, and in fact often served for the texts of the new Masses. The medieval history of the Chant of the Mass reveals a careful preservation of the precious heritage; the pre-Tridentine MSS. and printed books alike are in their contents practically identical with the oldest monuments of the Chant of the Mass from the 8th century onwards.

It is somewhat different with the Office. The music of the Nocturns as well as of the Day Hours at first exhibits the same tendency which governed the chant of the Mass in the Middle Ages, viz. the preservation of the primitive melodies unchanged. From the 10th century onwards we see a new departure, diametrically opposed to the earlier one. The new plan was, not to suppress the old Office-chants and replace them by new ones, nor merely to reform them,—such an idea was unknown throughout the Middle Ages—but only to abandon the primitive rule with regard to the new local Offices, (which became more and more numerous as time went on), and with the new texts to supply new melodies also. Each church naturally wished for beautiful Offices of its own saints and patrons; they could hardly be contented with the simple form in which the same feast was celebrated in other churches. Consequently there are a great number of Offices compiled and set to music from the 10th century onwards, which are of so peculiar a character as to make that date the starting point of a new era in the composition of medieval Offices. The melodic peculiarity of the new movement will be described later. So far as the text is concerned, most of the Offices belong to the class of the *Offices in verse*.

The starting-point and the rallying-point of all liturgical chant, both in ancient Christian times and in the Middle Ages, are the psalms and the other lyrical parts of Holy Scripture, *i.e.* texts in the form of prose. The ancient forms of the liturgical chant are adapted to them and presuppose them; had the founders of the ecclesiastical chant been confronted with metrical texts the music would have had quite a different development. The Hymns could not appropriate the older chant-forms: as little could the Sequences and Tropes; they created their own melodic ways of expression, suited to their own peculiarities. But when into the framework meant for prose texts there were inserted pieces in metrical forms, it was in no way an organic development, and the basis of the whole ecclesiastical chant might have been thereby placed in jeopardy. Happily the music acted as the preserver of the old venerable forms: the composers of the new offices, as a rule at least, treated their texts as prose, and in a different way from the Hymns and Sequences. Thus the structure of the Office-chant remained intact, in its main supports at least, although the new texts did not leave the musical forms quite unmodified. [1]

---

1 On metrical pieces in the Mass-chant *cf.* above, pp.61 and 68. Clemens Blume has discovered in a Vatican MS. of the 15th century (*Cod. Vat.* 1205) a metrical Mass of S. Achatio (*Liturg. Reimofficien des Mittelalters*, 5th series, p. 18) which is a curiosity, and is appended here:

Introitus.

Congaudentes laudent gentes
agmina nobilia,
militum crucifixorum
sancta dena milia,
per quos Deus mundo praestat
dona mirabilia.

Graduale.

Qui honorant crucifixos
cum pura instantia,
dena milia sunt semper
pro illis orantia.
Nunquam sinunt illos mori
sine poenitentia,
namque Deus donat illis
altum privilegium,
vincla solvens peccatorum
decenorum milium.
℣. Speciales horum servi
cum de mundo transeunt,
dena milia crucifixi
concurrentes veniunt,
Transeuntes adiuvando
precibus communiunt.
℣. Si poenarum loco dentur
et non aeternalium,

habent martyrum per preces
decenorum milium
Indulgentiam dierum
sic denorum milium.

Alleluia.

Sancta quippe mater tota
praedicet ecclesia,
quod per merita sanctorum
Deus dat auxilia,
poenitentibus confessis
donat indulgentiam.

Offertorium.

Cessent ergo malignantes
neque per invidiam
detrahendo molestare
martyrum potentiam,
ne in fine sint damnati
per Dei sententiam.

Communio.

Gloria sit crucifixo,
honor, jubilatio,
qui est rex crucifixorum,
vita, consolatio,
quos amavit, coronavit
in coeli palatio.

One can imagine the sort of music that would have to be provided in the various

In order to sketch the development of the new movement in its main outlines (more is not possible at present), it is advisable to examine some MSS. of Offices of different dates. [1]

The chants of the S. Gall Antiphoner (*Cod.* 390-1, the MS. of Hartker), composed in poetical form, may be divided into two groups. The starting-point of the whole movement is to be seen in pieces whose text was supplied by hymns already in liturgical use. Such is the 3rd stanza of the Christmas hymn *A solis ortus cardine*—*Castae parentis viscera*, which on p. 48 appears as the Verse of the ℞. *Gratulamini mihi omnes*, and on p. 118 as the Verse of the ℞. *Videte miraculum*; also the 4th stanza of the same hymn, *Domus pudici pectoris*, which on p. 49 is the Verse of the ℞. *Confirmatum est*; also, on the feast of the Exaltation of the Holy Cross, (p. 255) the ℞. *Dulce lignum, dulces clavos* with its ℣. *Crux fidelis*, taken from the Passion hymn *Pange lingua gloriosi praelium certaminis*. The introduction of these pieces into the Office may go back to the time when hymns were introduced into the Liturgy : in that case the germs of the poetical Office reach back very far; only the ℞. *Dulce lignum* cannot be older than the 7th century, in which the above-mentioned feast was introduced at Rome. [2]

Texts must be regarded as later which are drawn from poetry not used liturgically, or were composed on purpose for a particular feast. To these belong the Lauds Antiphon of Christmas, *Genuit puerpera regem* (p. 50) the source of which is the *Carmen paschale* of Sedulius (Book II, vv. 63 foll). As the stanzas of the hymn *A solis ortus* appear only as Respond-verses, and are thus connected with prose texts, the Antiphon before mentioned, which does not follow its original word for word, has rather lost its metrical character, especially in the second half. [3] On the

---

liturgical styles to suit a text of this sort. Dreves has found a similar Mass *De Immaculata Conceptione* in a Viennese MS. (*cf.* Preface to vol. 26 of the *Analecta Hymnica*). No proof is needed that works of this sort belong to the period of liturgical degeneracy.

1 Offices in poetical form are published in the *Analecta hymnica medii aevi* of Dreves, and later also of Blume, vols. 5, 13, 18 and 24-28. For their history *cf.* the prefaces of the volumes mentioned, also Blume in *Poésie des Kirchlichen Stundengebetes in Mittelalter*, in the *Stimmen aus Maria Laach*, 1898, pp. 132 foll. The material is not exhausted by the publications of the *Analecta hymnica*. The above-mentioned Offices of the Paris MS. for example have not as yet been published.

2 Duchesne, *Christian Worship*, 263.

3 The original runs (*Patr. Lat.* xix, 599) : 'Enixa puerpera regem, Qui coelum terramque tenet per saecula, cuius Numen et aeterno complectens omnia gyro Imperium

other hand the original form is kept by the R̥. *Continet in gremio* with its Verse *Maternis vehitur* (p. 49),[1] the similar Antiphon on p. 54, the Interrogation *Quid regina poli faciat nunc, dissere nobis* with the response *Nunc puerum Christum genuit gremioque locavit*, the Ant. *O Regem coeli* (p. 54),[2] the Ant. *In praesepio iacebat*,[3] which consists of four lines with a conclusion, and the Ant. *Praesepis angustia*,[4] composed of 2 hexameters clearly showing the repudiation of the laws of prosody (p. 55). All these texts belong to the Christmas Office.

In the Office of S. Benediçt we find (p. 129) the Antiphon, *Nutrici in auxilium*, consisting of four iambic dimeters[5] (also used as the Ṽ. of a Respond, p. 130); in that of S. Petèr, the text *Solve iubente Deo*[6] used as an Antiphon (p. 281) and as a Respond (p. 282), composed of two hexameters. I may further mention the Respond *in Nativ. B. Mariae* (p. 304) *Solem iustitiae* with the Ṽ. *Cernere divinum*,[7] consisting of 3 hexameters; two hexameters in honour of S. Othmar (p. 344),[8] and lastly

---

sine fine manet : quae ventre beato Gaudia matris habens cum virginitatis honore Nec primam similem visa est nec habere sequentem.' On the other hand the Antiphoner of Hartker runs thus : 'Genuit puerpera regem, cui nomen aeternum et gaudium matris habens cum virginitatis pudore nec &c. ;' thus it does not follow Sedulius word for word. Perhaps some other reading of Sedulius' poem is discernible here. It is remarkable that the Introit *Salve sancta parens*, which is first found in MSS. from the 12th century onwards, follows the original more exaçtly.

1 R̥. 'Continet in gremio coelum terramque regentem
    Virgo, Dei genitrix, proceres comitantur heriles,
    Per quos orbis ovans Christo sub principe pollet.

  Ṽ. Maternis vehitur, qui matrem vexerat ulnis,
    Bis seni comites, quem stipant agmine fido' (5 hexameters).

2 'O regem coeli, cui talia famulantur Obsequia stabulo ponitur qui continet mundum Jacet in praesepio et in nubibus tonat' (2 hexameters and 1 pentameter).

3 'In praesepio iacebat Et in coelis fulgebat Ad nos veniebat Et apud patrem manebat.'

4 'Praesepis angustia Christum portavit infantem Immensitas coeli Stephanum triumphantem suscepit.'

5 'Nutrici in auxilium Grande fecit miraculum Primum in partes divisum Reiunxit capisterium.'

6 'Solve iubente Deo terrarum, Petre, catenas, Qui facis ut pateant coelestia regna beatis.'

7 'Solem iustitiae regem paritura supremum Stella maria maris hodie processit ad ortum. Ṽ. Cernere divinum lumen, gaudete fideles.'

8 'Jam tenet Othmarus paradisi gaudia clarus Suppeditans agno date laudes robore magno.'

on p. 354 the ℣. *Nos sumus* (a *distich*) of the ℞. *Ora pro nobis* in the Office of S. Clement. ¹

All the metrical pieces named so far form a very small part of an Office which is otherwise made up entirely of prose, and they scarcely strike one, unless one examines the Offices singly and in detail with a view to this. They were still a long way from forming a complete Office in verse. This is to be found, in great part, in the *Officium de S. Trinitate* which stands in Hartker's Antiphoner on p. 101, and is used for a Sunday after Epiphany, not as afterwards (and in the case of the Mass as early as *Cod.* S. Gall 339) for the Octave of Pentecost. But even here the whole of the Office is not as yet composed in verse, though the greater part of it is. The 5 Antiphons of Vespers are: *Gloria tibi Triniïas, Laus et perennis gloria, Gloria laudis resonet in ore, Laus Deo Patri, parilique proli, Ex quo omnia*: perhaps the Ants. *Te invocamus, Spes nostra, Libera nos* of the 2nd Nocturn might also be counted, ² but in any case the ℞. *Gloria Patri genitaeque Proli.*

These texts composed in verse form a contrast to the others, whose language is in extremely sublime prose. Thus the Office does not make a harmonious impression; and the versified parts moreover do not all follow the same laws. First we have strophes of iambic and trochaic dimeters (Ants. *Gloria tibi* and *Laus et perennis*, and ℣. *Da gaudiorum*); then sapphic tropes (Ants. *Gloria laudis, Laus Deo Patri*, and ℞. *Gloria Patri*); then lines which are connected only by the assonance of their last syllables (Ants. *Ex quo omnia, Te invocamus, Spes nostra*, and *Libera nos*), if these can be regarded as verses at all. It is also remarkable that one and the same piece, the ℞. *Gloria Patri*, makes use of two completely different metres. All this either shews the author of the Office *de S. Trinitate* to be still feeling his way, and not quite clear as to how an Office composed in verse ought to look, or else shews the Office to be a compilation from various sources. Stephen, Bishop of Liège (†920), is mentioned as the composer of the Office, or rather his

---

1 'Nos sumus indigni promissa superna mereri, Sed tu pro nobis funde preces superis.'

2 These are inspired by the *Carmen de S. Trinitate* of Marius Victorinus Afer (*Patr. Lat.* viij, 1139 foll.). All the texts given above still stand in the present Roman Breviary, except the ℞. *Gloria Patri*, which may therefore be given here:

℞. Gloria patri genitaeque proli
    Et tibi compar utriusque semper
    Spiritus alme, Deus unus omni
        Tempore saecli.

℣. Da gaudiorum praemia,
    Da gratiarum munera,
    Dissolve litis vincula,
    Astringe pacis foedera. Omni tempore.

Ad Laudes

Ant. Cunctis valde venerandus
est beatus Arnulfus,
primum illis, quibus datus
est a Deo corpore.

Ant. Felix martir Arnulfus
coeli stemmate fisus
per corporis martirium
perenne sumpsit gaudium.

Ant. Metuende Deus semper,
O quam ammirabilis,
qui triumphum talem prae-
bes
militibus propriis

Ant. O athleta virtuose,
Arnulfe, suppliciter
ut pro nobis Deum roges,
precamur humiliter.

Ant. Laudemus dominum gaudenti
mente supernum,
laetificat tanto qui nos presente
patrono.

In Evang. Adest nobis dies gaudii,
qua beatus Arnulfus susceptus
est inter agmina sanctorum;
nobis ergo succurre, pie pater,
apud Deum.

Ad Magnificat

O martir propriam felix Arnulfe catervam
digna laude tui recolentem gaudia festi
semper sanctifica miti moderamine serva,
te duce christicolis iungatur iure perenni.

The further development of the versified Offices went on parallel to that of the Sequences. Beginning with a simple combination of portions in prose and poetry respectively, the whole Office soon came to be clothed in metrical forms, which at first appear in great variety, while no value is set on uniformity of structure. But no one could fail to see the defects of this stage, which merely represented a free compilation of the various parts, differing in their external form. The direction of the movement was determined from within: the whole of the *Historia* (the name for the sum total of the musical parts of the Office, especially those composed in verse-form [1]) ought to carry out the same metrical or rhythmical type from beginning to end, and by means of rhyme to unite the different parts of a strophe.

It has not yet been settled who made this important advance, and with it created the *Rhymed Offices*. Perhaps the Franciscan, Julian of

---

1 *Cf.* above, p. 115.

Spires, the highly gifted poet and composer of the Offices of S. Francis
and S. Anthony, [1] may be named as the perfecter of the movement. He
died about 1250 at Paris, where he had spent the greater part of his life.
We must thus place the origin of the uniform and completely-developed
Office in rhyme at the end of the 12th century or in the first half of the
13th; the period is not very far distant from the time of Adam of
S. Victor, and his Sequences must have influenced the Office-form. Both
of Julian's Offices form an organic whole of so perfect a character that
no further development was possible.

The structure of the Office of Julian is clear if one looks at its first
Antiphons :

Office of S. Francis   *Office of S. Anthony*

First Antiphon of the First Vespers

Office of S. Francis		Office of S. Anthony	
Franciscus, vir catholicus	a	Gaudeat ecclesia,	a
Et totus apostolicus	a	Quam in defunctorum	b
Ecclesiae teneri	b	Sponsus ornat gloria	a
Fidem romanae docuit	c	Matrem filiorum	b
Presbyterosque monuit,	c		
Prae cunctis revereri.	b		

The Office of S. Francis is written throughout in iambic, and that of
S. Anthony in trochaic verse, and the rhyme everywhere helps to round
off the distinct forms, so that the Antiphons and Responds often exhibit
a shape which has a similarity to the modern song-form. The Antiphons
or Responds belonging to one another, *e.g.* the Antiphons of Vespers, the
Antiphons and Responds of the first Nocturn, and so on, agree in the
number of their lines and the disposition of their rhymes. In the Office of
S. Anthony, moreover, all the Antiphons, those of Vespers as well as those
of the Nocturns, have four lines; only the *Cantica ad Evangelium* are,
according to the established tradition, properly treated in a more detailed
manner. It did not do to form the Responds and Antiphons alike; the
melodic execution demanded a greater number of lines for the former.

---

1 They have been published with the melodies by Father Fielder : *Die liturgischen
Reimoffizien auf dem hl. Franciscus und Antonius, gedichtet und componiert von Fr.
Julian von Speier*, Freiburg (Switzerland), 1901. Father Fielder has corrected in
some important points the statements of Dr. Weis in *Julian von Speier*, Munich, 1900.
The musical part of Weis's book is the least successful.

Julian's type of Office met with an extraordinary amount of favour, which, apart from the superior poetical and artistic capabilities of their author, is explained chiefly by the immense extension of the Franciscan Order and the Offices of its greatest Saints. For Offices of the Franciscan Saints, as well as for others, the forms of Julian were often imitated, not seldom with echoes of the original text, more frequently by simply adopting Julian's melodies. Such imitations are to be met with especially in books of Franciscan Use. Thus, to mention only a few, we find Offices in rhyme in honour of S. Clare, of S. Anthony the hermit, of S. Louis and others. The most important is one *De S. Trinitate* which begins with the words *Sedenti super solium.* [1] Its author is the Franciscan, John Peckham, Archbishop of Canterbury (†1292); in external structure it is an exact imitation of Julian's Office of S. Francis, with the melodies of which it is also connected. This new Trinity Office ousted the older one first from the Franciscan books, then from the Roman ones, which since Sixtus IV. had been edited by the Franciscans. To-day only the older one is in use.

The number of the Offices of the later Middle Ages is innumerable. Dreves and Blume have published many hundreds of them from MSS. and early printed books. Many Saints had several, *e.g.* 21 different rhymed Offices of S. Anne have been found. [2] In a few cases only have the names of the authors come down to us. Some may be given here to illustrate the extraordinary productiveness in the composition of Offices after the 10th century : we shall make no distinction between composers of poetry and prose respectively.

Alcuin is said to have composed an Office of S. Stephen and other pieces at Tours, though we are not told that he supplied them with melodies also. [3] His friend Angelram, Abbot of S. Riguier, is quoted as the composer of Offices of S. Valerius and S. Wulfram. Hucbald of S. Amand in Flanders, and Stephen, Bishop of Liège, have already been mentioned. The former, the celebrated theorist whose writings [4] have a unique interest because of the blending of the Latin theory with Byzantine ideas († *c.* 930), also composed chants for the Churches of Meaux and Nevers ; the song-school of Nevers had been under his direction for a long time. Stephen appears to have been very active, particularly in liturgical

---

1 Dreves, *Analecta hymnica* V, 19 foll.: *cf.* also XXIII, pp. 5 foll. and XXV, 5 foll.
2 Blume, *Zur Poesie etc.*, *l.c.* p. 133 foll.
3 Gerbert, *De Cantu* II, 33.
4 *De harmonica Institutione* ; see Gerbert *Scriptores*, vol. I.

matters, [1] as is also related of Franco, his predecessor in the See of Liège (856-903). [2] Ratbod, Bishop of Utrecht (c. 900), was considered to be the composer of the Office of the Translation of S. Martin, and Rainald, Bishop of Langres, to be the composer of an Office of the holy martyr Mammes, for which the poem of Walafrid Strabo supplied the text. Guido, Bishop of Auxerre (c. 950), is said to have set new texts in honour of a S. Julian, to the melodies of Hericus and Remigius, two monks in the monastery of S. Germanus at Paris, composed in honour of their patron. The same melodies were used at Autun since the 12th century for the feast of S. Lazarus also. [3] Abbot Folcvin of Lobbes (955-980) is the author of a rhymed Office on S. Folcvin, Abbot Odilo of Cluny (994-1048) in all probability of a similar one on S. Maiolus, his predecessor. Besides these, we may mention Letaldus of Micy near Orleans (end of 10th century), composer of a celebrated Office of S. Julian, the first bishop of Le Mans; he was admired for his knowledge of the old melodies which he took as his model, in contrast to other composers who allowed themselves licences and innovations. [4] About the year 936 flourished Marquard, a monk of Echternach, and composer of hymns, proses and other liturgical chants. One Remigius of Milan (about 980), at the request of Eckbert, Archbishop of Trèves, composed the Offices of SS. Eucharius, Valerius and Maternus, the founders of the Church of Trèves, as well as other chants. Bruno, Bishop of Toul, who ascended the Papal throne as Leo IX († 1054), deserves special mention. To him were ascribed Responds for the Office of S. Gorgonius, patron of the Abbey of Gorz, and Responds for the feasts of S. Hidulph, S. Ottila and Gregory the Great. If only Responds are mentioned, it must not be forgotten that they form the centre of brilliancy of the liturgical festival: on feast days

---

1 According to Sigebert (*De script, eccl. c.* 125 *Patr. Lat.* lx, 573) he sent to Bishop Robert of Metz a collection of Chapters, Responds, Verses and Collects for all the day and night Hours of the Church's year.

2 Gerbert, *De Cantu* II, 32.

3 For the following see Blume *l. c.* 137 foll., and Lebœuf, *Traité historique*, pp. 18 foll., also Gerbert, *De Cantu* II, 35 foll.

4 'Porro in componendo S. Juliani officio excedere noluit a similitudine veteris cantus, ne barbaram aut inexpertem melodiam fingeret : non enim mihi placet, ait ille, quorundam musicorum novitas qui tanta dissimilitudine utuntur, ut veteres sequi omnino dedignentur auctores.' *Annal. Bened.* I, 110. Lebœuf (*l. c.* p. 43) refers here to the gradual invasion of rhyme and metrical texts into the Office, and to some questionable licences which had already appeared in the compositions of Stephen of Liège, in the office *de S. Trinitate*,—a preference for the Tonic and Dominant at the end of the divisions and sub-divisions and a richer style of melody in the Antiphons.

all eyes were directed to the Cantor of the Mattin-Responds. Bruno also composed a celebrated melody for the *Gloria in excelsis*. [1] In later times still are mentioned Ingobrand, Abbot of Lobbes (12th century), and Peter, a Canon of Cambrai (end of 13th century), who set to music the Antiphons and Responds of S. Elizabeth, and who was also celebrated as the composer of the harmonized compositions called *Conductus*.

In Germany the rhymed Office was not in such vogue as in the countries of the French tongue : it was seldom the German way to rush into liturgical innovations. Nevertheless there was no lack of prominent men, poets and composers, who placed their great gifts at the service of the Liturgy. Berno of Reichenau (†1044) has been already mentioned in another connexion; from him comes an Office for S. Ulrich, perhaps also one for S. Meinrad, besides tropes and hymns as well. Hermann Contract is likewise already known to us as a composer. [2] To the 12th century belongs Udalschalc, who ruled the monastery of S. Ulrich and S. Afra in Augsburg (1124-1150). He was regarded with equal esteem both as a poet and a composer : he composed both the text and melody for the Offices of the two patrons of his monastery. [3] He is also said to have written the lives of S. Maurice and S. Mary Magdalen, and to have set them to music. [4] In later times there are two more writers of rhymed Offices to be named—Ghiseler of Hildesheim, and Leopold of Steinberg, who both laboured at Hildesheim about the year 1400; also Johann Hoffmann, Bishop of Meissen (middle of 15th century), and Johann Hane (end of same century). [5]

Still less attention seems to have been devoted to rhymed Offices in Italy. Alfano, a monk of Monte Cassino, afterwards Archbishop of

---

1 This melody is found in Schubiger, *Sängerschule*, No. 59 of the *Exempla*.

2 *Cf.* above p. 141, note, and p. 259.

3 The catalogue of the Abbots of his monastery praises him thus : 'Fecit inter alios cantus historiam totam de S. Afra. Similiter et historiam S ʋdalrici, ep. Aug., quem cantum ad episcopum Constantinensem Udalricum fecit : ita metro dyapente diatessaronque inducit, ac diapason consonantiarum concordi modulatione cum opportunis licentiis et figuris huius artis musicae utitur mirifice, ut in jocunditatem laudesque suaves Dei atque viri admirationem tristes quoque mentes quam facile excitari possint. Nec discors verborum sensus a melodiae concentu. Optimo enim metrorum genere Udalrici, Afrae autem prosa equidem a metri compendio haud multum distante, vitam pene omnem pariter ligavit ac comprehendit.' *Cf.* Hoeynck, *Geschichte des Bistums Augsburg*, p. 59.

4 'Versibus complexus est easque notis musicis composuit et ad publice decantandas in officiis ecclesiasticis destinavit.' Hoeynck, *ibid.*

5 Blume, *l. c.* 142.

Salerno (second half of 11th century), is the composer of a metrical Office of S. Sabina. A century later Reinaldus of Colle di Mezzo, also at first a monk of Monte Cassino, then (after 1140) Cardinal-priest, wrote an Office for S. Placidus. Lastly Raymund de Vincis, a Dominican, who lived at Capua towards the end of the 14th century, is spoken of as the author of an Office for the Visitation. The Roman Church held most faithfully to the old form of the Office, and pure Roman books seldom give admittance to a rhymed Office. Nevertheless they spread to England and Scandinavia.

Thus, gradually, the Office came under the influence of poetry, and its latest form, the Hymns, had almost completely assimilated all the older parts. Sooner or later a movement in this direction was bound to come, when once it became possible to adopt in the Liturgy texts not belonging to the Prayer book and Chant book of the Church, the Bible. The great liturgical reform of the 16th century ejected most of the later medieval Offices, and, by the movement towards uniformity in the Office, brought back the music to its first principles. The work of the Council of Trent was also a beneficent reform in this respect, even though the Church, by acquiescing in some rhymed portions, showed its readiness to incorporate all that is beautiful and good, so long as it submitted to those laws which were imposed upon the Office by its founders. Single rhymed Offices have been retained, chiefly in the Franciscan and Dominican Breviaries, down to the present time. As late as the 17th century David Furmann composed one for S. Florian, and a Viennese MS. contains a still later one for the Immaculate Conception. [1]

'Return to tradition' was the solution which the great Church assembly at Trent adopted for the whole province of the Liturgy. It was a necessity, as the liturgical innovations in the course of the previous centuries threatened to de-rail the forms of the prayers and also of the chants.

This 'Return' was attained, and the historian of ecclesiastical chant should offer hearty thanks for it to divine Providence.

The Tridentine reform awakened the Roman liturgy, established by

---

[1] Dreves, in the Preface to Vol. XXVI of the *Analecta hymnica*.

Gregory I., to a new and glorious life, so that the worship of the Church to this day rises up to Heaven in the old venerable forms. These have lost none of their power or freshness; they seem ever to grow in glory and beauty. But Providence has not only given us almost intact the forms of prayer: the music also which proceeded from them, born at the Altar, grown to greatness with the Church itself, and ordered together with its worship, has not been lost either. Hundreds of books preserve it down to the present time, and to-day it celebrates its resurrection under the *aegis* of an illustrious Pope. Thus the present and the past history of ecclesiastical music unite in showing forth the truth: may many powers unite in reforming the structure of the chant of Christian worship; the special providence, which has so wonderfully guided the fortunes of this glorious and sublime manifestation of the human mind God-ward, has always intervened at critical moments, and corrected the short-sighted attempts of the innovator.

APPENDIX

The Texts of the Antiphonarium Missae

The following tables give a summary of the texts of the early medieval Chant-book, with the indication of their origin. An ordinary figure after a text indicates the psalm concerned; the other abbreviations refer to other parts of Holy Scripture, *e.g.* Gal. 6 = Chapter 6 of the Epistle to the Galatians. Non-biblical texts are indicated by a? A comparison of these tables will prove the statements in Chapters 4—6 and 10.

The S. Gall MS. 339 of the 10th century is accessible to everyone in the phototype edition in vol. I of the *Paléographie musicale* of the Benedictines of Solesmes. Setting aside the few feasts of our Lord and of the Saints with which the Liturgy has since been enriched, the tables give the contents of the later medieval and the post-Tridentine books of chant, and will also prove of good service, should anyone wish for information about the present Gradual and the origin of its texts.

Almost the only variations in the MSS. are in the Alleluia-verses, the texts of which were probably not arranged under Gregory I (*cf.* p. 81). A comparison of the Alleluia-texts of Easter week, according to manuscript and printed sources from the 8th century till the Council of Trent, will show the difference.

The series of Gradual Responds for the Sundays after Pentecost, mentioned on p. 79, which surprise one in the Rheinau MS. and some others, is likewise given: they may be compared with those of *Cod.* 339 of S. Gall.

As the *Paléographie musicale* (I, pp. 71 foll.) shows in detail, the S. Gall MS. 339 exhibits the Roman Gregorian Chant-book in the condition in which it was in the second half of the 10th century. It is not impossible to evolve from this *Codex* the original form of the Gregorian *Antiphonarium Missae*: one has only to eliminate for that purpose the Masses and chants introduced in the 7th, 8th and 9th centuries: they are as follows:

1 All the Thursdays in Lent, which first received their Masses from Gregory II.

2 The feast of the Holy Trinity, first introduced in the 9th century.

3 The *Dedicatio Ecclesiae.*

4 The Sundays after the Ember days; of these the second Sunday in Lent still has no Mass in *Cod.* 339.

5 The Thursday after Pentecost.

6 The feasts of the Mother of God, and the Octave of Christmas.

7 The feasts of Holy Cross, which are furnished with Greek pieces.

8 Lastly, the following feasts of Saints: Lucy, Felix in Pincis, Gregory, Alexander, Eventius and Theodolus, Primus and Felicianus, Apollinaris, Agapetus, Hadrian, Gorgonius, Protus and Hyacinthus, Euphemia, Jerome and Martin.

In the tables, the post-Gregorian masses are indicated by brackets.

The texts printed in italics are indicated by only the first word in the MS. and without notes, because the chants in question have either already appeared before, or are given in full later on; *e.g.* R7. *Propitius* with ỹ. *Adiuva* for the Saturday before the 2nd Sunday in Advent and Thursday after the 2nd Sunday in Lent; R7. *Convertere* with ỹ. *Domine refugium* for the Saturday before the 2nd Sunday in Lent and the 6th Sunday after Pentecost; R7. *Salvum fac* with ỹ. *Ad te Domine* of the same Saturday, and the Wednesday after the 2nd Sunday in Lent; and the Tr. *Audi filia* for the Purification and the Annunciation.

I.

CODEX OF ST. GALL, 339.

INTROITUS	VERSUS	GRADUALE	VERSUS
Dom. IV ante Nativ.			
Dom.			
Ad te levavi 24	*Vias tuas* 24	Universi qui 24	Vias tuas 24
Dom. III ante Nativ.			
Dom.			
Populus Sion Isai. 30	*Qui regis* 79	Ex Sion species 49	Congregate 49
(Nat. S. Luciae)			
Dilexisti 44	*Eructavit* 44	Dilexisti 44	Propterea 44
Dom. II ante Nativ.			
Dom.			
Gaudete Phil. 4	*Cant. domino* 95	Qui sedes 79	Qui regis 79
Feria IV.			
Rorate Isai. 45	*Coeli enarrant* 18	Tollite portas 23	Quis ascendet 23
Feria VI.		Prope est dominus 144	Laudem domini 144
Prope esto 118	*Beati immac.* 118	Ostende nobis 84	Benedixisti dom. 84
Sabb. 12 lect.			
Veni et ostende 79	*Qui regis* 79	A summo coelo 18	Coeli enarrant 18
		In sole posuit 18	A summo coelo 18
		Dom. Deus virtut. 79	Excita domine 79
Dom. prox. ante Nat.		Excita domine 79	Qui regis 79
Dom.			
Memento 105	*Confitemini* 105	*Prope est dom.* 144	*Laudem domini* 144
Vigil. Nativ. Dom.			
Hodie scietis Ex. 16	*Dom. est terra* 23	Hodie scietis Exod. 16	Qui regis 79
Nativ. primo galli-			
cinio			
Dominus dixit 2	*Quare fremuer.* 2	Tecum principium 109	Dixit dominus 109
In primo mane			
Lux fulgebit Isai. 9	*Dom. regnavit* 92	Benedictus qui 117	A domino factum 117
In die			
Puer natus Isai. 9	*Cant. domino* 97	Viderunt omnes 97	Notum fecit 97
Nat. S. Stephani			
Etenim sederunt 118	*Beati immac.* 118	Sederunt princip. 118	Adjuva me 118
Nat. S. Johannis			
Ego autem sicut 51	*Quid gloriaris* 51	Justus ut palma 91	Ad adnuntiandum 91
Item ad Missam			
In medio Ecclus. 15	*Bonum est con-* *fiteri* 91	Exiit sermo John 21	Sed sic eum John 21
Nat. Innocentium			
Ex ore 8	*Dom. dominus* 8	Anima nostra 123	Laqueus 123
Nat. S. Silvestri			
Sacerdotes tui 131	*Memento dom.* 131	Ecce sacerdos Eccl. 44	Non est inv. Eccl. 44
Statio ad S. Mariam			
Vultum tuum 44	*Eructavit* 44	Diffusa est 44	Propter veritatem 44
Dom. I post Nativ.			
Dum medium Wis. 18	*Dom. regnavit* 92	Speciosus forma 44	Eructavit 44

ALLELUIA CUM VERSU	OFFERTORIUM	VERSUS	COMMUNIO
)stende nobis 84	Ad te levavi 24	Dirige me / Respice in me } 24	Dominus dabit 84
ætatus sum / Stantes erant } 121	Deus tu convert. 84	Benedixisti / Misericordia } 84	Hierusal. surge Bar. 4 & 5
)iffusa est 44	Offerentur...tibi 44	Eructavit / Adducentur } 44	Diffusa est 44
xcita domine 79	Benedixisti 84	Operuisti / Ostende } 84	Dicite pusill. Isa. 35
	Confortamini Isai. 35	Tunc aperientur / Audite itaque } Isai. 35	Ecce virgo Isai. 7
	Deus tu convertens 84		Ecce dominus veniet Zech. 14
Iym. 3 puer. Dan. 3	Exsulta satis Zech. 9	Loquetur Zech. 9 / Quia ecce Zech. 2	Exsultavit ut 18
Tractus Qui regis 79			
Memento nostri 105	Ave Maria Luke 1	Quomodo in me / Ideo quod } Luke 1	*Ecce virgo* Isai. 7
Veni domine ? (1st half Hab. 23)	Tollite portas 23	Domini est terra / Ipse super } 23	Revelabitur Isai. 40
)ominus dixit 2	Laetentur coeli 95	Cantate domino / Cantate domino } 95	In splendoribus 109
)ominus regnavit 92	Deus enim firmavit 92	Dominus regnavit / Mirabilis } 92	Exsulta filia Zech. 9
)ies sanctificatus ?	Tui sunt coeli 88	Magnus et / Misericordia / Tu humiliasti } 88	Viderunt omnes 97
'ideo coelos Acts 7	Elegerunt Acts 6	Viderunt faciem / Positis autem } Acts 6	Video coelos Acts 7
	Gloria et honore 8	Domine dominus / Quis est homo } 8	Magna est gloria 20
Iic est discip. Joh. 21	Justus ut palma 91	Bonum est confiteri / Ad adnuntiandum / Plantatus } 91	Exiit sermo Joh. 21
	Anima nostra 123	Nisi quod dominus / Torren. pertransivit } 123	Vox in Rama Matt. 2
nveni David 88	Inveni David 88	Potens es / Veritas mea } 88	Beatus serv. Matt. 24
	Offerentur regi 44	Eructavit 44	Simile est Matt. 13
Dominus regnavit ? 92	*Deus enim firmavit* 92		Tolle puer. Matt. 2

1 The MS. on p. 2 marks neither the *Offertorium* nor the second Alleluia-verse *Stantes erant.* For the *Fer. VI post Dom. II ante Nativ.*, which has the same Offertory *Deus tu convertens*, only the opening words are given, almost the only instance in the MS., except when the piece in question has already appeared in a complete form. Both pieces are given on one of the leaves of the MS. which precede the Gradual.

2 Of the hymn *Trium puerorum* only the words are marked, not the melodies also.

INTROITUS	VERSUS	GRADUALE	VERSUS
In Epiphania			
Ecce advenit ?	*Deus iudicium* 71	Omnes de Saba Is. 60	Surge Isai. 6
Dom. I post Theophan.			
In excelso throno ?	*Jubilate dom.* 99	Benedictus dom. 71	Suscipiant 7
(Nat. S. Felicis in pincis)			
Os iusti 36	*Noli æmulari* 36	Juravit dominus 109	Dixit dominus 10
Dom. II post Theophan.			
Omnis terra 65	*Jubilate Deo* 65	Misit dominus 106	Confiteantur 10
Nat. S. Marcelli			
Statuit ei Ecclus. 45	*Misericordias* 88	Inveni David 88	Nihil proficiat 8
Nat. S. Priscæ			
Loquebar 118	*Beati immac.* 118	Specie tua 44	
Nat. S. Fabiani et Sebast.			
Intret in 78	*Deus venerunt* 78	Glorios. Deus Ex. 15	Dextera tua Ex. 1
Nat. S. Agnetis			
Me expectaverunt 118	*Beati immac.* 118	*Diffusa est* 44	
Dom. III post Theophan.			
Adorate Deum 96	*Dom. regnavit* 96	Timebunt 101	Quon. ædificavit 10
Nat. S. Vincentii			
Lætabitur 63	*Exaudi Deus* 63	Posuisti domine 20	Desiderium 2
Nat. Agnetis (Octav.)			
Vultum 44		*Specie tua* 44	
(Purificat. S. Mariæ)			
Suscepimus 47	*Magnus dom.* 47	Suscepimus Deus 47	Sicut audivimus 4
Nat. S. Agathæ			
Gaudeamus ?	*Eructavit* 44	Adiuvabit eam 45	Fluminis impetus 4
Nat. S. Valentini			
In virtute 20	*Magna est* 20	Beatus vir 111	Potens in 11
(Nat. S. Gregorii)			
Sacerdotes Dei Dan. 3	*Benedicite* Dan. 3	*Juravit dominus* 109	
(Adnuntiatio S. Mariæ)			
Vultum 44		*Diffusa est* 44	
Dom. in Septuag.			
Circumdederunt 17	*Diligam te* 17	Adjutor in 9	Quoniam non
Dom. in Sexag.			
Exsurge 43	*Deus auribus* 43	Sciant gentes 82	Deus pone 8
Dom. in Quinquag.			
Esto mihi (70?) 30	*In te dom.* (70?) 30	Tu es Deus 76	Liberasti 7
Fer. IV in cap. jejun.			
Misereris Wis. 11	*Miserere mei* 56	Miserere mei 56	Misit 5
Fer. V			
Dum clamarem 54	*Exaudi Deus* 54	Jacta cogitatum 54	Dum clamarem 5
Fer. VI			
Audivit dominus 29	*Exaltabo* 29	Unam petii 26	Ut videam 2

ALLELUIA CUM VERSU	OFFERTORIUM	VERSUS	COMMUNIO
ʹidimus stell. Matt. 2	Reges Tharsis 71	Deus iudicium Orietur in diebus }71 Suscipiant	Vidimus stell. Matt. 2
ubilate Deo 99	Jubilate Deo 99	Ipse fecit } Laudate nomen 99	Fili quid Luke. 2
	Gloria et honore 8		Posuisti domine 20
ʹaudate Deum 148	Jubilate Deo 65	Reddam tibi} Locutum est 65	Dicit dominus Joh. 2
	Veritas mea 88	Posui } Misericordiam 88	Do. quinque Matt. 25
	Filiæ regum 44	Eructavit } Virga recta 44	Feci iudicium 118
	Lætamini 31	Beati quorum } Pro hac orabit 31	Multitudo Luke 6
	Offerentur minor 44		Quinq. prud. Matt. 25
ʹominus regnavit 96	Dextera domini 117	In tribulatione }117 Impulsus versatus	Mirabantur Luke 4
	Gloria et honore 8		Qui vult ven. Matt. 16
	Diffusa est 44	*Eructavit* } Specie tua 44	*Simile est* Matt. 13
ʹAdorabo 137} (Tract.) *Audi filia* 44	*Diffusa est* 44		Responsum Luke 2
TRACTUS			
ʹui seminant 125	*Offerentur* minor 44		Qui me dignatus ?
ʹesiderium 20	In virtute 20	Vitam petiit} Magna est 20	*Magna est gloria* 20
ʹeatus vir 111	*Veritas* 88		Fidelis serv. Matt. 24
ʹudi filia 44	*Ave Maria* Luke 1		*Ecce virgo* Isai. 7
ʹe profundis 129	Bonum est 91	Quam magnificata} Ecce inimici }91 Exaltabitur	Illumina 30
ʹommovisti 59	Perfice gressus 16	Exaudi } Custodi me }16 Ego autem	Introibo 42
ʹubilate 99	Benedictus es 118	Beati immaculati} In via }118 Viam iniquitatis	Manducaverunt 77
	Exaltabo 29	Dom. abstraxisti }29 Ego autem dixi	Qui meditabitur 1
	Ad te domine 24	Fac mecum } Da mihi intellec-}118 tum	Acceptabis 50
	Domina vivifica 118		Servite domino 2

INTROITUS		VERSUS		GRADUALE		VERSUS	
Dom. I Quadrag.							
Invocavit	90	*Qui habitat*	90	Angelis suis	90	In manibus	
Fer. II							
Sicut oculi	122	*Ad te levavi*	122	Protector noster	83	Domine Deus	
Fer. III							
Domine refugium	89	*Priusquam*	89	Dirigatur	140	Elevatio	I.
Fer. IV							
Reminiscere	24	*Ad te domine*	24	Tribulationes	24	Vide humilitatem	
				De necessitatibus	24	Ad te domine ⎫ Etenim universi ⎭	
(Fer. V)							
Confessio	95	*Cantate*	95	Custodi me	16	De vultu	
Fer. VI							
De necessitatibus	24	*Ad te domine*	24	Salvum fac	85	Auribus	
				Miserere mihi	6	Conturbata	
Sabb. 12 lect.							
Intret oratio	87	*Domine Deus*	87	*Dirigatur*	140	*Elevatio*	I.
				Convertere	89	*Domine refugium*	
				Propitius	78	*Adjuva nos*	
				Salvum fac	27	*Ad te domine*	
(Dom. II Quadrag.)							
Fer. II							
Redime	25	*Judica me*	25	Adjutor meus	69	Confundantur	
Fer. III							
Tibi dixit	26	*Dom. illumin.*	26	*Jacta cogitatum*	54	*Dum clamarem*	
Fer. IV							
Ne derelinquas	37	*Domine ne in*	37	Salvum fac	27	Ad te domine	
(Fer. V)							
Deus in adjutorium	69	*Avertantur*	69	Propitius	78	Adjuva nos	
Fer. VI							
Ego autem cum	16	*Exaudi domine*	16	Ad dominum	119	Domine libera	I
Sabbato							
Lex domini	18	*Cœli enarrant*	18	Bonum est confiteri	91	Ad adnuntiandum	
Dom. III Quadrag.							
Oculi mei	24	*Ad te domine*	24	Exsurge domine	9	In convertendo	
Fer. II							
In Deo laudabo	55	*Miserere mei*	55	Deus vitam	55	Miserere mihi	
Fer. III							
Ego clamavi	16	*Exaudi domine*	16	Ab occultis	18	Si mei non	
Fer. IV							
Ego autem in	30	*In te domine*	30	*Miserere mihi*	6	*Conturbata*	
(Fer. V)							
Salus populi	?	*Attendite*	77	Oculi	144	Aperis	I
Fer. VI							
Fac mecum	85	*Inclina domine*	85	In Deo speravit	27	Ad te domine	
Sabbato							
Verba mea	5	*Quoniam ad te*	5	Si ambulem	22	Virga tua	

TRACTUS		OFFERTORIUM		VERSUS		COMMUNIO	
Qui habitat	90	Scapulis suis	90	Dicet domino ⎫ Quoniam angelis ⎬ Super aspidem ⎭	90	Scapulis suis	90
		Revela oculos	118	Legem pone ⎱ Veniant ⎰	118	Voce mea	3
		In te speravi	30	Illumina ⎱ Quam magna ⎰	30	Cum invocarem	4
		Meditabor	118	Pars mea ⎱ Miserere mei ⎰	118	Intellige	5
		Immittit	33	Benedicam ⎫ In domino ⎬ Accedite ⎭	33	Panis quem Joh. 6	
		Benedic	102	Qui propitiatur ⎱ Justitiæ eius ⎰	102	Erubescant	6
Laudate dom.	116	Domine Deus	87	Inclina ⎫ Et ego ⎬ Factus sum ⎭	87	Domine Deus	7
		Benedicam	15	Conserva me ⎱ Notas fecisti ⎰	15	Domine dominus	8
		Miserere mihi	50	Quoniam iniquitatem ⎱ Tibi soli ⎰	50	Narrabo	9
		Ad te domine	24			Justus es	10
		Beatus est Exod.	32	Dixit dominus ⎱ Dixit Moyses ⎰ Ex.	32	Qui manducat Joh. 6	
		Dom. in auxilium	39	Exspectans ⎱ Avertantur ⎰	39	Tu domine	11
		Illumina oculos	12	Usquequo domine ⎱ Respice in me ⎰	12	Oportet te Luke 15	
Ad te levavi	122	Justitia domini	18	Præceptum ⎱ Et erunt ⎰	18	Passer invenit	83
		Exaudi Deus	54	Conturbatus ⎱ Ego autem ⎰	54	Quis dabit	13
		Dextera domini	117			Domine quis	14
		Domine fac	108	Deus laudem ⎫ Pro eo ut ⎬ Locuti sunt ⎭	108	Notas mihi	15
		Si ambulavero	137	In quacunque ⎱ Adorabo ad ⎰	137	Tu mandasti	118
		Intende voci	5	Verba me ⎱ Dirige ⎰	5	Qui biberit Joh. 4	
		Gressus meos	118	Declaratio ⎱ Cognovi ⎰	118	Nemo te Joh. 8	

286

INTROITUS	VERSUS	GRADUALE	VERSUS
Dom. IV Quadrag.			
Lætare Isai. 66	*Lætatus sum* 121	Lætatus sum 121	Fiat pax 12
Fer. II			
Deus in nomine 53	*Averte mala* 53	Esto mihi (30 ?) 70	Deus in te (30 ?) 7
Fer. III			
Exaudi deus 54	*Contristatus* 54	Exsurge domine 43	Deus auribus 4
Fer. IV			
Dum sanctificatus Ez.36	*Benedic. dom.* 33	Venite filii 33	Accedite 3
		Beata gens 32	Verbo domini 3
(Fer. V)			
Lætetur cor 104	*Confitemini* 104	Respice domine 73	Exsurge domine 7
Fer. VI			
Meditatio 18	*Cæli enarrant* 18	Bonum est confid. 117	Bonum est sperare 11
Sabbato			
Sitientes Isai. 55	*Attendite* 77	Tibi domine 9	Ut quid
Dom. V de Passione			
Judica me 42	*Quare me repu.* 42	Eripe me 142	Liberator 14
Fer. II			
Miserere mihi 55	*Conculcaver.* 55	Deus exaudi 53	Deus in nomine 5
Fer. III			
Exspecta dom. 26	*Dom. illumin.* 26	Discerne causam 42	Emitte lucem 4
Fer. IV			
Liberator meus 17	*Diligam te* 17	Exaltabo te 29	Domine Deus 2
(Fer. V)			
Omnia quæ Dan. 3	*Magnus dom.* 47	Tollite hostias 28	Revelabit 2
Fer. VI			
Miserere mihi 30	*In te domine* 30	Pacifice loquebant. 34	Vidisti domine 3
Dom. in Palmis			
Domine ne longe 21	*Deus, Deus meus* 21	Tenuisti manum 72	Quam bonus 7
Fer. II			
Judica domine 34	*Effunde fram.* 34	Exsurge domine 34	Effunde frameam 3
Fer. III			
Nos autem Gal. 6	*Deus misereat.* 66	Ego autem dum 34	Judica domine 3
Fer. IV			
In nomine Phil. 2	*Dom. exaudi* 101	Ne avertas 68	Salvum me 6
		Domine exaudi 101	Ne avertas / In quacunque / Quia defecerunt / Percussus sum / Tu exsurgens } 10
Fer. V *Nos autem* Gal. 6		Christus factus Phil. 2	Propter quod Phil. 2
Fer. VI		Domine audivi Hab. 3	In medio / In eo dum / Deus a Libano / Operuit cœlos } Hab.

Sabbato — CANTICA : Cantemus domino, Exod.; Vinea facta, Isai.; Attende cœlum, Deut.; Sicut cervus, 41. — ALLELUIA : Confitemini, 106. — TRACTUS : Laudate, 116.

TRACTUS	OFFERTORIUM	VERSUS	COMMUNIO
...i confidunt 124	Laudate dominum 134	Qui statis ⎫ Domine nomen ⎬ 134 Qui timetis ⎭	Hierusalem quæ 121
	Jubilate Deo		Ab occultis 18
	Exspectans 39	Statuit super ⎫ Multa fecisti ⎬ 39 Domine deus ⎭	Lætabimur 19
	Benedicite gentes 65	Jubilate Deo ⎫ In multitudine ⎬ 65 Venite et videte ⎭	Lutum fecit Joh. 9
	Dom. ad adjuvand. 39	Exspectans 39	Dom. memorabor 70
	Populum humilem 17	Clamor meus ⎫ 17 Liberator meus ⎭	Videns dom. Job. 11
	Factus est 17	Persequar ⎫ 17 Præcinxisti ⎭	Dominus regit 22
æpe expugnaver. 128	Confitebor tibi 118	Beati immaculati ⎫ 118 Viam veritatis ⎭	Hoc corpus 1 Cor. 11
	Domine convertere 6	Domine ne in ⎫ 6 Miserere mihi ⎭	Dominus virtutum 23
	Sperent in te 9	Sedes super ⎫ 9 Cognoscetur ⎭	Redime me 24
	Eripe me 58	Quia ecce ⎫ 58 Quia factus ⎭	Lavabo inter 25
	Super flumina 136	In salicibus ⎫ Si oblitus ⎬ 136 Memento ⎭	Memento verbi 118
	Benedictus es 118	Vidi non servantes ⎫ 118 Appropiaverunt ⎭	Ne tradideris 26
eus, Deus meus 21	Improperium 68	Salvum me ⎫ 68 Adversum me ⎭	Pater si non Matt. 26
	Eripe me 14	Ego vero ⎫ 14 Exaudi me ⎭	Erubescant 34
	Custodi me 139	Eripe me ⎫ 139 Qui cogitaverunt ⎭	Adversum me 68
	Domine exaudi 101	Ne avertas ⎫ Quia oblitus ⎬ 101 Tu exsurgens ⎭	Potum meum 101
	Dextera domini		Dom. Jesus Joh. 13
ripe me 139			

AD SALUTANDAM CRUCEM : Agios heos, Sanctus Deus.
Ant. Crucem tuam; Ecce lignum; Cum fabricator. Versus Fortunati episcopi. (Hymn. Crux fidelis.)

INTROITUS		VERSUS		GRADUALE		VERSUS	
Die Paschæ							
Resurrexi	138	*Dom. probasti*	138	Hæc dies	117	Confitemini dom.	117
Fer. II							
Introduxit vos	Exod. 13	*Confit. dom.*	104	,,	117	Dicat nunc Israhel	117
Fer. III							
Aqua sapientiæ	Ecclus. 15	*Confit. dom.*	105	,,	117	Dicat nunc 1	106
Fer. IV							
Venite bened.	Matt. 25	*Cantate dom.*	97	,,	117	Dextera domini	117
Fer. V							
Victricem manum	Wis. 10	*Cantate dom.*	95	,,	117	Lapidem quem	117
Fer. VI							
Eduxit vos	77	*Attendite*	77	,,	117	Benedic. qui venit	117
Sabbato							
Eduxit dominus	104	*Confitemini*	104			All. Hæc dies	117
Octava Paschæ							
Quasimodo	1 Pet. 2	*Exultate Deo*	80			All. In resurrectione ?	
Dom. I post Albas							
Misericordia domini	32	*Exultate justi*	32			All. *Surrex. dom. vere*	
Dom. II							
Jubilate Deo	65	*Canticum*	65			All. *Cantate domino*	
Dom. III							
Cantate domino	97	*Salvabit*	97			All. *Eduxit dominus*	
Dom. IV							
Vocem jocunditatis	Is. 48	*Jubilate Deo*	65			All. *Hæc dies*	117
S. Tyburtii et Valerii							
Sancti tui	144	*Exaltabo te*	144				
S. Georgii Mart.							
Protexisti	63	*Exaudi Deus*	63				
In Letania majore							
Exaudivit	17	*Diligam te*	17				
S. Vitalis Mart.							
Protexisti	63	*Exaudi Deus*	63				
S. Philippi et Jacobi							
Exclamav. ad te	2 Es. 9, 28	*Exultate justi*	32				
(Alexandri, Eventii, Theo-							
doli) Clamaverunt justi	33	*Benedicam do.*	33	*Gloriosus Deus*		*Dextera tua*	
S. Gordiani et Epimachi							
Sancti tui	144	*Exaltabo te*	144	Justor. animæ Wis. 3		Visi sunt	Wis. 3
S. Pancratii Mart.							
Ecce oculi	32	*Exultate justi*	32				
(Dedicat. Eccles.)							
Terribilis	Gen. 28	*Quam dilecta*	83	Locus iste	?	Deus cui astat	?
S. Potentianæ Virg.							
Dilexisti	44	*Eructavit*	44	*Diffusa*	44	*Propter*	44
In Ascens. Domini							
Viri Galilei	Acts 1	*Omnes gentes*	46			All. Ascendit Deus	46

1 Originally: Dicat nunc domus Aaron. Ps. 117. *Cf.* above, p. 79.

LLELUIA CUM VERSU	OFFERTORIUM	VERSUS	COMMUNIO
scha nostr. 1 Cor. 5 / ulemur	Terra tremuit 75	Notus in Judea / Et factus est / Ibi confregit } 75	Pascha nostr. 1 Cor. 5
rrexit dom. Luke 24	Angel. dom. Matt. 28	Euntes dicite / Jesus stetit } Matt. 28	Surrexit do. Luke 24
tulerunt Luke 24	Intonuit de cœlo 17	Diligam te / Liberator meus } 17	Si consurrexistis Col. 3
rrexit altissimus ?	Portas cœli 77	Attendite / Aperiam in parabolis } 77	Chr. resurgens Rom. 6
ntate domino 95	In die solemnit. Ex. 3	Audi popule / Non adorabitis } 80	Pop. adquisit. 1 Pet. 2
duxit dominus 104	Erit vobis hic Ex. 12	Dixit Moyses Ex. 14 / In mente habete Ex. 13	Data est Matt. 28
udate pueri / t nomen } 112	Benedictus qui 117	Hæc dies / Lapidem quem } 117	Omnes qui in Gal. 3
scha nostr. 1 Cor. 5	*Angel. dom.* Matt. 28		Mitte manum Joh. 20
ngel. dom. Mark 28	Deus, Deus meus 62	Sitivit in te / In matutinis } 62	Ego sum past. Joh. 10
nedictus Dei filius ?	Lauda anima 145	Qui custodit / Dominus erigit } 145	Modicum Joh. 16
rrexit altissimus ?	*Jubilate Deo* 65		Dum venerit Joh. 16
scha nostr. 1 Cor. 5	*Benedicite gentes* 65		Cantate domino 95
	Lætamini		Gaudete iusti 32
	Confitebuntur cæli 88	Misericordias / Quoniam quis } 88	Lætabitur justus 63
nfitemini dom. 106	Confitebor dom. 108	Adiuva me / Qui insurgunt } 108	Petite et accip. Lu. 11
	Repleti sumus 89	Domine refugium / Priusquam fierent } 89	Ego sum vitis Joh. 15
	Confitebuntur 88		Tanto tempore Joh. 14
	Repleti sumus 89		Justor. animæ Wis. 3
	Mirabilis 67	Exurgat Deus / Pereant peccatores } 67	*Gaudete justi* 32
	Confitebuntur 88		*Gaudete justi* 32
dorabo	Do. Deus in 1 Chr. 29	Majestas domini / Fecit Salomon } 2 Chr. 7	Domus mea Matt. 21
	Offerentur minor 44		*Diffusa est* 44
ominus in Sina 67	Viri Galilei Acts 1	Cumque intuerentur Ac. 1	Psallite Deo 67

INTROITUS	VERSUS	GRADUALE	ALLELUIA CUM VERSU I
Dom. post Ascens. Exaudi domine 26	*Dom. illumin.* 26		*Ascendit* 46
Nat. S. Urbani *Sacerdotes tui*	*Memento domine*	*Inveni David*	
Vig. Pentecostes			
In die Pentecostes Spiritus domini Wis. 1	*Exurgat* 67		Emitte spiritum 103
Fer. II Cibavit eos 80	*Exultate Deo* 80		*Cantate domino*
Fer. III Accipe jocundit. 2 Esd. 2	*Attendite* 77		Confiteantur do. 106
Fer. IV Deus dum egredieris 67 *Reminiscere* 24	*Exurgat* 67	*Dom. Deus noster* 8 *Beata gens* 32	*Lauda anima* 145
(Fer. V) Repleatur os 70 *De necessitatibus*	*In te domine* 70	*Convertere* ℣. *Dom. refugium*	*Redemptionem* 110
Sabbato 12 lect. Caritas Dei Rom. 5 *Intret oratio*	*Do. Deus salutis* 87	*Propitius* ℣. *Adiuva nos* *Protector* ℣. *Domine Deus virtutum* *Jacta cogitatum* ℣. *Dum clamarem* *Ad dominum* ℣. *Dom. libera*	*Eduxit dominus* 104 **Tract.** *Laudate dom.*
S. Marcellini et Petri *Clamaverunt justi* 33	*Exultate* 32	Clamaverunt justi 33	**VERSUS** Juxta est dominus 33
(S. Primi et Feliciani) Sapientiam sanc. Eccl. 44	*Exultate* 32	*Justorum*	*Visi sunt*
S. Basilidis, Cirini, Naboris et Nazarii *Intret in*		Vindica domine 78	Posuerunt 78
S. Marci et Marcelliani Salus autem 36	*Noli æmulari* 36	*Anima nostra*	
S. Gervasi et Protasi Loquetur dominus 84	*Benedixisti* 84	*Justorum*	*Visi sunt*
Vig. S. Joh. Bapt. Ne timeas Luke 1	*Dom. in virtute* 20	Fuit homo Joh. 1	Ut testimonium Joh. 1
Nat. S. Joh. Bapt. De ventre Is. 49	*Bon. est confit.* 91	Priusquam te Jer. 1	Misit dom. Jerem. 1
S. Johannis et Pauli Multæ tribulationes 33	*Benedicam do.* 33	Ec. quam bonum 132	Sicut unguentum 132 Mandavit

ALLELUIA CUM VERSU II	OFFERTORIUM		VERSUS		COMMUNIO	
Non vos relinq. Joh. 14	Ascendit Deus	46	Omnes gentes Quoniam domi- nus Subjecit populos	46	Pater cum	Joh. 17
	Veritas mea		Benedic anima		*Fidelis servus*	
Confitemini dom. 106 **Tract.** *Laudate dom.*	Emitte spiritum	103	Confessionem Extendens cœ- lum	103	U:timo	Joh. 17
Spirit. dom. replev. 67	Confirma hoc	67	Cantate domino In ecclesiis Regna terræ	67	Factus est	Acts 2
Emitte spiritum 103	*Intonuit*				Spir. s. docebit Joh. 14	
Non vos relinq. Joh. 14	*Portas cœli*	77			Spir. qui a Pat. Joh. 15	
Confitebor 137	*Emitte spiritum*	103			Pacem meam Joh. 14	
	Meditabor	118			*Intellige*	5
Dextera domini 117	*Lauda*	145			Spirit. ubi vult Joh. 3	
	Benedic anima				*Erubescant et*	
Non vos relinq. Joh. 14	*Emitte spiritum* *Dom. deus salutis*	103			Non vos relinq. Joh. 14 *Domine Deus meus*	
	Lætamini				*Justorum animæ*	
	Confitebuntur				Ego vos elegi Joh. 15	
	Exsultabunt	149	Cantate	149	Posuerunt	78
	Anima nostra				Am. dico vob. Matt. 25	
	Lætamini				*Posuerunt*	78
	Gloria et honore	8			*Magna*	20
Ipse præibit Luke 1	*Justus ut palma*	91			Tu puer Luke 1	
	Gloriabuntur	5	*Verba mea* *Quoniam ad te*	5	Et si coram Wis. 3	

INTROITUS	VERSUS	GRADUALE	VERSUS
Vig. S. Petri Dicit dom. Petro Joh. 21	*Cæli enarrant* 18	In omnem terram 18	*Cæli enarrant*
S. Petri Nunc scio Acts 12	*Do. probasti* 138	Constitues 44	Pro patribus 44
S. Pauli Scio cui 2 Tim. 1	*Do. probasti* 138	Qui operatus Gal. 2	Gratia Dei 1 Cor. 15 10
S. Processi et Martiniani Judicant sancti Wis. 3	*Exultate* 32	Exultabunt 149	Cantate domino 149
S. vii Fratrum Laudate pueri 112	*Sit nomen* 112	*Vindica domine*	*Posuerunt*
Octava Apostolorum *Sapientiam sanctorum*	*Cæli enarrant*	*Justorum*	*Visi sunt*
Praxedis, Virg. *Loquebar*	*Beati immac.*	*Dilexisti*	*Propterea*
(S. Apollinaris) *Sacerdotes Dei*	*Memento*	*Inveni David*	*Nihil proficiat*
S. Simpl., Faust. et Beatricis Sacerdotes eius 131	*Memento*	Sacerdotes eius 131	*Illuc producam* 131
S. Abdon et Sennen *Intret in*	*Deus venerunt*	*Gloriosus*	*Dextera*
S. Stephani papæ Justus ut 91	*Bonum est* 91	Just. non conturba. 36	Tota die 36
S. Sixti episcopi *Sacerdotes Dei*	*Memento*	*Sacerdotes eius*	*Illuc producam*
(S. Felicis et Agapiti) *Salus autem*	*Noli aemulari*	*Justorum animae*	*Visi sunt*
S. Cyriaci et Secundi Timete dominum 33	*Benedicam* 33	Timete dominum 33	Inquirentes 33
Vig. S. Laurentii Dispersit 111	*Beatus vir* 111	Dispersit 111	Potens in 111
Nat. S. Laurentii *Confessio* 95	*Cantate* 95	Probasti 16	Igne me 16
S. Tiburtii *Justus ut* 91	*Bonum est* 91	Os iusti 36	Lex Dei 36
S. Ypoliti Justi epulentur 67	*Exsurgat* 67	*Justorum*	*Visi sunt*
S. Eusebii *Os iusti*	*Noli aemulari*	Os iusti	*Lex Dei*
(Assumptio B. V. M.) *Vultum tuum* 44	*Eructavit* 44	Propter veritatem 44	*Audi filia* 44
Oct. S. Laurentii Probasti domine 16	*Exaudi Deus* 16	*Justus non conturb.*	*Tota die*
(S. Agapiti) *Lætabitur*		*Justus non conturb.*	
S. Timothei *Salus autem*	*Noli aemulari*	*Justorum*	*Visi sunt*

ALLELUIA CUM VERSU	OFFERTORIUM	VERSUS	COMMUNIO
	Mihi autem 138	Domine probasti / Intellexisti / Ecce tu domine }138	Tu es Petrus Matt. 16
Tu es Petrus / Beatus es } Mat. 16	Constitues 44	Eructavit / Lingua mea / Propterea bene-dixit }44	Simon Johannis Joh. 21
	In omnem terram 18	Cœli enarrant 18	Amen dico Matt. 19
	Gloriabuntur 5		Anima nostra 123
Laudate pueri 112	*Anima nostra*		Quicunque fec. Matt. 12
	Exultabunt sancti		*Justorum animae*
	Diffusa est gratia		*Simile est*
	Veritas		Semel juravi 87
Disposui	*Anima nostra*		*Ego vos elegi*
	Mirabilis		*Posuerunt*
	Inveni David		*Domine quinque*
	Inveni		*Fidelis servus*
	Gloriabuntur		*Ego vos elegi*
	Laetamini		Signa eos Mark 16
	Oratio mea Job. 16	Probavit ?	Qui vult venire Matt. 16
	Confessio 95	*Cantate dom. cantic.* / *Cantate dom. bened.* }95	Qui mihi Joh. 12
	In virtute		*Posuisti domine*
	Anima nostra		Dico autem Luke 12, 4
	Desiderium animæ 20	Vitam petiit / Lætificabis / Inveniatur } 20	*Beatus servus*
	Offerentur minor 44		Dilexisti 44
	In virtute		*Qui vult*
	In virtute		*Beatus servus*
	Mirabilis		*Ego vos elegi*

INTROITUS	VERSUS	GRADUALE	VERSUS
S. Hermetis			
Justus non conturba. 36	Noli æmulari 36	Justus ut palma	Ad adnuntiandum
S. Sabinæ Virg.			
Cognovi domine 118	Beati immac. 118	Specie tua	Propter veritatem
S. Felicis et Adaucti			
Sapientiam	Exultate 32	Gloriosus Deus	Dextera tua
(S. Adriani) Lætabitur	Exaudi Deus	Dom. prævenisti 20	Vitam petiit 20
(S. Gorgonii)			
Gloria et honore 8	Dom. dom. nost. 8	Posuisti	Desiderium
(S. Proti et Hiacinthi)			
Judicant sancti	Exultate iusti	Vindica domine	Posuerunt
(Exalt. S. Crucis)			
Nos autem Gal. 6	Deus misereat. 66	Christus factus	Propter quod
S. Cornelii Sacerdotes Dei	Memento	Sacerdotes eius	Illuc producam
S. Nicomedis Lætabitur	Exaudi Deus	Posuisti domine	Desiderium
(S. Euphemiæ) Vultum	Eructavit	Diffusa est gratia	Propter veritatem
Vig. S. Mathei Ego autem	Quid gloriaris	Justus ut palma	Ad adnuntiandum
S. Mathei Os iusti	Noli æmulari	Beatus vir	Potens in
(S. Cosmæ et Damiani)			
Sapientiam sanctorum	Exultate iusti	Clamaverunt	Juxta est
Dedic. Bas. S. Mich.			
Benedicite domino 102	Benedicamus 102	Benedicite dom. 102	Benedic anima 102
(S. Hieronymi)			
Sacerdotes Dei	Benedicite omnia	Inveni David	Nihil proficiat
Vig. Ap. SS. Simon et			
Judæ Intret in	Deus venerunt	Vindica	Posuerunt
Nat. eorundem			
Mihi autem 138	Dom. probasti 138	Nimis honorati 138	Dinumerabo 138
S. Nazarii Confessio 95	Cantate 95	Justus non conturb.	Tota die
S. iv Coronatorum Mart.			
Intret in	Deus venerunt	Vindica	Posuerunt
S. Theodori In virtute	Magna est	Domine prævenisti	Vitam petiit
S. Mennæ Os iusti	Noli æmulari	Inveni David	Nihil proficiat
(S. Martini) Sacerdotes tui	Memento	Ecce sacerdos	Non est inventus
S. Cæciliæ Loquebar	Beati immac. 118	Audi filia 44	Specie tua 44
S. Clementis			
Dicit dom. sermones	Misericordias 88	Juravit	Dixit dominus
after Is. 59, 21			
S. Chrysogoni			
Justus non conturba. 36	Noli æmulari 36	Gloria et honore 8	Quoniam elevata 8
Vig. S. Andreæ Ap.			
Dom. secus mare Matt. 4	Cæli enarrant 18	Nimis honorati	Dinumerabo
Nat. S. Andreæ Mihi autem	Dom. probasti	Constitues	Pro patribus
In Agenda Mortuorum			
Requiem 2 Esdr. 2	Miserere mei 56	Requiem 2 Esdr. 2	Convertere 114
(Dom. de S. Trinitate)			
(Benedicta sit) Tob. 12,6	(Benedicite) Dan. 3	(Benedictus es) Dan. 3	(Benedictus es) Dan. 3

ALLELUIA CUM VERSU	OFFERTORIUM	VERSUS	COMMUNIO
	In virtute		*Posuisti domine*
	Filiæ regum		Principes persec. 118
	Lætamini *Gloria et honore*		Quod dic. Matt. 10. 27 *Posuisti domine*
	Posuisti domine 20	Desiderium ⎱ Magna est ⎰ 20	*Posuisti domine* 20
	Gloriabuntur		*Anima nostra*
Dicite in gentibus *Disposui*	Protege domine ? *Anima nostra* *Gloria et honore* *Offerentur minor* *Gloria et honore* *Inveni David*	Salvator ⎱ Quia pro mundi ⎰ ?	Nos autem Gal. 6 *Quod dico vobis* *Qui vult venire* *Simile est* *Posuisti domine* *Magna est*
	Gloriabuntur		*Posuerunt*
Laudate Deum 102	Stetit angelus Rev. 8	In conspectu 137	Benedic.omnes Dan.3
	Veritas mea		*Beatus servus*
	Exsultabunt		*Justorum animæ*
	In omnem terram *In virtute*		Vos qui secuti Matt.19 *Qui vult venire*
	Anima nostra *Gloria et honore* *Desiderium* *Inveni David* *Offerentur minor*		*Posuerunt* *Posuisti domine* *Magna est* *Domine quinque* Confund. superbi 118
	Veritas		*Beatus servus*
	Desiderium		*Posuisti domine*
Dilexit Andream ?	*Gloria et honore* *Mihi autem*		Venite post me Matt.4 Dicit Andreas Joh. 1
	Domine convertere *Domine illumina* *Miserere mihi Dom.* Domine Jesu Christe ?		Dona eis domine ?
(Benedictus es) Dan. 3	(Benedictus sit) after Tob. 12, 6	(Benedicamus) Dan.3	(Benedicite) Tob. 12

INTROITUS	VERSUS	GRADUALE	VERSUS
Dom. 1. post Oct. Pent.			
Domine in tua 12	*Usquequo* 12	Ego dixi domine 40	Beatus qui 40
Dom. 2.			
Factus est dominus 17	*Diligam te* 17	*Ad dominum* 119	*Domine libera* 119
3. Respice in me 24	*Ad te do. levavi* 24	*Jacta cogitatum* 54	*Dum clamarem* 54
4. Dom. illuminatio 26	*Si consistant* 26	*Propitius esto* 78	*Adiuva nos* 78
5. Exaudi domine 26	*Dom. illumin.* 26	*Protector noster* 83	*Dom. Deus virtut.* 83
6. Dominus fortitudo 27	*Ad te do. clama.* 27	Convertere dom. 89	Domine refugium 89
7. Omnes gentes 46	*Subiecit popul.* 47	*Venite filii* 33	*Accedite* 33
8. *Suscepimus Deus* 47	*Magnus dom.* 47	*Esto mihi in Deum* 70	*Deus in te speravi* 70
9. Ecce Deus 53	*Deus in nomine* 53	Domine dom. noster 8	Quoniam elevata est 8
10. *Dum clamarem* 54	*Exaudi Deus* 54	*Custodi me* 16	*De vultu tuo* 16
11. Deus in loco 67	*Exsurgat Deus* 67	*In dom. speravi* 17	*Ad te* 17
12. *Deus in adjutorium* 69	*Avertantur* 69	Benedicam dom. 33	In dom. laudabitur 33
13. Respice domine 73	*Ut quid Deus* 73	*Respice domine* 73	*Exurge* 73
14. Protector noster 83	*Quam dilecta* 83	*Bon. est confidere* 117	*Bon. est sperare* 117
15. Inclina domine 85	*Lætifica anim.* 85	*Bon. est confiteri* 91	*Ad adnuntiandum* 91
16. Miserere mihi 85	*Incl. do. aurem* 85	*Timebunt gentes* 101	*Quon. ædificavit* 101
17. Justus es domine 118	*Beati immac.* 118	*Beata gens* 32	*Verbo domini* 32
Fer. IV mens. Sept.			
Exultate Deo 80	*Testimonium* 80	Quis sicut dom. 112	Suscitans a terra 112
Fer. VI *Lætetur cor* 104	*Confitemini* 104	Convertere dom. 89	*Domine refugium* 89
Sabb. 12 lect.			
Venite adoremus 94	*Venite exulte.* 94	*Propitius esto* 78	*Adiuva* 78
		Protector noster 83	*Dom. Deus virtut.* 83
		Dirigatur oratio 140	*Elevatio manuum* 140
		Salvum fac popul. 27	*Ad te dom. clamabo* 27
Dom. 18. post Pent.			
Da pacem Eccl. 36	*Lætatus sum* 121	*Lætatus sum* 121	*Fiat pax* 121
19. *Salus populi* ?	*Attendite* 77	Dirigatur oratio 140	*Elevatio* 140
20. *Omnia quæ fecisti* Dan. 3	*Beati immac.* 118	Oculi omnium 144	*Aperis tu* 144
21. In voluntate tua Esth. 13	*Beati immac.* 118	Domine refugium 89	Priusquam montes 89
22. Si iniquitates 129	*De profundis* 129	*Ecce quam bonum* 132	*Sicut unguentum* 132 ℣. *Mandavit*
23. *Omnes gentes* 46	*Subiecit popul.* 46	*Venite filii* 33	*Accedite ad* 33
24. Dicit dom. ego Jer. 29	*Benedixisti* 84	Liberasti nos 43	In Deo laudabimus 43

ALLELUIA CUM VERSU	OFFERTORIUM	VERSUS	COMMUNIO
	Intende voci 5		*Narrabo omnia* 9
	Domine convertere 6		Cantabo domino 12
	Sperent in te 9		Ego clamavi 16
	Illumina 12		Do. firmamentum 17
	Benedicam dom. 15		Unam petii 26
	Perfice gressus 16		Circuibo 26
	Sic. in holocaust. Dan. 3	Et nunc sequimur Dan. 3	Inclina aurem 30
	Populum humilem 17		Gustate et videte 33
	Justitiæ domini 18		Primum quær. Mat. 6
	Ad te dom. levavi 24		*Acceptabis* 50
	Exaltabo te 29		Honora dom. Prov. 3
	Precatus est Exod. 32		De fructu 103
	In te speravi 30		Panem de cœlo Wis. 16
	Inmittet angelus 33		*Panis quem* Joh. 6
	Exspectans 39		*Qui manducat* Joh. 6
	Dom. in auxilium 39		*Dom. memorabor* 70
	Oravi Deum Dan. 9	Adhuc me loquen. Audivi vocem } Dan. 9	Vovete et reddite 75
	Meditabor 118		Comedite Nehem. 8
	Benedic anima 102		Aufer a me 118
	Dom. Deus salutis 87		*Mense sept.* Lev. 23
Hymn. 3 puerorum **Tr.** *Laudate Deum* 116			
	Sanctificav. Exod. 33	Locutus est do. Oravit Moyses } Ex. 33	Tollite hostias 95
	Si ambulavero 137		*Tu mandasti* 118
	Super flumina 136		*Memento verbi* 118
	Vir erat Job 1	Utinam appender. Quæ est enim Numquid fortitudo Quon. non revertet. } Job 1	In salutari tuo 118
	Recordare Esth. 14, 12	Everte cor Esth. 14,13&14	Dico vobis gaud. Luke 15
	Sic. in holocaust. D. 3 De profundis cla. 129	Fiant aures Si iniquitates } 129	Amen dico vobis quicquid Mark 11

298

THE ALLELUIA VERSES

II.

THE ALLELUIA VERSES OF EASTER WEEK

IN

MSS. AND PRINTED BOOKS

DOWN TO THE COUNCIL OF TRENT

	IN DIE PASCHÆ	FER. II	FER. III
Cod. Monza Cent. VIII	℣ 1. Pascha nostrum 2. Epulemur	℣ Dominus regnavit, decorem	℣ In te, domine, speravi
Cod. Rheinau Cent. VIII	℣ 1. Pascha nostrum 2. Epulemur	℣ Dominus regnavit, decorem	
Cod. St. Gall 359 Cent. IX	℣ 1. Pascha nostrum 2. Epulemur	℣ Surrexit dominus vere	℣ Obtulerunt discipul
Cod. St. Gall 339 Cent. X	℣ 1. Pascha nostrum 2. Epulemur	℣ Surrexit dominus vere	℣ Obtulerunt discipul
Cod. Einsiedeln 121 Cent. X	℣ 1. Pascha nostrum 2. Epulemur	℣ 1. Angelus domini ℣ 2. Respondens autem	℣ Christus resurgens
Cod. Jacq. Rosenthal (Munich) Cent. XII	℣ 1. Pascha nostrum	℣ Nonne cor nostrum	℣ Oportebat pati 1
Cod. Paris nouv. acquis. 1235 Cent. XII	℣ 1. Pascha nostrum 2. Epulemur	℣ Surrexit dominus vere	℣ Eduxit dominus
Cod. Trèves City Library Cent. XIII	℣ 1. Pascha nostrum 2. Epulemur	℣ Nonne cor nostrum ℣ 1. Angelus domini 2. Respond. autem	℣ Christus resurgens
Grad. Sarisburiense Cent. XIII	℣ 1. Pascha nostrum 2. Epulemur	℣ Nonne cor nostrum	℣ Surgens Jesus
Cod, 445, Colmar City Library Cent. XIII	℣ 1. Pascha nostrum	℣ Nonne cor	℣ Stetit Jesus in medic
Cod. St. Gall. 353 Cent. XIII-XIV	℣ 1. Pascha nostrum 2. Epulemur	℣ 1. Angelus domini 2. Respond. autem	℣ Christus resurgens
Grad. Lausannense (Minorite Lib. Freiburg, Switzerland) Cent. XV, early	℣ 1. Pascha nostrum 2. Epulemur	℣ Nonne cor	℣ Surrexit dominus e
Cod. St. Gall 427 Cent. XV	℣ 1. Pascha nostrum 2. Epulemur	℣ Nonne cor	℣ Oportebat pati
Missale Lausannense (Minorite Lib. Freiburg, Switzerland) Cent. XV, late	℣ Pascha nostrum	℣ Angelus domini	℣ Surrexit dominus de
Grad. Franc. de Brugis, printed Venice 1500	℣ Pascha nostrum	℣ Angelus domini	℣ Surrexit dominus de
Grad. Lausannense, printed Lyons 1522	℣ 1. Pascha nostrum 2. Epulemur	℣ Nonne cor	℣ Surrexit dominus et
Missale Tridentinum	℣ 1. Pascha nostrum	℣ Angelus domini	℣ Surrexit dominus de

---

1 ℣ *Angelus domini* is also noted by a later hand.

FER. IV	FER. V	FER. VI	SABBATO
℣ Quoniam Deus magnus	℣ Lauda Hierusalem	℣ Surrexit altissimus	℣ Hæc dies
℣ Redemptionem mi-sit			℣ Laudate pueri
℣ Surrexit de sepul-chro	℣ Cantate domino	℣ Eduxit dominus	℣ Hæc dies ℣ 1. Laudate pueri 2. Sit nomen
℣ Surrexit altissimus	℣ Cantate domino	℣ Eduxit dominus	℣ Hæc dies ℣ 1. Laudate pueri 2. Sit nomen
℣ Oportebat pati	℣ In die resurrectionis	℣ Surrexit altissimus	℣ Hæc dies ℣ 1. Laudate pueri 2. Sit nomen
℣ Angelus domini 2	℣ Nonne cor nostrum	℣ Angelus domini	℣ Hæc dies ℣ Surrexit
℣ In die resurrectionis	℣ Angelus domini	℣ Benedic. es Dei filius	℣ Hæc dies ℣ Laudate pueri
℣ In die resurrectionis	℣ Surrexit altissimus	℣ Dicite in gentibus	℣ Hæc dies ℣ 1. Laudate pueri ℣ 2. Sit nomen
℣ Surrexit dominus et	℣ In die resurrectionis	℣ Dicite in gentibus	℣ Hæc dies ℣ 1. Laudate pueri 2. Sit nomen
℣ Surrexit dominus et	℣ Christus resurgens	℣ In die resurrectionis	℣ Hæc dies ℣ 1. Laudate pueri
℣ Surgens Jesus	℣ In die resurrectionis	℣ Dicite in gentibus	℣ Hæc dies ℣ 1. Laudate pueri ℣ 2. Sit nomen
℣ Oportebat pati	℣ Surrexit altissimus	℣ Crucifixus surrexit	℣ Hæc dies ℣ 1. Laudate pueri 2. Sit nomen
℣ Christus resurgens	℣ In resurrectione tua	℣ Dicite in gentibus	℣ Hæc dies ℣ 1. Laudate pueri ℣ 2. Sit nomen
℣ Surrexit dom. vere	℣ Surrexit Christus qui		
℣ Surrexit dom. vere	℣ Surrexit Christus qui	℣ Dicite in gentibus	℣ Hæc dies
℣ Oportebat pati	℣ Surrexit altissimus	℣ Crucifixus surrexit	℣ Hæc dies ℣ Laudate pueri
℣ Surrexit dom. vere	℣ Surrexit Christus	℣ Dicite in gentibus	℣ Hæc dies ℣ Laudate pueri

---

2 ℣ *Surrexit dominus* is also noted by a later hand.

III.

THE GRADUAL RESPONDS OF THE SUNDAYS AFTER PENTECOST

IN CODEX RHEINAU

ERRATA

Page 21, *last line, for* 'Greek' *read* 'Greeks.'

,, 75, *line* 19 *for* '*pulpitus*' *read* 'pulpit.'

,, 77, *line* 23, *for* 'Canons' *read* 'Canon.'

,, 120, *note* 2, *first line, for* 'Ordo' *read* 'Ordine.'

,, 144, *line* 6, *for* 'solus' *read* 'solis.'

,, ,, ,, ,, *after* 'Hostis' *insert* 'Herodes impie.'

,, 187, *note, line* 5, *for* 'beautiful' *read* 'florid.'

INDEX